The Strip Outlaw

L. J. Brooksby

PROCTOR PUBLICATIONS, LLC

Proctor Publications
P.O. Box 2498
Ann Arbor, Michigan 48106
(800) 343–3034

Printed in the United States of America

Publisher's Cataloging-in-Publication
(Provided by Quality Books, Inc.)

Brooksby, L. J.
    The strip outlaw / L.J. Brooksby. -- 1st ed.
    p. cm.
    LCCN: 99-74693
    ISBN: 1-882792-86-6

    1. Western stories.   2. Frontier and
pioneer life--West (U.S.)--Fiction. 3. Arizona
Strip (Ariz.)--Fiction.   I. Title.

PS3552.R65968S77 1999   813'.54
                QBI99-1229

ii

*Dedicated to
my wonderful wife,
Janetha,
who took the time to read,
edit, and enhance my book.*

The Arizona Strip

It is the intent of this author to capture some of the wild flavor and excitement of the Arizona Strip and to make the reader more aware of one of the last lawless areas of the old west. The footprints of time are being covered by the tire tracks of the present and soon no vestige of our past will be visible in the *No-Man's Land.* For many years, visitors have stood on the brink of the south rim of the Grand Canyon not realizing that across that great chasm lies an intriguing land. Arid and desolate though it may be, it is home to the Paiute and Navajo Indians.

In 1896 the US Congress set the Utah line a good hundred miles north of the Grand Canyon, cutting this strip of land from the rest of Arizona. The Colorado River, which flows through the Grand Canyon, effectively cut it off from the rest of the state, leaving a barren land which neither Arizona or Utah wanted. Consequently, those disaffected with society in neighboring states crossed either the Utah border or the Colorado River in order to disassociate themselves from the law. This naked land has always been home to more animals than humans and even the early Spanish explorers chose a much longer journey when traveling from west to east or north to south in order to avoid its harshness.

Major Powell was the first so called modern explorer to traverse this land in the mid 1800s, but even he didn't want to tackle it a second time. If dry bones of those killed on the Strip could talk, they would tell tales of the outlaws, the Navajos, and the Paiutes, for they are the ones who stalked the plains. The story is told of a Strip rancher by the name of Jacobs who entered the office of a sheriff across the Utah line, demanding action to stop the rustling of his cattle. The sheriff told him to raise his right hand. When he did, he was deputized. The sheriff's statement was, "Anyone who's fool enough to live on the Strip can do his own killing." Jacobs is also quoted as saying, "The Strip is the place God forgot and nobody else wants. It belongs to them strong enough to git and strong enough to hold — and you gotta be stronger to hold than to git."

The few hardy souls who inhabit this land are called Strippers. Until the early 1950s, no census was taken on the Strip and few lawmen stepped foot on it. The drunken courses of many washes twist across the dry land. Water holes are man-made, filled by infrequent thunder storms, and tend to dry up before the summer is spent, causing water to be more precious than the land itself. A traveler better pack plenty of liquid, because fresh water is hard to come by. What little water exists is brackish and full of alkali. When wells are drilled, it's common to not hit water till the bit bites through the 4000 foot mark. When a ranch is sold the water is what determines the price of the sale. Not too many years ago, a passing cowboy spotted a car high centered on the rutty road, the occupants stretched out under a mesquite bush with their tongues protruding because they forgot to pack water with them.

For all its faults, the Strip implants within the bosom of those who experience it a peace that transcends all the modern marvels of time and space. To stand on the red cliffs and watch the sunrise in the early morning, or to do the same thing as it sets in the evening, spreads the soul of man or woman just as the vastness of the empty Strip widens the vision of one's eyes. There is life here that flourishes among the sagebrush dotted landscape. A life that's free from worry if one lets his sense of time float by and isn't in a hurry to leave only his footprints in the earth. Traverse the land that the outlaws and native Indians roamed and let your eyes and mind take in the many magnificent colors of this country. You'll be glad you did.

L. J. Brooksby

The wagon bottom almost touched the high ground between the wheels in the deeply rutted road, making the wagon appear unusually small. A gray canvas top flapped wildly in the hard, biting wind that blew out of the west. Wild flowers struggled to bloom in the bone-dry desert and the wind-whipped dust tore at their petals, adding them to the sticks and bits of brush sweeping across the prairie. Juniper trees dotting the landscape had a permanent list to the east; even the sagebrush bent in the direction the wind blew. It seemed impossible there could still be dirt to blow away when the wind carried so much with it as it traveled across the surface of the earth. Surely, if this kept up, the western end of the Strip would be blown to the eastern end, causing mountains to accumulate there.

Two large draft horses pulling the wagon plodded with heads down and eyes slitted, trying to keep the dust from plastering

1

them closed. Hour after hour the wind blew, with not the slightest indication of a lull in sight. A brown haze covered the hot sun filtering through to the weary traveler in the wagon. Breathing became a chore as minute particles of dirt filled the driver's nostrils, even though a bandana covered his nose. The reins from the team of horses wound through a slit in front of the canvas cover, traveling back to long, fine-boned hands which grasped them tightly. These hands melded into strong, sinewy arms that were bare until they reached the shoulders, which were broad with muscles rippling when the team of horses needed a little more urging. His neck seemed too narrow for such broad shoulders, but his head, with the bandana covering the lower part of the face, was just right for a man of his young age. A floppy brimmed Stetson sat back from the furrowed brow, letting light sandy hair show beneath it. Somber blue eyes were hardly visible through the accumulation of dust bathing the lids.

Two bodies lay far back in the wagon, blankets covering their stiff limbs. The hands springing from the sides of each body and converging over the blankets about where the chest would be, indicated one of each sex. Those of the bigger body were rough and calloused, showing the many times they'd been used to toil the earth. The other pair of hands was soft and white, giving the impression of tenderness and love. It was evident from their stiffness that they had been dead for at least a day. No odor from the bodies permeated the air under the canvas top of the wagon, but he knew he must bury them soon.

Taut muscles of the team flexed and extended as they labored diligently to pull the wagon along the deep-cut ruts of the road leading to House Rock Valley, in which lay the Bar-H ranch headquarters. Sweat caked along the sides of each horse and foamy froth slid from the corners of their mouths where the bridle bits rested on their tongues. Both were a dark bay color with long manes and tails. Big bones in the head told of their draft horse breeding. They were well cared for, with hooves recently trimmed and shod. Sleek coats showed through the flecks of foamy sweat, with longer hairs protruding from around the fetlocks, swishing down and almost covering the walls of the hooves. Each foot lifted, then settled exactly where it would exert the most leverage to pull the wagon.

On closer inspection of the sides of the wagon, one could see where bullets had drilled their way into the wood. Even the canvas cover was pockmarked with bullet holes, letting small circles of light penetrate to the inside and flash on the two bodies, fireflies in a devil's dance. While the wagon jolted over the parched earth, the young man inside let his mind drift over the last two days since his parents met the train in Winslow, Arizona. He had been separated from them for four long years of study at an Eastern University, years in which he dreamed of the wild Strip country with its vast unspoiled beauty and honest, God-fearing folk. The clamor and bustle of the East did not appeal to him, and several times, after a particularly trying day, he was ready to chuck it all, wanting only to be back at the Bar-H in the comfort of friends and family. Then he'd remember his parents struggle to save enough money to send him to this school, their pride at this accomplishment, and he would return to his studies, determined to finish.

Their joy on seeing him at the train station made every sacrifice, his and theirs, worthwhile. He was sure they had told the station master, the telegraph operator, and the few hapless folks who also waited, about their brilliant, wonderful son. It was written all over their faces when he stepped onto the worn boards, and he would have felt embarrassed except for the understanding that accompanied those looks. His mother's warm embrace plus his father's hearty handshake banished any discomfort, and they were soon on their way home.

The attackers had come out of the night with lightning speed. Four mounted men, guns blazing, caught his father in the act of bending down to refill a cup with coffee. His mother rushed to her husband's side, only to be driven earthward by a hail of bullets. The wagon and canvas top were then methodically riddled with bullet holes.

"We sure fixed his hide fast. The youngun oughta know better'n to try hidin' in a wagon-- he's full a holes by now," came from the sneering mouth of one of the attackers just as a bullet sliced through his neck, almost decapitating him. Incredulous, the others turned in their saddles to meet a hail of rifle fire from the surrounding brush. The night cried with gun flame as hot lead sped between the lone rifle in the brush and those on horseback. Seconds later an unearthly stillness settled as four riderless horses pranced nervously, the light from the flickering fire casting shadows over the twisted bodies of six people lying in the semidarkness.

He moved from the brush with heavy steps, the barrel of his rifle still too hot to touch. The lead slugs had cut the attackers down so fast, their return fire had been completely ineffectual. They made sure targets with the firelight silhouetting them from behind; now they were lifeless forms already being covered by the blowing dust.

The Winchester lay cradled in his arms as he stood looking down at the two people who brought him into the world. Their empty eyes stared back at him while the firelight shifted over their faces, almost giving them irrational life. Except for the fact that he'd walked out from the fire a while ago to gaze at the star-filled sky, he would be lying with them. His old habit of always taking a rifle with him whenever he strayed into the brush had avenged his parent's deaths, but it didn't lessen the crushing grief that filled his body.

Why? What was the sense of this useless killing? His folks had always been well liked on the Strip. They went out of their way to help others who needed support. The old man was a leader in the community, giving of his time and money freely to make this land a better place for all. Now he'd been cut down by rifle fire, by the scum of the earth. Pushing all emotion deep inside and carefully placing a wall around it, the young man turned from their bodies to inspect those of the five attackers.

Each man had come heavily armed, with both rifle and a brace of pistols. None of them was familiar. Going through their pockets, he found several large bills but no identification on any of them. He took the hardware from their bodies and stored it all in the bed of the wagon. If possible, he would deliver everything to the cavalry post at Pipe Springs when he found the time to go there. Angrily he turned to free the horses, removing their saddles and checking for markings. Finding none, he opened the saddlebags. A Wanted dodger in each saddlebag specified a reward for the capture of the named individual. The faces on the dodgers matched those in the dirt. Their combined total added up to three thousand dollars. He stood staring at the posters, then deliberately strode to the fire and burned all four. His stomach churned at the thought of collecting a reward for the killing of those responsible for his parent's deaths. But he didn't burn the money. No, this he would use to find who had hired these men, for it didn't feel like a random slaughter, a spur of the moment escapade. Someone had planned this.

Two hours later, with the four outlaws buried and his parents loaded in the back of the wagon, he left the campsite behind. He would bury them on the knoll behind the Bar-H ranch house. Now he approached that ranch with a heavy heart, not knowing what would meet him there. Perhaps the hired hands would have an answer. The questions still filtered through his mind as he broke out of the stand of cottonwood trees in front of the ranch. His hands pulled the team up short as his eyes took in the incomprehensible scene before him.

Blackened ashes and charred pieces of wood littered the ground where the house and other buildings once stood. Not even the pole corral remained. His already stunned brain could barely comprehend this sight. The stone fireplace that he and his father built stood grotesquely amidst the burned timbers, a forlorn sentinel over a lost past. Much sweat and labor went into the building of that fireplace and those ranch buildings. Now they were nothing but ashes and charred rock.

Where were the ranch hands who helped his father? The count was nineteen when he left. His mother's letters made no mention of trouble at the ranch. Then the things which had been nagging at the back of his conscious began to take on meaning. He'd seen no cattle on the land since he crossed the part of the Colorado river that formed the eastern boundary of the Bar-H spread. There were a few buffalo, but no cattle. His mind, completely occupied with the death of those he loved and the reason for it, had failed to register what his eyes were telling him. Now he tried to figure out what all this meant.

His parents were obviously happy to see him when they met the train and no word was spoken of trouble being close by. A time or two he noticed his father looking at him steadily as though he wanted to say something, but before he could speak, his mother would drag up a funny episode from his past and they would all laugh and joke about it. He wished his father, for once, had disregarded his mother and said what was on his mind. But ever the gentleman, he died leaving his son in ignorance.

How long he sat immobile on the seat of the wagon he didn't know, since the dense dust haze covered the sun. Actually, he wasn't conscious of time at this point. Suddenly the wind stopped as though it sensed his indecision and didn't want to add to his grief. Silence surrounded him, almost deafening in its eeriness. His eyes roved over the valley where the burned remains of a ranch lay black and still, then swung to the knoll where he planned to dig two graves. The lushness of the grass proved a stark contrast to the dead earth it surrounded, and ran right to the edge of a stream ambling along its base. Life-giving water flowed, but there seemed no use for it now. Shaking the reins of the team, he started the wagon moving toward that knoll. Those bodies still had to be buried before he could concentrate on the puzzle laid out before him.

Going up the side of the knoll turned out to be easier than staying in the rutted road. Even with the buildings burned, the horses seemed to know their work was almost over and they put a spring in their stride. When they reached the top, he pulled to a halt and not looking back at the remains of the ranch, took the shovel down from its place on the side of the wagon and started to dig in the grass-covered dirt. He worked steadily till he completed the first grave. Crawling out, he strode to the water barrel on the wagon and dipped out a drink. Its brackish warmth made him wish he'd stopped at the stream for some cool water, but that would have to wait for the trip back down. His eyes surveyed the land in sight--nothing appeared to be living in all that vast area. Shrugging his shoulders, he went back to the shovel and as before, worked steadily till the second grave was dug.

Wearily he climbed out and came to a full stand, arching his back to relieve the kinks. He froze in this awkward position, brought up short by the sight before his eyes.

She stood beside the wagon, one hand holding the reins of a coal black mare and the other resting on the wagon's seat. Her gleaming midnight hair curled down her back below a white Stetson hat tipped slightly to the side. The skin in sight was a light brown, either from much sun or the nationality of her birth. It was hard to tell which. A man's pale blue western shirt was tucked into a split riding skirt covering the lower half of her body. A gun belt with a small caliber gun encased in a brown leather holster slanted across her waist and rested on her right thigh. The boots held no spurs and subconsciously this pleased him.

Cautious brown eyes steadily observed him. "This wagon belongs to the Hastings, but I don't recall you being one of their punchers." The words were soft but held a stern implication. Her hand left the wagon seat and dropped close to the butt of the revolver at her side.

He closed his eyes briefly as though to rid them of this apparition before him. When they sprang open, she still stood there with an expectant look on her face. There hadn't been enough time for him to change from the morbid musing he'd been experiencing while digging, to this new line of thought. Then his training came into play and the shades dropped over his eyes, leaving a blank expression in place of the surprised one.

"You're right about the wagon, ma'am, and if you look inside, you'll see the reason for the two graves."

A quiver went through her lithe frame at his words and she quickly walked to the back of the wagon. He waited for the gasp that would follow her discovery, but heard only silence. How had she been able to ride right up to the wagon without him hearing her? His time in the east must have dulled his senses to a great extent. Before he left for school no one, not even the best warrior of the Navajo tribe, would have been able to come that close without him knowing it. He would have to recover those senses since it looked like real trouble rode this range. Uh oh, the rifle leaned against the pile of dirt he'd thrown up at the first grave . . . too far away to have done any good if someone other than this young woman had caught him.

He stood leaning on the shovel, expecting to see or hear her at any moment. The silence continued, broken only by the chirping of the birds drifting up from the cottonwood trees in the valley. Once he thought he caught a sob emanating from the back of the wagon, but after a time decided he'd been mistaken. This young woman seemed to know his parents but he was sure he had never laid eyes on her before. She was someone who would not be easily forgotten. Her horse stood quietly as though sensing the sorrow enveloping the knoll. Time slipped by while his mind tried to grasp the significance of all that happened and the puzzle this young lady presented. There seemed to be no answers anywhere.

The spell holding him in place began to wear on his nerves. He shifted the shovel to his shoulder, walked to the wagon and placed it on its hooks at the side. He wanted to wrap each body in a couple of blankets for burial. He had expected to wrap his father in the large woven Indian rug that hung above the fireplace, and his mother in the soft down-filled cover that spread over their bed, but now only the rough, coarse, blankets used on the trail were available. He dipped another drink from the water barrel and wiped the sweat from his forehead, wondering how much longer she was going to stay with the bodies. She must have known them well to spend this much time.

Leaning against the side of the wagon, he let his gaze roam over the horse, a high-bred animal with not a white hair anywhere. The sleek and shiny coat blended into hooves that were well maintained. A large head with a slight roman nose, supported ears alert to any sounds from its mistress. Mane and tail showed good grooming and care. The saddle was handmade with stitching along the cantle and the skirts of the stirrup leathers. A thirty- thirty carbine rested in a saddle sheath on the left side, the butt protruding backwards. His attention was cornered by the saddle blanket. Its exquisite design showed the work of Navajo craftsmanship. Bridle and martingale were of matching stitched brown leather. This young woman came from a well-to-do family and he decided her skin color must be from her ancestry, rather than the sun.

His thoughts were interrupted when she stepped from behind the wagon. No trace of emotion was visible on her face, but he saw the telltale marks where tears had coursed down her cheeks. She walked to the fresh dug graves and gazed silently into them. Then her eyes lifted and took in the valleys on each side of the knoll. "They will be happy here. The land was part of them while they lived and now they'll be part of it in death."

The words were perfect and to hear them from a total stranger caused him to wonder what he had come home to. He left the side of the wagon and climbed in the back. Selecting the two best blankets from the bedrolls on the floor, he tucked them under his arm and climbed out. Spreading both on the ground, he reached in and lifted his mother's body out first, placing her on the nearest blanket. Returning to the wagon, he picked up the heavy body of his father as though it were weightless and placed it on the other blanket. He stayed in a crouched position, looking from one to the other, knowing he would never see their faces again. Almost, his emotions overcame him but only a tiny tightening of his muscles showed the strain. As his eyes left the bodies and roamed over the valley below, anger began to boil up inside his heart. This could be dangerous. He quickly squashed it and let his mind rest on the many fun events he'd experienced at the hands of these two people.

Time slipped by as he said his last farewell, then he pulled the blankets tight around each body and secured them with lengths of rope cut from a lariat. The girl stood quietly watching as he picked up his father and gently placed the body in the first hole. He did the same with his mother, feeling with his hand that of hers under the blanket. Then he stood and removing the floppy brimmed hat from his head, watched an eagle float in the sky above them. He wished he could be that eagle and see all that led up to this moment. It wasn't a prayer he uttered, but a pledge: those who instigated the trouble on this range would be dealt with harshly. His vow didn't escape his lips but from the set of his jaw, she knew what he swore and felt the rightness of it.

She was patient as he turned back for the shovel and began to methodically throw dirt into the final resting place of his parents. He didn't let up till everything was back as before. Even the grass sod had been saved to place over the fresh dirt, making it almost impossible for anyone to see where the graves were, but she knew both of them would know the spot anytime in the future. Wondering why he didn't want anyone to know where the graves were, she started to ask, then thought better of it. This silent man held his own council and she wouldn't intrude. By now she'd figured out he was the son named Colt. His parents had spoken of him many times since she came into the Strip country two and a half years ago. How did they meet their death? The bullet holes in the sides of the wagon and the canvas top attested to the fact that there had been gunplay, but when and why that took place was not yet known to her.

The shovel placed back on its rack, he climbed onto the seat of the wagon, starting the team downhill. No words had passed his lips since his first statement when she rode up and found him standing in the last grave, throwing shovel after shovel of dirt out of the hole. Stepping to the saddle of her horse, she watched the wagon rumble downward and stop at the stream. He got out and lay on the ground drinking in the cool water that flowed by.

Moments later he arose and taking an ax from its pegs on the side of the wagon, began to fell juniper trees that dotted the landscape. He trimmed the limbs from the first tree on the ground and cut it to the length of a post. There would be no time lost in the rebuilding of the ranch, and her heart was glad at the steadfastness of this young man.

He appeared to be a couple of years older than herself. The muscles rippled under his shirt as his arms rose and fell. She found it impossible to tear herself away from the scene before her. Deciding she wasn't any use just sitting here on her horse, she rode down the hill and taking her catch rope from the saddle, slipped the loop over one end of a post and drug it to where the corral had once stood. Flipping the rope off the end of the post, she went back for another one.

The sun tucked in its rays and settled behind the hills before Colt quit and placed the ax back on its pegs. He went to the stream to wash off sweat and dirt, then gathered some wood and built a small fire. She pulled a fry pan and some eating utensils from the wagon and put them beside the fire. Going to the stream with a coffee pot, she filled it with water and brought it back, setting it on a rock near the flame. He finished slicing steaks from a quarter of beef wrapped in a gunnysack hung from the roof of the wagon. Potatoes were laid out on the tailgate. These she took to the stream and washed, then brought back to wrap in some paper he handed to her. He pushed the fire to the side and with a stick dug a shallow hole, then he put the wrapped potatoes in the hole and covered them with a fine layer of dirt, finally scraping the hot wood back over them. She brought the slabs of meat from the tailgate and laid them in the frypan as he sat back on his haunches.

His voice was soft but the words were edged in steel. "Last night I buried the four men who did this, but the one who ordered it done is the one I want to get my hands on. Those men were only outlaws. I thought they might be acting on their own until I saw the burned ranch buildings and the empty range. Then I realized the killing was only part of someone's plan to get this ranch. That someone is in for a big surprise when he doesn't hear from his men and my parents don't show up back here."

Now she knew what he'd been thinking when he put the grass back in place over the graves: no one was to know what happened until he investigated the reasons for this atrocity. Her heart swelled at the confidence he placed in her, without even knowing her. He assumed already that she would never divulge his secret until he did so himself. The men sent to kill were lying somewhere in concealed graves and those they killed were also resting in hidden graves. The man responsible would have a fit trying to find out what happened. She had to smile a little at this. But who furnished the brains behind the trouble? Her own father lost cattle constantly, as did other ranches on the Strip, but none were hit as hard as the Bar-H, now almost devoid of cattle carrying that brand. It used to be the largest ranch on the Strip, separated from the others by the Kaibab mountain that rose from House Rock Valley to cut this section of the Strip off from the other side, where the town of Fredonia lay just below the Utah line.

She walked over to an old pine log by the fire and sat down. "How did you manage to kill those men who killed your parents?"

For a moment she thought he wouldn't answer. He picked up a stick, jabbed angrily at the fire. Then, eyes downcast to cover remembered pain, he said, "I was out in the brush where we camped for the night, looking up at the stars. You don't see stars like this in the East, and I just wanted to drink the sight into my soul. When the men attacked, my old habit of always taking a rifle with me made it possible to fight back. Dad got caught with the first shots, and Mom got it when she bent to help him. They riddled the wagon thinking I was in it. Unfortunately for them, the outlaws were back-lighted by the fire...as easy as shooting ducks in a barrel. That was their only mistake, and their last."

A chill hung in the air as she listened to his stone-cold speech. It contained no emotion at all over killing four men. Then she wondered if she wouldn't be the same way after seeing someone gun down her parents. "How horrible. Then to have to travel a full day and night with your parent's bodies in the wagon, must have made it that much worse." Her words were understanding and gentle as they reached across the space between them.

He stood up, his eyes still on the fire while his hand touched the heavy Colt forty-four-forty that rested in the holster on his right hip. "I'd like to thank you for your help today and for your thoughts about my parents. You must have been special to them."

Then he looked straight at her, his piercing eyes stopping any comment she might make, as his words continued. "Don't rightly know where to look for the dirty dog I'm after, but I intend to travel the country and see what might pop up. I've changed a lot since I've been off to school, and that should keep most people from recognizing me. With a little help from a beard and some hair dye, my movements won't raise any suspicions." He paused briefly, then continued, "You must live close by and I need a saddle horse. If your place has a good mount, I'm willing to pay for it."

"Actually, my home's on the other side of the Kaibab. I work in Fredonia at the hotel. I was traveling out to the reservation to visit my grandparents. Stopped to pay a call on your folks and saw the burned ashes and you up on the knoll. It took awhile for me to figure out who you were, Colt." To her surprise, the name fell naturally from her lips.

A smile split his face for the first time. "You have the advantage of me there. I don't know your name."

"Everyone in town calls me Shirley Pugh. I'm one quarter Navajo. On the reservation they call me Cunning Fox because of the tricks I used to play when my parents brought me to visit. I like my Indian name best since it denotes honor for those who use it." She waited for him to comment but when none came, she spoke again. "As to a horse, it would be best to get one from the reservation and put an unknown brand on it. Then you'd be even less apt to cause suspicion."

"That's good thinking, but will your people accept me under such false pretenses? It wouldn't be right to have any of the Navajo's get tangled in the mess here on the Strip."

Her pleasant laugh reassured him. "We'll arrange for you to steal it; there'll be no repercussions then if someone finds out where you got it."

"I see now why they call you Cunning Fox. And thanks, it sounds like a good plan to me." He turned back to the fire and proceeded to fork the meat from the pan to the plates. Moving the fire to the side with his boot, he dug up the well-cooked potatoes, wiped them with a rag, and put them beside the meat. Then he handed Shirley one of the plates.

While she ate, her thoughts were busy with this man who

seemed so natural in this setting. He'd been gone a while but the East certainly hadn't left any mark on him that she could tell. Oh, he talked a little differently, but his movements were sure and purposeful. A little sparse when it came to conversation, but she liked that in a man. Most of the fellows she met fell all over her trying to make some headway in courting, which she didn't have the least desire to accommodate. This man seemed to accept her as an equal, not giving the slightest indication of any difference between them. Come to think of it that could be a disadvantage--the least he could do was look at her as a lady. Then she smiled to herself: no wonder they said women were never satisfied.

As for Colt, his thoughts were locked solidly on the problem facing him. If by some chance he could pose as an outlaw, he may be able to work his way into the bunch causing all the trouble. They would now be short four men, so it might work. As he'd chopped the fenceposts earlier, he mulled over this possibility. If the Indians did let him steal a horse, it would start that disguise on its way. He could even hire some of them to come back and rebuild the ranch. Cunning Fox would know how to tell the Indians to do this and make it seem as though his parents were still alive and paying for the work. How fortunate she showed up when she did. It would take three or four weeks to grow the beard; during that time he could nose around quietly and maybe even make an outlaw name for himself.

"It's too late to continue on tonight, Colt. Why don't we sleep here and get an early start in the morning?"

Her voice snapped him out of his reverie. He noticed the depth of darkness and realized she made sense. Weariness overtook him. "Sounds good. Just hand me a couple of those blankets and

I'll bed down under the wagon. Also, my Winchester."

After handing him the blankets, Shirley returned to the tailgate. When she started to climb inside, it dawned on her that she'd be lying right where the dead bodies had recently lain. Her Indian side could feel their spirits hovering near. She muttered a pocket-sized prayer, grabbed two blankets, and joined Colt under the wagon. When he gave her a puzzled look, she replied, "Dirt's softer" and closed her eyes, cutting off further communication.

Colt shrugged and rolled into a cocoon with only his hand visible, wrapped around the rifle. Eyelids heavy, he thought again of becoming an outlaw. He never even considered the trouble he was letting himself in for.

The next morning dawned bright and clear with no sign of the hateful wind. By the time Shirley rose, bacon was frying in the skillet, eggs set by the side ready to cook.

"Watch this for me, will you? I have to get the horses and harness them to the wagon." Colt started for the meadow, not giving her time to answer.

Shirley dutifully turned the bacon, then headed into the bushes. Some things just couldn't wait. Hurrying back, she pushed the bacon to one side and dropped in the eggs just as Colt finished with the horses.

"Mmmm---smells good." He rummaged around in the wagon and came up with some hard biscuits. "They're only two days old; maybe we could soften 'em in the grease."

After scooping the eggs and bacon onto two plates, Shirley put the biscuits in the skillet, more-or-less frying them. They tasted pretty darned good, in her estimation. Colt simply ate, his mind obviously somewhere else.

"Do you think we can hide the horses and wagon on the reservation? I don't care if they're used, just so they're out of sight if somebody comes around."

"I'm sure no one will mind. In fact, some of the squaws will be delighted to have such big horses to pull the plow---saves them from doing it." Thinking of what she just said, Shirley was abashed. She shouldn't use the word 'squaw' . . . she should have said 'women'. While 'squaw' held no bad connotations on the reservation, it had become almost a dirty word in town. Knowing how hard the Indian women worked, Shirley wondered why this was so. But most worrisome to her was the fact that she'd used it without thinking. Yes, she was three-quarters white, but she loved her Indian heritage, and white or red, (or pink, she thought with a smile), she never wanted to demean another human being. Unless, of course, they deserved it.

Together they cleaned and put away the few cooking utensils. Shirley placed her saddle in the wagon and tied her horse to the tailgate while Colt hooked up the team. The morning dew was just beginning to dry as they set out, side by side, toward her grandparent's home.

2

"Have you heard the latest from down south, Shirley?" The woman stood behind the counter of the general store, filling Shirley's order for the hotel dining room. Tall and middle-aged, her rounded shoulders slumped constantly. Her long face always seemed to be contemplating something serious. The unbecoming dress she wore fell in barely broken lines to sensible brown shoes. The nicest thing about her was the blond hair done in a bun behind her head, but it didn't lessen the slyness of her eyes. Any tales coming her way would be passed on as soon as possible.

Knowing she was in for some gossip which she really didn't want to hear, Shirley smiled sweetly, "I've been too busy at the hotel to hear anything new."

The woman stopped filling the sack with supplies and leaned closer. "You'll never believe this one." The anticipation of what she was about to say gave her features more life than usual. "A dog helped rob the bank in Holbrook."

Shirley expected tidbits about other ladies in town, so this came as a real surprise. Then she laughed, "Someone must be pulling your leg, Peggy. Whoever heard of a dog robbing a bank?"

Peggy straightened, her eyes shining with triumph as she answered, "That's the strangest thing I've ever heard too, but word is the robber showed real ingenuity by training his dog to help. Sure would like to meet that young man--I'll bet he's really something." Her motions were momentarily suspended as she contemplated this thought.

Shirley wondered if this really could be true, and asked skeptically, "Who brought you the information?"

Peggy reluctantly left her dream to snug down her startling news. "You know the Captain out at Pipe Springs Fort? Well, he was in earlier this morning, saying it came over the wire from the Marshal in Holbrook. It said to be on the lookout for a young man with a black beard and a yellow and white dog."

Thinking back to the day Colt rode from the Indian village after supposedly stealing a horse from her grandparents, she remembered a yellow and white dog following him as he left. Was it possible he'd turned outlaw? She asked intently, "Did they give any more description of the robber or the dog?"

Startled by the sharpness in Shirley's voice, Peggy gave her a shrewd glance before answering, "Nope, that's all the Captain said. There sure hasn't been anyone fitting that description around these parts. If he were a member of the Hole-in-the-Rock gang, we'd have seen him by now. They all come here to do their drinking and gambling."

Shirley considered this statement, knowing the history of the town. Fredonia sprouted three miles south of the Utah border on the Arizona Strip. A small settlement, it consisted mainly of her hotel, a general store, blacksmith shop, and various other businesses, including the robust and rowdy, Lazy Lady saloon, every outlaw's mecca. Several homes were located back of the businesses. As with all small towns, the gossip spread mighty fast. When strangers arrived, they were quizzed quickly about the events taking place in other parts of the country, but when something came from the Captain at the Fort, you could pretty much count on it being more than idle talk. So there was no doubt that the bank in Holbrook, Arizona Territory, had been robbed. Shirley felt relieved that she heard the story secondhand from the store clerk. This gave her time to compose her thoughts before Captain Gregg came calling.

When he was in town, Captain Gregg made it a point to eat at the hotel dining room where he could continue his courtship of Shirley. She liked and respected him but love certainly didn't enter into the picture, at least not on her side. He didn't let this discourage him, however, feeling that one day she would come to her senses and appreciate his sterling qualities. Now, for once, she really looked forward to eating with him so she could hear the story firsthand.

Her order finally filled, she hurried from the store, going directly to the hotel. The Captain sat in a cane back chair on the porch and as she approached, he rose politely, taking the sack of groceries and slipping his arm in hers. He stood ramrod straight with shoulders back and a no nonsense expression on his face. The cavalry uniform he wore was always neatly pressed and the hat showed not a speck of dirt. The boots shone with recent polish, and the saber at his side caught the sunlight, reflecting it back toward her. If he would only smile occasionally, it would make him more attractive. She wondered, not for the first time, if he had any sense of humor at all. He carried the groceries back to the cook in the kitchen, then returned and pointed her to an empty table in the dining room.

As he held the chair for her, she considered what she knew about him. Captain Thornton Gregg the third came from a long line of military men. His grandfather was killed fighting the Apache Indians, and his father became a general after fighting brilliantly in the battle of Little Big Horn. Much had been expected of Thornton the third. From the day he was born, everyone felt he would surpass his predecessors accomplishments, and raised him accordingly. No time was wasted on frivolities: when other children were outside playing stick ball, he stayed inside studying battles and strategies. If he was caught gazing longingly at these other children, he got a sharp rap on the knuckles or head. No one asked, or cared, really, about the child's feelings, so he pushed them deep inside, and soon forgot that he had ever dreamed of being anything other than what his parents decreed.

All work and no play made Thornton into a strait-laced, up-tight, rather miserable man. He did everything he was supposed to, but at the age of twenty-eight, his future looked bleak. He was stuck at a small command post on the Arizona Strip, keeping an eye on the Indians and unable to do much about the outlaws. He often wished desperately for a war--even a small one would do--so his superiors could see how wasted the Captain's talents were at this post.

For now, though, his one bright spot was Shirley, whom he

felt he loved. Having never known love, he couldn't be sure, but she was pleasant and pretty and who knew, maybe having a wife would help his chances in the military. Accordingly, he saw her every chance he got, and today he had some interesting news to tell her.

When they were seated, he commented, "For the first time you seem anxious to eat with me. Always before you managed to take care of several tasks before stopping by my table for a short chat. Too short, I might add." He gave her a knowing look.

Shirley waited till the waitress took their order before speaking. "It's been rather a slow day and I have more time to relax. So why not visit with the most handsome man on the Strip?"

Captain Gregg studied her for a moment, not sure about this sudden change. "Thanks for the complement. Maybe I've made some progress with you after all. Lately I thought you weren't interested in the slightest sense."

Shirley laughed, "Now, Captain, you know you're the most eligible bachelor around." She wanted to get the story from as close to the horse's mouth as possible, but would wait patiently till he brought it up. Her wait didn't take long.

He kept watching her closely, wondering if he were reading her right today. It was so darn hard to tell when it came to women. In the end he gave up and decided to tell her some news that he imagined would fascinate her.

"One of our Sargent's came back from Holbrook this morning with the strangest tale." Then he took the next fifteen minutes to tell her the story while they ate.

Banker Jones left his home with a kiss on the cheek for his young wife, whom he'd recently married after his loving Jenny passed away. Strolling through town toward his office, he stopped occasionally to pass the time of day with friends and customers. He was a popular and gregarious middle-aged man with hair beginning to turn grey at the sides. Whistling, he stopped at the front of the bank, took out his key and opened the door. Kicking it shut behind him, he went through the office door toward his desk. Much to his surprise, a man slipped past him and sat himself down in the chair behind the desk, then propped his feet up and leaned back. His dark black hair flowed into a full black beard. The only visible part of the face was so darkly tanned, he looked like an Indian. He wore a floppy brimmed hat with the edges curled. It pushed back on his head, revealing a wide forehead over intense blue eyes, a startling contrast to the dark hair. A heavy six-gun strapped to his right thigh was aligned perfectly with a spot between the banker's eyes.

That huge round hole in the barrel of the gun looked bigger than death. The man hadn't even touched the gun or indicated that he might do so, but sweat began to form little droplets at Jones's hairline. "Good morning, Jonesy. Seeing as how it's such a clear, sun-drenched day here in Holbrook, I thought I'd take a long ride." A pleasant smile appeared on the man's face.

Jones tried to speak, but the words stuck in his throat. He never knew the man was behind him when he came into the bank--there hadn't been the slightest sound to warn him. He hadn't yet divined what lay in store for him, but with that gun lying along the leg resting on his desk, he doubted it would be pleasant. "Now what I want you to do is go back out front and lock the door. Then go to the bank vault, put all the money in one of your banks large delivery bags, and come back in here and sit down."

Just like that. He gave his order softly with no change of expression, and the smile still played around the corners of his mouth. Jones felt a tremble begin in his knees and slowly work up his back as he turned to do the task asked of him. For some reason it didn't even occur to him to object or try to make a run for it at the front door. Turning the key in the lock, he faced around to find the man standing in the office door, the smile still in place. It was hard to walk across the intervening space to the vault without shaking, but he made it. In all his days as a banker, he'd never been so scared. Attempted robberies occurred sometimes, but they were done by rough men who rushed through the front door with drawn guns and shot without warning. He always ducked behind his desk and the law usually caught up with the robbers before they were even out of town. Why was it that this calm young man seemed to spark such fear in him?

It took several tries to open the safe but finally the heavy door swung open. The sack was filled and he groaned as he handed it to the man still standing in the office doorway. "Now please sit down in your chair, Jonesy, and go on about your business. Don't leave the bank till my friend here goes through the back door."

Friend? What friend? There were only the two of them in the bank. If the robber talked this crazy, Jones felt he was lucky to only lose the money. A sickly smile spreading across his face, he sat down in the chair as he'd been told, his head resting in shaky hands. He didn't hear the back door open but when his courage rose enough for him to look up. A gasp left his lips. There, sitting on the floor wagging his tail, was the meanest looking dog he'd ever seen. The bared teeth didn't match the wagging tail at all. Smooth coated with large brown spots dotting the white coat, his medium size did nothing to alleviate the intensity of those yellow eyes. The ears stood erect and at this moment he looked as big as a cougar to banker Jones. Who would believe him when he said a dog helped rob the bank? They'd think he was crazy, or worse, a coward for not kicking the dog away and going to get help. A tentative movement on his part brought a low growl and tensing of muscles from the dog. Bile rose in Jones' throat, and he froze, defeated. It was almost funny, but he sure didn't feel any mirth, especially when the sight of that pistol barrel came back into his memory. You couldn't really call it armed robbery since the man hadn't made the slightest move towards the gun, but it was robbery nonetheless.

Time stretched forever as Jones sat there, those alert eyes and curled lips staring back at him. He knew he should get up and call for the Sheriff, but his legs wouldn't respond to his weak command. Suddenly the dog barked once, whirled, and darted out the back door, apparently left open. Jones had heard nothing but the dog must have. Wiping sweat from his face, he felt it drip down his back. He groaned again: what was he going to tell the Sheriff? He would be the laughing stock of town. Well, there was no other way--he'd have to confess and hope the law captured the crook soon. Pulling himself up, he stumbled from the office and unlocking the front door, began to holler that the bank had been robbed. People collected around him and Sheriff Johnson came on the run. "Which way did the robbers go?"

This brought Jones up short. "How in hell do I know? His dog held me at my desk till the man got away."

"What did you say?" Sheriff Johnson's voice vibrated with disbelief.

A murmur ran through the crowd, many wondering if their trusted and respected banker was having one of those 'hallucinatin'' spells. Perhaps his young wife was causing him to lose sleep. The men snickered while the women shook their heads at such a shameful thought.

Jones' legs were so wobbly that he sat down on the sidewalk. Spilling the story out in quick sentences, he finished with, "That man is a real killer."

The Sheriff threw him a disgusted look and sprinted through the bank to the back door. He saw no boot or horse tracks anywhere in the dirt. There were small dog prints running off toward the creek, but nothing else. Jones must not have been lying about the dog. He followed the prints across the prairie and down the bank of the creek to where they entered the water. Several horsemen arrived by this time and were watching him. "A couple of you fellows ride this side of the creek and a couple the other side while I go get my horse. When you see the dog prints leave the water, fire a shot and I'll come running." He hurried up the bank of the creek toward the livery stable.

He tossed the saddle on quickly, then mounted and galloped out of the stable, puzzled because no shot had broken the stillness. Horse and man raced toward the creek. Which way to go? Up or down? Since there'd been no pistol shot, he was confused. Deciding the robber would head upstream because it held more concealment, he angled in that direction. Within half an hour he came upon the men who had ridden this way. A good seven miles were covered with no sign of dogs tracks. "You see anything at all, Sam?" he asked one of them.

Shaking his head, Sam smirked, "That Jones must be runnin' a whizzer on us. Whoever heard of a dog helpin' rob a bank? 'Sides, Oscar ain't seen nothin' on the other side and there ain't been any shots fired from the ones what rode downstream."

Dumfounded, Sheriff Johnson began to curse. Then he turned his horse and spurred it into a fast run for town. He'd wring the truth out of banker Jones if it took a week. But when he got back to town the banker still seemed in a daze, having moved from the steps to a chair just inside the door, his face worried and confused.

Stepping from the saddle, Johnson blew up: "Dammit, Jones, what's this story you're trying to pass off on me?"

The words were barely audible. "Go look for yourself. The vault's empty and ten thousand dollars just walked right out by itself."

When he came back out of the bank, the Sheriff felt just as baffled as when he went in. The vault sure enough was empty. There were even scuff marks on the banker's desk where it looked like boots had been positioned. "Tell me the story again, Jones, and this time give me a description of the robber."

While the sun continued to beat down on the dusty street outside the door, the numbed banker pulled himself together and described the man. "Gosh . . . hmm . . . I'd say well over six feet tall. Broad shoulders, narrow hips, and a forty-four-forty as big as a cannon hanging from the right thigh." He paused to rub his hands nervously together before continuing. "Black hair and a coal black beard, mean blue eyes and a floppy-brimmed Stetson with the edge of the brims rolled slightly on each side. But it was that big vicious dog that scared me. He could have broken my neck with one snap of his jaws. I know he was just waiting for the chance."

Those paw prints sure didn't fit a dog as big as a cougar, but Johnson knew it wouldn't do any good to point this out to Jones.

"You see any identifying characteristics about the man? Like how he handled his gun, or walked, or something out of the ordinary?"

Face turning pink, the banker mumbled, "He didn't draw his gun. Just sat there in my chair with his feet on the desk and that gun pointing right at me."

"You mean he didn't threaten you with his gun?" Johnson tried hard to figure how a man could rob a bank without even touching his sidearm.

"Dammit, Sheriff, I was looking down the barrel of that cannon all the time. It wouldn't have taken him long at all to grab it and start shooting. Besides, he had the dog to help him."

This was too much for any lawman to have to put up with. "Well, I guess now we'll have to scour the whole country looking for a man and his dog." Disgustedly, he turned away. With no tracks to follow and a description that would fit fifty men, this case was hopelessly shot to pieces. It would be pure luck if they ever recovered the money. However, a stroke of luck--or carelessness-- did turn up the money, but not the robber.

A week after the robbery, several kids were playing hide and seek around the town. One youngster crawled under the back porch of the bank to hide from his playmates. When he finally came out, he clutched a large bank bag in his hand, still filled with the money from the vault. Sheriff Johnson and banker Jones were dumfounded by its sudden appearance.

Just as the Captain finished telling Shirley this part of the story, his lieutenant came through the door to the dining room.

"Sorry to bother you, Captain, but there's trouble at the fort. Old Bootstrap is drunk again. He's got several men cornered in the post dispensary, threatening to kill them."

"Blast it all to . . . oh . . . sorry, Shirley. Please excuse me." The Captain rose, gave a courtly bow, and followed by the lieutenant, who sneaked an appraising look at Shirley, hurried out. They mounted and somberly rode off to the fort.

Shirley didn't mind being left so abruptly. She wanted to think about the Captain's tale. It truly was a weird story and as the weeks passed, it spread across the territory like a wildfire. Every stranger coming through Fredonia retold it, with minor embellishments added.

Soon other stories just as bizarre began to filter in. The bank in Winslow had also been robbed by a man and a dog. Not a shot fired, not a gun drawn. The banker in Flagstaff was aroused from his bed by a dog barking in his room, then a man appeared and hustled him down to the bank. After cleaning out the vault, he left the dog to guard the banker till he got away, leaving no tracks at all. Each time within a week or two, the money was found somewhere in town, still in the bank's bag. From her position as the manager of the hotel in Fredonia, Shirley heard all these stories and began to seriously wonder if Colt might be the one involved in these shenanigans. To her, it sounded like something he might do. He wanted to build a reputation fast as an outlaw, and certainly this was faster than any she'd ever heard of before. Unfortunately, he also got the reputation of being dumb for leaving the money where it could be found.

Today she was busy helping seat the patrons coming for lunch when the local banker, Mr. Phillips, stepped into the hotel to eat his noon meal. A customer already there piped up, "Hey, Phillips, you better be careful. That robber will get around to you before too long."

Phillips's face darkened and he blustered, "If he knows what's good for him he won't come anywhere near my bank. Why, all the outlaws in the Strip would be after his hide."

This was true. Many of the outlaws who called the Arizona Strip their home deposited their ill-gotten gains in the Fredonia bank for safekeeping. Since no law existed on the Strip, the money would be secure and easy to get to when they needed it. Any man who even considered robbing the bank would be short of brains and soon short of life as well.

Listening to their conversation, Shirley hoped that if Colt was the one causing all this gossip, he wouldn't attempt such a dangerous task. But on second thought, it would be just like him to do so. His actions on those two days constantly crept into her mind, even though they were together for such a short time. Being unable to speak of the death of his parents or his plans for revenge, or even the fact that he was back from school, kept her on guard and unable to forget.

Shirley had arrived in Fredonia more than two and a half years ago with her parents after her father sold a lucrative gold mine in Nevada, fearing that one day someone would put a bullet in his back and steal the mine. Besides, his wife's parents often sent word about wanting her and their grandchildren closer. Her father was a white man who had scouted for the Cavalry, but had never been accepted in any local community because his wife was a Navajo. It didn't help that she was prettier and smarter than most of those women. Now they were living out their last years where they were accepted on merit, not color.

Shirley's two older brothers took a small share of the money and left for Sacramento. Neither one wanted a rancher's life, nor had they enjoyed working in the mine. The bustling California town was right down their alley, and there they opened a general store. From the occasional letters received, both young men were doing very well.

Since her mother's family lived on the Navajo reservation east of the Strip, they purchased the Circle-D ranch, about fifteen miles out of town. Shirley worked with her mother for about a year and many times worked with the ranch hands out on the range. She enjoyed the time there, but without anyone her own age and gender to pal around with, she became rather lonesome. Then the owner of the Fredonia hotel suddenly died, giving Shirley a way to be around others and make a life for herself by using the talents she knew were hers. She did some mighty hard talking and finally convinced her father to buy the hotel and put her in as manager.

None of the locals figured she'd last--just too young and inexperienced. Shirley could have told them that running a ranch and cooking for the cowhands was harder than running a hotel that already had a cook, a waitress, and a Chinese laundry just one block away. She truly enjoyed the job and met a lot of interesting people, and under her management it grew until business tripled.

Free time became illusory, so she hired Johnny, a traveling salesman down on his luck who wanted to settle somewhere and start a family. He worked diligently and proved his worth many times over. Shirley hoped he would be with her a long time.

After the lunch crowd left, she saddled Midnight and rode out to the Circle-D. Johnny and the old man who kept the hotel clean could handle everything until she returned. Being a Monday night, business would be slow, so if she decided to stay all night at the

ranch there would be no problem. Riding the fifteen miles between the ranch and town always refreshed her mind and body.
Midnight liked to travel and the first half of the trip went by fast.
Her mind went over the stories she'd heard lately and with the
horse moving along at a good clip, her thoughts centered on the
trouble here. The Circle-D employed quite a few cowboys, and
therefor the ranch didn't suffer near as much as others in the area.
Still, cattle came up missing at a regular rate.

The Bar-H lay on the other side of the Kaibab, and word from
that section of the Strip rarely reached Fredonia. Consequently
there had been very little talk of the Hastings. Someone coming
through told her several Indians were rebuilding the ranch, but
Mr. and Mrs. Hastings hadn't been seen for well over a month.
Speculation was that they took the train back east to pick up their
son from school and decided to stay a while. Shirley wanted to
ride that way several times but business being so good at the
hotel, she just couldn't get away. The last she saw of Colt was on
the reservation when he purchased a horse from her grandparents
and arranged to steal it sometime during the night. They all thought
this a big joke: buying a horse, then stealing it, showed just how
crazy white men could be. By bare dawn he was gone. She rode
back to the Bar-H with the Indians he hired to build the ranch house,
then went on to town after leaving them to their work.

The Circle-D seethed with turmoil when she arrived. Her father and several ranch hands, having just returned from a chase
after rustlers, pulled four bound and sore-footed men on tired
horses behind them. One of the rustlers sported a bullet-shattered
shoulder.

Her father met her as she rode into the yard. "You picked a

bad day to visit, Shirley. We got four rustlers to hang but we want to get some information from them first. They're all beat up but with a little encouragement, we're hoping to get one of them to break down and tell us who's behind all this trouble."

One of the rustlers looked familiar and she rode up to him. "Ollie, what are you doing with this bunch of outlaws? I thought you worked steady on the JP ranch."

Ollie stood about five foot four in his stocking feet. His ancestry appeared to be part Mexican but mostly white. He kept pushing back a mop of dark hair, revealing frightened brown eyes, high cheek bones, and a weak jaw. The mark where a belt and holster had ridden his hip showed plain in the hot sun. Unable to meet her eyes, sorrowful words spilled from his mouth. "Sorry, Miss Shirley. I was only planted there to make sure all the cowboys was busy somewhere else when the rustlers brung the cattle through. Made the mistake a tryin' to help these three others get 'em movin' faster. Mr Pugh and his men caught up with us 'fore I could get back to the JP."

"You've been on the side of the rustlers all along, Ollie? How could you? Don't you know what's in store for you now?"

"Yes'um, but it cain't be helped. I'd jist like to know who the jigger was what blocked the trail down the mesa and made us get caught. Hadn't been for him, the boys would'a got clean away."

Her father interrupted. "We got the story from Ollie but not who's back of it all. He says he collects his pay in town each month from a letter that arrives for him at the post office. No return address or anything--just money for the spy work he does."

Another puncher broke into the conversation. "I'm with him though, Miss Shirley. Who blocked that trail and stopped these boys cold in their tracks?"

Slowly she got the whole story with bits and pieces coming from her father, Ollie, and several of the cowboys. It was quite a tale. The cattle were stolen from the Circle-D range shortly after midnight. The three rustlers headed them west, planning to sell them in Nevada. Ollie joined them as they passed across JP range about midmorning. It was only a couple of miles to the trail down off the mesa to the valley below, then a straight shoot to the border. The problem came halfway down the trail. The cattle started milling and couldn't be pushed any farther. The rustlers rode to the front of the herd to see what was holding them up. They found logs and limbs piled in the trail, completely blocking it. As they started to dismount, a voice called from a forest of rocks about thirty paces away. "You boys don't want to spoil all my hard work now, do you?"

One of the rustlers didn't wait to answer. He went for his gun and a bullet sang from the rocks, catching him in the shoulder, spinning him from his horse. "Now why do you think he went and done that?" the disembodied voice asked as the other rustlers froze in place. "You lads unbuckle your gun belts and take them and your rifles and throw 'em over the rim of the mesa yonder. Oh, by the way, you better do it for your injured companion. He don't look like he's much interested in doing it himself."

The rustlers didn't hesitate to comply with this request. None of them could see the man hidden behind the rocks, but despite his joking manner, the sinister tone of his voice would make a snake shiver. They quickly stripped off their hardware, ashamed to look each other in the eye. When the guns disappeared over the rim of the mesa, he spoke again.

"Now unsaddle those horses and turn them loose. You ain't going to be doing any more riding for a spell." This task accomplished, the man fired several shots over the horse's heads and they took off back up the trail, chasing cattle as they went.

After the dust settled, the four rustlers stood dejectedly, hoping this would be the end of it.

"You boys ever walked barefoot over this desert country?"

A collective groan issued from the bunched rustlers. One of them got up the courage to whine: "Look, mister, we just do what the boss says. You oughta be huntin' him, not us."

"You squawk again and I'll bore you. Now do what I said."

The men, supporting their bleeding partner, scuffled slowly over to the mesa's edge, sat down and pulled their boots off, throwing them over the rim to join their guns and gun belts. They were about as helpless as a newborn baby and they knew it . . . it showed in the slumped shoulders and hangdog appearance as they stood knotted in the desert dirt, waiting for whatever came next. Moments passed with only the stillness and dry heat of the desert surrounding them. Finally getting up some nerve, Ollie sang out, "What you want us to do now?"

No answer came from the jumble of rough granite. Not knowing what to make of this, the men discussed their options. The injured man was lying on the ground, moaning softly. Ollie took his bandana and handkerchief to bind up the man's wound as best he could. The others stood around on the hot ground in stocking feet, trying to find a nonexistent cool spot.

After fixing the wounded man, Ollie straightened up and shouted, "For Pete's sake, fella, tell us what you want." Silence and the cry of a startled jay were his only answer.

Screwing up his courage, he started walking gingerly on tender feet toward the sunbaked rocks, expecting a bullet at any moment. To his relief, nothing happened. Upon reaching the granite pile, he paused to call out once more, "Hey, fella" then he nosed around them. Not a soul in sight . . . not even a boot print left in the dirt. Sitting down on a rock and wiping his sweaty forehead with the back of his wrist, he shouted back: "The guy done flew the coop. Ain't hide nor hair of him anywhere."

The others let out a whoop of relief and started tearing the branches away that blocked the trail. When enough had been removed so they could get past, they hotfooted it down to the bottom to retrieve their guns and boots. Ollie watched from the top, already suspecting what they would find. The heat scorching down from the sky and up from the ground added to the acute discomfort of the men as they searched everywhere for their possessions. Nothing could be found. "You might as well quit peckin' around, the varmint ran off with everything," he hollered down to them.

They tramped back up the trail, filling the air with curses and swearing death and damnation to the man who left them in such misery. Gathering in the shade of some of the rocks where the gunman had hidden, they tried to come up with a solution as to what to do. It was a long hike no matter which way they went. Sure, they still had water in their canteens on the saddles, but walking any distance at all on blistering earth and rock in nothing but stocking feet wasn't a pleasant thought.

Finally the decision was made to cut some leather from their chaps and tie it onto their feet, hoping they could walk without getting burned. This done, they agreed to strike straight north so as not to be caught by the Circle-D cowboys who were surely on their trail by now. The going was painful. The leather slipped now and then and their feet became more tender and sore with every foot placed in front of the other.

They managed to cover about five miles before reaching the shade of some scrub trees growing at the edge of the desert. Sinking down gratefully to rest and rub blisters, the sound of riders coming up their back trail started them to run for better concealment. The Circle-D men spotted them and easily overtook them. The rustlers lost their slipshod sandals in the mad dash to hide, and were hopping around trying to keep their feet from burning. It was so comical that the angry cowboys soon bent over double, laughing at the sight.

The rustler's horses were caught, saddled and with everyone mounted, the cowboys gathered the herd and drove them back to the ranch, wondering all the time who could have played such an appropriate trick. Whoever it was would get a hearty pounding on the back and a free drink if he ever made himself known.

When the story was finished, all but the rustlers laughed again. When this got around the range, the outlaws would be thirsting for blood from the man who ruined their plans. But it would definitely put a damper on the rustling.

Deciding to stay overnight at the ranch to hear what information could be pried from the unhappy men, Shirley unsaddled and went into the house to visit with her mother, who'd stayed on the porch listening quietly to the talk out front. "What do you think of that story, mother? Whoever stopped those rustlers was pretty slick. Sure would like to meet the gent."

Her mother laughed, "Now honey, don't go getting any romantic ideas about some kind of heroic figure. Luck probably played a big part and I doubt if he'll stay around here very long. He could be halfway to California by now, hoping none of the outlaws can track him."

"Mmm . . . I don't think so. Some awfully strange stories are floating around this territory lately and someone's responsible for them. I just wish I knew who. This story today may not be connected to the others but if somehow it is, it wouldn't surprise me at all."

Brows furrowed, the mother looked closely at her daughter as she asked, "What do you know about all this, young lady?"

Shirley told her mother about all the robberies that had taken place but didn't mention anything about her suspicions. Just as she finished, her father came through the kitchen door. "Looks like we ain't going to get any more out of those fellows. They're just common thieves--don't seem to know where the orders come from." He was discouraged. "We'll hold 'em till morning and see if anything changes, but it sure don't look like it will."

Supper wasn't exactly cheerful, despite the delicious pot roast and new baby peas. Doug Pugh started the mundane conversation by commenting on the heat wave covering the county. "I can't believe how hot it is. Was it this hot last year, Mother?"

"I think so, Doug. In fact, you asked the same question then." Turning to Shirley, she mentioned, "We heard from Junior a while ago. Seems he's found a girl he likes and might marry. If we decide to go to the wedding, can you watch the ranch for us?"

"Of course, Mom. It practically runs itself anyway. And we won't have to worry abut the rustlers for a while." This raised the specter of the four outlaws huddled in the barn, waiting for their inevitable death. Shirley couldn't take another bite. She laid down her fork and looked at her father beseechingly. "Do we have to hang Ollie, father? He didn't do that much, and we did get the cows back."

"You know we do, Shirley." The use of her given name showed how upset he was. Normally he called her 'honey' or 'sweetheart'. He deliberately hardened his voice as he replied, "It doesn't matter what job he did, he was part of it. The risks he took were obviously worth the risk of dying. He lost, and that's all. I don't want to hear any more about it." Doug Pugh pushed away from the table and stomped from the room.

Her mother let out a sigh and started collecting the dishes. Looking at the good side of this unfortunate mess, there was enough food left over so she wouldn't have to cook the next night. She sent her daughter an understanding glance. "I know it's not easy, honey. Sometimes in life you have to make hard decisions, and I'm mighty grateful it's your father's job to do it. He doesn't like it any more than you do, but if he lets Ollie go, who'll be next? And what does that tell the rustlers? That they're safe if they steal our cattle?"

Letting these questions hang in the air, she moved to the kitchen with a load of dishes. Shirley followed, her mind in turmoil. Of course her father was right, but this didn't make her feel any better. Now she was sorry she'd stayed--the next morning's necessary deaths hung in the air, dampening everyone's spirits. Even the cowboys were quiet . . . none of the usual chatter and laughter came from the bunkhouse. They heard the lonesome wail of a harmonica, playing a song about a cowboy who'd done wrong and was now being buried, still loved by his buddies. Shirley felt like crying.

Silently clearing the table and washing the dishes, Shirley and her mother said goodnight and went to their rooms. Doug sat for a time on the porch, rocking and smoking his corncob pipe, then turned in.

Nothing changed by morning and Shirley left the ranch before the rustlers were hung. She had no stomach for this sort of justice, but understood it. With no law around, the ranchers took the responsibility, otherwise chaos would reign. Pushing all these thoughts from her mind, she tried to enjoy the cool morning air, looking forward to her arrival in town, where even more surprises awaited her.

The horizon unveiled a pale grey haze barely lifting toward a few tenacious stars when Colt saddled and rode out of the Indian village. His gait was slow, easy and effortless, and by the time he crossed the Colorado River at Lee's Ferry, the sun's first rays slid over the burnt cliffs to the east to spread over the desert, heightening the varied colors of the rock formations. Traveling southwest, he angled toward the southern end of the valley where it met the Kaibab forest, knowing no one ever traveled that section of the Strip, it being too remote and isolated. By the time he reached the rim of the big canyon formed by the Colorado River, sundown slipped upon him. Hobbling his new horse, he fixed a cold meal, then lay out his bed roll and went to sleep with the brown and white dog lying beside him.

Morning found him up and cutting logs to form a small shelter in a deep canyon, backed by the pine-covered mountains. Three days later he had it completed and chinked so the weather would be kept at bay. A small corral leaned beside it but mostly he hobbled the horse and it stayed near the cabin. The cry of a puma on his second night there caused some worry, but when the dog began barking, he felt the horse would be safe. Plenty of water flowed from the stream that tumbled off the mountain and emptied into the river far below. He practiced every day with six-shooter and rifle to get his old skills honed as sharp as possible. His beard grew in fast and he figured another three weeks should see him to the point of showing himself to others, once his hair was coated with black dye.

The brown and white dog followed him everywhere and he found himself having conversations with it. He excused this by saying he was doing his planning out loud, but those intelligent brown eyes showed remarkable understanding. As the days passed he began to consider how this fact might be used to his advantage. The dog always followed him, whether on horseback or walking; if it were trained correctly, he might be able to use it in his plans.

Day after day he worked for several hours with the dog, making it sit on command and stay till he whistled for it. He would lie on the ground in front of the dog, staring in its eyes. The dog stared back for a short time, then would look off to the side, wagging its tail constantly. Every time the dog's look drifted, he would speak to it, causing it to look back at him. This was repeated many times and at the end of each session he rewarded the dog with a piece of jerky. There were times when he thought he'd never win, but the dog seemed so happy to be doing things with him that he kept at it. He found himself looking forward to being with the dog, and actually worried when it wasn't in sight.

When he finally got the dog trained so it would sit and stare at him for over an hour, he began to work on getting the dog to pull its lips back in a snarl, making him look mean as all get out and ready to attack at any moment. It took a lot of days to get the dog to hold that snarl till he blew the whistle. After this he moved farther away from the dog, each time making it hold its pose till the whistle blew, then reward it with jerky when it came to him. Soon he could stay out of sight for the full hour, blow the whistle, and the dog would come running. The dog learned fast and could hear the special whistle from as far away as two miles. Since they were always together, he named it 'Buddy'.

Where the man went, Buddy went, learning to almost read his master's mind. He slept curled up against the side or back of Colt. One time Colt awoke to find his arm circling the dog's stomach. Rising on one elbow and removing his arm, he gave the dog a piercing look, saying, "You're soft, warm, and don't snore, but I'm saving that spot for a special girl. Stick to my back, okay?" Buddy gave a mighty yawn and licked Colt's arm, tail thumping on the ground. Colt responded by rubbing Buddy's ears, eliciting a satisfied groan. Then, both happy, they rose together to begin the morning.

The bank job in Holbrook was the first time the two worked together. It turned out perfectly. With Buddy keeping the banker occupied, Colt deposited the stolen money under the rear porch and went to the creek behind the town, wiping out his tracks as he went. Crawling into a cottonwood tree with limbs overhanging the creek, he whistled and soon Buddy came bounding down the bank. Colt whistled again and it dashed into the water, swimming under the branch Colt clung to by his knees. Reaching down, he scooped Buddy up and climbed higher in the tree. The two of them were concealed comfortably in the top branches when Sheriff Johnson rode by, fuming and cussing.

The posse searched in vain. Colt smiled when the men gave up and went back to town. Not one of them looked up to the top of the tree. Their gaze remained fixated on the ground looking for tracks, while their quarry lay quietly above them, stroking the dog's head. Crawling down with Buddy hanging on his back, he walked upstream a way, crossed the creek and found his horse contentedly cropping grass a couple of miles west, close to where he left it. All in all, he'd succeeded in setting his plan into motion. He wanted to join the outlaws on the Strip and he hoped this would start the ball rolling.

Colt returned to his hideout and spent another week planning the job at Winslow. This time he waited till the bank closed, knowing the bank owner stayed a few minutes to check his accounts. When the owner opened the back door to go home, he found man and dog blocking his path.

"Howdy, Mr. Stewart. I need to make a withdrawal." Colt stood with one leg resting on the porch. This let the gun in its holster at his side point right up at Stewart's middle.

Stewart groaned. He'd heard the story of the Holbrook bank robbery and knew instantly what kind of a withdrawal the man meant. His eyes shifted to the dog sitting beside the man with its tail wagging and lips curled back. It did look big as a cougar, just like Mr. Jones said, and the barrel of that colt never wavered, even though the gun was not touched. Sighing, he turned back into the bank.

"Now just fill one of your large transfer bags with what's in the vault, then set at your desk for a while. My partner will keep you company."

When the job was done, Stewart sat at his desk wondering why he didn't have the courage to offer some sort of resistance. The robber and dog were such calm and deliberate characters that nothing he thought of would work. Suddenly the dog barked once and vanished through the door.

Hurriedly leaving the bank by the front door, he ran across the street for the saloon, shouting all the way that the bank had been robbed. When Sheriff Brown reached him, he was leaning on the bar, an empty glass in his quaking hand and his face ashen. The story spilled from his lips as skeptical men gathered around.

The story half finished, Sheriff Brown grabbed a lantern and rushed to the back of the bank. Not even dog tracks were visible this time on the hard-packed earth. Which way to go? He quartered back and forth over the ground, trying to pick up a clue. The hardscrabble land around Winslow would take a stick of dynamite to make a dent in it. Whoever robbed the bank could be anywhere. He could even be sitting in a chair on the hotel porch, watching the Sheriff hunt futilely in the dry dirt. Cold chills crept up the Sheriff's back and his glance swung that way. All he saw were three old codgers enjoying the excitement. He knew each of them and none of them fit the description of the robber. He continued his search for tracks but succeeded only in working himself into a frenzy.

Colt and Buddy were three miles out of town by this time, riding over the heavily-traveled trail between Winslow and Holbrook. The money lay hidden under the hay of the first manger in the livery stable. Might take a while for someone to find it, but it would eventually turn up. The hostler had been drinking in the saloon, so it was no problem hiding the money, then walking out of town by the back roads. When he got to his horse tied out in the brush, he whistled for Buddy. Now they would turn off the road about halfway to Holbrook and light out for his soddy on the Strip. Next week they'd take care of the bank in Flagstaff. That ought to give the folks enough to talk about. Then he'd head for the Strip and hope to make contact with the boss of the outlaws.

A week to the day found him camped back in the tall pines surrounding the town of Flagstaff, Arizona Territory. This being a larger town, he would have to be more careful. There were a lot of lawmen here, making his task more dangerous. He cased the town and discovered the law made its rounds each night till about midnight. They left one man at the jail. An hour before sunup, a couple of them made the rounds of the town again. Things seemed quietest on Monday nights so that's when he would strike.

Staying hidden till the weekend was over, he practiced constantly with his guns. He didn't shoot because the noise would attract unwanted attention, but he worked on speeding his draw from all sorts of positions. Buddy would watch him with one eye open as he lay on a bed of pine needles. At times he'd lift his head and listen, but when there was no alarm, he would go back to lying quietly and watching his master, the end of his tail moving every time Colt looked his way.

Monday night arrived with a real gully-washer thunderstorm blowing in about three in the morning. It dumped its load and wiped out any sign of Colt and Buddy after they robbed the bank. Despite his worry, he accomplished this rather simply:

Leaving the dog outside the back door of the banker's house, Colt picked the lock and tiptoed up the stairs where the banker slept, praying for no squeaky boards. The banker's wife and children were visiting relatives in Phoenix. The local barber divulged this little tidbit while Colt got a haircut. Amazing how men settled in the chair, a towel slid around their neck, and their mouths came open, spilling out all sorts of information. Perhaps they felt the barber wouldn't tell what he knew if they didn't reciprocate. The gleanings were sparse when it came to Colt, who managed to invent a few stories, which, it turned out, weren't really necessary. The barber's words kept time with the snipping scissors, giving Colt more news than he needed or wanted.

Colt crept noiselessly into the bedroom, watching the bed's occupant as he lay on his back, snoring softly. It must be nice to have no worries. Well, that was about to change. Moving quietly over to the tall wardrobe standing in the corner, he removed a suit and shirt, carrying it back to the bed. Next he found a drawer filled with socks and took a pair, placing them in a pair of high-topped shoes. Then pulling a feather from his pocket, he teased it back and forth under the banker's nose. The man's nose twitched, until finally a mighty sneeze shook the house. As his eyes opened, he saw a dark silhouette sitting in the chair at the side of the bed, his feet on the covers. A ray of moonlight illuminated the barrel of a six-gun pointed along the man's thigh, aimed a dead center at a spot between the banker's eyes.

This couldn't be happening to him. Arizona Rangers blanketed the town. If ever a town should be safe, it would be this one. He rubbed his hands across his face, hoping to obliterate what he thought he saw. But when his eyes focused again, the dark man drawled, "Good morning, Mr. Peters. We're going down to the bank and clean out the vault. Your clothes are laid out here on the foot of the bed."

As if on a cue, Buddy came into the room and sat, staring at Mr. Peters, his lip curled and his tail wagging. Having heard those other stories, Mr. Peters now knew how those bankers felt. This calm young man with hair and beard as black as midnight blended right into the darkness spread throughout the room. But those fierce blue eyes never so much as blinked and that gun did look as big as a cannon. Then there was the dog. Darned if it didn't look like it could break a man's neck with one flip of its head. Whoever said that a wagging tail meant a friendly dog, hadn't seen the huge jaws and gleaming teeth on this one. Why had no one noticed this man before, and where did he keep himself between holdups? Nobody ever reported seeing man and dog anywhere around. But why should they? In daylight, walking down a street, he would blend in with myriad others who calmly went about their business. Only now, in the darkness of night, did he become ominous.

Having heard that the money from the Winslow bank had been found four days after the holdup in a manger at the local livery stable, he began to hope this would be his fate also. But why did the man rob just to hide the money where it would eventually be discovered? Didn't make any sense at all?

After dressing, he walked in front of man and dog, leading them to the back of the bank, covertly sliding his glance from left to right. Dammit. Where were the Rangers when you needed them? He envisioned storming into their office and giving them what for--wouldn't they be surprised. They'd have a good excuse, and might even make some changes, but it would still be killing the coyote after the henhouse was cleaned out. Sighing, he took out his key and opened the back door.

Once inside he quickly filled a large canvas bag with money from the vault, handed it to the robber, and without even being told, walked into his office and sat at the desk.

"No wonder you're a banker, Mr. Peters, you learn awfully fast. Now set quietly till my partner leaves."

Mr. Peters wasn't a courageous man but he really wanted to know, so he managed to stammer, "What good does it do to rob a bank, then leave the money where it'll be found?"

Winking slyly at the banker, Colt remarked, "The fun of it, Mr. Peters, but maybe this time I'll keep the take. Looks like more than fifty thousand this haul."

That last statement removed all vestiges of hope from the banker and he closed his eyes. Moments drifted by until he figured enough time passed and he could go spread the word, but when he opened his eyes the dog still sat there, tail wagging, lips pulled back and a low growl in its throat. Just then the dog barked, ran to the door, and vanished in an instant. Glancing at the clock on the office wall, he noticed he'd been sitting there for almost three quarters of an hour. Plenty of time for the robber to have traveled several miles.

He groaned as he got up from the chair and staggered out of the bank to be met by a hail of cold rain. Slipping and sliding in the mud, he fell twice before he reached the Sheriff's office and burst through the door. The night man slept peacefully in his chair.

Mr. Peter's fist pounded on the desk. "Wake up, Vernon. That scoundrel just robbed the bank."

Man and chair almost fell over as the deputy came awake and tried to get a hold on the problem. "What you blabbering about, Peters?" Then his eyes widened. "You mean the same robber hit the Flagstaff bank?"

It wasn't possible-- there were too many lawmen around for that to happen. He grabbed his hat, rushed past the bedraggled banker and out the door. But he hadn't counted on the slippery mud, even though Peters was covered with it. His feet went flying and he went ass over backwards as he hit the muddy street.

Watching from the door, Peters broke out in a hearty laugh, relieving the tension inside him. "Won't do us any good to go after the man. This rain'll wipe out any tracks he might've left." For some reason, seeing the deputy turn that somersault in the mud lightened the banker's spirits; he only hoped the robber wasn't serious about keeping the money this time.

However, before the next two weeks were up he almost went wild because the money couldn't be located. Then luck smiled on him: his wife, finally back from Phoenix, found the sack of money under their bed.

This left the Sheriff's department and quite a few townsfolk wondering if Peters was pulling their leg. They couldn't believe someone would rob a bank and then conveniently leave the money under the banker's bed. On the other hand, why would the banker do it, make up such a wild story, and then just 'happen' to find the money? Only Peters himself knew the facts and he didn't want to go through it again. He knew that ornery bandit would be snickering in his sleeve when he heard all the hullabaloos going around town. Mrs. Peters tried to console her husband and eventually he began to see the experience for what it was: a joke on him. Even though he had a bad two weeks, he could now laugh about it.

Customers coming into the bank looked at the rough picture of the robber drawn up from Mr. Peter's description and were hard pressed to know whether their banker told the truth or not. With the mass of dark hair and heavy beard, facial characteristics were almost nonexistent. A drawing of the dog would have done more good. Even his young son and daughter were confused, but his wife knew her husband didn't have wits enough to make up a story like that. Besides, he'd been an altogether different person since they found the money. He seemed to revel in the stories floating around and became a lot more fun to be with. Secretly she thanked the young man for doing what he did, and if she ever found out who he was, she would grab him and give him a great big kiss and a hug.

In the meantime, Colt rode back toward his soddy at the edge of the canyon, passing by the Bar-H to see what progress was being made. The big Indian called Running Buffalo saw him ride in.

"What want you?" he asked gruffly. The Indian hadn't recognized him with the black hair and full beard. He held a rifle in the crook of his arm while the others went on with their work.

Colt pulled his horse to a stop and curled his leg around the saddle horn before he spoke. "You're doing a good job, Running Buffalo. Your Gods must be smiling on you."

Running Buffalo took two steps forward, peering hard at the man on the horse. Then his eyes shifted to the dog now sitting at its master's side. He grunted and a big smile spread across his

face. "You ugly now. Me see why bank man scared." The laugh
he emitted brought the other Indians running. They milled around
him as Running Buffalo began to talk, his arms going every which
way while stories filled the air.

They were all laughing by the time he finished. Colt didn't
understand all the fuss but the Indians were having such a good
time he hated to spoil it. Finally Running Buffalo broke from the
group and came over to the horse, putting his hand on its neck.
"You want eat turkey meat? We hunt last sun, find many wild
turkey. They good." His grin was still plastered from ear to ear.
Colt glanced down at Buddy, who gazed back with pleading eyes.
The smell of cooking meat brought slobbers to his mouth, which
he licked away with his tongue. The last time Colt ate a good
turkey dinner, his parents had been alive. Stepping down, he
patted Buddy on the head and ground tied his horse. Walking
with the Indians around the structure of the house, he saw a
smokeless fire burning and a large turkey gobbler roasting above
it. His hosts continued to jabber back and forth with each other,
apparently retelling some story they heard about him. He wondered how they knew he was the bank robber--did their Gods
see everything?

The squaws doing the cooking giggled and pointed at him as
the men and Buddy devoured over half the turkey. There were
wild onions, bread made from ground acorns, roasted squash
and roots from some sort of desert plant. All together, he decided
he'd been missing something by not stopping here more often.
Buddy agreed, going off for an enjoyable roll in the dirt.

As Colt licked his fingers, Running Buffalo inquired, "You like
house?"

The log sides were up but the roof was only half finished. "Looks like the one that stood here before. You're doing a bang-up job, Running Buffalo. The barn is almost complete and the corral looks big enough to hold a good amount of horses."

The compliment had its effect on the pleased Indian. His chest expanded as he talked. "Me figure you need big place after you find killers of women. Cunning Fox say you kill four white eyes. That good. We make good home for you."

Colt had almost forgotten Cunning Fox, but now, at hearing her name, he knew she lingered in the back of his mind most of the time. And on the spur of the moment he decided to ride on into Fredonia and see her.

The Indians went back to work as he mounted and rode away. Crossing the Kaibab mountain, he bedded down for the night on the other side where it met the desert. He always slept light so when Buddy gave a low growl, he came instantly awake, letting his senses test the surrounding air. The muted sound of horses and men moving out on the desert, drifted by. In this flat country sounds could travel for miles. Knowing that no honest rancher worked his cattle at night, Colt rose and finding his horse about half a mile away, saddled and rode toward the activity. Hidden by a copse of scrub pine, he watched as men gathered cattle from the range, then began to drift them toward the west end of the Strip.

An ingenious idea sped across his brain and without hesitating, he rode wide around the slowly moving herd, Buddy guarding his rear, aiming for the trail down the red cliffs from the top of the mesa. Once well out of earshot of the rustlers, he rode rapidly and by midmorning reached his objective. Roping several fallen logs, he drug them to where the trail narrowed and with a few loose limbs, constructed a barrier. He just had time to hide his horse and Buddy at the base of the trail and get back to the rocks before the herd reached the obstruction.

With all the guns and boots at the bottom of the cliffs, he wiggled down and gathering them up, strung them on his rope to drag several miles away. Satisfied, he turned and back tracked toward Fredonia. Tonight he would put one more part of his plan to work.

4

Morning exploded over the little town of Fredonia with a sudden blast of sun rays streaming from the east. White wisps of clouds floated through the lifting sky, occasionally blocking the rays from touching the desert below. It was so quiet you could hear daylight coming. Then the sounds of a rooster split the stillness and the peace that spread over the range was broken.

As the town came awake, people began to move around the streets. Shop doors were opened, sidewalks were swept and the hotel dining room began to pour sweet smells into the air. A few of the outlaw bunch had overdone their celebration the night before and being too drunk to stay on their horses, slept at the hotel. The noises this morning were beginning to tell on blurry eyes and aching heads. The first place these sorrowful boys headed was back to the hair of the dog that bit them, namely the saloon, to quench the torture in their throats and skulls.

Relief slowly beginning to come over them, they started a few games of poker while breakfast cooked at the hotel. It promised to be another scorcher of a day on the Strip and the ride to the outlaw camp seemed less and less appealing. Maybe they'd stay in town and pass the time inside where it was cooler. With any luck, they could play poker all day and get drunk again tonight. When they heard the triangle, clang at the hotel, they got up and tramped over to eat a hearty breakfast. The grub here was so much better than what they got at camp, that each of them vowed to stay over more often.

"Wonder how the boys what worked night 'fore last did with their cattle?" one of the outlaws asked as food dribbled from his mouth.

The apparent leader of the bunch hissed, "Shut your mouth, Hank. Won't do any good to spread word about us having anything to do with that job."

Hank kept a death grip on his fork and continued eating as though he hadn't heard a word. There were only two local people in the dining room and he figured they were far enough away, they wouldn't hear a thing. "Bill, what time was it when you left that little filly last night? Didn't hear you come in at all?"

With a laugh Bill intoned: "She hung onto me till just after daybreak. I sure hated to leave that warm bed behind."

The banter of the men went back and forth while they ate, then they filed out after paying, to amble back to the saloon. An hour went by before the rest of the business people started to open their shops. One of the outlaws watched the town from over the top of the batwings as Mr. Phillips walked jauntily down the street whistling a popular tune, stopped at the bank door, inserted the key and opened up. The shades over the bank windows went up with a snap and two customers went inside.

The cashier arrived and handled the transactions since they were only deposits from the night before's business. About an hour later Phillips greeted two Wells Fargo men who'd stashed twenty thousand in the vault for safekeeping last night. They would continue on their way to St. George, Utah, today. Paper work taken care of, he went to the vault at the back of the bank, dialed the combination and swung the door wide. A smile lit his face as he stepped into the vault with the two men right behind him.

"Yesiree, you certainly left your money in the safest bank in the country, gentleman. Why, there's never been even an attempt to rob this bank." Content with his banks infallible reputation, at first the significance of what he was seeing didn't register on his brain.

The two Wells Fargo men roughly pushed him aside as they rushed to the open strongbox. "Empty. By my mother's grave, the money's gone." They were standing as if in a trance, gazing down at the empty strongbox. The padlocks had been pried open and were lying brokenly on the floor.

Quickly Phillips eyes rose from the empty box to the shelves where the bank kept its money. Not a single bill remained on those shelves. It hit him with such force that he sank down to the floor, shaking his head and muttering "No, no, no."

Hearing the commotion, the cashier rushed into the room. It was as empty as a church on Saturday night, and he suddenly realized how stark and bare a vault could be without any money.

The leader of the Fargo men swore effusively in two different languages. "Phillips, you said your bank was safe. That's why we stopped here last night. Now there ain't a shred of money left in this cotton-pickin' place." Furious, his jaw clenched and his eyes roved around, trying to figure how the robber got in. Stomping back out of the vault, he examined the lock and found no signs of tampering. Both men then checked the locks on the front and back doors-- nothing had been forced. The locks worked perfectly and were still in place.

Going back to the vault, they hauled Phillips to his feet. With their help, he staggered to the chair in his office and folded into it. The two Fargo men eyed him, then looked at each other, simultaneously arriving at the same conclusion. Choking down his anger, the leader said "Okay, Phillips, this was an inside job. Try to think. None of the door locks or the vault lock have been tampered with. Who else have the keys and combination?"

Phillips' eyes dilated as the import of their words sank into his confused mind. "Why, I . . . I'm the only one with that information. No one else would be trusted with it." Then he groaned as the significance of his words spread through his body.

The two men eyed him contemptuously. "So where'd you put the money, Phillips? It ain't likely you could have taken it too far, seein' as how you don't ride a horse at all. Or did you have a partner in on this deal?"

Seeing no hope in the sternness of their faces, Phillips whimpered, "Honest Injun, I don't know anything. Why, the outlaws will string me up by my thumbs when they find out about this." All he could envision was what they would do to him now that their money was gone. The Wells Fargo men were insignificant in his thinking--the outlaws were the ones to be feared.

Disgusted with this line of questioning, the two men turned and hurried out of the office. They knew where Phillips lived and went directly there, pounding on the front door and scaring his wife almost to death. They searched the house from front to back and found nothing. All the while Mrs. Phillips wrung her hands and moaned because they were making a mess of her beautiful home.

Next they checked the livery stable to see if any horses or buggies might have left in the night. Word spread and the outlaws who stayed in town were soon following them wherever they went. The stable man assured everyone that the same horses which were there last night were still there this morning and no wagons or buggies were missing.

By now most of the town trailed behind them, and they returned to the bank where Phillips still sat in his chair, benumbed and ghostlike.

"Phillips, who did you have help you in this little caper?"

Startled from his reverie, Phillips' eyes focused on them. "Do you really think I'd be stupid enough to pull something like this?"

When they stopped to think about it, the two men realized they had jumped to conclusions and gone off half-cocked. "Well, how else would a person get into that vault?" one of the men asked testily. Then his mind clicked: no one had checked the ceiling while they were in it.

Dashing from the banker's office, they ran for the vault only to stand with puzzled faces as they contemplated a perfectly intact ceiling. It had to be an inside job . . . no other explanation fit. But not one person in town believed Phillips had the guts to pull off something like this. Besides, it was just too pat an answer. Such a plan could be so easily traced to the banker that he'd have been foolish to stick around.

Shirley rode in while they were still in the bank trying to figure out what to do. Noticing the people gathered at the bank door, her heart leaped into her throat. Surely Colt wouldn't have hit the bank here in Fredonia. Guiding Midnight to the crowd in front, she dismounted and asked the storekeeper what was going on.

"The bank's been cleaned out slicker'n a whistle, along with twenty thousand of Wells Fargo money left there last night. The Fargo men think banker Phillips did it, but knowing him, most of us doubt it."

"You got that right," one of the outlaws added. "Phillips would be plumb crazy to do this and stay in town. He knows we'd string him up pronto. I figger it's that smart aleck what's been doing all the robberies down south. He's mighty tricky, and who else could do somethin' like this?"

A young woman in back of the crowd said the obvious: "If he did it, all you have to do is wait a week or two and the money will show up. Seems like it's all a lark to him--a kid pulling a prank."

Shirley stood by her horse wondering if it really was Colt's doing. It didn't fit the way he normally worked, and if it were so, he'd bring every outlaw in the country down on his neck. She heard another man voice his opinion. "Whoever it was must be a whiz. Nobody can figure how the robber got inside the vault. Ain't clue one around to tip them off as to what happened. The money seems to have sprouted wings and flew off all by its lonesome."

"Yeah, maybe he's got a bird workin' with him now instead of a dog."

This brought a laugh from most of the crowd. They all believed it was the same robber, and felt the money would turn up sooner or later, so weren't truly worried. Shirley hoped it would be sooner, if it involved Colt---the longer the money remained missing, the angrier the outlaws would be.

Once the initial excitement passed, people began to eagerly search the town in hopes of being the one to discover the hidden money. All day they turned over rain barrels, scrambled under porches, the sidewalk, outhouses. They looked on roof tops and in every bale of hay in the livery stable, but uncovered nothing except a little trash, quickly tossed aside.

For three days this went on with not a place in the whole town left to ransack. More of the outlaw bunch came into town to help. Mitch, their leader, was jovial at first, but by the end of the third day his patience wore thin and he got meaner by the hour. The bunch gathered back at the saloon and Mitch sent two of them to the banker's house to bring him back for more questioning; this time without the gloves.

When Phillips came through the door, he looked like death warmed over. His pale, haggard face; sleepless, red-rimmed eyes; rumpled, odorous clothes, all spoke of the strain he endured. Although he'd expected a showdown with the outlaws, he still protested weakly as the two hauled him into the saloon.

Mitch sat nonchalantly at a table in the rear, tilted back in a chair, black Stetson slung low over hard, dark eyes. He removed the cigar from his mouth as his men dumped Phillips in a seat opposite him. In a voice as quiet as a graveyard, and somehow as deadly, he said, "We've got us a problem here, Philips. Your bank---a safe one, according to you---lost all our money. Now I know you didn't steal it yourself . . . you don't have the guts. But you're still responsible for it. Some of the men want to take it out of your hide, but I said your hide ain't worth that much. I might change my mind though, if you don't come up with a solution real quick like."

Phillips slumped lower in his chair, sniveling, "How am I going to get that kind of money? You know my money was in the bank too."

Hank banged his chair to the floor, rose threateningly, and slapped a meaty hand on Phillips' shoulder, saying, "Maybe you'll have to rob a bank." This brought a roar of laughter from the men.

Hopeless, all hopeless. He didn't know where the money was or how it got out of the bank. His nights were agony and his wife constantly wrung her hands, asking what they were going to do. They might as well shoot him now and get him out of his misery. He looked at the outlaw with so much pain in his eyes that Mitch involuntarily flinched. "Mitch, I don't know where the money is and there isn't any way I can ever get enough to pay you back, so just drill me and get it over with."

This abject statement brought a sobering air around the saloon. The outlaws realized their vicious attitude wouldn't get them anywhere, and they wondered how to proceed.

Suddenly the batwings flew inward as a man rushed into the saloon, shouting, "Phillips, we found how the robber got into the bank."

Mitch grabbed the man by the shirt collar, "What're you talking about? We went over that vault like a pack of flies on a fresh cow patty and didn't find a thing."

The young man pulled away from Mitch's grasp and took the time to straighten his shirt, knowing this was his moment. Still, he couldn't keep the excitement from his voice. "You know we looked under the back steps of the bank and didn't see anything out of whack, so we stopped at that. Well, I crawled under those steps tonight and guess what I found."

The barroom got as quiet as a held breath. No one wanted to miss the answer and the young lad beamed with pride as he said, "There's a hole that leads right up under the floor of the vault. Four bent horseshoe nails hold the board in place so someone walking over the board won't notice anything unusual. The robber pushed that board aside to get into the vault, then put it back in place after he had the money, bending the four nails tight against the bottom of the other boards."

Silence for a split second, then everyone made a mad dash for the door. Several men tried to get through it at once, blocking it completely. Seeing what was up, Mitch bounded out the back and around to the street, sprinting for the rear of the bank. The steps were shoved aside and sure enough, it looked like a hole going under the foundation of the bank went right into the vault. He noticed where the dirt from the hole spread across the ground, natural as all get out. Swearing profusely, he wiggled through and was in the vault when the first of the men from the saloon arrived.

Phillips, completely forgotten in all the commotion, stumbled from his chair to the street. Relief made his legs weak, but he continued on to the bank, going through the open door which hadn't been locked--with no money inside, why bother? When he got to the vault, several men were huddled inside. They parted so he could see the floor and the offending board. Pulling out a limp handkerchief, he mopped his brow.

Everyone began talking at once but Mitch shouted them down. "Phillips, I owe you an apology. This must be the way the robber chose to clean out the bank, all right. But who would ever a thought to dig up inside it? He worked mighty quiet digging that hole without anyone stumbling on to him."

"Hell, he coulda been working on it every night for a week for all we know." Hank wondered how long a job like that would take. He figured a good strong man could probably dig it in two, three hours. No one much came around the back of the bank at night, it being dark and isolated.

Phillips backed out of the vault and perched on a stool behind the teller's counter. Hand still clutching the damp handkerchief, he mopped his sweating face again. At least now they would believe him. But how to pay back the depositors, among which most were outlaws? He hadn't the foggiest idea.

Mitch strolled over, scratching his head. "The man who did this is slicker'n snot on a doorknob." His voice held a certain respect. "Sure would like to meet the fellow. We could use a man with brains in this outfit. If he's the same one who robbed the banks down south, we could really clean up the territory with him and his dog working for us. Fact of the matter is, we'd just lay around town drinking and gambling with the money he brought back."

Hank agreed, "That's the way I'd like to do business---just stay here and let the money roll in." A moment slid by before he added the obvious: "But if he gave the money back to the banks each time, we'd get nary a red cent."

"Still and all, we might change his mind on that little problem. At least I'd sure like to give it a try." Mitch wanted to get hold of the man responsible for the recent excitement and pitch him a humdinger of a sales talk.

"Sure ain't doing us no good to stand round here gabbing. Let's git back to the Lazy Lady and mebbe the whisky'll shed some light on what to do next."

They left Mr. Phillips sitting in the bank, his head resting in his hands. Not one of them felt sorry for the trouble they'd caused: their minds were on the robber and how to snare him. All sorts of suggestions were offered as they sauntered toward the saloon.

Mr. Briggs from the general store cornered Mitch as he passed by, anxious about the money. He hoped that if the outlaws knew how the robbery was done, they might also know where to find the money. He figured all outlaws stuck together. "Mitch, do you think we'll find where he left the money this time? I sure do need change occasionally and the bank is the only place where I can get it."

Mitch stopped as he considered Mr. Briggs. Didn't the man realize they'd been hunting the money for three days? What did these people use for brains? "Now how would I know that? That fool robber don't seem to take me into his confidence."

"I just thought you might have an idea since you know how robbers think." As soon as the words were out of his mouth, Mr. Briggs cringed. Mitch was sure to be offended. Although everyone in town knew he was an outlaw, no one actually said it. Sleeping dogs, and all that. He watched Mitch, eyes filled with worry.

Disgusted, Mitch moved on, throwing back, "Well I sure don't know how this one thinks." He continued to mutter under his breath, "I never heard of such goings on in all my days. A thief using a dog to help him rob a bank is just plain ridiculous."

Heidi, one of the bar girls who'd followed the crowd throughout the tumult of the evening, felt this was too much. "It worked, didn't it? And I don't care what the rest of you think--if that man ever shows up in the Lazy Lady, I'm going to buy him a drink and stay as close to him as possible. He's one whale of a man as far as

I'm concerned."

Another bar girl echoed the same sentiments. "If you get tired of him, honey, just toss him my way--I know how to catch."

"Aw, you girls would take any man that looked twice at you," Hank growled, tired of all this to-do over someone they didn't even know. Every time somebody different came along, they'd get all excited and fluttery. Made a man want to puke.

Heidi, practical as well as pretty, grabbed Hank's arm as they approached the door of the saloon. "Sweetie, I was only kidding. You know I'm yours whenever you want me."

"Humph," came his annoyed reply. But he didn't move her hand from his arm.

Oblivious of the group behind him, Mitch shouldered through the batwings, still mumbling about the robber. Two steps and then he stopped dead in his tracks. Hank, with Heidi on his arm, bumped into him while the rest of the crowd fanned out to see what was going on. A gasp of astonishment rippled through them. There, standing at the bar, nonchalantly drinking a glass of whiskey, stood a young man with coal black hair and a full black beard. His yellow and white dog stood on top of the bar lapping up a bowl of milk, his tail wagging back and forth in unison with his tongue. A colt forty-four-forty nestled in a brown leather holster on the man's right thigh. His right hand hung just at the side of the gun as he lifted the glass of whiskey with his left hand. A floppy brimmed hat with the outer edges curled up lay on the bar beside the dog, who ceased drinking and now watched them intently.

Neither of them moved when Mitch and the crowd stopped, but Mitch was aware of the stranger's watchful blue eyes resting on him in the mirror behind the bar. Mitch knew in an instant that man and dog were poised to react rapidly, depending on which way the wind blew. His senses told him to tread carefully: this man had done some amazing things in the past month. The gun looked well cared for and the holster, shiny with oil, made a fast draw a sure bet.

As Mitch stood undecided, nerves on the edge, he noticed a large bank bag sitting on the floor near the feet of this black haired stranger. A grunt of relief slipped past his lips while those behind him waited for some signal to tip the scales. Hearing it, Hank knew there'd be no fireworks, so eased around Mitch, heading for the sack. Careful of the dog and keeping a wary eye on the stranger, he nevertheless wasted no time in pulling the bag to him. Amazement spread across his face when he opened the top. "Gosh, I ain't never seen so much money in one sack in all my life."

Breaking out of his trance, Mitch covered the space to the bar in four long strides. Pike went behind the bar with a worried expression on his face. "Pike, pour drinks all around. We're going to celebrate the return of the bank's money."

The bartender relaxed as the crowd surged forward. They too had seen the bank bag on the floor, and that, plus Mitch's promise of free drinks, brought on a carnival atmosphere. Shouting and cheering, they pushed up to the bar only to be stopped short as the yellow and white dog lifted its lips and a deep growl pierced the room, silencing them all. Colt turned from the bar, leaving the bank bag where it sat, and ambled to a table at the back of the barroom. The dog ceased its growl, jumped down and followed him, then leaped to the tabletop as though waiting for food.

With the path to the bar clear, men and girls scurried over and began ordering all at once. Mitch grabbed a bottle and an empty glass, then carried both over to the robber's table. Not presuming too much, he stood as he spoke. "I gotta say, stranger, you sure know how to set a town on its ear. That dog of yours is right smart at his job too."

Colt reached over and rubbed the dog's ears, his eyes never leaving the outlaw's face. "You must be Mitch. I've heard a lot about you and the boys. People say you're the meanest and fastest in the west."

Subconsciously Mitch began to like this man. He hadn't heard any talk like that but it did his heart good to hear that this stranger heard it. "Mind if I sit down?"

Pointing to a chair across from him, the man drawled. "Go ahead. Buddy only attacks those I tell him to, or if someone wants to cause me trouble."

At this statement the dog growled again and Mitch, who had started to sit down, quickly reversed course and stood back up. Then somehow a signal passed between master and dog because Buddy jumped down from the table to lay at his master's feet. Since it now looked safe, Mitch gingerly took the indicated chair. The man sipped his drink without the slightest indication he'd noticed the actions of Mitch.

Pouring a hefty shot of whiskey and gulping it down, Mitch studied the person across from him. Talk about cool and confident! Nobody but a fool would want to tangle with this man and his dog. No wonder the bankers all capitulated so quickly-- if he were in their shoes he'd probably do the same. While appearing relaxed, this stranger gave the impression of fine-tuned alertness: his eyes never left those of Mitch as he sipped his drink, always with his left hand.

The minutes ticked by without so much as a breath of air crossing the man's lips. Finally giving up, Mitch broke the silence between them. "You the feller who caused all the trouble down south?" He knew this was true but wanted confirmation.

Those steely eyes grew tighter and Mitch thought he heard a growl low in the throat of the dog, then the man's words came out in a soft drawl. "You have any objection if I am?"

If any other man had spoken this way, Mitch would have slapped leather faster than a rattler's strike. However, this time he swallowed hard. He wanted this black-bearded stranger with his unusual ideas to be part of the gang. "Don't make any difference to me as long as you recovered the money from the bank here in Fredonia. Those Wells Fargo men are gonna be right happy to hear their twenty thousand's back."

His talk stopped when the batwings burst inward and Phillips came rushing through. His eyes locked onto the bank bag still setting on the floor and he ran to it, almost diving inside to see the money staring back at him. It was unusual in this hardened western desert to see a grown man cry, but tears rolled unashamedly down the banker's face as he hunkered beside the bag.

Heidi stepped over to him, lightly touching his shoulder. "Black Beard, the man sitting over there with Mitch, is the fellow who recovered the money and brought it back, Mr. Phillips. You should thank him."

Phillips remained immobilized, staring at the money, awash in a wonderful feeling of relief. His life had been restored. Folks would again look at him with respect, and he was sure the outlaws would bend over backwards being nice to him, trying in their own way to apologize for their harsh words and ungenerous thoughts. Best of all, his wife would be happy, bringing back the love and contentment to their home.

Finally Mitch called out, "Hank, you and a couple of others help Phillips over to the bank with the money. And while you're there, nail those floorboards down so tight it'll take a week to get 'em up again."

He turned his attention back to the man at the table with him. "Heidi seems to think your name is Black Beard. That the moniker you prefer?"

"She's a right pretty young woman, so that's as good as any." Not a trace of concern crossed his face.

Deciding he would wait till another time to learn more about this man, Mitch stood up from the table. "Well, guess I better get back to headquarters; the boys will want to know what's been going on."

No sign came from the man showing that he even heard the statement. He let his eyes switch to the dog and began to stroke its neck and back.

When Mitch exited the saloon, several gang members swallowed their drinks rapidly and followed him out. Moments later Colt stood up and with Buddy at his heels, left by the back door. Heidi had started over to sit with him, just as he got up to leave. Sighing, she turned back to the bar. A closer look at those blue eyes was enough to make her thankful for an ordinary outlaw like Hank.

A falling star split the black velvet sky, causing Colt to change course just slightly. He took his directions from the stars when he left the bank of Fredonia, heading toward the Circle-D. He would just have enough time to get there before the sun crested over the eastern hills.

After stopping the cattle rustlers, he stayed in the area to see what would happen. When the Circle-D cowboys overtook them, he headed straight for the bank in Fredonia. Reaching there about midnight, he dug his way into the bank and cleaned it out. A small cave above the town provided a perfect hiding place for the money. Now anxious, he rode quickly to get to the Circle-D before the rustlers were hung. If his calculations were correct, that would be done at dawn, and he wanted to be there, if possible.

Dawn lightened just as he reached the trees that grew a couple of a hundred yards in front of the ranch house. Dismounting, he hunkered down waiting for activity to get going around the ranch. Buddy lay at his feet content to chew on the jerky Colt gave him for breakfast. The last three days had seen them cover a lot of ground and his horse showed the strain. When this job was done, he should have a pretty good in with the outlaw bunch, as long as they didn't find out he was the one who stopped the rustlers yesterday. Then he could take a few days off and rest up till the next part of the plan went into effect.

An older man, probably the owner of the ranch, came out of the main house with four ropes in his hands. A hangman's noose dangled at the end of each rope. Striding grimly across the yard, the man entered the bunk house. A short time passed and he came out, followed by seven cowhands trudging behind him, angling toward the silent barn. A puncher sitting in front of the barn door with a rifle across his lap stood as the group approached, then turned to open the door. As the suns golden rays peeked over the trees in the east, the four wretched rustlers were led from the barn with their hands tied behind them. Several cowboys stepped into the corral to catch the horses belonging to the outlaws. Leading them outside the fence, they saddled and turned them toward the man who had come from the ranch house.

The ropes with the nooses at the ends were thrown over the plank extending from the loft that was normally used to haul cut hay into the loft. The man's voice carried plainly to where Colt waited, rifle ready. He'd have to work fast but with luck, he could accomplish what he wanted to do.

"You have any last words before you meet your maker?" The older man asked this question in a hard voice, his face a mask showing no emotion whatsoever. All feeling had been squeezed in a knot and tucked deep inside so he could get through this ordeal.

The rustler's gazed at the ground, trying to think of what to say. None of them wanted to beg for their life, knowing it would do no good. Neither did they look forward to hanging. As the moments drifted by, Ollie, eyes lowered, said haltingly, "Mr. Pugh, please tell Shirley that I'm sorry I disappointed her. She was always nice to me when we met in town--wanted to make sure things was going well at the JP ranch. She was this way to all us cowboys, so please give her the message."

Silence met his statement while Mr. Pugh waited for anyone else to speak. When no one had anything to say, he motioned the rustlers to mount their horses. Since their hands were tied, the cowboys helped them up and led them under the plank from the barn. "I'll tell her your last thoughts, Ollie."

On the hill, Colt closed his finger around the trigger of his rifle and waited. Mr. Pugh stepped back and the ranch hands placed the ropes over each man's neck. Other cowboys stood behind each horse, holding a quirt. Mr. Pugh raised his arm in preparation for the signal which would send the outlaws dangling from the end of the ropes.

Then a yellow and white dog ran out from the trees, behind the men in front of the barn. When his bark reached the ears of the cowhands getting ready to do their duty, they stopped, stunned as the dog ran toward them, barking furiously. The horses under the four rustlers grew nervous and began to prance. The dog ran straight for the horse's heels, barking so loud nothing could be heard. Mr. Pugh stood riveted, his arm still raised, as the men with the quirts waited, wondering if the dog was going to do their job for them.

Four quick rifle shots shattered the air. The horses took the bit in their teeth and bolted. To the surprise of Mr. Pugh and the cowhands, the outlaws on the horse's backs went with the horses, the nooses and a short length of rope dangling beside them. The remainder of the ropes hung from the plank, idly swinging back and forth. A rifle bullet had completely severed the rope circling each outlaw's neck, as the horses sped away.

The only man with a gun available was the guard who'd been sitting in front of the barn door. Before he could recover from the sudden turn of events, a thirty-thirty slug smashed into the shell chamber, making the gun useless and knocking the guard off his feet. More slugs began to splatter the dirt around the hanging party as rustlers and horses reached the trees, running full out to cover as much ground as possible. Ollie was the only one of the group to see the black-bearded man levering shells into his saddle carbine and pulling the trigger as fast as possible. The dog came running back as the last slug left the muzzle of the gun.

Colt sprinted to his horse, swung to its back, and pounded after the rustlers, Buddy leading the way. The men, back at the barn, stood in shock till Mr. Pugh recovered and started shouting orders. While one of the cowboys ran to get guns, the others vaulted the corral fence, going for their horses and saddles. Their haste and shouting startled the horses, who milled around in confusion. The more they were chased, the more the skittish horses tried to get away. Mr. Pugh climbed onto the top rail of the corral fence, waving his hat and shouting at his men to calm down. The only thing he accomplished was to add to the din. A buckskin became so frightened it tried to jump the corral fence. It didn't make it, but did succeed in knocking the top pole down. The other horses saw this as an escape route to freedom, peace, and quiet, and wasted no time jumping over. This left the frustrated cowboys standing in the corral with the one horse, who knocked the pole down in the first place.

Choking on dust, cussing, and sending shamefaced glances at their boss, the cowboys stood watching their horses disappear in the trees. What a washout. Who could have anticipated someone coming to the rescue of the rustlers, especially doing it the way it had been done? It would've been much easier for their friends to creep up on the guard during the night, overpower him, and let the rustlers escape. At least two or three men were in the trees firing at the ropes . . . no single man could've been that accurate with his rifle and thrown lead so fast.

When his thinking began to gel again, Mr. Pugh found his voice. "Cap, saddle the horse that's left and go round up some of the others. The rest of you men grab your hardware. We're going after that bunch." He slipped from the corral fence, running for the ranch house. The men headed for the bunkhouse, intercepting the cowboy laden with their guns. Unfortunately, there were no horses to ride for the next two hours. While waiting, two cowboys set out for the trees to check for tracks. They returned with an unbelievable story.

"You ain't gonna believe this, boss, but it was only one man firing those shots." They stood defiantly, knowing how unlikely this sounded.

"You're wrong!" Mr. Pugh, his blood already boiling, glared at them. The men were mistaken. But he knew they were good at tracking, the best around. If what they said was true, and looking at their stubborn faces he didn't doubt it, how was it possible?

And with a sharpshooter like that in the outlaw gang, what chance did the ranchers have? He simmered down and apologized. "Sorry, boys, I shouldn't doubt you. It's just beyond reason. Go see how the fellows are doing with the horses."

While the men at the ranch cooled their heels and Mr. Pugh became more and more exasperated, Colt pounded in a different direction from the rustlers, who headed toward the Hole-in the-Rock country. He wasn't ready just yet to make himself known to the outlaw bunch. Besides, when the Circle-D thundered out of the yard, they would follow the trail left by the four rustlers. At the time he didn't know of the fiasco going on at the ranch.

His horse carried him over the north end of the Kaibab mountain and by nightfall he was at the Bar-H. For the next two days he helped the Indians work on the ranch house, figuring most of the people on the Strip would be so occupied with the latest robbery and the rescue of the rustlers, that they wouldn't travel this far afield. He left the ranch in time to recover the money and arrive in Fredonia late in the evening.

Now as he left the saloon by the back door, he turned toward the hotel, anticipating a hot bath and a soft feather bed for the rest of the night. He'd already stabled his horse in the barn behind the hotel, where it would be handy if he needed it. But he really didn't expect any trouble; his standing with the outlaws should be good at this point, and because they more or less controlled the town, he could relax.

A rheumy-eyed old man lounged behind the hotel check-in desk. The man leaned close to see the name Colt wrote on the register, spelling it out slowly, then repeating it. "Black Beard. Say, ya any relation to the feller what killed all his wives?" The old man heard the story when he was a youngster but never attached it to a foreign land.

Colt chuckled. "He's a distant cousin of mine, old man; maybe I could introduce him to you some day. And his beard was blue."

The old man's eyes stared steadily back at him. "If ya don't mind, mister, I'd as leef not meet the gent. I got enough troubles 'thout bringing no more down on my head." He was so earnest with this statement, Colt decided to let it ride. No use trying to explain this late at night.

As he turned with the key toward the stairs, he asked, "Would it be possible to get a hot bath somewhere tonight?"

Coming from behind the counter, the man motioned him to follow. "Miss Pugh keeps a couple a pails a hot water on the stove for jist sich late arrivals. If'n you'll carry the buckets and foller me, ya can take as long as ya want ta soak." Staring at the heavy growth of hair on Colt's face, he mumbled, "If you'd like a haircut and shave, I kin do that fer a quarter."

"No thanks, just the hot bath tonight, although I'll take you up on that offer another day." Colt didn't know how long it would take to get the man responsible for his parent's murder, but after accomplishing that, he'd definitely want a haircut and shave.

Buddy followed the two of them, keeping a watchful eye on the old man until he left. When Colt poured the buckets of hot and cold water in the tub and started to step in, the dog beat him to it. So the two of them took a bath together, then dried off and went up to bed. Again Buddy beat him into bed. Colt had to smile: if he didn't know better, he'd figure the dog was a lot smarter than he was. It liked all the comforts the two of them had missed lately. This ritual was commonplace at his shack by the canyon, and Buddy seemed happy that things were partly back to normal.

The feather bed felt so good that neither he nor the dog wanted to get up the next morning, but he knew this day would either see him a member of the gang or he'd have to try something else. The breakfast crowd was thinning out by the time Colt entered the dining room, Buddy at his heels. He headed for an empty table in the corner. Sitting with his back to the wall, he observed the people eating breakfast. The folks were about the same as could be found in any other small western town. Mostly men filled the place, just a few women scattered here and there. A lot of them stopped eating and talking when he and the dog came through the door. After he sat down they went back to their meals, sending occasional wary glances his way.

A young lady came to take his order who appeared to be in her late teens or early twenties. The long blond hair flowing over her shoulders hung almost to her waist. There were a few small freckles sprinkled on a pert upturned nose that bisected two steady hazel eyes. Her gingham dress was partially covered by a rather frilly apron tied around her middle. An expression of cheerful anticipation covered her face as she approached the table. "Good morning, stranger. What would you like this morning?"

Colt let his glance rest on her for a moment, then drawled. "Steak and potatoes with eggs over easy, if you have them, and a big cup of black coffee."

With a twinkle in her eyes, the young lady drawled back at him, "Comin' right up, sir, and would four eggs do?"

Colt grinned at her imitation of his drawl. "Guess I've been out of touch with people too long--hadn't realized how gruff I sound. Yes ma'am, four eggs will do just fine."

Her gaze turned to two people entering the dining room. A tall, good-looking man in a Cavalry officer uniform, walked ramrod straight, his shoulders back and head erect. The saber at his side sparkled and Colt couldn't see a speck of dust anywhere on the soldier's uniform or boots. Shirley walked by his side, laughing lightly at something he'd said. The waitress turned back to Colt. "Mr. Black Beard, you better leave by the back door. That's Captain Gregg from the fort at Pipe Springs. If he sees you, there'll be trouble. Your picture is plastered on Wanted dodgers all over town." Her eyes were anxious as they looked at him.

Buddy growled low in his throat at the last statement. Colt reached down and petted the dog briefly. "Don't fret, miss. I won't make any trouble if the Captain doesn't."

"That's just it. Captain Gregg is a stickler for doing things by the book and he'll figure it's his duty to arrest you." Her eyes were big now as they swung back to the Captain, who was so engrossed with the woman at his side, he hadn't yet seen Colt and Buddy.

"You just round up my breakfast and I'll take care of the Captain, Miss----?." He left the sentence hanging in the air as his cool demeanor reflected back to her. There didn't seem to be any change of expression on his face, though it was hard to tell for sure with all those whiskers. However, his eyes still remained unconcerned. Trying to hold her voice level she told him her name. "Betty Jo Price is my name, but just call me Betty Jo."

Colt had forgotten about the Cavalry post being twenty miles to the east, so hadn't expected anyone from the fort to be here in town, especially the Captain. Too late now--he'd have to bluff his way through this encounter. That is, if the man ever looked anyplace other than at Shirley. For some reason his constant attention to her began to rub Colt the wrong way. His stubbornness began to assert itself and he decided a confrontation with the Captain would be just dandy.

"Thanks for your concern, Betty Jo. Now just go back to the kitchen and fetch my breakfast." He leaned back, lifting a booted foot up to the chair across from him. This action brought Buddy's head up, alert for danger.

Shirley's gaze roved around the room, stopping abruptly when it fell on Colt. Her eyes dilated and the smile on her face disappeared. The Captain stood holding a chair for her and missed the change of expression. By the time he seated her and walked around to his chair on the other side of the table, she found the control needed to let the smile return. It had been quite a shock to see the man she suspected of being Colt, sitting at a table in her dining room, obviously without a care in the world. She held her breath, waiting for the explosion to come. She couldn't be sure this man with the black beard was Colt since he appeared to have changed so much, but if it were, he must realize the danger of being in the same room with the Captain.

Captain Gregg never took his eyes off Shirley as he rounded the table and sat down. He was so used to eating here that he rarely noticed the patrons. To him they were always the same and definitely unimportant. He came to see Shirley, not the other inhabitants of the town. "So the robber showed up at the saloon last night and gave the stolen money back to Phillips. That's one man who must be crazy in the head. Why go to all that work just to turn the money back to the bank?"

Trying to keep him occupied so he wouldn't see the man at

the back of the room, Shirley gave an opinion. "Perhaps there are other reasons for making himself known around the territory. Some folks just want the recognition. And since he returns the money, people take it as a joke on the bank. They're happy because the banker gets to have the joke turned on himself occasionally. The robber has actually become a folk hero in the eyes of most folks, especially some of the women."

The Captain focused on the last part of her speech, not realizing conversation around them dwindled when he came through the door. The patrons knew who sat at the back table with his dog, and they were all waiting for the Captain to tumble to the same thing. But Captain Gregg focused only on Shirley. "Don't tell me you've been taken in by this shyster after what he did to your father and his men. Stopped the hanging when those rustlers should have been sent on to their maker. Now they'll be more bold than ever."

Still concerned that sooner or later Gregg would notice the man sitting quietly and now eating the breakfast that Betty Jo brought him, she latched onto this opening. "Actually, I think Dad was kind of glad the man stopped the hanging. Dad's not a violent man at heart, so it saved him some sleepless nights." She conveniently ignored the question of being taken in by the robber's daring escapades. The Captain, his mind aghast at her opinion of her father, forgot his insinuation.

"You can't really believe that. Why, if those rustlers aren't caught and hung, there'll never be peace on this range. One has to be a little harsh sometimes in this violent land or the outlaws would rule the country." Sure of himself, he leaned back in his chair, his eyes lifting to Betty Jo who stood blocking his view of the back table.

"Good morning, Captain Gregg. Good morning, Shirley. What would the two of you like this morning?" Betty Jo's voice contained only happiness as she stood there. The position she had chosen didn't escape Shirley and she reminded herself to thank the young lady later.

Annoyed at this minor disturbance, the Captain only gave her half his attention. "Whatever Shirley is having is all right with me." Then his gaze ranged back to the woman sitting across from him and he took up the subject again. "The outlaws running this town are a menace to all of us and the sooner they're gone the better. If I had more authority over civilians, I'd clean up this whole Strip country. There wouldn't be one outlaw left on the place."

Shirley reached her hand across the table to rest on his arm. "I know, Captain Gregg, and it would be nice to have the town a little safer, but that doesn't mean my father has to do something he isn't really cut out to do." Raising her gaze to Betty Jo, she said, "Just a cup of coffee will do for me." She wanted to get the Captain outside as soon as possible, despite the fact that she really felt hungry this morning.

The Captain was annoyed at the small order she gave, but he'd committed himself to whatever she ordered and he didn't want to go back on his word, so he ordered the same. Turning back to Shirley, he spoke in a condescending tone: "I know it's difficult for a woman to see the drastic measures that must be taken occasionally, but this time your father is wrong. Those men need to be caught and strung up, but all I can do is hope they get what's coming to them in the near future. However, if that bank robber shows up here, I'll arrest him and hold him for the Sheriff to come pick him up."

Betty Jo left, going for the coffee they had ordered. Shirley, seeing his eyes start to turn in the direction of the back table, squeezed his arm, causing him to look back at her. "You may need help in that chore, Captain. Those who saw him last night say he looked mean enough to take on the whole place. Even Mitch didn't want any trouble with him, and you know how tough Mitch is."

"There's another one who ought to be hung. I know he bosses those boys at the Hole but there isn't a Wanted dodger on the man anywhere. How he's gotten away with things for so long is beyond me. He must have some powerful pull somewhere. It's the only way he could continue to dodge the Sheriffs around the country."

Now that his attention had been diverted, Shirley wanted to get off this subject. "There's a dance at the school Saturday night. Do you plan to go?"

His countenance darkened. "I intended too, but orders came through this morning to take a patrol toward the Nevada line. A killing out there of some nester family needs investigating and the Sheriff wants me to look into it. If it's anything serious, I'll wire him back and he'll take over. If it was done by Indians, then it'll be my responsibility."

"Well, if you get back in time for the dance, I'll see you there." Shirley thanked Betty Jo as she set the coffee cups on the table. She drank hers so fast it made her wonder if the Captain would notice, but his mind was still occupied elsewhere. While he drank, she chatted with the waitress, who again stood blocking his view. The two of them talked about the dresses they would wear to the dance and all the things they'd have to do to get ready for the big night.

Finishing his coffee, Captain Gregg stood and Shirley quickly rose in order to precede him out the door, hoping this would keep his eyes on her. But it didn't work. For just that moment the captain let his eyes drift around the room and being taller than Betty Jo, got the shock of his life. Sitting at a table in the rear was a black-haired, full-bearded man. The next instant Buddy rose up and a low growl began to issue from deep in his throat. His wolfish eyes locked onto the Captain, never leaving him. Everyone in the room knew that the dog read the Captain's mind.

Before the Captain recovered from his surprise, Colt waved his arm, motioning the man toward his table. "Captain Gregg, how fortunate to meet you here. Folks have been telling me you were going to throw me in the guardhouse at the fort, but I didn't believe it. Why, a genteel man like you wouldn't do a lowdown thing like that, would you?"

Shirley stopped in her tracks, astounded at the brashness of the man. The room was unnaturally still, the diners suspended in motion. Even the rattle and din of the town seemed to recede before the immediate situation. Speechless, the Captain couldn't figure how to answer this man and his dog. The dog appeared to be the real threat--the man sat so relaxed you would have thought him just there for a leisurely breakfast. Not a worry showed on the man's guileless face. Shirley noticed his leg resting on the chair across from him and the muzzle of that six-gun pointed right at the Captain's chest. She inhaled sharply, not sure whether the Captain saw the gun or not. If he did, he paid no attention to it.

Colt turned his smile on Shirley. "Miss Pugh, you'll have to excuse the Captain. It seems as though he's forgotten his manners this morning. When a man escorts a lady to breakfast, he ought to at least have the decency to escort her home again. 'Course, since this is your hotel, the Captain may figure you're already home, but if you were my girl, I'd still escort you out of the room and come back later to unfinished business."

A look of pure hate momentarily crossed the Captain's face, then quickly faded as he regained control of his emotions. He gave a brief bow in Colt's direction, took Shirley's arm with a firm grip, and led her out of the dining room. When the door closed behind them, a collective sighs rose from everyone in the restaurant. The next thing they saw was Black Beard going through the side window, followed by the yellow and white dog.

The smoke-filled room reeked with sweat and stale beer as the tin covers over the kerosene lamps reflected back onto the crowded barroom. Men were everywhere, boisterous and having a rip-roaring good time. Some wore overalls indicating they were of the Nester Bunch; cowboys with guns hanging from cartridge belts mingled with pale-skinned men who spent most of their time in underground mines, and a few who came to Fredonia to hock their wares were duded up in white shirts with string ties and fine shoes. The fancy-dressed saloon girls swirled among them, laughing and flirting, giving a colorful atmosphere to the place. The gaming tables were full of an assortment of men, each trying to win a bundle of money.

At a secluded table near the back of the room, Heidi talked quietly to Hank and Mitch. "The Captain sure met his match to-day. Why, Black Beard never so much as moved a muscle, but the people sitting where they could see said the muzzle of his six-gun was aimed and ready. When Captain Gregg came storming back into the room with his gun already unlimbered, he was mad clear through to see his quarry gone. Those still in the dining room said they'd never heard such language spurt from the Captain's mouth. He dashed to the open window but found nothing except sweet-smelling morning air out there."

Heidi took a great deal of satisfaction in the Captain's misfortune and her eyes sparkled while she told the story. Mitch figured the whole town enjoyed the show at the hotel earlier, many comments having been made to him when he entered the saloon with Hank. "That man sure made a reputation fast. Wonder what would've happened if he'd stayed till Gregg came back."

Hank felt pretty sure as to the outcome of such an encounter. "You can bet we'd be minus one Captain tonight if that happened. Black Beard sure don't seem like a mean soul, but one look at his eyes puts the kibosh on any action against him. All I can say is the Captain's just plain lucky the man chose to make himself invisible."

A tremor rippled through Heidi. "You're right on that account, Hank. The man's as dangerous as a keg of gunpowder with a lighted short fuse. Most of the men witnessing the confrontation should have figured Black Beard to be a coward for slipping out the window, but it isn't what they think at all. It's utterly amazing how every one of them figures the same way you do. Black Beard just didn't want to soil the dining room floor with the Captain's blood."

"Well, we sure could use a man like that, but no one seems to know where he came from or where he stays between shenanigans. Ollie thinks he's the greatest man ever lived. I figure Ollie would do anything for him. 'Course, I probably would too if he saved me from a hanging at the last minute." Hank still couldn't figure how one man could cause so much ruckus in a short two months.

"I talked to Betty Jo and she says Black Beard acted so calm and relaxed all the time he ate his breakfast, she couldn't believe it. The whole place held their breath waiting for an explosion which never came. And the way he told the Captain off, was something to behold. I think that young lady is head over heels in love with Black Beard. Fact of the matter is, she's not the only one, from what I hear the women saying around town today. The Captain used to be all the rage-- now he takes second place, much to his dislike, I'm sure." She felt sooner or later Black Beard would show up again and something else would happen to talk about. The man made news just by his presence.

The thought barely crossed her mind when the swinging doors burst open and Spuds, the stagecoach driver, catapulted into the room. His disheveled hair, dusty clothes, and wild eyes captured everyone's attention. They waited expectantly while he staggered to the bar. Pike quickly poured him a drink, which he swilled down so fast, he choked. Sputtering, he shuttled his gaze to the faces around him. "That Black Beard done took the money them two Wells Fargo men was transportin' ta St. George. Slickest piece of work I ever seed and I seen a whole bunch a stagecoach holdups in my time."

Life returned in the saloon as men crowded around and began yelling questions at the driver. As the liquor took hold of his system, he relaxed and began to enjoy the attention. Taking another drink offered to him by one of the businessmen, Spuds downed it again in one gulp. "Yessiree, that man's a whiz. We was roundin' the corner by Molly's Nipple when we come face ta face with that yeller 'n white dog a his. He sat smack-dab in the middle a the road with his fangs bared an tail waggin'. I sure pulled them horses to a sudden stop. Course, it weren't too hard since they din't want no part a that dog." He stopped as another drink appeared in front of him and everyone waited for him to continue.

"Well, for heaven's sake, what happened then?" one of the cowboys hollered, causing Spuds to almost choke on the drink.

Getting himself under control, he let them have the whole story. "Heck's fire, I jist sat there lookin' that dog straight in the eye while them horses pranced around. Ain't no way I'd let him stare me down. I tried my damndest ta win the starin' contest and figured the battle almost won when this feller dropped from a overhangin' tree limb. Din't want ta take my eyes off'n the dog, but on t'other hand, I sure wanted ta know who sat beside me. Why, it coulda been any old outlaw an he might already be coverin' me with his six-gun. I din't hanker ta be shot when I wasn't lookin', but that there dog din't want ta give up neither."

He was interrupted by a businessman, who passed him another drink. "Come on, Spuds, skip the dog and get to the man."

Spuds reared back, scrinched his eyes up, and slanted his gaze at the businessman. "Who's tellin' this story anyway? You want ta hear the whole thing or jist part of it?"

A savvy bar girl shot a withering look at the businessman, then turned to the driver and said, "You go right ahead and tell it like you want, Spuds. If this greenhorn interrupts again, I'll yank his hair."

This brought laughter and salty comments from the rest of the saloon: "Better watch it, fellow," "Ain't that the truth," and "She's a ornery one," were heard. Mollified, Spuds moved his attention back to the crowd, throwing his chest out a little. "Course I knowed who was sittin' aside me since that there dog's so popular 'round this Territory. An you know what? When I turned my head ta look at the man, he jist sat there in the seat with a blade a grass 'tween his teeth and smilin' up at the sky. Why, he never so much as made one threatenin' move toward the big ol forty-four-forty hangin' in his holster, brushin' my thigh. I started ta say somethin' when that there dog jumped onto one a the horse's backs, spookin' the animal terrible. This got the whole team ta goin', now that the dog wasn't in front a them no more. All I got ta see was them blue eyes as they turned my way 'fore that dog bounded up ta the man's lap an the team took off, runnin' like the devil hisself was comin' after 'em."

Spuds took another swallow, enjoying everyone's undivided attention. "One a them Wells Fargo men had stepped outta the coach to see why we'd stopped. I heard him holler when we left him standin' in the dust but ain't no way I coulda held them fool horses. Seems when a team gits somethin' like that in their noggins, neither hell ner high water's got the ghost of a chance a stoppin' 'em. I snuck a glance agin at that black haired feller, and he jist set there relaxed as all get out, watchin' the scenery whiz by. Me, I was scared spitless. I been drivin' one coach with a runaway team afore and I'm tellin' ya, it's a hair-raisin' event, but he din't seem ta have a nerve in his body, jist enjoyed the ride."

The businessman couldn't control his impatience. "That why you look so beat and tired? The coach rolled over, spilling all of you?"

Spuds reached over and unexpectedly pulled the man's derby over his eyes. "Ya can't keep yer trap buttoned while I tell this here story, then go somewheres else."

Mitch moved to the bar, standing beside Spuds while he talked. "Ah, don't pay any mind to the tenderfoot, Spuds. Just finish telling us what happened."

"Well, them horses finally run themselves out, an I was sure wore to a frazzle by the time they come to a stop. When I snuck a look at Black Beard, him and the dog weren't nowhere around. Couldn't figure anything exceptin' they'd been thrown clean off the seat of that gyratin' coach. Served him right fer not payin' attention and hangin' on tighter. I let the horses blow and the passengers all got out ta git a breath a fresh air, after all the dust blowin' inside the coach."

He took another swallow, letting the tension build before he drawled again, "Yep, the Wells Fargo feller was purely upset at me fer lettin' them horses run like that and leavin' his partner behind. That man can shore cuss when he's of a mind to. So I told him what happened ta cause the trouble and if'n he din't like the way I drove, he could walk the rest of the way ta St. George." Spuds chuckled softly at his remembrance of this, before starting again. "He finally quit his bellyaching' and they all climbed back in the stage. I turned it around ta go back fer the other agent. When we got there he was settin' on a rock, ready ta bite my head off. Then his face goes white as I whipped the coach around ta head back ta St. George. He tried ta speak but nothin' come out, jist a sorta croak. His partner got out ta help him and happened ta look up on top a the coach. Damned if he din't go white as a sheet to an the two of 'em jist stood there, frozen like."

When he turned to the bar for another glass of whiskey, Pike had it ready and shoved it forward. "Get on with the story, man.

Black Beard must've been sitting up there with a gun pointing right at those two."

Letting his gaze rove up and down Pike, Spuds intoned, "Now it's you wants ta tell the story. Well, go right ahead, if'n yer so smart."

Mitch interposed, "Pike's just like the rest of us, Spuds. You got us so all fired worked up, we can't wait to hear what happened next."

Spuds turned back around, clutching the drink in his hand as he leaned against the bar and smiled benignly toward his captive audience. "I couldn't figger what them two was so scared of. Weren't no man on top a that stage when I looked where they was lookin'. Then it hit me like a ton of dirt throwed in my face. You know what had 'em so worked up?" Here he paused to let the tension build. Satisfied that he had their undivided attention, he took a sip, drawing this out as long as he could. When he saw the smoke, begin to float up from some of those watching, he decided the time was right.

"That strong box with twenty thousand dollars in it what set on the top a the stage when we left here, wern't there no more. Why, that dad-burned Black Beard musta got up on the top a the stage with them horses runnin' like mad, pushed the box off, then jumped after it. The yeller 'n white dog musta went with him."

The barroom was as quiet as the whisper of leaves on a calm day. Spuds stood waiting for the explosion. It came suddenly with everyone trying to talk at once, sounding like a herd of long yearlings in a branding pen. Spuds, a grin plastered from ear to ear, turned back to the bar. He sure had set the barroom in a tailspin and he thanked Black Beard for providing this moment of glory. Did a man's soul good to see these hombres hanging on every word dropped from his lips. He poured another slosh of whiskey down his gullet, then swivelled back around, raising his hands in the air, trying to get the crowd to button their lips. But the babble of sound only got louder, as everyone wanted to give their opinion.

Pike grabbed the shotgun from under the bar and let er' rip, blowing the back door off its hinges. The smoke-filled room immediately came to a standstill, leaving stunned people with open mouths and gesturing hands frozen in midair. A breeze wafting through the missing door shoveled out some of the smoke and Spuds flapped his lips again. "That ain't the half a it. But if y'all don't keep yore lips locked tight, I'll go ta bed and wait till tomorrow ta tell the rest of it." By golly, he had their attention again...funny what the blast of a shotgun could do.

"You ain't saying Black Beared showed up at that point and gave the money back to those two Wells Fargo men, are you?" Mitch pulled his hat off, mopping his face with his neckerchief.

"Now it's you what wants ta tell the story. Well, go right ahead, since yore so all fired smart." It wasn't often Spuds got a chance to knock Mitch down a peg or two and this was a God given opportunity.

During the hullabaloo, Heidi had slipped to the bar and now stood beside Spuds. She laid a soothing hand on his arm. "You go right ahead and finish the story, Spuds. Pike won't let off the other barrel of that scattergun unless someone else wants to interrupt."

He didn't really want to hear the gun go off again so close to his ears, so he unlocked his jaws. "You never heerd such cryin' in all yore borned days. Why, them two men jist couldn't stand losin' that cash twice in one week. Made a feller feel downright sorry fer 'em, and me bein' so bighearted," he paused to glare at the crowd, daring anyone to dispute this fact, "I suggested we pile inta the coach and backtrack till we cut the tracks a Black Beard and his dog. When they found 'em, they could cut a couple a the horses outa the traces and ride after him. They figured it to be a right smart idear, so we done jist that. Only thing was, by the time we covered ground fer the third time, there weren't track one in sight. Now how you figure that strong box got throwed offa that stage without leavin' a hole in the road big enough ta drive a mule through?"

Silence ruled the barroom as the import of this struck home. Spuds waited but no one wanted to hear the scattergun again, so he meandered on. "Well, we put our heads together with ta'other men on the stage an decided two of 'em would walk out from the road 'bout ten feet on the way back ta where the coach stopped the first time. Din't have no more luck then than the time afore. It jist din't scratch any part a our brains as to how that box disappeared. I declare, Black Beard musta had wings under his shirt ta git away from a job 'thout leavin' no sign." The next drink he took went down fast, "Finally the good fairy musta tapped me on the shoulder. While we was tryin' ta come up with a answer, that narrow section a road come into my noggin. When they heard my idee, we piled in the coach so fast it'd make yore head swim. Ya know what we found when we got back ta that spot? Where the road narrows goin' through a stand a large poplar trees on each side?"

Hank started to open his mouth, then closed it as Spud's eyes bored into him. "By grab, ya could see the rope burns on the trunks a two trees jist as plain as day, once ya looked close enough. Black Beard musta strung a rope cross the road 'tween them trees sometime afore the coach got there. Then he left his horse, walked back up the road with his dog ta where the coach first stopped, climbed a tree, 'n dropped offa tree limb onto the seat beside me. Now the big question laid hold af our minds all at once. How in God's world did he manage ta grab that rope from the back of a fast movin' stage, a strongbox in one hand and his dog in t'other? I tell ya, nothin' made sense. Them rope marks was there all right, but it'd take a superhuman to pull off a stunt like that. Oh, the marks was deep enough to let ya know a terrible force had pulled on the rope, but it woulda pulled the arms of a strong man right outta the sockets."

Spuds turned back to the bar, motioning Pike to refill his glass. The effects of all these drinks were making him groggy and addling his mind, so it took him a few minutes to figure out what he said last. Things were getting mighty fuzzy around the edges. "That sure nuff was the place where Black Beard, his dog, and the strong box left the coach, though, and it was plain as day ta all of us. So we scattered out from the road ta hunt fer tracks. Three went offa one side a the road an three went t'other way. We scoured the land like a buzzard huntin' dead meat. Wasn't no more successful then, than the time afore. The bunch I was with give up, headin back ta the coach. Only ya know what?"

Heidi couldn't stand the suspense anymore; she breathed softly over his shoulder, "The coach wasn't there."

Spuds didn't become offended at her interruption. Besides, she was a right purty little filly and smelled mighty nice. "Naw, the coach was there, all right. But jist as we got purt near, it started ta move, and sneaky ol' Black Beard, his dog, and the strong box was sittin' right on top. Danged if my jaw din't fall in the dust and my sore eyes settled on some sorta sling hangin' over the side a the coach. Black Beard stood up as he drove the coach away, wavin' ta us. We stood there feelin' as helpless as a fart in the wind."

"So that's why you're so tuckered out. You walked all the way back here to spread the word. But what did you mean by a sling?"

Spuds eyes were seeing double images at this point. He squinted at Mitch, trying to capture only one image. "It took purt near the better part a the walk back here fer me to figure that one out. Them Wells Fargo men ain't inta walkin' an t'other guys decided weren't no use in anymore'n one man goin' fer help, so I come all by my lonesome."

He stared at the glass in his hand but darned it there weren't three or four of them, and he couldn't decide which one to drink from. Wiping the back of his hand across his eyes, he squinted, searching hard for the real drink. He swayed toward Heidi, hoping she might be of some help, only there were three of her too. Well by golly, too many whiskeys and too many Heidi's wasn't such a bad deal. But if he was going to enjoy this, he'd better finish his tale, so he tried his voice again. "He musta had a sling made from ropes with a hook on it. Dropped it on top a the stage when he slipped from that tree limb. All he had ta do was crawl outta the seat beside me," a loud, rolling burp caused him to pause briefly, "slide inta the sling, put the box on his lap with the dog settin' on top, and when the horses pulled that wild gyratin' stage under the rope crossin above, he held the hook up and swish---it plucked him right off'n that there stage top and left him swingin' in the breeze.

Not a sound could be heard in the barroom as they all visualized Black Beard with that strong box and yellow and white dog lazily waiting for the swing to stop. Son of a gun, if that young man couldn't think up more ways to get money than a cat had lives. It'd take a real educated fellow to figure out all the things he'd done, and you couldn't rightly figure why he spent such talent robbing banks and stagecoaches. Mitch turned to the bar, signaling Pike for another drink. He saw Heidi leave the side of Spuds, who staggered toward Hank, still at the table where they left him. Then his eyes widened as Spud's image in the mirror slowly sank out of sight.

When he pushed back and glanced down, Spuds lay snoring up a storm on the barroom floor. This broke the spell and the men and ladies erupted into laughter. Soon talk took its place and the air became charged with speech as each person gave their opinion of where the strong box rested now.

A couple of the local businesspeople approached Mitch. "What do you think about going out after those stage passengers tonight?"

He gave it a quick thought, then shook his head. "Nah, that's near twenty miles from here and it's getting pretty late. Might be best to wait till morning when we can send a wagon out. Won't hurt any of them to spend a sleepless night on the ground. But I sure would like to know the whereabouts of Black Beard."

The two agreed with his assessment of the situation, not really wanting to ride a jolting wagon along that rugged wheel-gutted road at night. "We might as well pack it in. Come daylight, we'll have to decide who gets the honors of picking those fellers up."

Hank came over to the bar with Heidi on his arm. He stood letting his eyes rove over the sleeping Spuds. "Think we should leave him there or pack him over to the hotel?"

"Well, he looks mighty comfortable right where he's laying, but I feel sorry for the old codger. After walking twenty miles, he deserves a good bed tonight. Haul him up to my room and I'll sleep at the hotel. I saw a light still on in Shirley's room and she probably wonders about all the excitement taking place over here, so I'll fill her in before going to bed." Heidi only hoped that her generosity wouldn't be regretted by Spuds vomiting his voluminous amount of whiskey. "Make sure you put the chamber pot close to him. Right under his nose, okay?"

"You got it." Hank picked two husky punchers to help carry Spuds dead weight up the stairs. When he returned, he was surprised to see Heidi waiting for him.

"I thought we could walk to the hotel together, it being such a nice night and all," she said. Of all the men on the Strip, Heidi fancied Hank, but wasn't completely sure of his feelings for her. A woman could usually tell these things, and Hank did occasionally give the impression that Heidi was his girl. But no absolute commitment had been made, so she took every chance to strengthen the bond.

Hank gallantly took her arm, and they strolled together in the moonlight, neither one in a big hurry. Eventually they arrived at the hotel, where they reluctantly parted. Heidi went to Shirley's door and rapped lightly. It immediately swung open. The expectancy in Shirley's eyes told Heidi she'd made the right choice. Heidi wasn't sure why Shirley concerned herself with the gang, and especially Black Beard, but lately she always managed to bump into Heidi, wanting to know if anything new presented itself. Having been friends since Shirley took over the hotel, Heidi noticed how animated Shirley became upon hearing Black Beard's name. Heidi couldn't help but speculate as to the reason.

Trying to tell the story just like Spuds did, she observed Shirley hanging on every word. When she finished, the two of them sat there in silence, Heidi waiting for a comment and Shirley absorbing all the information. Finally Shirley got off the bed, and went to the window to stare out at the star- studded sky magnified by a full moon. She stood still for so long that Heidi became concerned. Suddenly Shirley whirled, rushing out the door of her room like a dog after a cat.

Bewildered, Heidi jumped up, running after her. It was one o'clock in the morning and surely no one would be up at this hour. Dashing through the front door of the hotel, she plowed right into Shirley's back, almost knocking her off her feet. Grabbing the porch post to right herself, Shirley hissed, "Look. You see what I see?" Her finger pointed to the edge of town.

It couldn't be. There just didn't seem to be any rhyme or reason to the apparition they were sighting. The stagecoach rolled into town, turned toward the stage office, then proceeded toward the corral behind it. A man in a floppy-brimmed hat sat on the seat, one hand holding the reins of the six-horse team. Both ladies shrank into the shadows of the hotel, fearing he would see them. But he never even so much as glanced their way as he drove the stage up to the gate. Stopping, he slid down, followed by the yellow and white dog. Then he unhooked the teams, led them into the corral and removed all the harnesses, after which he went into the barn. He must be feeding the horses, since they followed him inside.

Heidi whispered, "Do you think he'll sleep in the loft tonight or ride back out of town?" Before Shirley could answer, he stepped back out, going to the horse tied behind the coach and stepping into the leather. Expecting to see him leave, they held their breath as he turned toward the hotel, riding around behind it as though he were going to the hotel barn.

After he disappeared around the corner, Shirley dashed back through the front door with Heidi right on her heels. They sprinted through the kitchen, trying to be as light on their feet and as quiet as possible. Standing with their faces glued to the back window, they waited, wondering what the man wanted to stir up this time. Shortly, he came through the barn door, ambling toward the back stairs of the hotel. Shirley swore he raised his arm and waved at them as he mounted the stairs and she jerked back instantly, her heart in her throat.

Heidi's voice slid shakily into the dusky room. "You think he actually saw us?" It couldn't be possible for him to have seen them in the hotel, but he may have seen them on the front porch when he rounded the corner, even though they were in deep shadow.

"I don't know, but I wouldn't lay any bets on the fact that he didn't---that moon's awfully bright." Shirley actually felt her heart pounding as her words tumbled softly into the air.

Not wanting to go back through the lobby to get to her room, the two of them waited tensely for what seemed like hours before creeping out of the kitchen. With every stealthy step, they expected to hear his voice issue from the top of the stairs. To their great relief, nothing happened. Once inside Shirley's room, they sank to the bed, holding each others clammy hands, not able to speak at all.

Finally Heidi whispered, "Would it be all right if I sleep in here with you tonight? I don't hanker to go up those stairs to an empty room."

Suppressing a nervous giggle, Shirley answered, "I don't blame you. If I were in your shoes I'd stay put too. It wont be any trouble at all and we'll both feel safer. I know wild horses couldn't drag me out of this room tonight. When I open that door into the lobby, I want full daylight to hit me square in the face."

Despite their foreboding, Heidi definitely agreed with that sentiment.

Life in a small town can be rather drab for some people but those living in Fredonia certainly were filled with excitement lately. The appearance of Black Beard sparked a whale of a lot of talk. To think the man who did all the bank jobs in the southern part of the Territory now showed up in their town, made everyone feel important. The tale of the stagecoach fiasco spread so fast, the dining room of the hotel was packed wall to wall for breakfast the next morning. Betty Jo couldn't handle all the traffic so Shirley enlisted Heidi in the task of serving. No one seemed to mind that a saloon girl waited on them and Heidi enjoyed the change of pace.

When Mitch and Hank were through eating, Hank decided to hang around the hotel for a while. He felt really good about Heidi helping out at such a respectable place---might turn into a permanent job for her and he'd like that. Of course, his being an outlaw didn't enter into the situation . . . as long as he didn't shoot women and children, a man could be considered honorable. Robbing banks and rustling cattle didn't denote the highest moral principles, but if done well and not too often, people sort of admired it. He'd never stopped to analyze why, just accepted it as fact.

Eyes bleary and red, skin grey, clothes wrinkled and stinking, a shaky Spuds staggered through the door as Mitch went out. Mitch almost turned back to help, but Hank took the man by the arm, led him to a vacant chair and sat him in it. Spuds sure looked like the devil had been wrestling with him most of the night. His grey hair stood up on end and his breath would flatten a horse.

Squinting up at Hank, Spuds groaned, "How many drinks you fellers pour down me last night?"

Shirley arrived to take his order, carrying a large cup of steaming black coffee which she placed in front of him. "Actually Spuds, I understand you did all the pouring; the rest just stayed listening to your story. You sure all that really happened?"

Up to this point Spuds brain existed in a bowl of mush. His head pounded so cussed bad it took real effort to think what she flapped her mouth about. He took two big gulps of the coffee, waited a moment, and then it all started to slide into place. "Heck's fire, ya bet yore bottom dollar it happened and jist the way I said. When Black Beard comes back, he'll tell ya it did."

Hank took up the talk. "You figure he'll show his face in this town again, Spuds? Why, he won't only have the Captain after him--those two Wells Fargo men are out to nail his hide to the barn door."

Voice rising to a fever pitch, Spuds gave his opinion. "Hell, why would somebody what kin disappear into thin air worry bout them three measly excuses fer men? Black Beard'll jist blow on 'em an knock 'em into the next county." He chuckled at his own assessment of the situation.

Shirley wondered how a man who had been made to walk twenty miles could be so taken in by the one who caused his trouble. Yet it appeared to her that Spuds was singing the praises of said man. "You figure he's that tough, Spuds?"

"You got any beer in this place? I kin talk a lot better if'n you'd corral me a large schooner a beer 'stead of this coffee."

The room settled into a hushed silence as Spuds talked; everyone present wanted to hear what he said. Shirley smiled as she went toward the kitchen: this must be the most exciting thing to ever happen to him, and he was going to milk it for all it was worth. She wouldn't be surprised if they were still hearing about it years from now. She came back in a flash, handing a big mug of beer to Spuds. He tipped it up and they watched half of it disappear down his gullet. Wiping his mouth on his dirty shirt sleeve, he looked up at her. "Thankee, that sure cut the dust from my throat. Do I think he's that tough? Why, if'n the captain brought his whole gol-darned troop after Black Beard, he'd go back ta the fort empty handed, his tail showin' 'tween his legs. I seen his eyes yesterday an' there ain't no way you could pay me enough ta go up against that hombre. If'n he want's my money, he kin have it and anything else I got."

Several diners were on his side and a chorus of amens came through the air. Betty Jo stopped by the table as he finished. "That don't jibe with what I saw at breakfast yesterday morning. He seemed the perfect gentleman and those blue eyes were soft and gentle."

Spuds took another swig of beer, letting his mind go over what he saw in the robber's eyes. "Okay, I'll agree with you there, Betty Jo. But if you'd a seed 'em when he first sat on the coach seat, you'd be thinkin' different. I 'spect he aimed ta know which way I'd jump 'fore he relaxed, and one glance at him pointed me in the right direction. But when I roved my eyes over him while the team was runnin', he looked plumb gentle. Cain't quite figger ta this minute how he slipped away without I knowed it. Course, I sure had my hands full with them six horses."

He sat trying to figure how a man could move so quickly and not be noticed. Shirley remembered Colt telling of killing those four outlaws, plus the shooting of the four hangman ropes, and decided he moved like lightning when needed. "What do you think those Wells Fargo men will do when they get back to town?"

A laugh came from Hank. "I'll tell you, if they know what's good for them, they'll find the stage and take it to St. George. It's a sure bet Black Beard'll show up here before too long and they won't want to tangle with him face to face."

Mitch came tramping back in. "You gonna drive the wagon out to pick those boys up, Spuds? It's already an hour past sunup and they'll be chomping at the bit to get back to town."

With a groan Spuds mumbled, "Someone else outta do it. I jist ain't up ta tacklin' that there road this mornin'."

"There isn't anyone else in town who works for the stage company but the clerk over at the company office, and he's not much of a driver. He'd probably turn the wagon over on that rutty road. Might be best if you picked them up and went on to St. George, where they have a bigger office. They'll want to notify their main office of the missing money anyway." Shirley wanted to get the Wells Fargo men out of town before Black Beard showed up. She didn't know if he was still up in one of the hotel rooms but thought he might be---it had been pretty late when he went to bed.

"A man cain't get no sympathy 'round here this mornin'. Why, I'd a thought you'd all be grateful for the story I brung ya last night." Spuds glanced hopefully up at her, to no avail. Damn. He'd have to make the trip no matter how he felt. The company would have his hide if he didn't get those passengers on to their destination.

Shirley decided to make his going easier. "Just think, Spuds, you can tell your story all over again; the folks in St. George will be hanging on your every word. You'll be almost a hero, figuring out how it was done and walking all that way to get help."

Ah, such a glorious thought. Spuds face lit up, and his mind immediately began to embellish the facts to make it sound even better. And think of all the free drinks he could get--the surety of another hangover never entered his mind.

Hank stepped into the conversation. "I'll go hitch up a wagon, Spuds, while you feed your face. By the time I get done, you should be ready and I'll pick you up out front."

Shirley volunteered to fix something for the passengers to eat on their trip, then left for the kitchen to get an order of pancakes and sausage for Spuds. Betty Jo and Heidi continued to serve the customers still in the dining room, but just below their smiling exterior lay the worry of when Black Beard might show up. By the time they heard wheels grinding on the gravel out front, Spuds had finished his meal, ambling toward the lobby where he picked up his hat and set it gently on his still throbbing head. Everyone in the dining room finished quickly and along with Shirley, Betty Jo, and Heidi, followed him outside.

The three ladies were right behind Spuds when he went through the front door, plowing into him when he came to a sudden stop. All four of them hung on to each other as their glance settled over the stagecoach squatting on the road, Hank on its seat. Spuds stood blinking his eyes, afraid last night's boozing was having a delayed effect. A grin spread across Hank's face as his gaze roved over the crowd on the porch. "Darned if this coach didn't step out and bite me when I went to get a wagon. It set right there in front of the company office and all six horses were fed and watered with their harnesses hooked up, standing in the corral just waiting for me." He scratched his head. "Now who do you think would go to so much work this early in the morning?"

Spuds grabbed his hat and slammed it in the dirt just off the porch. "That dadburned Black Beard's a doin' it." His glance ranged over the town and its people, expecting to see the man standing in the street somewhere, a smirk on his face.

He tramped down the steps, retrieved his hat and moved toward the stage. "Probably left the money inside the coach where we kin find it easy. Be jist like the feller ta do somethin' like that."

Hank shook his Stetson-crowned head. "Nope, I already searched this coach from top to bottom, thinking the same thing, Spuds. There ain't a lick of cash anywhere on it. I figure he hid it somewhere else, which may take a little time to find. He likes to keep the suspense up as long as possible. Left the coach so those men still out on the road could get on their way."

Folks crowded around the stage, opening doors, looking in the boot, crawling on top as well as underneath, trying to find the strong box. It just didn't reach out and snare any of them. The three ladies stood on the porch, silently watching this inspection.

Finally Spuds stepped up to the driver's seat. "Okay, everbody, git away from here. Might jist as well get er rollin'. If'n the box ain't there, it ain't there." He snapped the whip, causing the team to lunge into the harness. The coach rolled out of town as the sun sent lemon yellow rays through the dust kicked up by its passage.

The people who'd been involved in the inspection wandered off in small groups, discussing where the strong box might turn up. Moving as one, the three ladies drifted back to the dining room, not mentioning anything, but thinking plenty. The place rang with dishes being carried back to the kitchen. Tables and counter cleared, they began to help the cook clean the dishes. Chatter filled the air since the three were close enough together to talk.

"Why do you think Black Beard, if that's his real name, keeps doing all these crazy shenanigans?" Betty Jo wanted to believe he meant good but the picture being tossed out made his motives suspect.

Heidi puzzled over this too, but felt she knew an answer. "He wants to make a name for himself. A lot of these outlaws are braggarts, doing all sorts of things to get attention or prove their manhood."

To Shirley, it didn't seem possible for the young man she met on the Hastings ranch to be the same person being talked about all over the Strip. However, there were just too many similarities.

The floppy-brimmed hat with the edges curled up, the yellow and white dog that used to live on the reservation, and the keen blue eyes. The build presented the same picture but the black hair and beard certainly didn't fit her memory of Colt. The real clincher, though, was her heart, which began to beat faster every time she saw Black Beard. She figured he wanted to gain a reputation fast, which he had, but the way he went about it was risky.

Most of the folks considered him a hero of some kind, but the Captain and those Wells Fargo men would not be so generous.

The dishes done and the cook carrying the pan of dishwater out the back door, the three untied their aprons and put them over the back of a chair. "Thanks so much for helping this morning, Heidi. If you ever want to quit the saloon, just give a whoop and a holler. I'll put you on steady anytime."

"You may get a new hand sooner than you think, Shirley. I enjoyed working with you two. Besides, I get the feeling Hank wants me to change jobs. But the money at the saloon is pretty enticing."

They shouldered through the kitchen door, going to the dining room with Betty Jo right on their heels. Because breakfast ended some time ago, they didn't expect to see any customers in the room. All three became rooted to the floor as the vision of a man with black hair and a full black beard, sitting at the counter, stunned them to silence. A dog perched on a stool beside him.

"Howdy, ladies. I know it's late but I sure am hankering for some steak and eggs. My stomach feels like the inside of an empty gunny sack, and Buddy sure would like a good bone with lots of meat left on it."

Being the first to recover, Shirley felt her heart vibrate in her chest. That voice positively fit Colt and she almost called him by name before her thinking took hold. "The cook won't like to stay but I'll be glad to fill that empty stomach for you." She turned back into the kitchen, hoping Heidi would follow, but no such luck.

Recovering from her surprise, Heidi leaned on the counter. "Where did you put the strong box, handsome?"

Despite her words, Colt knew by her attitude that she just

wanted information. "The last I saw that box, it rested on top of the stage. Why, something happen to it?" Betty Jo stood in a trance, admiring him, her eyes wide and her mouth turned up into a smile.

Heidi felt confused for a moment, then decided he was only joshing. "The stagecoach driver said you took the strong box with twenty thousand dollars off the stage yesterday. Don't rightly seem possible there'd be two fellers on the Strip with the same description and a yellow and white dog, does it?"

Shirley came back through the door with a cup of coffee and a bowl of milk in her hands. Setting the coffee in front of him, she walked around the counter to set the bowl of milk on the floor for Buddy. She patted the dog on the head, scratching his ears when he hopped down to drink it. "He doesn't look the least ferocious. Why did those bankers think he's mean?"

Colt swung around on the stool. "There's not a mean hair on his whole body. Does anything I want him to and travels with me all the time. Keeps a man from getting lonesome while on the trail. That's why his name's Buddy." At the mention of his name, Buddy looked up at Colt, milk drizzling from his jowls, and wagged his tail furiously.

Betty Jo came out of her trance and went over to pet Buddy. She'd always liked dogs, and felt sorry for the strays. Quite a lot of kitchen scraps ended up behind the hotel at the end of the day, and she always made sure they were divided evenly and quickly to keep the dogs from fighting. "You sure you're safe here this morning, Black Beard? The Captain may come in anytime." She didn't want anything to happen to the man who'd put excitement in all their lives.

His quick laugh gave out a mellow sound. "Captain Gregg's off chasing some wild story about a family being killed over near the Nevada border. Don't figure he'll be any problem for at least a week."

"How did you know the Captain went out to check on that? And why do you think it's a wild goose chase?" Shirley was a little indignant that he knew what the Captain told her.

He turned back to the counter as he glanced at Betty Jo. "You think that steak might be getting about right?"

She stood up, giving the dog one last pat, then hurried into the kitchen. "Why, everyone in the dining room heard the Captain tell you, Shirley, but since you ask, I bumped into Ollie yesterday and he told me part of the gang came back from that section of the Strip last night, saying the story was a hoax, planted by some outlaws wanting to get the Captain out of the road for a while." His eyes settled on those of Heidi, but his next words didn't address the point at all. "What were you two doing up so late last night?"

"So you did see us at the window." Her statement pushed a breath of exhaled air behind it.

The coffee cup reached his mouth and he studied both ladies while drinking. "You were easy to see when you came out on the porch---the moonlight shone right on you for a moment."

Heidi laughed. "I guess it'd take someone getting up real early to put one over on you, Black Beard. By the way, is that really your name?"

Shirley held her breath as his glance swung to her, then back to Heidi. "I figure more than half the people living on the Strip are using a different name than the one their parents plastered on them, so it's as good as any for now."

Betty Jo came through the kitchen door carrying a platter with a huge sizzling steak, three eggs, hash browns and toast, setting them proudly in front of him. On another small plate were two T-bones that customers hadn't finished. Black Beard picked up one of the T-bones, tossing it to Buddy, who caught it in strong jaws before it hit the floor. The three stood watching him as he dived into the food. Again, as yesterday, he ate like he was famished. "You sure you eat regularly? Every time you're in here you put away the food like a starving man. You might think about coming in more often." Betty Jo's dreamy eyes didn't want to leave him.

"Actually, the food here is so much better than my own cooking, I can't wait to get around it. And the coffee is just superb. Think I'll stick around for a week while the Captain's elsewhere so I can fatten up a little. That is, if the room I slept in last night is available for that long."

Shirley glanced at the other two ladies, who watched her hopefully, willing her to say yes. "What if those Wells Fargo men come back with Spuds when he returns?"

His eyes steadied on her. "Since they have their money back, I doubt they'll press the issue."

A stunned silence met this statement. "Just how do you plan to get the money back to them, even if you're really the one who took it?" Shirley wanted to know.

"When I left the stage at the company office last night, the strong box sat right on top Figured with everyone asleep, it would still be there this morning."

"That might not have been a smart move---it wasn't there when Hank hooked up the teams before Spuds left." Heidi felt disappointed that he'd do something so stupid.

He continued eating as the three looked at him. Their accusing stares eventually got to him. "What can I say? That's where I left it.

If it disappeared during the night, it means someone in town took it. You know anyone who either lives in town or stayed here last night who'd steal a strong box?"

Shirley began to wonder if he deliberately left the box where it could be stolen. But if he did, what would be the motive? "I'm sure there's several folks who'd fit that idea; the Strip is a haven for rustlers and outlaws. You give them a chance at an unguarded strong box and they'll take it."

Colt pushed his empty plate aside and picked up his coffee cup. The only sound heard in the dining room came from Buddy gnawing on his second T-bone. Betty Jo's disillusioned words slid across the counter, speaking for all of them. "You didn't really leave the money there for someone to steal, did you, Black Beard?"

"Now why would I pull a crazy stunt like that? And why does everyone think I'm the one who took the box? The coach swayed and jerked so much, it could've bounced off. I just wanted a joy ride and Spuds didn't object at all."

"Then how did it get back on top of the coach where you left it last night? You must be the one who stole it. The men riding in the coach saw you drive away with it." Heidi tried to figure where all this led.

"Did they say they saw the box up on the coach when some man drove it away? Could they actually tell who it was? Why, there would've been dust everywhere hindering their view. What if I found the stage out in the desert and drove it into town last night? Can anyone prove different? Why would I bring the coach back if I were really the one who stole it?"

Shirley tried to follow all these questions but realized there were too many holes poking through to get a handle on things.

"How can you deny it? You're accused of doing similar things to the banks down south and the bank here in town. Buddy is the spittin' image of the dog that helps rob banks and you definitely fit the description on the Wanted posters. Plus you brought back the money stolen from our bank. So it fits that you would bring the coach back." She was fit to be tied at him thinking they were dumb.

"Tell you the truth, I don't recall saying anything about the bag of money on the saloon floor that night. Maybe it set there when I came in. Someone else could have brought it in while you folks were over at the bank seeing how the job got done. From what I hear, the bank-robbing dog is mighty ferocious. Does Buddy look mean to you?" At this point Buddy rose, carrying the bone daintily through the door to the lobby, where he paused expectantly. Colt went to let him out. When he returned, the three girls hadn't moved.

"Now if you don't mind, I'd like to get a little sleep; it was pretty late when my head hit the pillow last night. You two might consider the same thing-- you were up even later than I was." His eyes momentarily rested on Shirley and Heidi.

"Oh, by the way, Betty Jo, would you let Buddy back in when he scratches at the door? I'll leave the door to my room ajar for him. He knows how to push it shut after he's inside, so that won't be anything for you to be concerned about." Tipping his hat to the three of them, he strode out of the dining room and up the stairs.

Heidi walked to the window, watching the town going about its business. Wagons rumbled down the dirt road; men on horseback shouted greetings to friends, most of them entering the saloon; businessmen and ladies bustled in and out of the stores. Just another ordinary day in Fredonia. No one seemed worried about the robber, or his dog, or the missing strongbox, except the three of them. "What could Black Beard have in mind by bringing the coach back, then leaving it where someone could remove the strongbox? It doesn't make sense."

Shirley moved over beside her. "You're right. I can't figure it out either, but it seems he may have done just that. Maybe he didn't sleep at all last night. One of the empty rooms faced the street where he'd have a clear view of anyone approaching the stagecoach. That could be why he's tired this morning. If I'm right, he knows who took the box. The question is, why did he want that information and what will he do with it?"

Betty Jo joined the two talking at the window. "You think he's a lawman and here to apprehend a dangerous criminal?"

"If he is, why let the three of us in on the secret? He's bound to know we'd consider something like that." Shirley couldn't quite believe Colt carried a law badge, especially since there were so many dodgers out with his description plastered all over them. On the other hand, he may now know a little more about who killed his parents. At least she wanted to believe that was her reason. But no way could she tell her suspicions to the others.

"He sure does some mighty peculiar things. I don't believe for a minute that someone else brought the bank money back to the saloon that night. He's right--no one saw him bring it in, but there's no other person I can think of who'd do it." Heidi knew all the outlaws in the gang and if any of them did the job, Hank would have told her.

"Whatever his reasons are, I figure there's more surprises in store for us with him saying he's going to stay in town this week. Something's in the wind and it'll probably pop before too much time elapses." The worry began to gnaw on Shirley that Colt would dig into things which would overpower him.

"I guess I better get back to the saloon. I'll keep my eyes open and let you know if anything unusual happens." Heidi hurried out the door, moving rapidly toward the saloon. Buddy used this as a chance to get back in, and trotted up the stairs. The two women soon heard a door closing softly, and smiled at each other.

A deafening wind howled across the desolate land, raising a shield of dust to hide everything in its path. Sweeping tumbleweeds crashed into themselves and any other obstacle that might impede their progress. Tree limbs bent over so far some of them were touching the ground, causing them to appear as ghosts hovering over the earth. With the dust so thick, there were times Ollie got the distinct impression they just might be ghosts. His hat was tied on his head with the bandana that usually lay around his neck, leaving his face exposed to the whims of the dirt. It was a toss up as to which would be the best way to use that bandana, but he decided his hat meant more to him than keeping the dust from his nose and eyes. He'd hunched his shirt up enough so most of the dirt was filtered out and with his eyes nearly shut, he gave the task of keeping on the road over to the horse.

Since the morning Black Beard shot the rope from his neck

and set him free, he pretty much stayed around the Hole-in-the-Rock hangout. But today he just couldn't stand being cooped up any longer, playing endless games of poker which he usually lost, so he braved the wind and when his butt hit the saddle, he let the horse have its head. He knew there could be trouble if he showed his face in Fredonia, but things were happening there since Black Beard showed up. Ollie now considered he owed his life to the man and wanted to thank him. Besides, after that close brush with the hangman, he spent a lot of time considering what the future might hold and decided the life he'd lived up to this point wasn't what he really wanted.

The horse's head hung low as they entered the town. Buildings were shaded in a hazy brown color, almost indistinguishable from the road and the sky. His throat told him he needed a drink but his stomach said food would do him the most good. Plodding to the tie rail in front of the hotel, he stopped, considering what to do. His decision made, he turned the horse, heading for the livery stable. Be best if he put the horse up out of this wind first, then took care of his own needs. If trouble found him, he wanted his horse to be in the best of shape.

Dismounting in front of the closed stable door, he shouldered it open, leading the horse inside. Relief from fighting the wind came suddenly. He chose the closest of three empty stalls, pulling the saddle and bridle off, then climbed the ladder to fork down some hay. His foot had barely touched the floor of the stable again when Drew, the stable owner, shuffled out of his office. Drew stopped in surprise when he saw his visitor. "What you doing in town, Ollie? If any of them fellers from the Circle-D show up, your life ain't worth a plugged nickel. I figured you'd a left the country by now."

Ollie slapped the dust and chaff from his pants, furtively shifting his gun to a better location on his hip. "Them boys' will be busy trying' to keep their cattle from drifting all over the Strip. A cow purely hates to face the wind, so they'll drift wherever the wind blows. You won't see any Circle-D fellers till a day or two after the wind stops."

Figuring Ollie probably read things correctly, Drew warned, "Well, you better be long gone when that happens." He started back to his office.

Words drifted to him: "You ain't seen that Black Beard feller around, have you? Kinda like to meet the gent so I could thank him."

"Heard by the grapevine he was sleeping at the hotel. Don't rightly know it that's the straight of it but it wouldn't surprise me none. He don't seem to let anything much bother him."

Glad to hear this, Ollie figured he'd fill his belly next and left the stable, hustling over to the hotel. The wind blew him through the front door and he slammed it shut behind him, causing the wall to shake briefly. Betty Jo hustled from the dining room to see what had blown in. When she saw him standing there slapping dust from his shirt and pants, she asked, "What're you doing in town, Ollie? You want to get your neck stretched for good this time?"

Betty Jo was definitely his idea of an angel, but she never paid the slightest attention to him when he entered town. "That all you people think about? Drew wanted to know the same thing. I don't figure any of the ranch crowd will be in today---they'll be chasing cows with this wind blowing them from hell to breakfast."

"Watch your tongue, Ollie. Just cause you run with outlaws don't give you any right to use language like that in a lady's presence." Annoyed, she huffed back into the dining room. He sheepishly followed, straddling a stool at the counter.

"Drew said Black Beard was poundin' his ear in one of the hotel rooms today. Figured I'd like to thank him for savin' my life."

The mention of Black Beard brought a sudden change to the face of Betty Jo, and it made Ollie wish he hadn't brought the subject up. He could see right then and there that this young lady stood in awe of the man. She told him the truth, "He's here all right, but don't you go disturbing him . . . he ain't looking to be fawned over by an outlaw."

Son of a gun, if this didn't beat all. She was so wrapped up in the man she wanted to protect him from everything. "I weren't figurin' to wake him up. Just wanted to fill my belly with some of that good cookin' you serve here." Now that he had the information he sought, he sure hoped she'd get off the subject of Black Beard.

"We don't serve lunch for another fifteen minutes, so just cool your heels till I ring the dinner bell." She vanished into the kitchen, leaving him sitting with nothing to occupy his attention.

Ollie was born to cattle and the open range, and his personal knowledge of women wasn't enough to fill a cartridge shell. They got all excited over fellers who probably filled their spare time drinking and carousing, and never noticed the gem right under their noses. It didn't set right with him that Betty Jo should be so all-fired spurred up over this stranger. If it weren't for the fact of the stranger saving his life, he could grow right fond of hating the man. He felt like going in that kitchen and letting her know he stood on the same amount of ground as that feller did, and he forked a saddle the same way too. Course, when it came to sling-ing lead, he didn't have the chance of a Chinaman in Hades of shading the stranger's accuracy. He didn't know of another person in the world who shook lead out of a rifle as fast and accurate as Black Beard. Gave a man chicken skin just thinking on it.

His mind wallowed so deep in self-incrimination, he didn't even look up when the front door banged open and then shut. A gust of wind entered the dining room, causing dust eddies along the floor. The visitor took a seat right beside him without saying a single word for several minutes. Ollie still hadn't climbed out of his trough when the first words from the newcomer charged the air around him. "Didn't figure on meeting you here, Ollie." There appeared to be another person in the room, but his thoughts just wouldn't track anything other than that voice. It sent shivers up his spine, and the urge to run for the windblown dust outside almost over powered him.

Before he could gather his legs under him, a feminine voice perforated his befuddled thinking. "Dad, you wouldn't do anything here in the hotel you might regret, would you?" Shirley let her body slack onto the stool the other side of Ollie.

Mr. Pugh tried hard to work up the anger necessary to handle this rustler, but his daughter could see he was losing the struggle. Ollie found his voice, even though it didn't ring out the way he hoped it would. "Since you got so close to stretchin' my neck, Mr. Pugh, I turned over a new leaf. That's why I'm in town. Can't stand bein' around that bunch. The other three you had in your clutches that day gave up and left the country, but I didn't feel like runnin'. Seems to me I oughtta fess up and face the music. Sure don't hanker to swing a wide loop no more."

Shirley latched onto this line of thinking right quick. "See, Dad, if you'd hung Ollie, he wouldn't have the chance to make things right. Now he can work at a respectable job and maybe become a leading citizen."

Her father eased the tension by slapping Ollie on the back. "Guess my daughter has a point, but this rustling business needs to be brought to a stop. Nobody's figured a way to do that yet-- cattlemen are still losing herds right and left. Just got word that a big bunch of JP cattle were run off last night. When I saw you here, I figured you might've had a hand in it."

Ollie let his eyes hang steady on those of Mr. Pugh. "No sir, I weren't in on it, and can't say any of the other men from the Hole was either. Since the shindig at your place, everybody's layin' low. If a jag of cattle was run off, it was done by someone outside the gang."

Pugh lifted his hat from his mop of dark hair, letting it rest on the counter. "You think someone else is pulling part of the jobs around here?"

"Well, the JP outfit hugs the Nevada border pretty close and it wouldn't be any big deal for a few boys from the other side of the line to hop over and collect a passel of cows."

"Ollie might be right, Dad. If there are other gangs with a craving for Strip beef, it'll really put a crimp in things." Shirley envisioned the ranches on the Strip being as barren of cattle as the Hastings spread.

Pugh squinted at Ollie. "You think that fellow doing all the bank robbing might be trying to set up shop on this range, planning to clean out the cattlemen?"

"You figger the man kin fly? It's all over the county that he held up the stagecoach, then brung the coach into town last night. Besides, Betty Jo says he's upstairs sleepin'. Unless he's got wings somewhere under that shirt, it ain't humanly possible to be two places at once." Ollie sat thinking on the trust he already placed in Black Beard, reckoning he didn't fit the picture of a cattle rustler.

"What made you think he took part in the rustling last night, Dad?" Shirley felt like Ollie did. Her father's reasoning didn't strike her as even a possibility.

"Word's going around saying he's the one let Ollie and his three friends off the hook out at our place. If so, it seems logical he'd be in with the rustlers."

"Nope, yore bayin' at the wrong moon if you believe that, Mr. Pugh. Ain't none of us ever seen the feller before. That's all the boys been talkin' about lately and nary a one of 'em knows where he hails from. Seems he just dropped from nowhere and started pullin' jokes on all the bankers. If he'd been mixed up with rustlers, one of us would of gotten wind of it."

"There has to be a big boss somewhere who's trying to ruin us all. Shirley says the Hasting's ranch is almost stripped clean of cattle."

Hanging his head with eyes downcast, Ollie owned up to his part. "Ain't nothin' to be proud of, but I did my share. We got orders to see those folks moved off that section of the country as fast as possible, so we done it."

"Who rode with you on those assignments, Ollie?" Her father now figured he held the right slant on there being a head honcho bossing things. Orders came from someone to the gang and they carried them out.

Ollie might do a lot of bad things, but he wouldn't rat on his friends. He scratched at his head, pretending to think. "Can't rightly remember who was with me. Seemed there weren't any shortage of gun-hands wantin' to do a little night ridin'."

"Dad, if a man's worth his salt, you know he isn't going to answer a question like that. But I think the same as you about there being a big auger doing all the planning. Whoever it is has easy access to what goes on." She didn't really want to bring up Colt's activities but decided it needed to be talked about. "When Black Beard came in for breakfast this morning, he mentioned he left the strong box on top of the stagecoach last night, but Hank didn't find it when he hitched up the teams. Do you think there's any significance to that?"

"The significance I'd put on it is the man's a liar if he robbed the coach, then said he left the strong box on top of it."

"What about the possibility of someone here in town seeing the coach parked in front of the company office, then stealing the box?" Shirley wouldn't give up on her belief in Colt.

"Can you put a name to who it would be?" He didn't wait for an answer. "Of course not. Some of the outlaws might have stolen it, but no one living here in town would do such a thing. No, Black Beard is lying and I'll bet he knows where the money is."

"You're right on one of those accounts, Mr. Pugh, but I don't figure to tell anyone else where it is. That money stays put till the proper time comes to turn it loose." The voice from the dining room doorway turned them all around just as Betty Jo came from the kitchen to ring the dinner bell.

She stopped short on seeing Black Beard leaning against the door jamb. "Black Beard, what're you doing up now? Thought you wanted to sleep most of the day." She reached down to pat Buddy, standing just behind his master.

Colt's drawl reached them all. "The wind coupled with the

banging of the front door kinda gets under your eyelids and pushes 'em open. But it's mostly those great cooking smells drifting up to the second floor that sprung them wide."

Ollie left his stool, crossing the floor with long strides and extending his hand. "Man oh man, it's good to see you, Black Beard. Been wantin' to thank you for savin' me from a necktie party. Only got a glimpse of you that mornin' but it sure set a pretty picture in my mind." He sent a sly glance at Buddy. "And thanks to you too, fella, for your part."

Colt took the proffered hand. "Mr. Pugh still seems to be on speaking terms with you, Ollie. At least there's been no sound of guns talking."

"So, you're the rip-snorter causing all the talk on the range. You don't look big enough to fill shoes like that. I've been of the opinion that you fit the bill as more of a troublemaker than a practical joker." Pugh sure didn't want to give out he held the wrong slant on things.

Colt shrugged his shoulders. "Don't really care one way or the other what you think, Mr. Pugh."

Pugh shifted off the stool as his hand flashed hip-ward. He hadn't even touched gun butt before he found himself staring into the black muzzle of a loaded six-gun and a snarling canine right beside it. He caught his breath, expecting to see flame and lead sprouting from the large hole gaping at him. As suddenly as the gun appeared, it slipped back into the brown leather at Colt's side, but the dog continued to watch, a low growl sending warning. Colt looked not at Mr. Pugh but at Ollie, who sported a very white face.

"You don't owe me anything, Ollie. As long as you walk the

straight and narrow from here on, it'll have been worth it."

Trying to get his thinking off the speed of that draw, Ollie mumbled, "Still, if it wasn't for you, I'd be hot and humble, shoveling coal for the devil." Then it dawned on him that Colt shook hands with his left hand turned so it would grip Ollie's right one. He sleeved a drop of sweat from his eye. He hadn't noticed it because he was watching Black Beard's face. A chill ran through his body: must be a natural way for Black Beard to shake hands, thereby freeing his right hand to come into play when needed. In all his days he'd never encountered a man who did that.

Shirley gripped her father's arm while her heart began to slow and recede to its proper place in her chest. One glance at her father told her he felt the same way. The hair on the back of his neck was standing up and his eyes showed unbelief. In his younger days he'd handled a gun with the best of them, but today he witnessed something he never hoped to see again, at least with him on the receiving end. Betty Jo couldn't quite grasp the situation either-- she'd expected to hear a six-gun thunder, but none split the silence.

Ollie took matters into his own hands by grabbing Black Beard's left arm and pulling him toward the front door. "Let's go somewhere so we can talk, like the saloon. We can come back and eat after the rush is over."

Colt let the outlaw lead him out of the hotel across to the saloon. Buddy went right along, although the idea of another steak was mighty tempting, and he sent a hopeful look in Betty Jo's direction. Nevertheless, his duty belonged to Colt, and also his heart.

When they were gone, Shirley heaved a long sigh of relief. "Dad, you still believe he's responsible for the trouble on this range?"

Pugh dropped his weight to the stool behind him, pulling his bandana up to mop his face. "Guess I must be thinking like a tinhorn. A man with such ability don't need to steal cows to make a living. But why stop a hanging if he ain't in with the bunch doing the dirty work?"

Shirley put a lot of thought into this, but didn't know whether she should broach her conclusions. Finally she told him. "Maybe he figures you can catch more bees with honey than you can with vinegar."

This turned on a new light for her father. "You may have something there. About three months ago I wired Captain Smith of the Arizona Rangers for help in stopping the rustlers up here. You think he's the one they sent?"

His statement worried Shirley. "If that kind of thinking got loose on the range, Dad, his life wouldn't be worth a plugged nickel. Please keep it under your hat."

Betty Jo started to say something, then shook her head, agreeing with Shirley. "Wild horses couldn't drag those words from me. From now on my lips are sealed." She dearly wanted to believe Black Beard was a lawman.

"I guess you two have the straight of things. Trust an old fool to let his lips flap when they shouldn't." Patting Shirley's hand, he said, "Well, honey, guess I better get back to the ranch while I'm still among the living. Remind me to never touch the butt of this gun again unless I'm facing something that can't shoot back." A rueful smile spread over his face.

When his silhouette receded through the door, Shirley went to the kitchen while Betty Jo proceeded to the outside to ring the dinner bell. She was immediately covered over with a cloud of dust as several hard-eyed men pulled rein in front of the hotel. They sprang from saddle leather, tramping inside, the wind moving along behind them, ignoring her as she wiped grit from her eyes. She recognized none of them.

Movement in front of the saloon caught her attention. Peering through the dust, she pinpointed Black Beard with Ollie at his side, pushing through the saloon doors. It crossed her mind that the men who just entered the hotel might cause trouble since they appeared so tough, but she shrugged it off. Ornery strangers were always slipping into town, and usually nothing happened. It was the number of them in this bunch that caused her to fleetingly sense a problem.

When the batwings banged shut behind them, Colt spotted Mitch and Hank playing cards at a table with three other men. Angling that way, the two dropped into chairs at the next table. Hank squinted at them. "What you two doing in town? Someone's liable to stretch both your necks for the things you been doing."

Mitch laid down his cards, letting his eyes rove over Black Beard. "You figure to hang and rattle in these parts for a time?" He completely ignored Ollie.

Leaning back in the chair and hoisting his boots up to the table top, Colt let time drag for a moment. "What's in it for me if I do?"

A frown crossed the rugged face of Mitch. "Look, mister, you've pulled some pretty unbelievable stunts lately but that don't cut the mustard with me. We could use a good man, but he'd have to take orders and no questions asked. With an attitude like you just displayed, you might not be happy with the bunch running this Strip."

Colt's flinty eyes were locked on Mitch, his voice steady. "You run roughshod over all your men that way, Mitch?" He sat his chair with his boots on the table, easy as pie. Buddy, however, rose to his feet, his shackles up and teeth bared.

Shoving back his chair, Mitch rose menacingly. "The other night when you brought that money back, I felt beholden to you, even though you were the one stole it. But today ain't a particulary good day for us. If you want to argue who bosses the outfit, just pull your iron and get it over with." Sending a venomous glance at Buddy, he added, "And keep your damn dog out of it."

"How you figure I brought the money back? Could've been anyone. All of you were over at the bank that night. The money could've been there on the floor when I came through the door. If that's the case, how you going to know if I stole it? By the way, this dog of mine is a friend. Be careful how you talk about him."

His temper hanging on tight, it took a minute for Mitch to digest this new thought. When it slowly began to weave its way through his mind, his mouth fell open and his hand dropped from his gun butt. Then he connected with the idea tossed out by Colt. "You ain't saying someone else robbed the bank, are you?" It sure was hard to chew this possibility.

It might not have been a wise move, but Hank stepped into the argument. "If you didn't do it, who else would've had the smarts to pull that stunt?"

Colt's eyes never left those of Mitch. "Thanks for the compliment, Hank, but it could be one of those tough hombres who just pulled up in front of the hotel. Last Ollie and I saw of them, they were heading through the doors like a pack of wolves."

That six-gun lying alongside Colt's leg and the muzzle pointing right at him soon got Mitch's thinking running in a different direction. He hadn't understood why Black Beard sat down that way, but it slowly came to him as the two argued. Now his stare shifted to Ollie. "You see who those men were?"

"I never got a good look at 'em, but what I saw didn't ring no bells. They was five or six and they looked like back-shootin' gun dogs to me." Ollie, too, had discovered the way Black Beard's gun rested and he reminded himself how lucky he was that the man liked him.

Seeing the tension relieved, the men sitting around the table got up, moseying over to the batwings with Mitch in the lead. The horses standing hipshot at the tie rail, their tails facing the wind, stared back at them. "That ain't a brand what's slapped on anything around here." Mitch said.

No sooner had the words left his mouth than a woman's scream carried across the wind from the hotel, followed by several shots. Instantly Colt went slamming through the batwings, his gun out, ready for battle.

9
AS

Betty Jo passed through the dining room door left open by the men who preceded her. Her glance roved over them. They wore common range garb, dust caked in the creases of their shirts and pants. Their hats rode mops of different colored hair, but the gun belts hanging from their hips were almost identical. Spurs drug along the planking as they drifted toward tables. Hooking chairs with booted toes, they sprawled into them, spirals of dust floating up.

Some instinct made her hesitate before stepping in their direction, then shrugging her shoulders, she moved toward them. Their eyes boldly ravaged her as she stopped at the table, trying hard to keep a smile on her face. By now she wished she were miles away. Men stared at her all the time, but these ruffians made her skin crawl. 'Respect for women' wasn't in their vocabulary. Leers spread across several faces as one thug rasped, "Say honey, you want a real man to take home tonight?" His guffaw sailed from thick lips almost hidden by a drooping mustache.

Another tough kicked his chair backwards and was beside her before she could move a muscle. Too late, she tried to step back but his arm swung around her waist, pulling her against him. Getting control of herself, she lifted a knee with surprising force. The man's face took on a sudden pained expression and his arm fell away. She shifted to the side to get away from the table, stepping into the waiting arms of another of the bullies, who had risen from his chair while she was occupied with the first one. His arms tightened around her as his head lowered, biting her on the neck. Kicking back with the heel of her boot, she felt it connect with flesh and bone. The man hollered and his arms loosened, making her stagger away from the table.

"Hey, you boys tangled with a real wild cat. I bet she'd keep a man plenty warm at night, once she's tamed down," came from a smirking, heavyset man, the apparent leader of the bunch.

Betty Jo got her balance, ready to hotfoot it out of there, but afraid to turn her back. Just then a cold voice drove through the air, diverting them from their sport. "You men want to eat lead or food today."

Heads swivelled, finding Shirley standing in the door to the kitchen with a six-gun in her hand. The muzzle set steady on the middle of the man who last spoke.

"Now, ma'am, ain't no need to get excited. The boys was just having a little fun. Ain't no harm done except to Mort's and George's feelings."

"You haven't said yet which you want, mister." The words speared the man as Shirley never shifted the bore of that six-gun a fraction of an inch.

His eyes blazed momentarily, then his head dropped as he turned back to the men sitting at the table. His body blocked the view Shirley wanted of the man across from him. She took a step to the side to bring him into her line of vision. Too late. His gun lay along the table with the muzzle pointing her way.

Betty Jo saw his finger tighten on the trigger. Her scream ruptured the silence, causing the man to jerk slightly. The bullet from his gun traveled along the table, veering upward to pass over Shirley's head, burying itself in the door jamb behind her. Her gun exploded, sending lead into the man sitting next to the leader of the gang. He slumped to the floor, and all hell broke loose.

The leader let his weight carry him from the chair as he slapped leather, bringing his gun in line with Shirley. Realizing her danger, she dropped behind the counter as a bullet whined above her. Betty Jo darted for the door to the lobby, planning to grab the rifle behind the check-in counter. Her knees bent as a body tackled her from behind. Three more guns added their voice to the din, pouring lead into the counter shielding Shirley.

Above the roar the leader shouted, "Let's get out of here before the whole town corners us." Fitting action to words, he ran for the door, snatching Betty Jo by the arm as she tried to stand up. The man behind her bounded to his feet, grabbing her other arm. The two men propelled her through the door, the other three following. Guns were fired back at the counter to keep Shirley pinned down.

With Betty Jo screaming at the top of her lungs and trying desperately to pull away, the bunch charged through the front door of the hotel. Before they knew it, lead sang its deadly song to them. Colt's forty-four-forty spit flame and death as he tore along the walk for the hotel. Out of nowhere a wild dog charged into the melee, ripping and biting at their legs. The man who'd tackled Betty Jo and now held one of her arms, caught a bullet in his chest and wilted to the ground. The leader began to pull Betty Jo in front of him as one of the men behind fired at Colt. His bullet took her in the back, causing her legs to fold, spilling both her and the leader to the churned earth among the milling horses. The bullet from Colt's gun, meant for the man still holding onto Betty Jo, tore over their heads, finding the man who'd loosed lead into her back, splattering his blood in all directions as it sliced through the carotid artery in his neck. He staggered backward, dropping his gun and grabbing his neck, trying to stop the spurting blood.

Colt sank to his heels, trying to dodge the bullet from the gun of the man to the side of the one spurting blood. Centering his gun on one of the remaining toughs, he pulled trigger and saw the man thrown backwards by the heavy lead. A bullet sang over his head and he heard a grunt behind him. That sound could only mean one thing: someone running behind him took the bullet meant for him. Another leaden death pellet sped over his head, droning in the other direction. The last tough staggered sideways, trying desperately to bring his gun into line and fight off a mad dog at the same time. Realizing only one bullet remained in his gun, Colt sighted and shot just as the man's gun spit lead. His target faltered, buckled at the waist, then sank slowly to the dust of the street.

Colt stayed where he knelt, punching empties out of his six-gun and reloading from his belt, knowing that if one of the toughs still breathed, he may need the loads. He heard sound behind him and the words, "Ollie took one in the shoulder."

Shirley came running from the hotel as Colt sprang to his feet, hoofing it toward Betty Jo who lay on the ground, unmoving. Buddy lay beside her, licking her hand. Approaching, he noticed no breathing from anyone lying in the dirt. Shirley reached Betty Jo at the same time he did, flinging herself down beside the young girl. Her eyes were pleading as they lifted for a quick glance at Colt.

"She's dead, Colt." Her mind didn't even register the use of his real name. He knelt beside Betty Jo and lowered his head to let his cheek rest just beside her nose. His actions were quick when he felt a weak stream of air slide against his skin. Ripping his skinning knife from its holster, he split the girl's dress down the back, exposing the angry hole just off to the right side of the backbone.

"Good." His voice was soft as it reached Shirley's ears. The one word brought her thinking back to speed, realizing there still may be a chance of saving Betty Jo. Her hands moved rapidly as she tore a strip of white cotton from her slip.

Handing it to Colt, she sobbed out the words, "You think she has a chance?" The bullet fired point blank surely would have torn things wide open inside the girl.

His hands moved expertly as he padded the wound in the back. Wrapping another strip of cotton from Shirley's slip over the padding, he gently turned the girl over. His knife flashed again and a piece of cloth came free from over the girl's midsection, showing a much larger hole where the lead exited. Gently his fingers probed over the abdomen.

A crowd had appeared around the three by this time, everyone holding their breaths. Colt got the distinct impression that everyone in town approved highly of this young woman. "It doesn't feel like any of the vital organs were punctured, except maybe a lobe of the liver. That's what's causing the dark blood to seep and mix with the normal red blood coming from the skin and underneath tissues. Since there's no gas issuing from the wound, the bowels were pushed aside by the heavy slug. She's unconscious because she's in so much shock."

Glancing up, he saw Heidi bending over them and said, "We need to move her into a room at the hotel and out of this dirt. Get a couple of men to find the back door Pike blew off the saloon the other night--we'll carry her on that. I noticed he hadn't fixed it yet."

Immediately Heidi disappeared from his vision and his eyes dropped back to his work. "If one of you will bring a bottle of whiskey, I'd like to pour some in this wound before she starts to wake up. It'll burn like fire if she's awake."

Pike leaned down with a bottle in his hands. "I've seen a lot of gut-shot men in my time, so I fetched a bottle when I left the bar."

"Thanks, Pike." Colt took the bottle. Wiping off the blood from around the wound the best he could, he poked the head of the bottle into the wound and tipped it up.

Bubbles drifted to the bottom and he pulled the neck back out of the bloody hole. The size of the crowd diminished greatly during his ministrations: white-faced men and women stumbled away from the bloody sight, gasping in huge gulps of air. Shirley, pale and nauseated, hung in there and passed him another pad of cotton which he gently placed over the gaping hole, tying it tightly into place with the strip from the girls back.

By this time two men came up with the door he'd requested. Colt placed it next to Betty Jo's side. Several outlaws helped roll her gently onto the door. "When we get her on a bed, we'll roll her off so she's lying on her back. Now you two carry her to the hotel while I check Ollie. Don't move her from the door till I get there. Shirley, you go with them to show where she's to be put." He stood up, striding back to where Ollie sat leaning against a man's legs. A sickly grin spread across Ollie's face. "Sure beats all, the way I'm constantly beholden to you, Black Beard. One of these days you better let me return the favor."

Colt slit the shirt over Ollie's wound with his knife. "If I hadn't dropped to the ground when I did, you wouldn't have taken the bullet meant for me, Ollie."

A grimace spread across Ollie's features when Colt began to probe the wound with his fingers. Moments passed as his hands covered both front and back of the shoulder. Then he leaned back, smiling at the man. "Nothing broken, but it's too bad it was your right arm --you won't be able to handle a gun for awhile."

Ollie pointed at his right hip. "You see a holster nestled there?" At the sudden knowledge spreading over Colt's eyes, he tried to laugh but it came out as a groan. "I'm a southpaw."

A ripple of laughter rang out from the crowd. "I guess it just slipped my mind in all the gun talk, Ollie."

Mitch and Hank were busy inspecting the toughs where they lay sprawled grotesquely around the front of the hotel. They straightened the bodies, putting them in a line. Not one of them was alive; the short gunplay lasted only minutes, but six men met their fate in a hail of lead. Mitch detailed two men to carry the one in the hotel dining room outside and lay it alongside the others. "There ain't a familiar mug in the whole bunch. Wonder where they come from." Raising his eyes to search the town for answers, he asked an obvious question, "Why'd they picked here to start trouble?"

Colt began to clean Ollie's shoulder. Ollie gritted his teeth and his eyes watered when the whiskey ran into the raw wound, but he made no outcry. The man Pike had ordered to fetch bandages from the undertakers arrived with several rolled strips of white cloth, handing them to Colt as he needed them. With the wound cleaned and disinfected by the use of the alcohol, Colt began to wrap it with the cloth. By the time he finished, Ollie's face was white as a sheet. "You're going to stay at the hotel for a couple of days, Ollie, till we're sure there'll be no more bleeding. Then you can go where you want."

Despite the shock and pain, Ollie mumbled through slitted teeth, "You figger Betty Jo's gonna make it?"

Looking into the man's worried eyes, Colt got a glimpse of what the young girl meant to this outlaw. "She took a wicked hit from that slug but as near as I can tell, nothing vital was damaged. The liver repairs very rapidly once the bleeding stops and if none of the intestines or the stomach were touched by the lead as it passed through, she should heal all right. But it'll take a long time. If the bullet had penetrated the opposite side of the spine, the spleen would have been ruptured and caused fatal internal bleeding."

Ollie stared at him, mouth open, not understanding a word Colt said except that Betty Jo had a chance. "You better get up there to her-- these other fellers kin help me to the hotel." His voice broke slightly as Colt stood up. "See you handle her with kid gloves, Black Beard. Everyone in town loves that youngster."

Nodding, Colt swung toward the hotel, his stride carrying him rapidly through the front door. The rachet of his boot heels on the stairs telegraphed his passage to Shirley as she huddled over the white-faced girl lying on the door. Heidi, with another lady from the saloon, stood by the bed patiently waiting for Black Beard. They had removed the girl's shoes and set them sedately by the washstand, and tried to fix the torn dress to look decent.

The room was warm and quiet when Colt came in, going immediately to the bedside. Bending down to examine the girl, he picked up the arm closest to him and finding a weak but steady pulse, let his eyes seek Shirley. "Where are the men who carried her here?"

"We asked them to leave while we straightened her clothes. I guess they decided we could handle everything, and I think we can."

"All right, then, if the two of you will take the feet, I'll handle the shoulders and we'll roll her off the door. Move as gently as possible but don't hesitate in the rolling process."

Seconds later Betty Jo lay on her back and the lids covering her eyes began to slowly spread apart. At first there didn't appear to be any recognition in the depths of her eyes. Shirley brought a wet cloth from the night stand and laid it over Betty Jo's forehead. The cool moisture caused her eyes to spring wide open and her lips began to move, but nothing escaped them other than air.

Taking the girl's hand, Shirley leaned toward her. "You took a bullet in the back, honey. You must lay as quiet as possible. Black Beard cleaned the wound and bandaged it. He figures you have a fighting chance."

Resting her eyes on Shirley, a faint smile drifted across Betty Jo's lips, then her gaze slowly shifted to rest on Black Beard. She didn't try to speak but her eyes told what she would have said if she could. Realizing the girl may need a little more explanation, Shirley whispered, "Those terrible men have gone to where they'll roast forever. Not one of them escaped with his life."

Her pain-filled eyes again shifted to Shirley, then closed slowly. Momentarily, Shirley felt fear engulf her. Then Colt's soft voice dissipated that fear. "What she needs now is rest and quiet. I'll look in on her again in an hour. If one of you will stay here with her, you can let me know if anything changes." He moved quietly from the room and down the hall. The lobby stood packed wall to wall with men and women waiting to get the word on Betty Jo's condition. Shirley appeared by his side as he walked down the stairs. At the bottom she stopped, lifting her voice slightly. "Betty Jo came awake for just a minute, then drifted back to sleep. Her pulse is weak but steady. Black Beard feels she has a chance if we can keep things quiet around here. I know none of you have eaten yet and we won't be serving in the dining room at all the rest of the day. However, I'll have Andy fix plenty of food which will be sent to the saloon for you men and to the school house for you ladies. Most of it we cooked in preparation for lunch before this happened, so it will only be a short time before it arrives at those two places. Now, if you'll clear the hotel and keep things on the quiet side in the street, it would be appreciated."

Everyone began to file slowly out the front door. Colt started to move after them but she touched his arm, signaling him to follow her. Giving orders to Andy, who stood with a gravy pan in the kitchen doorway, she continued on into the storage room with Colt. "You seem pretty adept at handling wounds, Black Beard. Would it be too bold of me to ask where you learned your skill?"

He let his eyes wander over the supplies stacked on shelves. "Not at all. I had a couple of medical classes at school. We got mostly thugs and gangsters at the infirmary. They were always using knives or guns to eliminate each other and those they didn't cotton to, so there were plenty of wounds to practice on."

As he finished speaking, Hank came quietly through the door. "Heidi's gonna stay with Betty Jo most of the afternoon, then someone else can spell her." He leaned his weight against one of the shelves beside Colt. "I can help Andy by distributing the food to the saloon while he takes it to the schoolhouse."

Shirley let her eyes inspect Hank's face. "From the look you gave Black Beard, you have something else on your mind. What's the problem?"

Colt suddenly came to attention and remembered that when she called him 'Colt', Hank stood right beside him. No one else was close enough to hear her. He didn't try to beat around the bush. "What do you intend to do with the information, Hank?"

Hank's eyes turned speculative as they bored into Colt. Shirley hadn't yet grasped the gist of Colt's words. Hank's voice barely reached her ears. "So you're Colt Hastings. Mitch and the boys been wondering what happened to you and your folks."

The intake of breath as Shirley gasped caused Hank to look at her. "Why are you so surprised? After all, the name 'Colt' came from you when you talked to him over Betty Jo."

Mortified, Shirley looked at him with pleading eyes as Colt drawled, "She didn't think anyone else knew who I was, but it accidentally slipped out. Now that you know, I guess there's no use pretending any longer."

Hank straightened up, walking to the door and back several times. Finally he reached a decision. "Your secret is safe with me. You've gone to a lot of trouble making a name for yourself, so you must have a good reason. But you better be real careful. If

Mitch ever finds out who you really are, he won't waste any time stomping you. If you planned to join the gang, no matter what your motive, you better think twice--you'll be in the lion's den at all times. I'll do what I can to help, but it might not be enough."

"Why would you want to play along this track, Hank?" Colt couldn't figure the man out. He was definitely a trusted member of Mitch's team and hiding this information could get him in a heap of trouble . . . maybe as much as Colt.

"Let's just say I have my own axe to grind and let it go at that. Now if that grub is ready, I'll get it over to the saloon." Hank turned abruptly toward the kitchen.

Shirley hung her head and waited miserably for Colt to say something. Unintentionally or not, she'd really messed up. If Hank didn't keep his word, Colt's plans and all his actions so far would've been for nothing. She wanted to just flat out die.

"Hey, don't take it so hard. Hank's the only one who knows, and he won't tell. I might've done the same thing, what with all the confusion and worry." His sympathetic tone heartened her, and she raised her grateful eyes to his. Too close. Too soon. He took a step back, an easy smile planted firmly on his face. "Let's go check on Ollie. I want to make sure the move to the hotel didn't caused any serious bleeding." They left the room, relief overlaying longing in both of them.

Ollie lay tense in the bed, showing the pain he felt. "That whiskey burns as much on the outside as it does inside, Black Beard. I sure hope you ain't planning to dump anymore where it hadn't oughta be."

"Buck up, fellow. Most of the pain you're feeling is due to the wound, not the whiskey. It'll be with you for several days. I'll try to get some peyote for you. Looks like the movement hasn't caused any more bleeding, so no major vessels were ruptured." Colt rechecked the bandage, happy that Ollie was doing well.

"Guess I shouldn't be complaining too much . . . Betty Jo took a lot bigger hit than me. You still think she'll pull through?"

"I won't lie to you, Ollie. The whiskey will help keep infection down but if there's more damage inside or infection takes over, she'll have a rough time of it. A week will tell the story. After that, if she's still with us, it'll only be a matter of time."

"You gonna stay around to look after her?" Ollie had a lot of faith in this man who continued to pull him out of tough spots.

"I'll be around all the time unless the Captain gets back and decides to press things. If that happens, I may have to pull a disappearing act."

"Don't you worry none. I'll put a bee in Mitch's ear and he'll see the Captain stays outta things. We all like that little gal and no yellow-striped uniform is gonna cause her the slightest problem."

Smiling at the serious expression on Ollie's face, Colt walked to the door of the room. "You do just that. Now I need to get back up and make sure she's resting quietly. You better get some sleep yourself. You won't do Betty Jo any good if you don't heal fast."

After the door closed, Ollie lay there wondering what Colt meant. This was sure a terrible time. Why did those six men come into town huntin' for trouble? It just beat all what could happen so fast. With all of them dead, the mystery would never be solved. His eyes closed as his body relaxed, and soon he was snoring softly.

Colt and Shirley stepped quietly into the room where Betty Jo lay sleeping. Colt noticed a little more color in her face and the breathing, though still weak, was steady. Shirley whispered to

Heidi, "I'll be up to spell you in a couple of hours. She seems to be getting the rest she needs. And have you noticed-- there isn't nearly as much noise in the streets as usual."

"Yeah . . . I know people are praying for her. Look, hon, when Hank gets back from taking meals to the saloon, tell him to stick around. I'd like to talk to him about where he thinks those toughs came from and what business they might have here." The fact that six men rode into an outlaw town to cause trouble just didn't trigger any sane reasons, as far as she could tell.

Shirley nodded her head to show she understood and left the room with Colt. The air was tense between them when they descended the stairs to the lobby. She wanted to ask him what his plans were, but hesitated for fear of invading his privacy. Men could be so touchy. Only, Colt seemed more level-headed and responsible, somehow, than the usual run of the mill cowboy. This gave her courage.

When they reached the empty lobby, she timidly asked, "What are you going to do now?"

He knew what she was driving at, but evaded the real answer. "With two patients to look after, I figured to stay around town for a week at least. Might even consider going to the dance you folks been planning on Saturday."

"You think that's wise? If Captain Gregg gets back in time, it's the first place he'll come and he may have some of his officers with him."

Colt turned to her. The afternoon sunlight streamed through the large front window, back lighting her and putting a glow of subtle fire in her hair. Her soft lips were slightly parted, and as Colt stood speechless, drinking in her beauty, the concern in her eyes disappeared, replaced by tenderness and a deeper feeling he was not yet ready to face. With profound regret, he pulled himself together and said lightheartedly, "Apparently he hasn't asked you to go with him. That leaves you free to accept my offer to take you."

Shirley felt his withdrawal and wisely let him go. Although she wanted nothing more than to be with Colt, her initial fears returned. She said, "You know you could be committing suicide if he shows up."

Colt winked at her. "You let me worry about that. I'll pick you up a few minutes before the dance starts. Then I can see which box lunch you packed and bid on it."

Despite her worries, she began to feel excitement building in her. "All right, but don't say I didn't warn you." She still wanted to know if he would go ahead with his plans and join the outlaw bunch, but since he avoided mentioning it, she figured she already knew what his answer would be.

Colt walked to the front door and Buddy came up off the floor where he'd been sleeping. "I'll be at the saloon the rest of the day. If anything changes with either patient, let me know. Otherwise I'll check on both of them in a couple of hours."

He let the door close quietly behind him, sauntering along the boardwalk, heading for the saloon. The air smelled of dust but the wind hadn't resumed its travel over the town. Everywhere he looked, he saw tumbleweeds blown in off the desert, creating a scene of desertion about the place. Dirt lay piled up against the side of the boardwalk and in front of closed doors.

Reaching the saloon, he turned in at the batwings. A layer of dust on the floor was being shifted around by the barrage of boots tramping through it. Mitch sat playing poker with three others at a table in the back of the room. Colt turned his steps their way, hooked an empty chair with his boot toe and dropped into it as Buddy curled up on the floor beside him. The men around the table ceased the card play when he sat down, and Mitch let his eyes range over Colt.

"For a bank robber, you're pretty handy with the medical duties. Mind telling me where you learned your trade?" Mitch was suspicious, showing a guarded acceptance of Colt.

"Not at all, Mitch. I suspect you could do as well--you've probably seen a lot of men take a bullet while riding the outlaw trail. Any man who picks that as a mission in life is going to get plenty of opportunity to practice a little medicine, especially out here where doctors are few and far between. I've seen my share of gunshot wounds." Colt pulled some money from his pocket, laying it in front of him while waiting for the game to resume.

Mitch studied Colt for a couple of minutes. "Before the gun talk, you were acting pretty high on the post. You still want to throw your gun against me?"

A low laugh came from Colt's lips. "Seems to me it was you wanted to test my skills, Mitch. I've got no quarrel with you. I figure the excitement is over for one day and a nice quiet game of poker would ease some of the butterflies in my stomach."

The others at the table thought this was funny and laughed at Colt, but Mitch gave him a hard stare before he turned to his cards. The game got under way and the next hand played brought Colt into the game. He hoped all was forgotten, but he wasn't sure Mitch felt the same way until four hands later when Mitch broached the subject. "You interested in joining the bunch or are you off to pull another job on your own somewhere?"

Colt examined his cards as the outlaws around the table went silent. "Might just as well throw my rope with you fellows. You seem to eat regular and still have time to play a lot of poker. But I'm not up to a lot of night riding. I like my sleep, so leave me out of any wild cow-chasing activities."

Mitch leaned back in his chair, suddenly tense. "You swing your loop with us, you ride when I say. You don't like that, then roll your heels somewhere else."

The challenge whistled through the air. Colt realized Mitch wanted to establish once and for all that he was boss. Deciding to see how far the man would go, Colt threw down two cards. "I'll take two. You boys always play cards with your tempers hanging on the edge? Me, I like a good friendly game."

All movement ceased as the men held their breath. Mitch let his chair down slowly. Laying the cards on the table, he glared at Colt. "You're just asking for it, ain't you."

A surprised expression crossed Colt's face. "Now there you go again. Who put the burr under your saddle this morning, Mitch? Any of you other fellers getting raked over the coals like he's doing me, or am I just special?"

The whole saloon went quiet, as the men around sensed something going on at the table where Mitch and Colt eyed each other. Silently, those watching made bets with themselves that Colt would come out on top. After all, they saw him throw lead at those toughs about as fast and accurate as they ever witnessed.

Mitch couldn't decide whether Colt deliberately antagonized him or if the man just naturally craved trouble. If it were the latter, he could sure use a man like that. One who goaded the tiger in his cage, no matter what the risk, could come in mighty handy. Most men arriving on the Strip were run of the mill outlaws who did just what they were told and nothing more. A man who acted the way Colt did, may have enough brains in his noggin to help plan a few things. He certainly showed a lot of ingenuity when he took on a bank job. With that trained dog of his, now sitting alertly beside him, future bank jobs might be a lot less risky. Making up his mind, he picked up his cards and leaned back in his chair again.

"You came in to play cards. Let's see if you can do it as good as you shoot your mouth off." Mitch wanted the last word and that fit in with Colt's feelings as well. He knew now he was in with the bunch. A decision had been made by Mitch to accept him for the time being.

Colt studied the other players as the game got under way and those in the saloon resumed their conversations. There would be no gun play for the present and many of them were disappointed.

The three other card players wore the normal range denims with various colored cotton shirts. A heavy cartridge belt with a six-gun in the holster rode on each hip and a blue bandana around each of their necks finished off their attire. One man topped six and a half feet with no hair showing under the black Stetson on his head. His face was angular, sporting a brown mustache curled at the ends. He seemed to be the quietest of the three. The man next to him came only to his shoulders, giving the impression of being very short when sitting next to the bean pole. His hair flowed out from under the hat tipped to the back of his head and the shine of a clean-shaven face made another contrast to the tall man. His eyes constantly shifted around the table, staring at each of the other players in turn, trying to read their minds. The third player sat hunched over his cards with his head tipped down, causing his face to be shielded by the wide brimmed hat pulled over his forehead.

The tall hombre dealt the next hand while Mitch raked in the pot from the last play. He flipped the cards to each player with a flourish. Colt's eyes narrowed when he caught a shift of the hands that the other players apparently hadn't noticed. Wondering what the man's game was, Colt picked up his cards and stared at three aces. Nothing crossed his face as each man picked up his hand to decide what to discard. They all threw one to three cards into the discard pile and replacement cards were dealt to them. Colt took two, one of which glared back at him: another ace.

The dealer shoved fifty dollars into the pot, making Colt consider wether or not to stay in this game. Beanpole certainly wanted something to happen, but it was hard to figure what. To Colt's surprise, Mitch matched the amount and raised twenty. The two others in the game threw their hands into the discard, taking them out of the play. A slight tension built as the two still holding cards watched to see what he would do. Four aces would be hard to beat but the dealer had bet fifty right off the bat. Colt felt sure he dealt cards exactly where he wanted them. It was evident that this hand meant more than just a game . . . a test of his ability must be in the wind. Now the question came hard into his mind: should he bet on what he was holding or fold, being certain the dealer had a better hand? He figured the play had been rigged, with both Mitch and Beanpole in on it.

His face remained expressionless as he let his gaze rest first on Mitch, whose features were also blank, then on the dealer, who avoided his eyes but had a slight upturn at the corners of his mouth. Reaching for more money in his pocket, Colt laid out an even hundred made up of five twenty-dollar gold pieces. He let the pile sit in front of him while he considered his options.

The others stared at the gold coins while a speculative look came into Mitch's eyes. He knew the Wells Fargo money consisted of mostly gold coins of high denomination, with only a few twenty dollar gold pieces in the bunch. His body tensed when Colt started to push the money toward the center of the table. Then Colt's hand stopped halfway to the pile. His eyes again roved over the faces of his two opponents. "You fellers have set me up for a fall and I'm wondering why. I think I'll just fold." He pulled the coins back to the edge of the table in front of him.

A sigh left the lips of the man next to him as Mitch leaned back in his chair with a grin spreading across his face. Beanpole, eyes sharp with anger, let his hand drop below the table. "You saying I dealt you a crooked hand?"

"Not at all. I think you dealt me a very good hand, but yours or Mitch's would be even better."

Mitch laughed out loud. "By golly, Pole, he's got you there. The man must know his cards to have seen you deal 'em where you wanted."

Pole took his time putting his hand back up on the table. He laid his cards down and a grin spread across his face. The cards showed a straight flush topping the four aces. "You're a tough nut to crack, Black Beard. No wonder the bankers all let you take their money with no complaints." A grudging respect showed in Pole's eyes.

Mitch stood up from the table. "All right, Black Beard, it's time for me to get back to the Hole-in-the-Rock. You might as well come along so you can meet the boys. We got a big job coming up and the details need to be worked out."

Colt frowned. "I sure would like to get in on something that big, Mitch, but with two patients to look after, I guess I better stay put. Betty Jo is a fine girl and if something happened to her while I went with you, I'd be in a lot of trouble."

This wasn't what Mitch wanted to hear but he didn't want any more trouble for Betty Jo. Besides, the folks around town wouldn't appreciate having the only person capable of taking care of her, gone for two days. "You won't share in any of the profits, if you stay here."

"Can't say I need any extra cash just now. I'll wait for the next trip." He reached for the gold pieces in front of him, slipping them into his pants pocket.

Mitch chuckled. "No, I guess you oughta have enough to last a while, since that strong box ain't been located yet. None of us care if you put one over on those Wells Fargo boys. We planned to do the same before you beat us to it. But don't monkey with Phillip's bank again--most of our spare cash rests in his vault."

Having said that, he motioned to the other three and they joined him as he left. Colt sat for a while looking over the patrons of the saloon. Two men were busy putting the door on the back room while Pike sweated to serve the ones crowding the bar. It seemed since the shooting there were a lot more people in the place and the noise sailed to the rafters, bouncing back to cause a constant din pounding on his ears. A bar girl flounced over, dropping into a chair across from him. "You really came on fast today, Black Beard. I have my own private room upstairs . . . any time you want to get away from the crowd, just let me know."

"Thanks for your concern, ma'am, but it looks like I'm going to be kept pretty close to the hotel for a while." He read disappointment in her eyes.

"Well, remember the invitation's always open." She sat with her eyes boldly roving over him, then coyly said, "My name's Ardyth."

He decided he might as well get as much information from her as he could. "Well, Ardyth, Mitch said he and the men were going on a big job but he neglected to mention what it would entail. You wouldn't happen to know what I'm missing out on, would you?"

His engaging smile and keen blue eyes completely disarmed her. She wanted to please him, so didn't hesitate to say, "He spends a lot of time here and did mention something about traveling west into Nevada. Said he'd bring me back a gold necklace. The gang don't broadcast their intentions when they plan a chore-- someone traveling through might tip off the law. I guess you'll have to wait till Mitch gets back to find out what you missed."

It sure seemed to be common knowledge around the saloon when the gang planned an activity, and everyone accepted it. He remembered Fredonia being a pretty wild town the few times he came here with his father when he was younger, but the acceptance of the gang as citizens of the place seemed a little bold, especially with the Cavalry post just fifteen miles away. But the Cavalry's responsibility dealt mainly with Indians, and with no other law on the Strip, he guessed the men were right to feel safe here.

"Sure hate to blow a big take, but guess this one will slip by me. Do you know if Hank is going with Mitch this time?"

"Hunh-uh. The best place to find out is by talking to Heidi. She keeps him pretty well to herself so none of the rest of us are privileged to his plans."

"Guess it's about time I checked on the two patients anyway. I'll keep in mind your offer of assistance. Hope next time the men pull a job I'll be able to role my hoop with them." He stood up, striding toward the door. The difficult part of his plan was over. It would be just a matter of time before the subject of the Hastings spread came up among the gang, and now that he would be with them, he'd hear the information he wanted.

His thoughts turned to the dance coming up and anticipation began to work into his gut. He wondered if Mitch and the men would be back in time for it, then decided they may not be welcome at a town dance in the school house. The local folks would put up with a lot, but they might draw the line when it came to outlaws hobnobbing with respectable ladies. They may even be adverse to him being in attendance, but after today and with Shirley on his arm, he figured he'd get along with them all right.

10

The quarter moon rested on its back in the black velvet sky, waiting like a bowl for stars to fall its way. Night sparkled down on those making their way to the dance at the school house, which sat a couple hundred yards from the outskirts of town. Crickets added their unique song to the happy sounds of expectant people. Wagons stood silent as ghosts in the night. Occasionally the rustle of harness and stamp of a hoof broke the evening's gentle breath.

Drawing close to the activity surrounding the school yard, Shirley let her arm rest on Colt's, holding the box lunch in her other hand. Buddy trotted close on Colt's heels, enjoying the delicious smells of ham, chicken, and beef that lingered after the women went by. His immediate future looked good. A few men leaning against their horses were discussing conditions on the range as the trio strolled past.

One voice sailed over the others. "If something ain't done soon, we'll all be out of work. Those night riders have stripped the Hastings spread clean. I rode over the other day to see if the owners were back yet and I didn't encounter one cow branded Bar H. When they get back from the east, they'll have to go into raising buffalo--it's all that's left on their range."

Another angry voice was heard. "Maybe he's the only smart one of the bunch, going back east at a time like this. Won't need to ride his backsides sore hunting for cows that ain't there."

The bitter laughter dwindled as Colt and Shirley proceeded on to the school. Shirley's fingers involuntarily tightened on his arm when she heard the men talking. She felt keenly the loss of her two friends and knew Colt felt it even more. The overheard conversation saddened them until they entered the door to the school, when their mood soon changed as the festivities surrounded them. The place sounded like a henhouse, chatter coming from all directions. The musicians were tuning up their instruments, adding squawks and screeches to the tumult.

Shirley smiled up at Colt. "It's amazing how a Saturday night dance can bring so many people into town. Most of the time you think the Strip is deserted---you can ride for days without seeing anyone. But put on a dance and they come out of the woodwork." Her excitement dispelled the seriousness that occupied her thoughts just moments before.

Colt's eyes slid over the crowd. He wondered if he should stay put or run for cover; gave a man goose bumps to be in a room with so many happy, talkative folks. He'd attended many parties in the east, but they didn't hold a candle to this. The folks attending those activities were more straightlaced and, to him, they

157

seemed to want to show who they were and how much money they had. Here punchers chatted with the wives of businessmen while ranch owners discussed work with nesters. Children raced around the room, yelling from sheer exuberance and excess energy. Pretty young girls wearing long party dresses sat on benches placed against one wall, while scrubbed, hopeful cowboys stood at the opposite wall eyeing them.

Kerosene lamps hung brightly from the ceiling, casting flickering shadows through the mass of people. Colt could feel rice rolling under his boots. Someone sprinkled it on the wood floor to make it easier for the dancer's feet to glide over the rough surface. Shirley left his side to take her box lunch to the makeshift stage to put with rows of other pretty boxes, surrounded by wilting wild flowers.

Colt stepped to the coat closet where guns were being checked. Unbuckling the cartridge belt, he handed it to Cyrus, the grocer's gangling son, who tagged it and placed it on a shelf among several others. Then he reached down, patted Buddy on the head and told him to stay with the gun. Buddy settled down with a disgruntled sigh.

"We were hoping you'd show up, Black Beard." Cyrus's voice cracked as he spoke earnestly to Colt. "What you done for Betty Jo in the last three days sure upped your standing in this neck of the woods. If it hadn't been for you acting so quick, those hoodlums would've got clean away and taken her with them." He choked up, then regained control and continued. "I hear she had a pretty rough time of it, but your doctorin' skill pulled her through. Folks are mighty thankful for you being there."

"If I hadn't done the job, one of you would have, so don't give me too much credit." Colt felt embarrassed with so much attention being slathered on him. "Is it all right if my dog stays here to keep you company?"

"Sure thing, sir. I'll keep an eye on him." Cyrus happily bent down to pet Buddy, who rolled his eyes at Colt and let out a bit of gas to show his true feelings. He wanted to be back in their small hut in the forest, alone with his master.

Ignoring Buddy's plaintive look, Colt turned from the boy and his glance ranged around the room. Strands of popcorn hung from the ceiling, crisscrossing above and almost touching the heads of some of the taller men. Colored paper cut and linked into chains had been placed around the edge of the room, where stalks of corn and bundles of straw were sitting, adding to the rough western look of the place.

Shirley touched his arm when the band struck up a Virginia reel. He felt himself propelled into the group by Dave, the owner of the general store. He and Shirley squared off with the other dancers while hands clapped, skirts swished merrily, and feet stomped the floor. Mingled in all this could be heard the laughter of those left on the sidelines. Shirley danced lightly in his arms. Before he knew it, she swung away with another man and he found a different lady in his arms. The caller shouted at the top of his voice and the band tried desperately to drown him out, but the man bellowed even louder and the dancers never missed a call.

The reel ended and someone hurriedly claimed Shirley, so he found himself facing a shy young girl with long, gold-flecked hair and freckles across the nose. He had noticed her earlier dancing with a tall, bowlegged cowboy and when his eyes lifted from her, searching for Shirley, he saw the same cowboy leading Shirley to the middle of the floor. The girl's smile was sympathetic as his glance came back to her. The music started immediately and the two of them were swept into the melee as her laugh reached his ears. He attempted to talk to her but this time the caller called a square dance and she glided off on the arm of another man while he bore a plump middle-aged woman on his arm. He saw the girl several more times during the dance, but they were changing partners so fast he never even got her name. When the caller stopped, he found himself with a tall, slim, haggard-faced woman who must have spent a lifetime at hard labor, but whose eyes were lively and mouth edged in a smile. A man stepped forward, taking her by the arm, and Colt found himself standing at the edge of the crowd looking on. Sweat dripped from his forehead and he pulled his pocket rag to wipe it off.

He spotted Shirley in the arms of a bull-necked farmer in bib overalls and bulging muscles that were squeezing her a little too tight. He caught her glance as they whirled by. Sensing her predicament, he stepped onto the floor and tapped the man on the shoulder. This signal always meant another man wanted to dance with the girl being held by the man who got tapped. Colt expected the same thing to happen this time, but he was mistaken. The man dropped his arms from around Shirley and pivoted on his heels, bringing a haymaker up from the floor. Having spent some time at school wrestling at the gym, Colt slipped inside the punch, grabbed the man's head with both hands, and using the man's forward momentum, tucked the head under his left arm. Then slipping his hands under the man's armpits and around behind him, Colt clasped his fingers together over the farmer's back. His left arm clamped down on the farmer's neck, locking his head in a tight grip between Colt's chest and his arm. The man struggled to get out of the headlock, but with his back bent and Colt's feet spread wide, he couldn't get enough leverage to break free. Colt saw Buddy standing in the doorway watching, but the dog made no move toward the tussle. He guessed the dog figured he could handle this all by himself.

The music came to a halt and three ranchers rushed to the two struggling men. One of them tapped the head sticking out from behind Colt with a bung starter. The farmer went limp as the other two caught him by the arms and drug him from the room. His heels bounced on the steps as they tossed him off the porch into the dirt. The cowboys still outside saw the man coming and seeing it was a farmer, ringed him with their bodies. The two men who threw him out turned back inside, knowing trouble from him would be over for the night.

The man who had cold-decked him with the barroom brawl-stopper chuckled. "Every time we have a dance, Ed gets thrown out. He don't like anyone cutting in on his dances. Usually though, it takes four or five of us to subdue him after he's laid the feller out cold that tapped him on the shoulder." He scrutinized Colt. "You sure don't look strong enough to hold a feller that big until we got here. I saw you start to cut in and grabbed a couple of men to come pick up the pieces, knowing what'd happen. At least what I thought would happen. You ever want a job on the Lazy J, give me a holler. Where did you learn to handle a man like that? Smoothest trick we ever saw."

Again Colt felt embarrassed at all the attention they were giving him. "Had a good wrestling partner once who saw to my training in the ring. Thought he'd break my neck with that hold and this seemed like a good time to see if it'd work for me."

Shirley waited by his side during this discussion. Now she took his arm, sensing his uneasiness with the incident. "You men get on with your gabbing. The dance still has more than half to go and I want to finish it with Black Beard."

The man doing the talking signaled the bandleader and the music took up right where it left off. Colt could see this was an expected thing . . . there wasn't even a change in beat. He slipped his arm around Shirley and the two of them were immediately engulfed by dancers. Her eyes poked at him as he guided her among the crowd. He mostly read her lips, since it was almost impossible to hear above the noise. "Would you like to step outside for a breath of fresh air?"

Realizing action would fit better than words, he swung her to his side and they wended their way through the dancing couples to the back door. Cool air brushed their faces as the door opened, filling them with a refreshing sense of being. He steered her toward the bench setting under the trees. Another couple occupied half of it, disregarding the two as they stepped up to sit down. Shirley suddenly pulled him around the bench and they walked into the trees.

Stopping with the lights from the dance still visible, she faced him. "You're the master of a lot of talent, so why continue on this wild scheme of yours? You could set up a medical practice until this trouble blows over, then start ranching again."

His eyes turned hard and she knew the wrong words had been said. "I got in with the gang like I wanted. Now I'll get the man I'm after."

"What if they get you first? After all, Hank told you there'd be

162

trouble for you and he seems to have a level head on his shoulders."Again the wrong words had come out.

"Meaning I don't?" His sarcasm cut deep and a gasp left her lips.

"I didn't mean it that way. Why are you always so defensive?" Tears stung Shirley's eyes. She only wanted to help, to keep him alive. Why couldn't she find the right words? She hugged her arms to her chest, afraid to say any more.

Several moments passed before his eyes softened and he sauntered off a ways from her. "I guess the last few months have seen a surge of the darker side of my makeup. I've killed nine men and helped in the elimination of another in that time. The responsibility for that hangs heavy on me. I shouldn't have come to the dance tonight."

Now it occurred to him that he voiced the wrong thing . . . her face went a shade lighter in the starlight filtering through the leaves. "Don't you think I feel the same way? My bullet snuffed the life from one of those men. I too spend nights soul-searching for an answer as to why it had to happen. But with things happening so fast, there wasn't any time to think."

He stepped toward her, taking her in his arms and pulling her close. Her head dropped to his shoulder and he felt moisture through his shirt. The two stood that way for some time, communicating with each other silently. The other couple left the bench, so after a few minutes, he led her over and they dropped onto it. Buddy had come up and sat by the side of the bench, keeping an eye on them while they were back in the trees. He now curled up on the ground.

Shirley spoke first, holding her voice low, for his ears only. "Colt, this is a dangerous game you're playing, so be careful. I felt almost the same about your parents as you did, but maybe vengeance isn't the way to go. However, if you're determined and that's what you still intend to do, I'll help all I can."

His heart swelled at the trust she placed in him. The urge became so strong to fold her in his arms, and kiss her tears away, that it took all his willpower to hold back. His life may not tread on this earth for much longer and, to him, it wouldn't be right to leave her a widow. He started to speak, to say a little of what was in his heart, when an uproar erupted from the school house. "Sounds like trouble. Maybe we better go back; your medical services might be needed again."

Shirley unwillingly left his side, and he took her arm as they hurried to the back of the schoolhouse. His glance backward showed Buddy still lying beside the bench, apparently preferring the quiet of the trees to the noise inside.

Passing through the door, they saw the dancers begin to move to the center of the room as two men drug another one across the floor, shoving him outside. This time it was a cowboy who felt the weight of the bung starter. Colt decided that these western dances could get out of hand if it weren't for a few good men acting as bouncers. "That there cowboy drank a little too much of the punch that old Pike spiked. Sure going to have a sore head tomorrow, what with all the liquor and the rap on the head." The speaker was the tall skinny man with the haggard wife.

Shirley smiled at the woman as the music started. "We better get these two men onto the dance floor before something else happens." A slight smile of acknowledgment crossed the face of the other woman as her husband swung her into the crowd.

"Mrs. Riley always seems unhappy. I wish there weren't so many troubles on this range . . . then people could relax more." Shirley knew things might never change, but she could always hope.

"That's another reason why I need to stay with what I've started." His voice became indistinct as the music drowned him out.

A business man tapped him on the shoulder about halfway through the dance and Colt found himself facing the freckle-faced young girl again. He swung her into the middle of the dancers and her laughter lightened his mood. The tune ended after a couple of minutes, but without a pause, the caller stepped to the front, his words sallying forth over the hubbub. "Grab your partners, swing them high."

She swished away from him in the arms of a young cowboy and Colt felt his shoulders squeezed in a grip so tight he thought a man had grabbed him. As he faced around, the lady's arms encircled him, propelling him into the dancing crowd. She stood a good six feet with broad shoulders and arms bulging with muscle. "Why don't you stick to a real woman, Black Beard? Why, I'd take such good care of you out at my farm, you'd think you'd died and gone to heaven."

How had he been so lucky as to have traded the young, slim, freckle-faced girl for this massive woman? He didn't want to anger her--she looked tough enough to eat cactus and enjoy it. Diplomacy was definitely called for in this situation. "Yes, ma'am, I'm sure you're right, but Mitch would be more of a match for you than I am."

Her laugh drowned out the caller and as the square formed she was whisked away by the man opposite them. Colt relaxed as he found himself again swinging Shirley. "Take your partners round the pole, come back fast and let 'er show." Suddenly the caller's voice trailed off and the band came to a grinding halt. His back to the rest of the room, he swung Shirley to a stop, thinking another fight must have broken out. One glance at her face showed him it was more than that. She had gone white, unable to speak. He heard feet shuffle behind him as dancers stepped back. When he turned to see what caused the sudden curtailment of all activity, the silence fell in on him.

A space opened between him and the ramrod straight uniform standing about ten feet inside the door. Colt had known this might happen and he kept his face blank as he spoke. "Howdy, Captain, looks like you've finished your hunt down south. Most of us still have enough energy for several more dances, so grab your partner and join in."

A collective sigh whispered through the room. The Captain paced forward, stopping within arms length of Colt. His face was set in granite and his eyes as hard as whetstone. "You must be the world's dumbest outlaw, Black Beard, to show your face around here again. This time you won't be able to talk your way out of the guardhouse trip."

Shirley started to step forward but Colt's arm reached out, preventing her from proceeding. "Way I always heard it, Captains were supposed to be gentlemen. Guess the folks who told me that must of never met the right Captain." His eyes were joined with those of the man in front of him.

The captain stood straighter and his face began to darken. "You, sir, are a scallywag from the word go. Why these fine people let scum like you come to a dance, I haven't found out yet, but if you will step outside, my men will escort you to the Post."

Shirley wouldn't be quiet any longer. Her voice shook with

anger. "Captain, you're out of bounds here. This man saved the life of Betty Jo and helped rid the town of six hard cases who were trying to abduct her. To all of us, that makes him as welcome at this dance as anyone. If you can't stand to be in the same room with such a man, then it's you who should leave."

The fire in her eyes set the Captain back a pace. Maybe he'd stepped into something he should have left alone. His eyes roamed the faces around him and he saw the same expression on all of them. How stupid to let jealousy trap him in a circumstance like this. He'd stepped through the door, seen Shirley in the arms of this Black Beard, and all reason vanished. Now he better make apologies fast if he wanted to get back into her good graces.

His back bent as he bowed to her. "I'm truly sorry for causing you discomfort before knowing the whole story. If the man has been of service to this community, then of course he's welcome at the dance. I'd be obliged if you would tell me all that's happened since I left." His hand captured her arm to lead her toward the punch bowl.

She didn't want this but could see no way to get out of it. At least Colt would be safe for the time being. Her head swung back, catching a glance of him striding toward the front door with people closing in behind him, trying to talk him into staying. From the set of his shoulders she knew her fun with him had ended for the night. Turning back, she walked beside the Captain, both of them listening to the chatter behind them while the band struck up a quick tune.

"Looks like this Black Beard's wrapped the whole town around his finger." Immediately he sensed his words were wrong, but jealously still racked him.

Shirley left his side in a flash, squeezing through the throng of people, leaving the Captain standing alone and unhappy at the punch bowl. An outraged cry followed her, and Buddy dashed by headed for the door. At this point she hoped the dog had bitten him.

It took time for her to squeeze through the crowd. By then Colt had buckled on his shell belt and stepped into the night. The man with the club in his hand caught her arm. "I'm sorry, Shirley, but the look in his eyes when he left here raked me pretty hard too. I don't think he wants company tonight."

She shook his arm off. "He may not want it, but he brought me to this dance and he's going to take me home."

Colt's pace held steady, Buddy matching his stride, when Shirley caught up to him and slowed her gait to fit with theirs. They continued in silence till the edge of town became visible through the darkness. "You told Gregg the last time you two met that if you took a lady to dinner you would see her home. I guess that doesn't hold for a dance."

The boot sound stopped. He turned to her, repentant but with a teasing curl at the corners of his mouth. "If my temper got away from me when I was a youngster, my mother always washed my mouth out with soap. Do you have a good-tasting kind at the hotel?"

This broke the spell and she grabbed his arm, starting him forward again. "Maybe both of us ought to use a little--I got a little hot under the collar as well. But Gregg takes too much for granted sometimes. I know he hates the fact that the town is more or less run by outlaws and he can't do much about it since the rangers won't come up this way. Although he still shouldn't have said what he did to you."

Reaching the steps of the hotel, Colt answered, "If he'd have said that anywhere else other than at a dance where everyone was having fun, I'd a called him. Guess that would only make things worse. It's a good thing it happened where it did. Now I have to check on a couple of patients. Thanks for sharing a night of fun and peace with me. From now on it probably won't be possible, and I'd like you to know I had a great time."

Her eyes were soft as they held his. "Colt, be careful wherever you go. It won't only be the law you have to worry about, but also the bunch you'll be running with. And Captain Gregg will be even more against you."

Before she could see the longing in his eyes, he opened the door, ushering her inside. After saying goodnight, he left her in the empty lobby while he and Buddy climbed the stairs. Ollie's door came first, so he knocked. No answer came back to him. He knocked again with the same results. He decided Ollie must be asleep and continued on.

His footsteps were let down softly as he approached Betty Jo's door. Tapping lightly, he heard boot heels clomping on the wooden floor as they crossed the room. She must have a visitor, he thought, until the door opened. Then he looked into the grinning face of Ollie. "We figgered it must be you. Ain't no one else would disturb someone's sleep this late. Since everyone else took off for the dance, I figured Betty Jo might like some company. We been playing checkers but I have to make her moves for her. She can't set up and moving her arms still causes a lot of pain in her back. Even with that handicap, she still beats me every game." He winked at Colt.

Smiling, Colt pushed into the room and went to her bedside. He saw a little more pink to her cheeks than should be expected, but ignored it. He bent over and pulled the covers down to her waist, checking the bandage with light finger pressure through her nightgown. His gentle fingers probed around the abdomen and he watched for any sign of pain in the steadiness of her breathing. Only when he felt close to the bullet hole did he sense the slight intake of breath. "Young lady, if you continue to improve for the next couple of weeks like you have since I went to the dance, Shirley will have you up waiting tables in no time."

She started to giggle, then stopped suddenly. He took her hand, checking the pulse. "Still don't want to have a good bellylaugh, do you?"

"Not if I can help it. But do you really think my progression is better than normal?"

"I guess it's the young vibrant time of youth that's moving you along so good. An older person like Ollie here would be in bed for weeks, moaning and groaning." There was a sputter behind him and he saw her catch herself before she laughed.

"By golly, Black Beard, you just bring a horse around and I'll show you how an old codger can heal fast."

"Can't do that yet, Ollie, but come next week you can get out to the stable and clean the stalls if you want. Now we need to let this young lady get some sleep. You two can talk tomorrow and the next day. You're both doing well, and I need to be gone for a couple of days. Just don't keep her up too long. Shirley and Heidi will make sure the two of you are taken care of till I get back. "

When the door closed, they each went to their own rooms, Ollie's admonition following Colt. "You better be careful if you go out to the Hole-in-the-Rock. Mitch might not be back yet and most of those boys don't know you. Might be trouble."

"Thanks, Ollie. Hasta la vista."

Once inside his room, Colt spun around to Buddy. "And where were you, big guy, when the Captain arrived? Out rolling in the grass, dreaming of some female? I know, you think I can handle anything." He reached down and fondly rubbed the dog's ears.

Buddy's tail happily thumped the floor, and a grin spread across his canine face. He'd done his duty by lifting his leg and showering the captain's pant leg. It showed contempt far better than a bite.

Colt gazed into Buddy's adoring eyes. He could almost swear the dog was trying to tell him something. "It's all right, fella. Let's get some sleep."

Buddy beat him to the bed.

Darkness still flowed over the town when Colt saddled, stepped his boot into stirrup and swung onto his horse. The hoof falls raised small flurries of dust as the horse carried him out of town, Buddy trotting behind. Day broke over the Kaibab mountains, showering the earth with lemon-yellow rays of sunshine. While the brightness latched onto the various layered colors of the cliffs around him, he relaxed in the saddle, letting his thoughts drift along unpleasant lines. There would eventually have to be an understanding between Captain Gregg and himself. He figured the Captain didn't appreciate him taking Shirley to the dance. He also figured she'd be better off with the Captain than with him-- his immediate future would play out pretty rough. Sure, the town liked him and that felt good, but placing Shirley between the two of them would only lead to heartache, so he better make his visits to town short and professional, then get on his way.

Perhaps his quest for vengeance would put him on the outlaw trail for the rest of his life. So far, the only thing they could really get him for would be the loss of the money from the strong box and without proof that he took it, he'd be pretty safe. Once he went on a raid with the gang, no matter what kind, he would be a marked man. Mulling this over as the trail slipped behind and time drifted, he found no solution other than the one he seemed destined to take.

The offer of a job at the Lazy J seeped into his mind. Realizing he would be passing the turnoff to that spread on his way to the Hole, he decided to have a look at the ranch. When the wheel ruts cut off to the north heading toward the land called Scutumpaw, he followed them. This end of the Kaibab mountain didn't jot his memory much . . . he only came over the mountain with his father a couple of times when he was younger, but he figured he rode in the right direction.

Trying to remember what the spread looked like, he topped a knoll and there below him lay a green valley. Sunlight glanced off a small lake in front of the ranch house, striking the cliffs behind from a different angle, highlighting more colors which clashed with the green leaves of the cottonwood trees surrounding the houses, barn and corral. Lifting his leg to swing around the saddle horn, he pulled in, letting the scene before him refresh his memory.

The stream running through the valley and into the lake wandered out on the other side, quartering through the corral and into the cottonwoods. As his eyes surveyed the front porch of the main house, he pictured the one time his father brought him here. There had been cowboys everywhere, horses being worked in the corral, fence mending, as well as a man on the roof doing repairs. He remembered a small, yellow-haired, freckle-faced girl with long pigtails running down her back, about six years old, sitting on that porch. Her eyes followed him the whole time his father talked with one of the men. Being about twelve, he tried to ignore such a young child. Letting his horse swing over to the corral, he watched the men work the horses. When his father finished the business he came for, Colt followed him out of the yard. A glance back showed her gaze still latched onto him with those steady eyes.

Now things were different. Nothing moved in the yard between the lake and the house. There were horses in the corral and smoke curling lazily up from the cook shack chimney, but no evidence of any men anywhere. A cottontail scurried from under the bunkhouse to the water trough by the corral and stood up on its haunches, sniffing the air for danger. Not sensing anything out of place, it scurried on, passing under several horses and disappearing into the grass on the other side. The whole ranch appeared deserted.

He waited, trying to decide whether to ride on down and talk to the cook who evidently had a fire going, or continue toward the Hole. Deciding his time would be wasted if he didn't at least inspect the place, he swung his right boot toward stirrup, slouching to the left side of the saddle slick with his right thigh resting on it. His presence in the yard seemed undetected until he glanced at the cook shack door as it swung open.

A short pot-bellied man stepped out the door, red long johns showing under the suspenders holding up his pants, a knife in one hand and a potato in the other. He wore no shoes or socks, and thin grey hair scraped across his head, not doing much in the way of covering a large bald spot. His bare feet stirred the fine dirt of the yard as he aimed for a rocking chair setting beside a bucket of spuds. The arm carrying the knife waved to Colt. "If it's a drink you want, there's a bottle in the shack, or the water in the stream's cold as ice."

Flicking the reins against the horse's neck, Colt rode toward the stream. Lifting his right leg on over the saddle, he slid to the ground. He dropped one rein so the horse could drink, then bellied down on the grass as Buddy began to lap eagerly. Leaning over the water, he let his lips touch first. The man spoke the truth. The icy water slipped down easily. The horse snorted once then stuck its nose in, blowing and drinking at the same time. He felt that between his horse, himself, and Buddy, they would drink the stream dry. Coming up for air after a few moments, he rolled over to a sitting position while Buddy curled up beside him.

She stood there with a smile and the freckles still in place across her nose, but instead of pigtails, the hair hung down her back and he remembered now why she seemed a little familiar at the dance last night . "That ride out from town does kinda make a feller thirsty, don't it."

A cotton dress covered her from neck to ankle and she too stood barefooted. Chuckling, he drawled, "You got that right. I wanted to drink the stream dry, but after a time I could see it would end up the winner."

The laughter reaching his ears lifted him out of the serious thoughts which filled his mind moments before. She spoke in a light, pleasing voice. "Saw you top the knoll up there. Wasn't sure you'd come on down. Ain't many men ride into a strange ranch setting half in and half out of the saddle."

"Figured my presence would be less threatening that way. Sure looked like the place stood deserted, except for the smoke from the cook shack. Wanted to see if the cook knew where everyone went."

She squinted at him. "You forgot this is Sunday and we cut the rug at the dance pretty late last night. Why, there ain't a man on the place who didn't go to the shindig, and most of them tipped the punch bowl up too many times."

"Guess my thinker isn't working very fast this morning. Seeing you here came as a real surprise. I enjoyed dancing with you-- you're light as a feather."

Her musical laugh rang out again and she stepped over to his side, plopping to the grass and spreading her skirts around her legs, which she brought up so she could rest her chin on her knees. "My names Millicent, but folks call me Millie, unless they're mad about something. I know they call you Black Beard---can't imagine why." She rounded her eyes and tried to look innocent, but her mobile mouth couldn't keep from smiling, and they both broke up. "You sure are full of malarkey this morning. I bet you got up before the crack of dawn to reach here so soon. My pa won't be up for awhile, so you can tell me whether you're going to take the job or not."

"The fellow doing all the head thumping last night is your pa? With a billy club to keep the crew on the move, maybe I better say no to his offer. And I don't remember seeing you around anywhere when he asked that question."

This time she didn't laugh. "You're right on that point. I rode on the tailgate of the wagon on the way home so my feet could drag the grass growing between the ruts. When it pulls through my toes, it feels real good. Anyway, dad talked with mom about it most of the way. Seems like he figures with your help, he can get the other ranches to band together and solve the rustling. He wants to get you on our side before Mitch buttonholes you into riding with him."

She waited for an answer to her implied question, but he didn't have the one she wanted. Vengeance just wanted to stay with him. "You mentioned you saw me stop on the knoll. Sure didn't see anyone down here the whole time my eyes watched the place."

An impish grin crossed her face. She pointed up to the second floor of the house. "See that big cottonwood tree with the limb hanging conveniently outside the window? I can climb on it from my bedroom. You'd be amazed at what can be seen and heard when no one knows you're around. The punchers are pretty free with their speech early in the mornings when they're trying to catch and saddle. The words floating up to me would burn a hole right through the toughest cowhide." She stopped talking as she tried to decide if she should tell him any more.

He let her think on the subject while he picked a blade of grass and began to chew on it. She did the same, then finally spoke as her fingers lazily scratched Buddy's stomach, which he'd conveniently exposed. "Sometimes I wish I were a cowboy and could go into a saloon. They tell all sorts of wild things about what goes on there and I don't know whether they're true or not."

"I suspect most of them are full of hot air and brag. The only thing I usually run into in a saloon is trouble, so you better steer clear of places like that."

Her mind puzzled over something and he waited patiently. "Sometimes they talk about a girl coming from New York or Boston or Philadelphia, like those places really exist and a girl coming from there is really something. There ain't no such places, is there, Black Beard?"

Trying to keep a straight face, he filled her in. "Yep, they do exist, but I wouldn't trade what you got here for the bunch of them. You can stand on the streets running through those cities and get a crick in you neck trying to see the top of those brick buildings. Why, they go up seven or eight stories high with people living inside them, one on top the other. You can hear a boot drop when they go to bed at night and when trouble in a family breaks out, everyone on the floor above and the floor below knows about it. There's factories making trains, railroad ties, pots and pans, buckets, stoves, beds, clothes, dresses like the one you're wearing and everything else that people need. The place is a bundle of noise day and night, with people coming and going to work or to other activities. You don't see many stars at night or the sun much in the day. Makes a person feel all cooped up."

"I know most of the things you talk about, but what do you mean by a brick building, and how do they keep it from falling down when it gets that high?"

He thought a moment, then scraped the grass away from a small spot in front of her. Taking a stick, he drew the shape of a brick. "You know the adobe blocks some folks use to make houses out of? Well, these brick are the size of this drawing. They're made out of a substance called cement, which when it dries, is very hard. The bricks are stacked on top of each other with more cement holding them together and keeping them in place. You can stand at the bottom of one of those buildings looking up and not one brick is out of place all the way to the top. When you look around, there are brick buildings everywhere. Can't see anything but buildings and people."

Her eyes were wide and riveted on him as he continued. "There's no place to look, like you got here. You can see clear to the top of the Kaibab mountain 'thout anything getting in your road. Take a morning like this, the air still and quiet---makes goose bumps crawl up your back when the sun glances off the lake and brings out the color of the cliffs behind your ranch house. Yes ma'am, there's a peace that settles over a person. You won't find it in those places. The policemen have their hands full with men fighting all the time because they feel so penned in. 'Course, they mostly use only knives and their fists, but a lot of them get killed just the same."

"This policeman you talk about, he some kind of king that rules the place?" Her attention stayed right on him as he talked.

"A policeman is like a sheriff in this country, only where we may only have one Sheriff to take care of many miles of territory, there are ten, twelve policemen in an area the size of that lake out there. They don't carry guns on their hips in those cities. They use a big billy club similar to what your father used last night. They're made out of real hard wood and can crack a man's skull open in nothing flat. Nope, you can have all the East you want. Me, I saw enough of it, and believe me I'll take a place like this anytime."

Silence held them in place as the cook gently swayed back and forth in his rocker with the bucket of spuds on his lap. The knife expertly sliced the peels off, which dropped in a pan beside him. The chickens, who roamed the yard earlier, now pecked at the peels, paying no attention to anything else.

Finally she broke the silence. "You sure tell it scary. I thought only young girls lived back there from the way the cowboys talk. Oh, I went to school for a couple of years, but I thought those pictures in the books we had were just make believe. Now I guess they must have been the real thing." She paused, then continued, "But still, I'd like to go there someday and look up to the top of one of those buildings. But all those people in such a small space — why, I'd rustle my heels back home after the first look."

Colt pulled his feet under him and stood up, gathering the reins of his horse. His boot found the stirrup and his body settled into place against the cantle. "Looks like your pa needs more sleep than you do. Tell him I'll stop another time to talk to him. It's been a real pleasure visiting with you." He touched his hat brim, pulling the reins over the neck of the horse. It cantered out of the yard, Buddy right beside them. When he looked back from the top of the knoll, everything still remained the same. She sat on the grass where he left her and seeing him turn in the saddle, waved dejectedly. Lifting his hat, he waved it above his head, then rode down the other side of the knoll. Those moments had been pleasant but now he must face the men at the Hole-in-the-Rock.

11

Black clouds rolled across the night sky as a few drops of rain splattered the dust-choked earth. A stout wind danced the tumbleweeds around the small shacks standing like sentinels in the dark. Now and then a horse snorted in the corral and the scream of a puma rent the brittle air. Suddenly the clouds let loose their fury and jagged streaks of lightning split the sky, lighting the earth with momentary brightness, followed by the boom and crack of thunder. Rain drops blossomed in size, bringing sheets of water to pound the shacks as well as animals. Moisture the thirsty ground needed came slashing down, causing streams to flow where moments before only parched dry ground sprawled. The tumbleweeds were washed from their perches against the shacks, tumbling over and over in the now gushing water.

The door to the makeshift barroom banged open, letting in gallons of water and a stiff wind before Hank could get up to close it. Feet slipping on the rain-soaked floor, he finally made it back to the chair he'd left. Slacking into it, he looked at the three men sitting at the table with him. Their hard eyes studied the cards, not in the least mindful of the storm raging outside. They'd drifted into the gang's headquarters in the Hole about an hour before the storm hit, along with a message from Mitch that he would be detained for another two days. None of the three registered any recollection in Hank's memory. If it hadn't been for the note, he wouldn't have told the guards posted at the entrance to let them in. At this point he felt even that would turn out to be a mistake.

The short-coupled one of the three ran his hands over his cards. "I think you're bluffing, Hank. You been getting a muscle jerk in your neck every time you've bluffed tonight, so I'm raising ten."

The tall man with bushy eyebrows sitting to Hank's left, tossed in his cards. "You boys been sparring with each other since we started this game. I guess it's time for me to let you go at it. Ain't no skin off my nose one way or the other."

Hank tapped his cards on the table. "You sure you're reading things right, Shorty? Might be I been setting you up for just such a mistake."

Shorty swore under his breath, but decided to push it. "One way to find out is for you to match my ten."

The fourth player threw his cards into the discard also. "Ort, this may end in a fight. Maybe we better go start another game across the room."

"Pace, it wouldn't do any good . . . they'd probably pull iron and shoot both of us by mistake." Ort showed evident disgust at the way this game seemed to be going.

Pushing the money in front of him to the center of the table, Hank said mildly, "I'll see your ten and add everything I got on the table."

This hadn't been what Shorty expected and his face scrinched up as he tried to decide if he faced a bluff. His thinking took on the storm raging outside, causing him to wonder if the muscle in Hank's neck jumped to the sudden clap of thunder and flashes of lightening. If he matched that amount of money and lost, he'd be broke till they went on another raid. Since he didn't know Hank at all before tonight, his observation may have led him to an erroneous assumption. His eyes sought help from the two other men in the game.

Pace pulled out the makings, rolling a cigarette with one hand. "You're a big boy now, Shorty, so either call him or fold so we can get on with the game. Ain't no use going to bed with that thunder sounding off so often."

Hank sat relaxed in his chair, then remembered the way Black Beard sat when there might be gunplay. His boots came off the floor and the spur rowels cut into the top of the table, his six-gun's gaping muzzle lined up with Shorty's chest.

It took a moment for Shorty to realize the danger. He began to push his stake into the middle of the table when his eyes grew big and round. His fists suddenly stopped with the money half-way there. He tried to let his eyes drift elsewhere but they wouldn't respond. Now he remembered Mitch's warning to not question Hank's authority when they rode into camp. He hastily pulled the money back and flung his cards face up on the table. There, staring at everyone, were three kings.

Hank nonchalantly tossed his hand into the discard pile and raked in the pot.

"Hey, ain't you going to show what you held?" Shorty's querulous voice revealed his anger.

"Why would I want to do that, Shorty? This way you'll never know when I'm bluffing or packing a royal flush." The smile on Hank's lips never got close to his eyes. Ort slapped his thigh. "Now I know why Mitch keeps you in charge when he's gone, Hank. I figure I'd of folded too, with that pistol staring me in the chest."

"I picked that little trick up from a friend of mine who uses it very successfully. Between him and his dog, he's able to intimidate even Captain Gregg."

The mention of the Captain's name brought a laugh from all but Shorty, who wished he'd called Hank's hand. "You put those boots down and stand up like a man and I'll show you a trick of my own." Shorty just wouldn't let things drop.

"What do you think, Pace? You figure your friend is full of wind or can he sling lead as fast as he indicates?"

Shorty's chair went crashing backwards as he came to his feet, his gun coming up. Hank had been confident the man wouldn't act and surprise slowed his hand as it darted to gun butt. It was plain as day he'd never reach it in time.

Gun thunder sang out over the sudden silence. Ort and Pace expected to see Hank tip over in his chair. It didn't happen, yet his gun hadn't fired. Their glances switched to Shorty who stared at his stinging gun hand, pain and confusion in his eyes. The stark white face of Hank contrasted noticeably with the dark blue flannel shirt he wore. A voice coming from the back door leading to the storage room swept their glances that way.

"You men figure to wipe each other out over a card game? Why, when Mitch hears about this, he'll skin you alive, Shorty. Hank, unless you're prepared to use that trick, don't count on it.

Your balance is off so far it's a wonder you didn't tip your chair over trying to reach your lead thrower."

The man stood punching out the empty as he spoke, then reloaded and slipped the forty-four- forty to leather. As it nestled back in the soft holster, a curl of smoke issued from the muzzle. A sinister dog skulked just at his heels. "You fellers better sign off the poker for tonight--I got some things to talk over with Hank. Pick up your money and find your straw tick. When you show for breakfast in the morning, if you can't eat without causing trouble, leave your pistols on your saddles."

Pace started to say he wasn't in on the ruckus, but those flinty eyes meeting his discouraged any comment. Turning on his heel, he shrugged, padded to the door and looked out. The storm had eased a lot in the last few minutes. These sudden thunder storms were violent but short. Hunching his shoulders, he pushed through the door with Ort right behind him.

Shorty whined, "What about my hand? It stings like fire. I need a doctor."

Hank got his voice back. "Hell, it's your gun that took the slug. Your hand stings from the shock of the gun butt twisting out of it. Since your gun ain't going to do you a lick of good anymore, follow your partners out that door and be careful where you tread from now on."

Shorty took one look at the cold icicle eyes of the man whose shot saved Hank and decided he got off lucky. And if the truth were to be told, he was more afraid of being torn up by that snarling dog than of a gun. Swiftly tromping to the door, he went out, leaving the two men in the makeshift barroom in silence.

Colt dropped into a chair. "Didn't know for sure whether you were here or not Hank, so I injuned up the back, hoping to see the lay of the land before I made myself known."

Hank wiped sweat from his face with his pocket rag. "Your timing couldn't have been better, Colt. I figured I'd be buzzard bait by now. Seems like I owe you my life. Guess it wasn't too smart, using that trick of yours without some practice first."

"I thought you'd have gone with Mitch on the last raid. Didn't really expect to find you here or I would have ridden straight in."

"Good thing for me you didn't. Besides, there's too much of a reward hanging over my head-- I stay pretty close to the Strip while Mitch and some of the others do most of the work. Another reason is, I'm a short-timer . . . only been with the bunch a couple of months. They're not sure I can pull my own weight yet."

"I saw your picture hanging on the wall of the Flagstaff bank when I was there. Ten thousand dollars for your hide would make a lot of men haul you off to the nearest lawman. How come Captain Gregg doesn't latch onto you like he's been trying to me? You're certainly worth a lot more than I am."

"Seems to be a matter of a certain young lady that makes the Captain like you so much, Colt. He figures she may be attracted to you, but with me he don't have a thing to worry about."

Colt picked up the cards, pushing them together and shuffling, "He won't have to worry none about that. She's just a good friend who helped me one time when I needed it. Figure it'll be some time before I go after any lady--he's free to plow that field alone. When you expect Mitch back? Think he'll complain about me being here?"

"He'll be happy to have you, don't worry. How'd you get by the guards without being challenged."

"Figured when the storm hit, I could ride right past them without being seen. That proved to be a correct assumption. I lay watching them for a while, waiting for the lightening to strike. When it did, my opportunity came quick."

"This place must not be as safe as I thought-- a whole passel of law dogs could've done the same thing as you and been on us before we knew it. Might have to make some changes around here. When Mitch gets back, I'll take it up with him. How's your two patients doing?"

"I'll ride in tomorrow night to check on them . . . so far they're both doing fine. Besides, Heidi and Shirley are capable of nursing them unless something goes wrong, and I don't expect that to happen. How come you and Shorty were tying into each other?"

"That's kind of hard to figure. None of those three ever been here before--don't even know where they came from, but he packed a note from Mitch saying they were okay. The more we played, the more I felt they were cut from the same mold as those six toughs you planted in town the other day. What puzzles me is why Mitch sent them here."

"Maybe Mitch didn't have any say about it. They're tough enough to have just horned in on their own. You sure that note came from Mitch?"

Hank let his mind dwell on this for a few moments. "It looked like Mitch's scribble all right, but those boys are mean as a she bear who's just lost a cub. I shoulda known better than to egg Shorty on that way." He sat trying to puzzle something out. "What you mean by saying Mitch might not have any say in the matter? He pretty much bosses this bunch and he ain't wanted nowhere that I know of. He handles things in town for us, and with him keeping our money in the bank, it keeps the people more or less on our side."

"What about the rustling going on? The Strip ranchers will get tired of it one of these days and band together. Won't matter then what the town folk say, you'll have a fight on your hands."

"That worries me somewhat, but Mitch says there ain't any of those fellers able to organize the cowmen except for Mr. Hastings, and since he ain't around at present, Mitch figures he has some time left. You wouldn't know where your old man is, would you?"

Ignoring the question, Colt mentioned another cowman. "I stopped by the Lazy J today. Seems like Mr Jefferies may be the one to corral them other ranchers and get 'em off their duffs."

Hank sat quietly, letting his eyes study Colt. "That makes me wonder if your old man turned the task of solving this rustling problem over to you, which is why you're here."

Colt met Hank's steady stare. "I suppose one could read things that way. But why would I have taken the Wells Fargo money if that were the case, besides all the other bank jobs I've pulled?"

"You got me guessing there. Someway you're after something other than just being a member of the gang. If Mitch ever tumbles to what that reason is, you're dead meat."

"Where do you stand with that little suspicion in your noggin, being you're a solid member of the gang?"

"I told you before I have my own axe to grind. Since you just saved my life, I guess I'll just string along and see how you make out in whatever game you're playing."

"That's fair enough, Hank, but there may come a time when you'll have to jump one way or the other. That could be risky."

"You let me worry about that. Now lets find you a place to bed down. I'll show you around the place tomorrow and introduce you to the men staying here. I won't mention how you got here undetected--- it might spoil the guard's breakfast."

The mud clung to their boots as they slogged through the drizzly night to a shack next door. Hank pushed the door open and motioned Colt inside. "You take the bunk in the corner; I'll get someone to stable your horse."

"No need for that. I put him in the stable before I came inside. Buddy and I will make out fine right here." He reached down and scratched the dog's ears, whispering something, and the dog immediately went to the bunk, slinking under it.

Hank prepared to cook up a steak for each of them as Colt stoked the fire in the two hole wood stove. Hank propped the door open so the room wouldn't get too hot. Fresh, sweet-smelling air drifted in, replacing the smell of unwashed bodies and dirty clothes. Once the meat was sizzling in the fry pan, he slouched into a chair. "Where you figure those three toughs came from? We've been a pretty tight organization up till now and the rest of the men ain't goin' to like splitting takes with these hombres."

The same question nagged at Colt. If these three were from the same gang as the six who tried to abduct Betty Jo, how many more were there, and what did they want? "Maybe there's another organization wants to take over the Strip and run this gang out, but I can't figure Mitch inviting them here. Still, someone else may have figured out that you men have a good thing going, with the town being more or less in your pocket."

Thinking this over, Hank finally lodged his opinion. "Maybe so, but it would be a lot easier to just join the gang, rather than try to crowd us out." Something jogged his memory. "We had a bunch come through here a couple of months back--old friends of Mitch.

They stayed a couple of nights then took off. Ain't seen hide nor hair of them since. But Mitch seemed pretty upset 'cause they didn't come back." He rose to turn the steaks over in the pan. "Those four fit the mold of these other toughs and it kinda surprised me that Mitch let them stay. I'd only been with him a short time when it happened, so didn't question it. Now I'm beginning to wonder if all these men are somehow connected."

He didn't notice the slight tension in Colt at the mention of four men sent out to do a job, then not returning. Colt's voice stayed level when he offered a suggestion. "That bunch may have run into trouble and been thrown in the lockup somewhere. From what you say, it seems Mitch is controlling these men or at least giving them their orders. A new setup may be on the way for the old timers here."

Shaking his head, Hank took a fork and put two steaks on tin plates and set them on the table, flipping the third one under the bunk for Buddy. He smeared a piece of bread with thick yellow butter, slapped the steak on it and began to munch while his mind worked. "I sure can't figure a reason to do that. Mitch's got it made: he lets others do the dirty work while he stays out of sight. That's why you don't see any dodgers pinned up with his name on them. If he lets broncos like these toughs take over, he might not have it so easy." On hearing this, Colt felt confident he now knew who had given the men their orders to kill him and his parents.

For a time the two sat shoveling bread and meat down. But something kept nagging at Colt: why did Shorty pick a fight with Hank? Sure, it looked like it was because Hank bluffed him out, at least that would be the general consensus around camp. When he put his mind to it though, there would've been only a little over a ten dollar loss for Shorty. Why pull a gun on another player for such a small amount? The other angle may be more correct: Mitch wanted to get rid of some of his men so these new ones could have all the rewards. Hank, being the newest member, would be the logical one to start on.

These speculations were banging around in his head when Hank got up to toss his steak bone to Buddy, who'd already gnawed his to shreds. He leaned down as he tossed it, and noticed the dog rising, hackles up and teeth bared.

At first Colt thought a crack of thunder split the air, then he saw Hank roll to the floor with one arm flopping at an odd angle. Instantly he kicked his chair back, diving for the open door. He slammed it shut just as another slug buried itself in the wood. Jumping for Hank, he pushed him under the bunk as Buddy began barking. His next move snuffed out the lantern and pitch dark surrounded them. Enough starlight filtered in for Colt to grab Buddy's muzzle to quiet him. The growl low in the dog's throat and his ears pointed toward the only window in the shack alerted Colt, who snapped up his gun. The light from the window momentarily dimmed and he squeezed the trigger. A window pane shattered, then he heard the distinct sound of a body splash in the mud. "Shorty's done for--lets hightail it outta here. Mitch'll blow his stack when he hears about this foul up," came drifting through the jagged glass.

Silence as thick as a stone settled on the shack. Even Buddy ceased his growl. Then Hank groaned from under the bunk. Quickly Colt slithered over to him, gently grasping him by the legs and pulling him into the open. His fingers explored the arm he had seen flop crazily. He felt blood stream down it and found the bullet hole in the upper biceps. His hand clamped on the muscle above the wound. Blood caked heavily around the side of Hank's chest, and Colt, his eyes adjusting somewhat to the darkness, barely made out where the bullet grooved along the ribs and exited through the skin of the chest. He probed the ribs finding two of them broken by the force of the bullet. It was a good thing the slug went through the arm first or it would have had enough force to push right on through the ribs, penetrating the lungs, and Hank would be dead.

Quickly removing his bandana, he tied it around the arm above the wound, then took his gun barrel and slipped it under the bandana, twisting it tight to shut off the flow of blood. With only the pale glow from the stove to work by, he cut Hank's shirt away with his knife. Reaching up, he pulled a corner of the flannel sheet from the bunk. He slit it and arranged the piece into a thick pad, then cut some longer strips to be used to tie the pads in place. Then he stood, took the lid off one of the stove's holes and placed the iron lifter into the hot coals inside.

His eyes had adapted well to the pale light by this time. Buddy sat patiently with his ears erect and his nose constantly sniffing the air. Colt kept one eye tuned to the dog, knowing he would put those ears back if anything stirred outside. Hank started to sputter and tried to sit up. Colt said "Sorry, fellow" pulled his gun, and rapped Hank smartly on the head. Hank sank back to the floor without a sound. This next piece of surgery would not be any fun for a man awake. He wished he had ether available, but in a small outlaw town with no doctor, ether was impossible to attain.

When the poker blazed red at the tip, Colt wiped the wounds on both the arm and chest as clean as possible, then rapidly stuck the hot end into the bullet holes and quickly pulled it back out. Hank's body stiffened, and a groan escaped from his mouth, but he would never remember that sudden pain. Untwisting the pistol slowly, Colt watched for a renewed flow of blood from the main artery of the arm. As the tension released and no fresh blood appeared, he heaved a thankful sigh. The cautery had done the job of sealing the severed artery.

He fumbled around in the semi-dark until he found a half bottle of whiskey in the cupboard. Pouring some in both the entrance and exit holes in the arm and over the ribs, he proceeded to bandage the arm and rib cage, hoping the blankets were at least partly clean, and thanking God for the drinking habits of cowboys. The arm would have to be splinted but for now he would leave it.

Going to the door with Buddy at his side, he cautiously eased it open. The clouds had dissipated, leaving the star-shine bright enough for him to see a body lying in the mud. He stepped out and toed it over. The sightless eyes of Shorty peered into the heavens, the closest he would ever get to that hallowed place. Buddy sniffed the corpse, then deliberately turned his back and tried to scratch some dirt over it, but ended up frustrated by the mud.

Colt reentered the shack, covered the window with a blanket and only then lit the lantern. No use taking any more chances, even with Buddy guarding the door. He selected the smaller of the two chairs and broke the legs from it. After ripping more strips of flannel from the sheet, he carefully aligned the ends of the broken bone, then put two chair legs along Hank's arm and held them in place as he wrapped them snugly. After much grunting and groaning, he finally got Hank into a sitting position so he could strap the arm to the man's side. From there he lifted him onto the bunk. Hank's breathing was regular, displaying no apparent sign of trouble from the blow to the head.

Shifting the other chair over to the bedside, Clot collapsed onto it. One fact glared at him: the danger Hank would be in if he left him here at the Hole. Mitch apparently prearranged this right from the get-go: himself being gone, the three outlaws setting up Hank, and Shorty doing the shooting. Colt figured he'd have to move him to a safe place and that place would be his soddy at the edge of the canyon. The question worrying him was what would happen when Mitch returned. He decided something really serious would soon break over the Strip with all these new men coming in, and Mitch was the key. After tonight Colt may not be one of the gang. He could only hope Mitch would see his actions tonight as simply helping Hank, who he'd left in charge. Hank's shooting may have been the very reason he was left in charge, thus assuring his presence when the men came to kill him.

There were no solid answers to any of these conjectures, but he continued to wrestle with them. He'd get one of the men staying here to watch Hank tomorrow, leaving Buddy with instructions to guard Hank all the time. The ride to town would be a fast one to check on Betty Jo and Ollie, then back to pick up Hank and take him to his shack at the rim of the canyon. That is, if something else didn't sidetrack him.

12

Sometimes on the desert when the sun peeks its nose above the horizon, its reflection off the clouds causes the land below to be bathed in flaming fire. The apparition is so spectacular one pauses to watch the ball of flame move upward. Time stops as body and soul fill with the wonder of nature. This morning found Shirley standing in awe as she stepped from the hotel's back door. She remembered an old adage her father used many times: "Red sky in the morning, sailors take warning. Red sky at night, sailors delight." Trying to push the saying from her mind, she wondered if it were true, and if so, what danger might lie in wait for them this day.

She truly loved a sunrise like this, and felt foolish thinking something bad might happen before the day ended. Her thoughts turned to the dance last evening, bringing up the obvious dislike Captain Gregg showed for Colt. She noticed on the hotel register that the Captain took a room for the night. Glad that she didn't know about it till this morning, she walked down the back lots of the town to the creek behind. Pulling her skirts around her, she sank to the dirt of the creek bank, staring at the moving water below. Now the rays of the sun were glancing off that water in almost blinding flashes of light. Momentarily her vision disappeared. When the light dispersed, she saw three horsemen crossing the creek about a hundred yards from where she sat. Her position lay shielded from their sight by a large wild rosebush. They looked to be as tough and thorny as cactus as their mounts carried them up the bank and into town.

The vision of the man she killed sprang into her mind. These men were similar in the attitude emanating from them and a premonition went through her body. As they disappeared around the side of the blacksmith shop, she sprang to her feet, running for the back of the hotel. Now she felt glad Captain Gregg stayed in town last night. He may be needed today and she hoped some of his men were with him.

Racing to the back door of the hotel, she shoved it open and ran through the kitchen and up the stairs, stopping only when she arrived at Colt's room. Pausing a moment to catch her breath, she wondered if her nerves weren't getting the best of her. Never mind--better safe than sorry. She knocked lightly on his door. Nothing. She knocked again and receiving no answer, stood undecided as to whether to knock again. Clenching her knuckles, she rapped sharply on the door. After a spell, when there came not the slightest sound from the room, she twisted the knob and went in. The room stood empty. Her heart sank. Colt must have risen early to walk Buddy. Since she hadn't seen him out the back of the hotel, she hurried down the stairs to the front door. Shading her eyes with her hand, she panned the street, not seeing the man she looked for. The three toughs were not in sight either.

Turning back to the door, she bumped into Ollie coming out. His arm steadied her as he sang out. "Hey, settle down, little gal. I heard you knock on Black Beard's door. He ain't here today. Said last night he'd be gone for a couple of days and that you and Heidi would look after his patients."

Desperate, she asked, "Have you seen the Captain this morning? He stayed at the hotel last night."

Squinting in the bright sunlight, Ollie told her, "The Captain left the hotel shortly after Black Beard did this mornin'. I figured he wanted to get back to the fort before his men started the days work. Why? You think those two might've tangled outside 'a town?"

Damnation! Where were the men when you needed them? With both the Captain and Colt gone and three tough hombres in town somewhere, there might be no one left to stop trouble if it started. But it wouldn't be any surprise if Captain Gregg followed Colt, then got the drop on him and carted him off to the guardhouse. She let her eyes rove over the street again, trying to see if the toughs had tied up at any of the hitch racks. They hadn't, as far as she could tell. They must have ridden on out of town toward the Hole-in-the-Rock. "I don't know, Ollie, but it worries me. Those two seem destined to tangle their ropes together and knowing how the Captain is for going by the book, it would be just like him to haul Black Beard off today."

Ollie shrugged. "Don't think I'd let that put a burr under your saddle. If the Captain tries something like that, he'll end up tied to a tree somewheres and Black Beard'll go on his way."

"When do you figure Hank and Mitch will be back?" If the three men she saw cross the creek were still hanging around, she better alert Mr. Briggs, the store owner, so the town wouldn't be completely caught off guard.

"Don't figger either will be back to town for at least a week. Mitch is off scoutin' in Colorado and Hank is forted up at the Hole while Mitch is gone. Why're you so all fired interested in where everbody is this mornin'? Ain't like you to be nosin' around in other people's business."

Her eyes sought his and he saw the concern there. "Three tough men crossed the creek a little while ago, coming into town. They looked to be cut from the same cloth as the ones who put a bullet in your arm. I don't figure there's anyone in town who could handle those men if they started to play rough."

"We been seein' several of that stripe comin' 'round the Hole lately. Can't figure what's up but they sure are mean sons a guns. Look like they been fightin' a war and ain't goin' to give up on it. Hank's been worried since the last bunch came, then disappeared. Where you think those three are now?" His glance roamed the street as his brow puckered.

"I don't see them or their horses. Maybe I'm jumping the gun thinking they mean trouble for the town. But after what happened to you and Betty Jo, I think some of the men better be alerted. I'm going over to roust Pat from his home behind the store." Having said that, she stepped off the porch and walked rapidly across the street.

Watching till she disappeared around the back of the store, Ollie swore, then padded down toward the saloon. He felt good enough today to be of some use and he figured Pike should be alerted to possible trouble. He pushed through the batwings to see Pike ambling in from the back of the barroom, his fingers combing through his hair and bags under his eyes. Pike glanced up, noticed Ollie. "What you doing up and around? Thought you liked that soft feather bed so much you'd never leave it." His chuckle floated across the room.

"You better make sure that shotgun of yours is loaded and handy, Pike." Ollie let his hand rest on one hip, close to gunbutt, the other arm in a sling hanging from his neck.

Pike stared at him, the grin on his face fading. "What you up to now, Ollie? Ain't you had enough gunplay for a while?"

"Shirley says she saw three toughs ride across the creek and come to town. They's just like the ones shot up the place the other day. Figgers there may be more trouble." Ollie moved toward the bar as he spoke.

Hurrying around the end of the bar, Pike stooped down, reaching the shotgun from under the bar and laying it on the surface. "Those boys come in here, they'll drink with a shotgun pointing at them. Won't turn business away, but they'll know I won't put up with any monkey stuff. Where the heck is Black Beard?" He didn't wait for an answer. "You better get over and roust him out, Ollie."

"Black Beard left early this morning; so did Captain Gregg. Ain't no one here but us peons if trouble starts. And I ain't much good at throwing lead by myself. Always have someone with me when it's called for."

The shotgun cradled in the crook of his arm, Pike stalked to the batwings, peering over them, first up and then down the wide dirt road. Words skimmed over his shoulder: "Don't seem to be any strange horses tied anywhere and the street looks plumb peaceful.

Maybe Shirley's getting antsy after the ruckus the other day."

Ollie snorted, "You ever see her go to pieces when trouble hits? Nope, that's one lady could beat the pants off most men 'thout half tryin'. Look what she done with the pistol she keeps at the hotel. Finished that hombre off while he slung lead at her as fast as he could. No sir, if she says those three are part of that bunch, she knows what she's talkin' about. Me, I aim to keep my eyes peeled and my gun handy till we know for sure where those boys are and what they want."

"Guess you're right on that count, Ollie, but I sure wish Black Beard would've stayed in town-- we need somebody like him around with these toughs rolling in all the time. Captain Gregg talks a lot, but he stays out of local trouble. 'Sides, he ain't no match for toughs like those men. Why you figure there's been so many of them lately?"

"Nary a reason's crossed my mind. They seem to get along with Mitch, but the rest of the gang don't cotton to any of 'em."

Pike gave this some thought. "You think there's a new breed coming here to take over things?"

"Hank kinda leans that way, but he don't see any reason for it. We been pretty safe in this neck of the woods up to now, but if toughs like them get the upper hand, you better look for greener pastures, Pike."

Finished with his examination of the street, Pike ambled back behind the bar. "Well, we'll just have to wait and see what happens along. If Black Beard would stay around, things would be all right. Can't figure where he came from but sometimes I get the feeling I've seen him before-- just can't put my finger on where." He poured Ollie a drink.

One gulp and the liquid vanished down Ollie's gullet. He set the glass on the bar. "Thanks, Pike. I gotta rustle back in case trouble pokes its head up in that direction. Wouldn't want anything to set Betty Jo back a spell." He hurried out the door, almost running to the hotel as his mind started to envision her alone and no one there to help if trouble did come.

Rushing through the front door, he bounded up the stairs two at a time, but all seemed quiet so he slowed his pace, creeping silently to Betty Jo's door. When he put his ear against the panel, no sound came through to him. He twisted the knob softly and opened the door just enough to peek in. Heidi sat in a chair beside Betty Jo's bed, her head bent to her chest and her eyes closed. Shifting his glance, he saw the patient also sleeping peacefully, even breaths causing her chest to rise and fall. Gently closing the door, he heaved a relieved sigh and walked quietly back to the stairs. Halfway down, the front door opened and Shirley slipped through. Her glance picked him up as she started toward the dining room. "You see anything of those men, Ollie?"

Going on down the steps, Ollie squinted at her and replied, "Not one shaggy dog hair of any of 'em. Pike's got his shotgun handy. If they come in, he'll show 'em what-for. I hope they head for the Hole and leave us alone. We got to talkin' 'bout why so many of 'em are suddenly showin' their faces in this section of the country. Can't see any gol-darned reason for it."

"If they're still in town, they'll probably show up for breakfast, so the sooner I get things rolling, the sooner we'll know." She hurried on into the kitchen while Ollie hunkered down in front of the big window facing the street.

While Shirley banged on the triangle in front of the hotel, she watched anxiously, fearing to see the three men show from somewhere along the street. The normal breakfast crowd gathered without any sign of them. For the next hour her mind stayed occupied on their whereabouts, only half listening to the conversations around her as she served breakfast.

Heidi came down the stairs after most of the folks left for their daily tasks. "That young lady upstairs is anxious to be back to work. She woke up this morning feeling lots better. Ollie took breakfast up and said he'd stay with her. After I eat, I'm going over to my room at the Lazy Lady and sleep for a week." She perched on a stool at the counter.

"What sounds good to you this morning, Heidi? You've been such a help during this crisis-- name whatever you like and I'll do my darndest to serve it." Shirley felt as tired as Heidi looked. The way things were going, maybe they'd both catch up on their sleep before long.

"At this point anything that'll go down fast and easy is all I care about. Ollie mentioned there could be some trouble from toughs again in town. I want to catch as much sleep as possible before the next disaster hits." Heidi's callous words made them both wince.

Shirley left and returned with two steaming bowls of oatmeal and a pitcher of thick cream. Scooping a spoonful of sugar from the sugar bowl on the counter, Heidi smiled. "I couldn't have done better if I'd ordered myself. This is perfect. When that warm oatmeal hits my stomach, I'll sleep like a hibernating bear. Unless the roof falls in or the town burns up, I don't want to be woken up by anyone."

Since everyone else was gone, Shirley perched on the next stool and the two fell to getting around the bowls of oatmeal.

They finished at the same time. Shirley stood up to take the bowls back to the kitchen while Heidi headed for the door. Just then Captain Gregg arrived. "Good morning, Heidi. How're the patients doing this morning?"

Hearing his voice, Shirley turned, setting the bowls back down as Heidi answered. "They're both keeping each other company this morning and I'm headed for bed." She brushed by him as quickly as possible.

He continued on to the counter, spying the empty bowls. "That smells like the oatmeal my mother used to make. The stuff the Mess Sergeant stirs up makes a man want to leave the cavalry."

"I'm glad you're here this morning, Captain. Ollie said you rode out of town earlier. Something wrong that you came back?" She wanted to ask point blank if he knew where Colt went, but realized it could cause discord, which she wished to avoid.

He studied her for a moment, wondering at the slight tartness in her question. "I intended to, but as I topped the mesa west of town, I glanced back and saw three riders leaving, going the other way. When I put the glasses on them, they resembled the description of those who caused havoc here recently, so I swung around to follow them. They're headed in the direction of the Hole-in-the Rock and that spells trouble in any man's language. Once their destination became plain, I turned around to come back here, hoping they hadn't caused any problems. When I passed the saloon, Pike told me all stayed peaceful. I got the distinct impression he may have seen them and expected the worst."

"They crossed the creek early this morning. Ollie and Pike were getting ready in case they came back."

His brow furrowed like a newly plowed field, and he tried to choose his next words carefully. "I know you mean well, Shirley, but Ollie is a known rustler and should be hauled to jail."

A moment before she'd been happy to see him . . . now his unforgiving attitude got under her skin. Before she let off steam, she went to the kitchen. Shortly she returned with a bowl of oatmeal and slapped it down in front of him. He caught her arm as she headed back to the kitchen. "Looks like I put my foot in my mouth again. Please don't look at me like I'm some kind of monster. You know my military training makes' it hard to see how these outlaws have everyone around here in the palm of their hands and not be able to do anything about it."

She turned back to him, realizing that he meant well but his thinking was as ramrod straight as his carriage. "Since the shooting, my nerves are strung pretty tight, Captain. I tend to flare up at the slightest incident. It's nice of you to think of us by following those men. I felt they might be here to cause more grief and it's a relief to know they're headed elsewhere."

He sprinkled sugar on the oatmeal, then poured a heavy portion of the thick cream on top. She leaned on the counter and watched when he began eating. "You think we'll ever get to the bottom of the trouble on this range, Captain Gregg?"

He swallowed and replied, "Because of the last fracas here, I wired the Rangers again to send some help. No response came back other than to say they were working on it. That's all I ever receive. The southern part of the territory doesn't give a hoot what happens up here. And since it involved outlaws shooting outlaws, they're happy with the outcome." His glance focused on the kitchen door as he contemplated how to get better response, so missed the sudden change of expression on her face.

Why did he continue to say things that irritated her? Going back over the two and a half years of their acquaintance, she realized he always treated her with respect and many folks in town figured the two of them would marry, but when he brought up the subject something in her inner being refused to let her accept. After she met Colt at his parents grave, the Captain took a back seat in her thoughts and she wondered if things would ever be the same between them again.

He was speaking when she came back to the present. "I've also petitioned Washington to give me blanket orders to clean up this Strip country because so much deviltry's going on, but no answer's been received. If they finally get around to it, my troops will patrol the country and the rustling will come to an end."

"I guess perhaps that's best, Captain, but it would be dangerous work for you. The Hole-in- the-Rock is a mighty rugged area. A lot of men could be lost if you attacked it."

He smiled at her. "On the other hand, if we ringed it with troops, we may be able to stop them from getting out or in, causing them to eventually give up."

To her, this was a pipe dream. "You know it would take the whole United States Army to ring that place. You'd never receive enough reinforcements. Besides, Washington and the four states bordering this area don't care about what happens here. They figure local law in those states will eventually take care of the outlaws when they leave to rob and plunder other areas."

"That's why it's so hard to stay within the regulations the army imposes on me. To know I might be able to stop this nonsense and then have my hands tied, just galls the heck out of me. I know you like this Black Beard fellow, Shirley, but look what he's done with his life. Why, he robs and kills all the time."

She tried to keep her voice level as she answered these unfair accusations. "Captain, the men he killed were abducting Betty Jo. If he hadn't acted so fast, they would have gotten away with it. And the money he's taken has always been found somewhere and returned to the banks."

Not wanting to meet her eyes, he let his gaze wander out the window. "I know this sounds rather rough, but if they'd succeeded in taking her, the Rangers might have been sent in immediately. To get a response from that outfit, all it takes is for a woman to be molested or kidnaped."

The gasp from her throat told him he should have buttoned his lip again. "Captain Gregg, you can't really mean that. Why, think of what the poor girl would have gone through if they took her by force."

He tried to wiggle out of the hole he'd dug for himself. "Look what she's going through now. A bullet almost snuffed out her life because Black Beard tried to stop them. He should have been more careful, with her in the line of fire."

Flushed with anger, she spit out hot words: "Damn you, Gregg! Thinking like that's what keeps these thugs in business. If more of us stood up to them, they wouldn't have a chance in hades of molesting people. You go talk to Betty Jo. You'll see she thinks Black Beard is the greatest man in the world for saving her. Besides, if you got the story straight, I fired first at those men. Would you like it better if they'd killed me in the process? That would have brought the Rangers in, wouldn't it?" Having made her point, she stomped into the kitchen, leaving him staring at the slammed door.

She literally shook with rage. The cook took one look at her expression and immediately went back to his dishes. Suddenly she stood beside him. Grabbing up a plate, she heaved it at the door, gaining a sense of satisfaction as it shattered to the floor. Another one followed and he scurried out the back. Seeing him run brought some semblance of normality to her. The third plate she set back on the sink, but her body still trembled. Moments later she heard the front door close and knew the Captain had left.

Talk about jumping from the frying pan into the fire . . . now the Captain would have no reason at all to hold back on trying to arrest Colt, since he'd figure he didn't have any more chance with her. Fear began to build inside. She refused to let it get the upper hand, hoping Ollie would be proved right if the two ever came to a confrontation. Kicking the broken dishes aside, she went through the dining room and climbed the stairs, knocking at Betty Jo's door. Boot sounds came from the other side and the door swung open, revealing Ollie with a broad smile on his face.

"Come on in, Shirley. This little lady says the food this morning tasted great and she ate most all of it. Figure she's on the mend if she can eat like that."

Betty Jo's voice came weakly from the bed. "Ollie's been telling me about Black Beard's exploits out at your ranch. I've never heard the full story of what happened there. Ollie says he owes his life to him . . . talks like he's a God."

The shine in her eyes told Shirley where this girl's heart rested. "Ollie will be interested to know that the Captain just finished breakfast and made no mention of seeing Black Beard. He also said he followed those three men for a ways making sure they headed for the Hole." At the look on Betty Jo's face, she realized Ollie hadn't told her about the three men because he didn't want her to worry. Quickly, she explained: "Three travelers came into town headed for the east end of the strip- the Captain just wanted to make sure where they were going. You know how he hates strangers who ride through here and join the gang. One of these days he'll get the authority to police this Strip — then he'll be truly happy."

Betty Jo's smile told her she'd smoothed the slip of the tongue. "He won't have anything to do after Black Beard demolishes that bunch. Ollie says the Rangers could've sent Black Beard to scout out the gang's headquarters and that's why he came to this area. Those bank jobs were just a smoke screen."

Shirley realized Ollie built Colt up as much as he could for this love-struck girl. She also knew what Ollie felt for Betty Jo, and realized the agony going through him at the girl's constant talk of her idol. For that matter, her feelings were similar to his in that she didn't really know how Colt felt. He seemed gentle with her, like the night in the trees at the dance, but his actions were more like a brother than someone in love, and this young girl certainly would be attractive in any man's eyes. None of these thoughts showed in her face as she bent over straightening out the covers on the bed and checking the bandage. They still looked clean with no new blood showing. Probing gently around the area like she had seen Colt do, there appeared to be even less pain.

"Ollie must be right about you being on the mend. It's amazing how fast you're responding."

Betty Jo laughed lightly. "With all you people taking such good care of me and with Black Beard's expert medical abilities, it's no wonder I'm doing well. Ollie stayed close the whole time and told me what's been happening while I was so sick . . . you and Heidi are excellent nurses. It's so nice to have friends like you three."

"Thanks, honey, but you'd do the same for any of us. Now it's time I got back to the kitchen, so you two go on with your stories." She walked to the window to check the street. For some reason, despite the assurance of the Captain, she felt anxious. Something kept nagging at her, not letting her forget the three toughs. Seeing nothing to arouse her suspicions, she left the room and went to the kitchen. The morning passed and the noon meal went smoothly, so she prepared to go upstairs to spell Ollie at Betty Jo's bedside for the afternoon. One foot on the stairs, she heard a fast running horse pounding down the street outside.

It was as if her fears were being realized; without hesitating, she ran for the door. As she reached it the door burst open, almost knocking her down. An agitated cowboy dashed inside. His face was flushed and dust caked him from head to toe. Pulling off his hat, he quickly glanced around, shouting, "Where's Black Beard? We need him quick at the Lazy J."

Fear ripped through her body. The Lazy J lay between town and the Hole and those three toughs had ridden in that direction.

"What's happened, Grady?"

He gulped air and licked his lips. "I came awake at the ranch when I heard rifle fire. Bullets were flying everywhere. Once the fire stopped you could see the place was shot up terrible. Mr. Jeffrey and his wife are shot mighty bad . . . ain't no sign of Millie anywhere. Looked like tracks of maybe three horses leaving the place. Bob and a couple a hands saddled and started following. I figured to do the best I could with the Jeffreys, but saw right away they needed more help than I could give, then lit a shuck for Black Beard."

"He isn't here. Ollie said he left for the Hole-in-the-Rock early this morning." She heard footsteps upstairs as she finished speaking, then Ollie's voice issued from the second floor.

"So, those vicious hombres did have evil in mind. Grady, it ain't possible for you to get into the Hole without being shot. Get to the stable and start saddlin' my horse . . . I'll ride with you as far as the Lazy J, then I'll head on out to get Black Beard." He hurried down the stairs as he spoke.

Grady left without question. Shirley caught Ollie's arm before he went out the door, "Saddle my horse too. I'll go to the Lazy J to do what I can till you get back with Colt." The use of his real name slipped out in her excitement. A curious look spread over Ollie's face, but she thought he wasn't sure she should ride with them. Not wasting any time, she dashed to her room to change into riding clothes and strap on a gun, not even realizing her error.

It seemed to Colt that his eyes barely closed when a horse came galloping along the wagon ruts in front of the shack. One glance showed Hank sleeping peacefully, not having moved since his placement on the bed. Going to the door of the shack, Colt pulled it open. An exhausted rider pulled up in front of the makeshift bar room. The early light of dawn crept over the shacks as the man left the saddle, hitting the ground on a run. Colt stepped outside, thinking it looked a lot like Ollie, even to the sling around his neck. Nothing would bring a wounded man on a ride like that unless real trouble had risen it's ugly head.

He covered four running steps toward the lathered horse when Ollie burst back through the door of the makeshift barroom. Spying Colt, he shouted something that sounded like Millie, but the words were not discernable. The two closed the space between them rapidly. Fresh blood showed on Ollie's bandaged arm and his face gleamed whitely in the dimness of dawn. He panted to a stop and Colt put out an arm to steady him. Words making no sense tumbled from his lips.

"Whoa up, pardner. Take a deep breath and then tell me what's eating you." He held the man tight, thinking he may collapse at any time. As Ollie steadied out, Colt adjusted the bandage after taking a quick look at the bullet hole. Bleeding was minimal . . . with some rest, Ollie would be okay.

"Three villains attacked the Lazy J yesterday. Both the Jeffreys are shot up bad and Millie ain't nowheres around. You got to get there fast, Colt, or them two are going to kick the bucket." On the ride from town, Ollie gave a lot of consideration to Shirley's use of the name and came to the realization that this man in front of him was the Hasting's boy. He made no mention of it during the ride, not wanting Grady to know. One thing for sure--wild horses couldn't make him divulge this man's secret where anyone else could hear it.

"You think you're up to looking after Hank?" At the puzzled expression on Ollie's face, Colt elaborated: "Hank took a bullet from one of the same three last night. He's in the shack now with a broken arm. I planned to ride to town today to check on you and Betty Jo, then get back here to hide Hank from Mitch. Looks like you'll have to do the latter for me while I head for the Lazy J."

Things were coming too fast for Ollie in the last twenty-four hours. "What you talking about, hiding Hank from Mitch? They're both part of the gang."

Leading Ollie toward the shack where Hank lay, Colt filled him in. "I may be wrong but I think Mitch is back of all this trouble. For some reason, which I haven't figured out yet, he wants Hank dead and sent those three toughs to carry it out. I killed one of them last night after he shot Hank in the upper arm and chest. The other two have probably skedaddled by now, going back to report to Mitch. You have to take Hank to my shack at the south end of House Rock Valley. It sets on the edge of the rim; I'll detail Buddy to show you the way. Stay there till I come for you or till you're both healed properly. Your arm will be okay if you relax some on this next ride. It'll take you most of the day to reach my place. We'll get Hank on a horse and the two of you on your way before full light settles in."

They were inside the shack by now. Hank's eyes were watching them both. The urgent sound of their voices had woken him. "What the hell you doing here, Ollie? I thought you were laid up in town."

Colt cut in, "No time to explain anything, Hank. Ollie's taking you to my place. You'll have to ride slow and easy or neither one of you will reach it. Tell me where your horse is and I'll saddle while Ollie gets a little grub packed to eat on the way. He can explain what's up while I'm gone."

He strode from the shack after Hank's quick instructions as to where his horse was stabled. The shacks around the area were still dark. Apparently those living here were accustomed to fast ridden horses coming into camp, paying no attention to the one this morning. Finding Hank's horse, he saddled quickly, then led it to the shack where the two men were just finishing the task of stuffing jerky, biscuits, and hardtack into a gunny sack. Ollie had told Hank what Colt said about Mitch. Hank's face showed pale as he hobbled around, yet his eyes were determined. His thinking came around to that of Colt's, causing him to figure if he was still here when Mitch returned, he'd be dead meat. No more safety at the Hole for him. He sure wasn't hankering for that long ride today, what with sore ribs and a broken arm, but it was either that or prepare to fight and he wasn't in any shape for the latter, either.

Putting an arm around Hank's waist and pulling his good arm over his shoulder, Colt half carried him to the waiting horse and boosted him up. Ollie mounted his own horse, tying the sack of food to the back of his saddle. Colt knelt down by Buddy and put a hand on each side of the dog's face. Buddy gazed at Colt trustingly. "You've got to do a job for me, fella. We have to split up for a short time. I need you to lead these guys to the soddy--the soddy, remember? Take them there."

At the woebegone look on the dog's face, he added, "I'll be back with you soon. I promise. Then he put his arms around the dog and hugged him, whispering "thanks, pal" in his ear.

He rose, slapped both horses on the rump, then ran for the stable where he'd left his horse last night. Saddle in place, Colt vaulted to the horse's back and raced toward the Lazy J. Would his troubles never end?

Since returning from school there seemed to be a constant spate of things happening and now he had the death of one more man on his hands. This range stood peaceful when he left for the East four years ago, but now trouble stalked at every twist of the road. The thing he couldn't figure was why Mitch stirred things up so bad. He already had the Strip in his pocket, why keep pushing on those living here? First his parents, now the Jeffreys. Who would be next, and where had Millie disappeared? Cold icewater went down his spine as he thought of that lovely girl in the clutches of Shorty and his two companions before they showed up at the Hole.

He tried to assess the time element from when he left the Lazy J till he found the three in the makeshift barroom playing cards with Hank. He'd wasted more than a couple of hours, waiting outside the guarded camp till the rain began--that wouldn't leave much time for the three men to attack the ranch, abduct Millie and get to the Hole. Now he wished there were more time to search the shacks before leaving, but with her parents critical, he'd have to hope she would be safe wherever they left her. Course, she may be hidden somewhere on the Lazy J, afraid to show herself, since she seemed pretty adept at spying on folks.

He continued to brood over the mess on the range. Bringing in a new breed of outlaw would stir the town's people up and the Cavalry or the Rangers would eventually be called in to quell the violence those men would perpetuate. Why kill the owners of the ranches? At first he thought they wanted just the end of the Strip where the Bar-H lay, since it would be isolated from the rest of the Strip country. But with this new violence, there must be more to it. The thing sticking in his craw was the abduction of Millie, if it actually happened. Mitch certainly seemed smarter than to order something like that. Nevertheless, men carrying Shorty's brand wouldn't let anything stop them when lust reared its ugly head.

Since Shorty now lay dead back at the Hole, where would the other two lite out for and would they take Millie with them, providing she was still alive? His eyes roved over the terrain as the horse pounded along the trail. There were tracks going in and out of the entrance to the Hole but he didn't have time to stop and decipher their meaning. Passing the guard that suddenly came awake at the sound of hoof beats, he waved his hand. The startled expression on the guard's face disappeared in the cloud of dust thrown up by his horse's feet.

Glancing at the ground occasionally for more tracks, he rode on. It always amazed him how quickly the ground dried out after a heavy thunderstorm. In this arid desert country, the water seemed to run off as fast as it fell from the clouds. If it weren't for the large water tanks scraped out of the dirt where a wash cut a course through the land, there'd be no water collected for any cattle to drink. At least after last night's rain, the tanks he passed were brimming full and the ranchers could heave a sigh of relief for a couple of months.

The steady ring of the horse's hooves over the hardened land seemed to pound more questions into his head. All he'd wanted at first was to buttonhole whoever ordered the killing of his parents. That took second place now, as finding the reason for the killing became paramount. This whole range would blow up if that motive wasn't discovered before too long. The only way for him to find out was to stick close to Mitch, who appeared to be the key, but by saving Hank's life and spiriting him away to safety, he may have ruined any chances he had there. Oh well, first things first. He better have a good story to spin for Mitch's ears or his days would be numbered. The tight rope he walked before these latest events suddenly seemed loose and shaky.

Weary horses stood ground-tied in front of the Lazy J when he vaulted from the saddle, running towards the front door. It swung open as he reached it, showing Shirley with a white face and a worried expression. "Thank the good Lord you're here. They're both hanging on but only by the skin of their teeth."

She hurried to the bedroom where Millie's parents were lying side by side on the bed. Colt stood for a moment assessing their breathing and facial color. Then stooping, he felt for a pulse in each patient, finding them both weak and erratic. Bandages were wrapped around the chest of Mr. Jeffrey and around the middle of his wife. Taking his knife, he slit the bandages, pulling them off to uncover the gaping wounds. Bubbles of air pushed through the bullet wound in the man's chest, red frothy blood surrounding it. Dark blood and droplets of foul, smelling gas oozed from two holes just above the navel of his wife.

Making his decision on what to do, he barked orders to Shirley. "Get four of the strongest men you have on the place. I'll need a cup of vinegar and a couple bottles of whisky. Send someone to the stream for a good two hands full of green moss, unless you can find a jar of Vaseline. Get water boiling on the stove and make sure one of the pokers is placed in the coals to heat. I'll need some lightweight fishing line and whatever sewing needles are in the house. Have one of the men cut off some bark of the willow tree at the side of the house and put it on the stove to dry out. We'll crush it when it's dry and mix it in coffee. The last thing I need is a mix of half vinegar and half honey in a cup. Hurry."

Shirley turned to do his bidding. "I brought all the bandaging material I could get from the undertaker in town." She pointed to the pile on the night stand as she scurried out.

Colt could hear the orders she gave to different individuals and the activity it generated as he knelt down and began probing with gentle fingers around the wounds of each patient. It would take more medical skill than he possessed to pull these two through, and for a moment he almost threw in the towel. However, his father always said to do your best and let God take over from there, so he squared his shoulders and started to cut away the puckered skin at the edge of the wound in Mr. Jeffrey's chest. Rolling the man over, he did the same for the enormous hole in his back. By the time this was accomplished Shirley stood beside him, holding the things he wanted. Four husky men came into the bedroom, one carrying two full bottles of whiskey.

Mr. Jeffrey's eyes followed his every move while he worked, but not so much as a groan escaped his lips. "Mr. Jeffrey, drink as much of that liquor as you can. If you don't get enough of it down, I'll have to knock you out and that would worsen your chances of survival. Now, drink till you can't take any more."

One man stepped forward, put a hand under Jeffrey's head and taking the bottle of whiskey, began to slowly pour it down the man's throat. Colt turned his attention to Mrs. Jeffrey who lay unconscious, and began to clean her wounds. "If one of you could get the mixture of vinegar and honey down her, it'll help keep infection down in the gut and clear away any mucus in the back of the throat. The bullet tore the intestines inside. I'm going to have to make an incision through the abdominal wall, find the torn gut, and sew it up. She has one chance in a thousand of living through this procedure, but if it isn't done, she has no chance at all."

Shirley sat on the other side of the bed and began to spoon the liquid very slowly down Mrs. Jeffrey's throat. Half the bottle of whiskey had disappeared down Mr. Jeffrey. Colt took the bottle and poured some over the bullet holes in both patients, then handed it back to the man who was forcing it down Mr. Jeffrey. "I'm going to cauterize both front and back wounds with a red-hot poker, Mr. Jeffrey. Don't try to hold the pain in . . . if you holler no one will think less of you. After that I'll suture the wounds closed, getting as deep as I can with the needle. I'll tell you when I want you to take a deep breath and hold it. That'll hurt like fire, but it helps expel as much excess air from your chest cavity as possible, causing the lungs to expand after being partially deflated. I'll do this when I tighten the last stitch in your chest. If it works, you'll be able to breathe better as each day passes and unless there's a large vessel torn inside, you'll have a chance to live. Now finish that bottle of whiskey while I get everything ready."

Picking out the largest sewing needle he could find from those in the basket, he threaded the fish line to it, then dropped line and all into a cup of whiskey. Going to the kitchen, he returned with the red-hot poker. "You four men grab his arms and legs. Don't let him move any more than you can help."

When the four husky men grabbed hold, Colt quickly rammed the hot poker into the chest wound, twisting it one turn, then pulling it back out. Jeffrey bucked against the pain and his lips parted but no sound came forth. Sweat beaded his forehead and his eyes were momentarily wild. Glancing up at those holding him down, Colt saw sweat dripping off each man. "Now turn him over. That was the easy part--this hole in the back is going to hurt even worse."

While the men rolled their patient, Colt quickly wiped off the wound with a small cloth, removing the accumulated blood. Then he cautioned: "Hold him tight."

The still red-hot poker thrust into the gaping hole and twisted back and forth. Jeffrey bucked his whole body upward, almost tearing loose from the men holding him and this time a curse left his lips. Then he went limp. Grabbing the needle and fish line,

Colt began to sew the wound closed. With that done he took bandages and placed a pad, after smearing it with Vaseline, over the wound in the back. Signaling the men holding the arms to lift Jeffrey into a sitting position, he wrapped strips around the back, bringing the ends to the front as he told them to gently lay the man back down.

He placed the needle in the front wound, taking as big a bite as possible. The bubbly froth oozed from the still open wound each time the man breathed. "He just fainted. With his body flat on the bed it won't be long before he comes around. Then he'll have to take that deep breath before I pull this suture tight."

They all relaxed as the wait began. The cowboys wiped the sweat dripping down their pale faces while Colt checked Mrs. Jeffrey. Shirley still spooned the vinegar and honey mixture slowly down her. He said a prayer of thanks that the woman lay unconscious, hoping she would stay that way till he completed surgery. Never in all his time at school did he see this procedure performed, but he'd read several surgical books and talked to one surgeon who'd done the operation. "If two of you men could carry Mrs. Jeffrey into the kitchen and lay her face down on the table, we'll work on her there. If she starts to wake up while the surgery is in progress, one of you'll have to knock her out. Be gentle but make sure you put her out with the first blow."

Two men picked her up and carried her out of the room, Shirley following. Mr. Jeffrey showed signs of waking up: his head moved from side-to-side and his eyes fluttered open. The color of his skin matched the whites of his eyes. Touching his forehead, Colt felt cold clammy sweat. The man would be lucky if he survived this ordeal. "Can you hear me, Mr. Jeffrey?"

The man's eyes focused on him and after a moment his head nodded. You could see the determination begin to form behind his look. The lips moved but no sound came out. "All right. I'm going to pull the last stitch tight. You'll want to exhale at that point, but don't. You must keep your lungs expanded as much as possible, so hold all the air inside you can. Now take a deep breath and hold it."

His eyes closed as he pulled air into his lungs. Quickly Colt prepared to pull the stitch tight, closing the wound as frothy air came rushing out. When it looked like Jeffrey could hold his breath no longer and air ceased to escape from the wound, he tightened the fish line, tying it firmly, then proceeded to sew the skin around the wound, reinforcing the inner stitches. Next he poured whiskey over the area and padded it with a Vaseline smeared pad, wrapping the strips from the back over the front and tying them tightly.

Jeffrey lay as though he were dead. Only by close observation could Colt tell he still breathed. His pulse was weak but steady. Pulling the covers over the man, he said, "The rest is up to him and the Lord. Now we've got another patient to work on, so let's get at it." He left the room, sure that his body would drop from the strain of working on two patients in less than twenty-four hours, with hardly any sleep the night before, coupled with two long rides. But the hardest task of all now stared him in the face. Could he pull it off?

Shirley sensed the strain on this man as he came through the kitchen door with the cold poker in his hand. He hung it on the cook stove, squared his shoulders and bent over the wounds in the woman's back. Rolling her gently over onto her side, he studied the entrance holes. Luck ran with her in that the bullets were from high-powered rifles and in driving through her body, missed the spine and major artery. The speed with which they traveled must have left only minor damage inside, since there was no evidence of bright red blood showing at any of the four holes. The fact that she still lived after having so much time pass, meant the spleen or the liver were not touched. But with the gas that occasionally slipped out of the front wounds, he knew a bowel had been torn. It would have to be sutured or peritonitis would soon set in, causing slow, agonizing death.

He couldn't find a reason for her to be unconscious at this point, but would take anything that helped . . . he'd hunt for the reason later. "Shirley, bring in a clean sheet to spread over her while I work. That way things'll stay as clean as possible and there'll be less chance of more infection causing trouble. You men stay handy---you may need to hold her down."

The cowboys weren't happy about all this. Branding cattle and sewing torn skin was the extent of their knowledge, and the way they liked it. A big gaping wound, such as the Jeffreys bore, meant the person would flat-out die. It was normal. The sickening stench of burned skin, the putrid gas, the blood frothing and bubbling, all of it, made even the hardiest want to puke. However, the West toughened even the most unlikely of men. No matter how revolting the task, if it would help someone, they would do it.

Colt took the second bottle of whiskey and dribbled some over both front and back wounds. "I'll take care of the back wounds once I'm through with the problems inside." He padded it with bandage material, then gently turned her onto her back. Taking his knife, he poured whiskey over it, then slit the sheet that now lay over her. He leaned over the patient to cut away more of the sheet and her clothes. After rinsing his hands with more whiskey, and saying a silent prayer, he poured more whiskey over the knife and sliced the skin between the two bullet holes, extending it another two inches on either side. Shirley wiped the oozing blood out of the cut, giving him a vision of the tissue beneath the skin. His knife stabbed gently through the muscle and lining of the abdomen. The first finger of his left hand pushed through the stab wound and he lay the blade of the knife along this finger, slitting tissues without damage to underlying organs.

As he spread the incision edges, a sigh escaped his lips. There lay a loop of intestine with a hole through it. If this were the only damage done, his work would be much easier. Lifting the loop out and laying it on the sheet, he wiped it clean with bandage material which Shirley handed him. "Thanks. Now pour a little more whiskey over the bowel."

This done, he took up the needle and fish line and proceeded to sew the entrance wound and the exit wound in the loop of gut. Once he completed this, he had more whiskey poured over the sutured area, then dropped the loop back into the abdomen. Spreading the wound edges as far apart as possible, he checked the many loops of gut by spreading them apart with one finger. Everything else appeared in one piece and he couldn't smell any more gas or see it bubbling.

Finished with his examination, more whiskey went inside. He took up needle and thread and sewed the abdominal lining and muscle together, finally placing stitches in the skin to close the wound. Almost done. Shirley patted the sweat running down his face. He stretched his shoulders again before beginning the final procedure. Then he turned the woman over and sutured the wounds in the back after pouring more whiskey over them. The bottle was almost empty. He took a big dab of Vaseline and packed it around the wounds both front and back. They then set her up so he could bandage all the way around the mid-section. "Let's carry her back to the bed. I've done all I can--the rest is up to a higher power than what we have here." Three of the cowboys hurriedly left after helping him. Colt walked back into the kitchen leaving Shirley and one cowboy in the bedroom.

Cleaning up at the wash basin, he stood drying his hands when Shirley entered the kitchen. He said, "The one thing puzzling me is why Mrs. Jeffrey is unconscious. I didn't notice any bumps on the head or bruises on the jaw."

Shirley stopped in front of him. "According to the man who rode to town trying to find you, she lay that way when the men found them after hearing shots. They were asleep in the bunk house when the rifle fire broke out. Both the Jeffreys were lying like they were dead on the front porch, apparently having just come outside when the bullets hit them. Mr. Jeffrey mumbled something about wanting Millie, and his wife said she heard Millie scream, then she went quiet. By the time the men got them inside and on the bed they were both out cold. The cook bandaged them as best he could but I guess the shock of seeing Millie taken by force, plus the bullet wounds, put Mrs. Jeffrey out."

"That sounds as good as anything. I wonder if she'll eventually come out of it. If not, well, we did our best with what we had to work with. Someday we'll have a qualified medical doctor in this area."

"Where did Ollie catch up with you?" Shirley asked as she

stood looking at his tired face.

"He came to the Hole just before dawn. I sent him with Hank and Buddy to where I have a soddy. It's on the rim of the canyon, at the southern part of the Bar H. Both men are wounded so it would be good if you could get Heidi to go there and help them." He then gave her directions to the soddy.

"What do you mean, both men are wounded?" He didn't get time to answer.

One of the men who'd assisted him, came from the bedroom. "Black Beard, Mrs. Jeffrey woke up when her husband's hand fell on her face. She wants to talk to you."

Dropping the towel, he sprinted for the bedroom. Her eyes were closed when he stopped at the bedside. Mr. Jeffrey still lay with no sign of consciousness. His wife's hand rested on his two big rough and hairy ones and her eyes fluttered open. Words barley audible pushed through her teeth. "They took . . . Millie. Leader . . . short man. Threw her over . . . neck of horse . . . rode off. Find her...before something terrible . . . happens." Her eyes closed again and her lips were still. Colt could see the steady rise and fall of her chest, but there wasn't a lot of force to it. Mrs. Jeffrey lay with tears running down her checks.

"That girl is tough as whang leather. If Bob gets to her in time, she'll be all right," the man beside him muttered. He explained further, "Bob, the foreman here at the ranch, took two men with him to see if he could work out the trail of the skunks who did this. Me and some of the men will go with you to look for them, if you'd like."

"Thanks, I appreciate your offer, and you or any of the other punchers are more than welcome. The short leader of the bunch is already dead. They came into the Hole last night, got in a poker game with Hank. Shorty took a shot at him later that evening, breaking his arm and two ribs. I was lucky to get Shorty right after he fired but the other two got away. I patched Hank up and he and Ollie are riding to a safe place now. There was no sign or mention of Millie during the time the killers were there--that may indicate they cached her somewhere. We'll head right for the Hole and watch for tracks as we get close. Bob and his men are probably already there, but they won't get into the Hole. Let's ride."

He whirled to the door, striding outside to find his saddle, with rifle butt protruding, on a rangy bay gelding. Two cowboys were waiting with extra horses for Colt and the man with him- they had anticipated his next move and were ready. Vaulting to the saddle, the four of them pounded from the ranch yard, leaving a pall of dust and distress to settle over the place. It would be dark by the time they reached the Hole, and if Bob and his men hadn't picked up any tracks coming out of the Hole, indicating the killers were gone, they'd still be there. He would search every building until he located either the two men or Millie. However, it wouldn't be that easy.

The floppy-brimmed Stetson with the edges curled up, dropped out of sight behind the knoll. The dog's tail gave its last wag before it too disappeared. Millie strolled lazily up the sloping grass covered hillside. Something kept dragging at the edges of her awareness as she talked with Black Beard and that something still hung in there. Topping the rise, there was no sign of the man, horse, or dog. She dropped to a sitting position on the grass and watched the open meadow about two miles farther out, waiting for him to appear.

Time passed, then she saw him, stopped just at the edge of the trees on the far side of the meadow. Oh, he was smart all right. He skirted the edge of the open space until he got just inside the trees, to see if anyone followed him. Then he slipped into the foliage and she lay back on the grass, smelling the freshness of the morning and chewing on a stem of grass. Her mind pictured him as he had ridden down this knoll earlier. Horse and man seemed to be one in movement as they neared the ranch house. Her dreams last night had been of this man she'd danced with and the stories that went around about him. He was becoming the most talked about outlaw in the whole country, and being held by him while they swirled around the dance floor, made her want to stay clasped in his arms forever.

His steel blue eyes reminded her of someone, but she just couldn't put her finger on who that someone was. She knew sometime in the past she either saw him or somebody just like him. Letting her thoughts drift over her past experiences while growing up, she tried to get a handle on this puzzle. Something about a man visiting her father came to mind, but she couldn't tie it in with Black Beard. Giving up after a while, she rolled over on her stomach, raising up to look off in the direction he traveled. Her eyes dilated, and her body stiffened, but she let no other indication of worry show on her face.

Three men with horses standing behind them were only twenty feet away, watching her. The soft grass must have cushioned their approach, or else she was so wrapped up in thinking about Black Beard that her ears were plugged. The short one of the group let a lecherous grin spread across his face. "Hey, boys, look what we got here. Just layin' there waitin' for us to have fun with."

Millie didn't move a muscle till he started forward, then she bolted down the side of the knoll at a run. The long dress got tangled in her legs and she sprawled forward, skinning her arms and legs in the rough dirt. Desperately she tried to get back on her feet when a body slammed over the top of her, smashing her to the ground. Foul-smelling breath made her gag and she struggled to slide from under the dirty, stinking, man.

"You ain't gittin' away from me, missy," he whispered savagely in her ear. He grabbed both her arms, stretching her out flat, her face pushed in the dirt.

"Come on, fellows, let's get a taste of this fireball."

The words laid a cold hand on her heart. Where was her father---the ranch hands-- anybody? If she broke free for only a second, a scream might bring them running. The two outlaws with Shorty pulled him up slightly, wanting to be in on the action. Pressure relieved, she took a deep breath, trying to roll her body out from under him and yell at the same time. He caught her by the long hair, shoving her back down.

"Now, missy, you ain't goin' nowhere till we git the job done we come fer. Then you're gonna keep us company till we git plumb tired a you." He rolled her to her back and stuffed his filthy pocket rag in her mouth. Frantic, she squirmed and fought, but his massive arms were too strong. Standing up, he jerked her to her feet by her hair, while the other two outlaws pinned down her arms. She tried not to cry, but the pulling of her hair with such force hurt so much, tears rolled down her cheeks.

"I'll handle this wildcat. You two numskulls' git the rifles from the saddles. Old Jeffrey will be comin' outa the house soon and we better be ready. The boss said to git it over with fast-- the punchers'll be sleepin' late on a Sunday mornin'."

His words sank deep into Millie's brain and she struggled with all her might. His hairy hands clung tight to her wrists. Her knee came up but he must have expected this--his hip swung forward and took the blow meant for another spot. She managed to spit out the dirty rag, screamed, and latched onto his wrist with her teeth, exerting all the power she could into biting. One hand let go of her wrist and the other slammed into her jaw.

The next thing she knew, sounds of rifle fire blossomed around her. The blue sky above swam into her vision, then his leering face blocked it out. He grabbed her by the hair again, stepped foot to stirrup and dragged her over the pommel of his saddle. Her dress caught on a bush, tearing part of the bottom off as the horse whirled away, pounding down the far side of the knoll. Every bounce of the horse pushed the saddle horn agonizingly into her stomach. Despite how she hated to do it, she squirmed closer to the outlaw to shift off the horn. This brought some relief. The steady bounce still sent stabs of pain through her body, but there didn't seem to be anything else she could do.

Her eyes saw the grass of the meadow flash by, causing hope to rise in her: they were headed in the same direction as Black Beard. Surely he would hear them coming and rescue her. But only moments later, as they reached the trees on the far side, the horses swung to the right, pounding at right angles to the path he would have taken. Her mind screamed with frustration. Abruptly the horses came to a stop and she tried to slip off the saddle. Her feet touched the ground and she tore off as fast as her legs would carry her. Suddenly her arms were pinioned by the coarse feel of a rope and she spilled to the pine-needle-covered ground, many of the needles puncturing her tender skin.

Millie wouldn't give up. Rolling, she came to her feet, trying desperately to shake off the rope snagging her legs. Then two others flashed out, one circling down her body, the other her neck. The ropes sang tight, cutting off air and tripping her to the earth again. Grasping the rope around her neck, she succeeded in getting a much needed breath of air.

Then Shorty stood beside her, face pushed close to hers and that evil grin spread across it. "You're sure a wild un'. It's goin' to be plumb pleasurable tamin' a spitfire like you. Why, me an the boys are gonna have the time a our lives when we git you put away where no one can find you. And with your old man and woman dead, ain't nothin' anyone can do about it."

All Millie's struggles stopped at the import of this statement. Now she knew what the rifle fire meant. While she lay unconscious, they had waited on the knoll till her parents came running from the ranch house, then cold-bloodedly shot them down in their tracks. A numb, passive, feeling settled over her and she didn't care what happened from that point on. She knew what awaited her . . . it was plain as day. They would use her and when all were satisfied, her throat would be slit. Her fate would be the same as Betty Jo's would have been if Black Beard hadn't arrived in time. Western men were supposed to respect women, but these three were the scum of the earth.

She became limp as a dishrag while they bound her and set her on the saddle behind Shorty. At least this was more comfortable than riding belly down over the saddle horn. They removed the rope from her neck, but with her feet tied under the horse's stomach and her wrists tied to each side of the saddle, her body was forced to bend forward, pushing against Shorty's stinking back. Every now and then he'd turn and grin at her. His fetid breath and rotted teeth made her stomach churn, but she would need every bit of strength possible to last through this ordeal, so she fought to keep the contents down.

Miles drifted behind and pine trees grew scarce as scrub cedars began to show and sagebrush dotted the landscape. Soon large boulders thrust up from the land, scattered haphazardly by capricious, unknown hands. Millie looked up to the top of the red and white hills before them. At first she thought they angled toward the outlaw village at the Hole, but now she noticed they would be more to the south. Trying to remember any place down there which would serve their purpose, she couldn't recall a thing. This remote area never saw much travel by the cowhands; the country seemed to have been dumped here like refuse, and there wasn't enough grass to support even one cow.

The rays of the sun slanted from the west and she reckoned they must have been riding for more than four hours. Not one of them offered her a drink when they stopped briefly but she held her silence, not wanting to draw their attention any more than necessary. Her mouth felt so dry she'd probably have to prime it to work up a good spit. The little left of her dress didn't hide much of her legs and she felt the sunburn already taking its toll. Glancing at her bare arms, she saw the skin bright red and from the feel of her face, figured she'd look like a roasted chicken by the time the sun went down.

The lead horse pulled to a stop and its rider, who'd been relishing the idea of Millie, said, "It's going to be pretty late when we reach the shack. How we going to do anything with this tender morsel if we're supposed to be at the Hole by sundown?" The breathless excitement in the man's voice conveyed his unwillingness to wait.

Hoof fall echoed again as they started on. Shorty's rough voice scratched the air. "The boss'll skin us alive if he finds out we got her. So I figger we'll have to postpone our fun till we git that other job done, then go collect the rest of our money. After that we kin git back and have ourselves a party."

"Shoot fire! That'll take most of the night and tomorrow. You 'n Ort oughtta be able to handle that pesky job 'thout me tagging along. I kin stay and guard her till you get back."

Shorty gave a brittle laugh. "You think I'd trust you with her alone? When the time comes, it's goin' to be me gittin' first crack at this little filly. Besides, if you don't come, you can't share any of the money."

Silence met this announcement and sneaking a glance at the man who first spoke. Millie could see him weighing whether the money would be worth the wait. He started to speak when Shorty cut him off. "The boss said that gunslinger, goin' by the name a Black Beard, might be at the Hole and if he is, it'll take all three a us to pull this off, 'thout one a us gittin' a blue whistler through his gut. So that settles it. We're all goin'. We'll leave her tied to the bunk with the door and window wedged shut. Ain't no way she'll escape. By the time we git back, she'll be so happy to see us, she'll fall all over us."

Crude laughter made Millie's skin crawl. There must be an isolated shack somewhere that stayed hidden from the normal honest cowhand. At least she'd be alone for a while when they dropped her off to head out for whatever it was the boss wanted them to do. Her former passivity changed to determination. In that time she'd use all the abilities she possessed to escape. Her mind still ran over this possibility when the horses stopped in front of a weather-beaten old shack.

Shorty swung his right leg forward, sliding down from the saddle. He untied her, then reached up, grabbed her roughly by the arm and pulled her off. Her legs wouldn't support her weight and she crumpled to the ground. This didn't slow him down one bit. He got a handful of her long hair and yanked her into the shack, taking more skin off her legs as they drug along the rough dirt floor. With one powerful jerk, he slung her by the hair onto the bunk at the back of the shack. Her body bounced off the wall before settling to the straw tick.

The outlaw called Ort strode in with two ropes in his hand. Shorty grabbed one, throwing a loop around her neck again, then wrapping the rope down around the legs of the bunk. He left just enough slack in the rope for her to barely breathe, after which he wrapped it over her body several times, tying her tight to the bunk. He took the other rope and secured her legs with another loop before cinching it tight to the underside of the bunk. All she could move were her fingers and eyelids, and fear began to well up again. Not giving in to it, she forced her mind to start a plan of escape even though it would probably be fruitless. She knew if her thoughts dwelt on the hopelessness of the situation, she would go stark, raving mad.

The door to the shack slammed shut, causing dirt and dust to trickle down from the rafters. She closed her eyes as it settled over her. Blowing upward through her lips caused the dust to shift on her face so she could at least open her eyes. Deciding she better start wiggling her arms and hands before they became numb, she struggled against the ropes. Nothing gave at all. Steeling herself, she kept at it till sweat began to mix with the dust and her breathing came rapid and short. If possible, her mouth felt even dryer and fear again took a turn at discouraging her. Why not just lie here till her whole body went numb? Perhaps she could just pass out.

A horrible thought came into play: what if the three outlaws were killed trying to do the job they talked about? No one knew where she was. Unless someone came to this shack by accident, she'd lay for days until she finally choked to death. From the looks of the dust accumulated inside, it never received any visitors. Perhaps Shorty was right: by the time they came back, she might be begging them to do what they wanted, then kill her and get it over with. At that point, death would be welcome.

She wondered if Bob or any of the ranch hands would be able to follow the trail from the ranch to this shack? Hope flaired like a burst of fireworks in her mind, until she remembered the miles of volcanic rock they crossed early in the afternoon. No one could track horses over that turned-upside-down country. The bend her captors made leading off in another direction came to her. Trying to think where it was, she recalled it to be about halfway through the volcanic rock. Ort had dropped back from the others when they came out of the rocky ground. He must have wiped out the tracks of the horses leaving the volcanic rock, so even if the trackers circled the massive area searching for tracks, they would find nothing. Despair overwhelmed her.

A noise outside the wall near where the bunk sat began to make its way into her consciousness. It sounded like someone digging. Turning her head carefully so the tight rope wouldn't cut her skin, she saw a hole coming up from under the wall of the shack. Suddenly a head poked through, almost scaring her to death. A porcupine's quills followed the head. One slap of it's tail in her face would send sharp quills into her skin. She remembered seeing an unlucky ranch dog after it tangled with one of these creatures, and how painful it seemed to be. The cowboys tied the dog down and his mouth shut so they could extract the quills from its face and neck. Even the front legs were covered with quills. Well, no one would have to tie her down . . . she was already tied. But with nobody to pull the quills out, she'd have to suffer in pain till Shorty came back or she died. No matter how she looked at it, pain and death were inevitable.

From working with the cattle on the ranch, she knew if a person stood still, not moving a muscle, the cattle would walk right by, not even aware someone stood there. Breathing as light as possible, anxiety cruising through her body, she became immobile. The animal nosed around the shack, tipping over a bucket that almost made her jump at the noise. When the bucket tipped, it distracted the animal so it didn't see the involuntary muscle contractions of her legs and arms. Hours passed, at least it seemed like it to her, before the porcupine completed its inspection of the inside of the shack, and scurried back through the hole under the wall.

Relief washed over her. It must have hoped the recent visit of humans left something for it to eat, and came inside to check things out. It, too, would be disappointed at the callousness of her captors. Never in her wildest dreams could she have imagined something like this happening to her. Her mind conjured up the outlaws who took her captive. They didn't ride like a true cowboy and their speech did seem a little different, but it didn't ring a bell at the time. These men must be imports from back East or somewhere.

The light coming through the shut window began to fade. Darkness settled in, causing the inside of the shack to become as black as a chuck wagon skillet. Being tied to this bunk in the daylight had been bad enough, but when night covered the land, pure fear curled through her body. Time was passing, and she must escape.

No matter how she tried to loosen the ropes binding her, she made little progress. But determination again took over and she struggled constantly. As the blackness grew even more dense, she finally discovered some looseness in the ropes. She could move her legs back and forth, but the scratching of the rough ropes caused them to bleed. At first this stopped her struggles, until twisting one leg, she felt it move easier from the blood, making the rope more slippery.

Another cowpuncher fact flashed into her mind: new ropes were often stuck in water, then stretched between two posts to dry so they would be more pliable and longer. Hope surged through her . . . a wet rope would stretch. Frantically moving her arms under the ropes, she felt blood begin to coat the ropes. Gritting her teeth against the pain, she slowly worked at stretching the rope, now wet from her own sweat and blood. It seemed like hours before her right arm came free. Exhausted, she closed her eyes to rest a moment. The next thing she knew, sunlight hit her in the face.

Daylight. Shorty would be here sometime today. If she were to escape, she'd have to maneuver fast. Why did sleep overtake her? If she could have worked at the ropes all night, she might be free by now. Feeling down the rope on her right side, her fingers touched the first knot tied to the leg of the bunk. Could she undo that knot with one hand? Sweat began to bead her face. Sweat. What did she use for brains last night . . . sweat worked as well as blood. Struggling with the knot at her finger tips, she moved as much as possible as sunlight streamed through the cracks in the shutter nailed over the window, causing her to sweat even more. She could feel it running onto the rope around her neck and legs. Moving all her muscles, she felt blood mixing with the sweat. She worked at the knot with renewed desperation, feeling her fingers begin to slide in the mix of sweat and blood. To her relief, the knot began to loosen. How much more time would it take before she was free? With the knot loose the rest of the rope would soon slip from her. Did she have that much time before Shorty arrived?

15

His heart pounding, Bob quickly saddled a horse while two punchers did the same. They vaulted to saddles, the horses already on the run. Reaching the top of the rise in front of the Lazy J, they immediately cut the trail of the three horses running fast in the direction of the outlaw village at the Hole. Pounding along, the tracks plain in the soft soil, they figured the men to be only thirty to forty minutes ahead. With luck, they would overtake them before they reached their destination.

Bob felt his whole life had spun out of control. Since hiring on at the Lazy J as a young seventeen year old, he spent a lot of time dreaming of the time when Millie would notice him and he could ask her to marry him. When he worked up to the top job as foreman of the spread, he figured he would be in a position to pop the question. Months drifted by and each time he felt inclined to ask her, his courage failed. He planned to take the plunge when he rode behind the wagon going toward the ranch after the dance, but all she talked about was that fellow Black Beard and he again delayed the question. Now she'd be taken to the outlaw's village and who knows what her future would be. Well, whatever happened to her, if she were still alive, he still wanted to marry her . . . his love was constant and deep. His concentration on these thoughts caused him to miss the sudden change in direction of the tracks they followed.

Barney pulled up when his eyes spotted the direction change. It took a minute for Bob to realize his two companions were not trailing him. Twisting in the saddle, he saw them strike out to his right. One look down at the ground showed him the tracks of only one horse going toward the Hole. The tracks of the three horses weren't visible. His ears caught Barney's shout and he spurred in their direction. Catching up to his two companions, he saw the tracks of the three horses now traveling so they would shoot straight for the ferry at the Colorado River. The three weren't going to the Hole after all. This would be better--they'd be in the open most of the time and he wouldn't have to figure a way to get into the Hole undetected.

Mile after mile flashed behind the pounding horses. The trail entered the massive lava rock country and disappeared. Keeping to the same direction the tracks had been leading, the three riders slowed their pace over the rough surface so as not to cut their horse's hooves. To Bob, it seemed an endless trail over the lava rock and his patience wore thin by the time they reached the end of this massive, rock strewn, area. It didn't surprise him when they saw no tracks from the three horses coming out of the lava bed--the three may not have tracked the same direction all the time, but he figured they would cut their tracks in a short while. He went one way searching for tracks and Barney went the other, while Ed continued on for a mile in the same direction as the tracks led when they angled off on the lava. If one man spotted tracks, he would fire three shots to signal the other two.

Time drifted by as Bob rode, circling the outer limit of the lava, watching close. Hoping one of the other men was more successful, he turned back after several miles. He reached the spot where they came out of the lava and saw Ed waiting. "Did you pick up any sign of them?" he asked as he approached.

Lifting his hat and scratching his head, Ed answered, "Nary a track. Those boys coulda cut back or turned again to throw off anyone followin'."

"If they did, it'll take a couple of days to work out their trail. We don't have that much time to waste. Millie needs help as soon as we can get to her." Bob tried to figure what would be the best course to take now that the trail appeared to be lost.

"We could cut around to the side of the lava that leads to the Hole, and see what tracks lie in that direction. It's pretty plain they didn't keep heading to the Ferry, and I can't recall anyplace else in this God-forsaken country where they'd take her." Ed too worried about the amount of time which would pass before the trail came again into view.

Gigging his horse into motion, Bob sighed, "Let's get after Barney. He headed in that direction and may find something by the time we catch up to him."

Ed swung his horse alongside as the two of them pounded around the edge of the lava field. An hour later they spied Barney riding toward them. Pulling his horse to a sliding stop, signs of hope clothed his face. "I didn't hear any shots--did you find anything?"

Stopping in a cloud of dust, Bob squinted at him. "We were hoping you might've stumbled onto something. Neither one of us cut any sign at all."

Barney's face took on a pained look. "Nothing we're looking for. I saw the tracks of one horse going toward the Hole, they looked fresh but everything else was too old. Followed them a ways to see if any others joined them, but no luck."

The weight of the world sagged onto Bob's shoulders. "You know anyplace else they could take her? You've been on this range a lot longer than either of us . . . don't you know of somewhere that would fit their purposes?"

Barney strained to remember such a place. "Can't rightly recollect any. There's a few old miners' shacks scattered around the country, but they're not fit for three men to hole up in for any length of time. I figure they either headed for the Hole or the Ferry. Since I didn't cut their trail in the direction of the Hole, they must've headed for the Ferry, intending to hide on the reservation somewhere or go on down south toward Flagstaff. One way to find out would be to line out for the Ferry and check with Josh as to whether they crossed the river there."

His mind trying to figure the best way to go, Bob became more agitated. "It'll be way after dark by the time we get there and if Josh ain't seen them, then we'll have a long ride back this way."

Barney mentioned, "Josh's run the ferry for over twenty years. If they didn't go that way, and with no tracks leading to the Hole, maybe he'd know the best place to look. He talks with men crossing the river all the time and might have a notion about where they're headed."

With a groan, Bob decided. "That sounds reasonable, but if he hasn't any ideas, we'll be way behind those boys and Millie. Cold-blooded killers like them won't let any grass grow under their feet before they use her, then kill her."

Seeing the anguish in Bob's eyes, Ed made the decision for him. "Still and all, that seems to be our best option. We start now and push the horses as much as possible without foundering them, we can have an answer before sunset. If things turn out bad, we can trade horses at the Ferry and ride back this way."

Turning their horses and gigging them into a rapid trot, Ed and Barney led out with Bob now bringing up the rear. Dust boiled up to hang momentarily in the air before settling back to earth. Both horses and men were wet with sweat and dirt before the river came into sight. Another three miles brought them to the buildings on the west side of the river crossing.

To Bob's consternation, Josh was just pulling his ferry to the far bank, letting off several horsemen and a wagon. It took several minutes for them to disembark and for two horsemen to spur onto the plank-covered ferry before Josh started back. Fidgeting like a kid in school, Bob slid off his horse and waited for the ferry to bump the bank. With twenty feet to go, he shouted at Josh. "Josh, you seen three men come this way with Millie Jeffrey?"

Spewing a cud of chewing tobacco, Josh pulled his long pole up from the bottom. "Ain't seen that youngster in quite a spell. What fer she doin' with three men anyways?"

This news sent Bob into total discouragement. "Three men shot the Jeffrey's this morning and kidnaped Millie. We lost their trail over on that big lava bed--thought they might of headed this way."

By now the ferry had reached the bank and as Josh let the

poles down so the two horsemen could go ashore, he spat out another cud. "Was one of them three a short stocky hombre built like an oak tree?"

The two horsemen stopped on the bank to listen to the answer Bob gave: "We didn't see what they looked like. The rifle shots came from the knoll in front of the house. We were still sleeping off the effects of the shindig in town. When we got to the front porch of the house, Mrs. Jeffrey managed to gasp that they took Millie, then she fainted. Both the Jeffreys were shot up pretty bad; don't really expect them to live."

One of the horsemen spat, then opined, "If those are the three who stopped the stagecoach between Holbrook and Window Rock three, four days ago, you might as well stop looking for this girl you call Millie. When they finally found the stage, all inside were dead. Looked like the women were used pretty bad before the outlaws killed them."

Dropping to a rock, Bob put his head in his hands. Barney sent him a sympathetic glance and took over the questioning. "These three we're after must've crossed here for you to mention a short, heavyset one. Did they say anything that might give us a lead as to where to look for them?"

Another plug of tobacco went into Josh's mouth before his lips parted with speech. "Now that I kin answer. The short one seemed to be the leader of the bunch and he mentioned they was headed to Fredonia to meet a gent, then they'd be stayin' at the Hole-in-the-Rock fer a while. Struck me kinda strange that men as mean and dirty as them three would join the Hole gang. If that's what's comin' into this country, I gist might quit the Ferry business. Them boys was gist plain ornery and looked like they come from somewheres back

243

east. They ain't got the western cut 'bout 'em at all. Fer that matter, there was six others of the same stripe crossed a few days afore this bunch did. You think there's more on the way?"

Hearing this latest statement, Bob came out of his doldrums. "I don't have any idea---I haven't seen any of the men you're talking about. We're going to need three fresh horses. When we get this job over with, we'll bring them back to you." He sprang up and raced toward the corral where Josh kept several extra horses.

Josh looked at Ed and Barney. "You fellers et anything since mornin'? It might be smart if'n you could get Bob to slow down enough to fill your bellies. Cain't do much fightin' on a empty stomach, an the missus should have grub on the table by now. 'Sides, it ain't likely Millie is still alive at this point, so hurry ain't goin' to get you nowhere."

Reigning his horse around, Barney threw words over his shoulder. "I'll see what I can do to talk sense into Bob. If you think of anywhere else those mean sons might of holed up, let us know."

It took some hard talking to convince Bob to take time out to eat, but Barney finally accomplished it by mentioning Josh might have an idea as to where the three could be holed up, if they didn't head for the Hole. With three fresh horses saddled, they stopped at the main house where Josh and the two horsemen were just sitting down to supper. Josh's wife already had three filled plates on the table for Bob's bunch. Falling into chairs, they began to eat fast.

Talking around a mouthful of food, Bob looked Josh in the eye. "We didn't find any tracks leaving that lava range in the direction of the Hole-in-the-Rock. You know of anywhere else those boys might be headed?"

Stabbing a piece of steak with his knife, Josh grunted, "Hell, there's more old prospector's shacks 'round this country than you kin shake a stick at." He crammed the steak in his mouth, chewing rapidly. "If them boys are eventually headed for the Hole, they may stash Millie in one of those shacks to hold till they get through with her. That bein' the case, they'd hunt fer a place close enough to the Hole where they could ride to easy. Or they might keep her in one of the shacks at the outlaw village. My bet'd be they'd take her to the Hole first, but if Mitch hollered 'bout it, they'd stash her in a prospector's shack somewheres close."

"If they did that, where would be the closest shack for their purpose?" Bob could eat no more; his stomach churned with worries about Millie.

A mouth full of meat could be seen going down Josh's skinny neck as his adam's apple bobbed up and down. "There's one ol shack 'bout five miles north of the entrance to the Hole, and another 'bout four miles south at the rim of the river. Ain't been to either of 'em in years and don't know of anyone usin' 'em of late. They're probably ready to fall down, but those're the closest. If it was me and I was as mean as those three looked, I'd go right on into the village at the Hole and tell Mitch if he didn't like it, to lump it."

One of the horsemen added, "We ran into Mitch and several of his boys down around the Gap trading post--they were headed for a job over Colorado way, from what we heard. He won't be back to put up a fuss about what those three do."

Bob pushed back his chair. "Thanks Josh, we'll be riding fast for the Hole now; ought to get there about late afternoon tomorrow. We'll have to figure a way to get into the place when we get there. Don't suppose that'll be easy to do." Having said that, he hustled for the door with his two companions cramming the last of their food between two chunks of bread and sprinting after him.

By the time they reached the top of the wind swept mesa above Lee's Ferry, it was as black as a miner's tomb. There were still many miles to go. Barney pulled alongside Bob's galloping horse. "We keep goin' at this pace, in the dark, we'll cripple a horse or two. Best we slow up before that happens or you'll never get where you're going, unless you want to hoof it on your shank ponies." *(shank ponies are the two legs God gave to every man.)*

Several minutes passed before Bob let reason take over and pulled his horse to a walk. "I guess I've been going off half-cocked since we started. Thanks for horning in, Barney. We better come up with a plan to get into the outlaw village and how to search it."

Sounds of light hoof falls spread out from their passage over the juniper and sage-dotted landscape. "That job seems near impossible. Those outlaws keep a guard on the alert all the time and he ain't going to let three cowboys from the Lazy J do no snooping around. We get in there, we'll have to do it sneaky-like and on foot. That place is a forest of rocks and crevices, we'll be lucky to get in sight of the village even on foot."

Silence held as each tried to work out a way to accomplish the rescue of Millie, if she were still alive. Barney squinted in the dark at Bob--the set of his shoulders and the way he held his head told plain as day that he wanted to strike out at anything in his path. Trying to allay the fears in all their hearts, he drawled, "That girl's a fighter and always has been. You know how she bosses all us men around. Why, if they lay a hand on her, she'll scratch their

L. J. Brooksby

eyes out. Sure wouldn't want to tackle that female if she didn't want to be tackled."

Endless miles drifted behind and as dawn's cruel breath enveloped them, they crossed their tracks leaving the lava bed that were put down yesterday. Eyes sharpened as they continued on, watching for any sign of the three outlaws' travel. Midday came and went with nothing to shout about, poking into their silent journey. Each man pulled his belt another notch tighter. The horses were now alternately trotting, then loping, causing the dust to churn up from their hooves and bringing them closer to the entrance of the Hole.

Full dark settled over the land before they reached their destination. The moon sent its glow over the boulder strewn area, casting the rugged scenery into shadow. The men moved warily, expecting to see gun flame spear toward them any minute. This would be the second night since Millie disappeared and Bob's hopes of finding her alive were all but vanished. A small spot of optimism still burned, however, and he continued to hope.

They sat in darkness, each of them suggesting a way to enter the outlaw enclave without being seen, and how to search the place after gaining entrance. The more plans suggested, the more hopeless it seemed. Bob ventured out along the trail in stocking feet to see if he could slip by the posted guards. He didn't cover much more than a couple of a hundred yards before a rifle bullet chipped rocks near him. Sweat trickled down his face as he sprinted back to where his two companions waited.

"Well, that's the end of that scheme. We might as well trail over to the north and see if we can find another way in," Barney said doubtfully. They knew the country lay right at the edge of the

247

cliffs above the Colorado River, and getting down those cliffs in the dark, without a trail to follow, would be about as successful as throwing a two thousand-pound bull by the tail.

"We could rush the guard. With the three of us, at least one would get through." Bob just wanted to be doing something other than talking about it.

"Then after rousing the whole village, how're we going to find Millie? If we're going to help her, we got to figure a better way than killing ourselves before we get the job done." Ed knew someone in the group needed to keep a sane head. He understood Bob's frustration, but wasn't willing to die for it.

The sound of running hoofs thudding against the earth broke the silent night air. They were coming from the outlaw village, heading toward the entrance to the Hole. Drawing guns, the three Lazy J cowboys crouched in the brush, hoping this would be the three men they were after. Tense moments drug on while the horses drew closer, then stopped at the hail of the guard. "Where you fellers going now? Didn't you come back no more'n a couple of hours ago?"

A steady drawl reached their ears. "Couldn't even work up a good poker game with anyone. Thought we might find things more interesting in town. We know it's late, but if we ride hard, we'll get there in time for at least one drink of Pike's fine liquor."

The laugh of the guard came clearly to the three cowboys as Barney leaned toward Bob, whispering in his ear. "Sure sounds like that Black Beard feller. You don't suppose he's one of the ones we're after, do you?"

Bob whispered back, "Josh would've mentioned him if he was one of those men, so I don't figure he's in on the killing of the

Jeffreys. When they ride by, we'll stop them at gunpoint and find out if the men we want came into the Hole with Millie."

Guns drawn, they waited tensely until the gab ended between the guard and Black Beard. The creaking leather and occasional snort of walking horses drew near. Soon four horses showed against the starlight. Men sat in three of the saddles, followed by a horse carrying no rider. This fact didn't register on Bob and his companions till Bob spoke. "Stop right there, fellers, we got you covered."

Surprise lay bare in the voice of the man on horseback closest to them. "That you, Bob?" Then the voice leveled out. "Where the heck you been for the last two days? We cut your tracks headed toward the Ferry. Black Beard figured you were checking it out to make sure Millie wasn't taken that way."

The three cowboys crept out of the brush, looking up at the three horsemen who were part of the Lazy J crew. "We been riding solid since leaving the ranch. Ain't caught the slightest indication as to where she's been taken. Josh figured the three would bring her to the Hole, what with Mitch being gone and all. So we been trying to figure a way to get in there and search the place."

Barney cut his eyes from looking at the horse with the empty saddle to those sitting saddle, and a creepy feeling began to spread along his spine. "I reckoned the voice talking to the guard belonged to that Black Beard feller, but I might of been mistaken."

The men on horseback leaned back in their saddles, grins spreading across their faces. "You reckoned right Barney, but you see, while Black Beard talked to the guard, he spotted the starlight glancing off one of your gun barrels. So we rode ahead while he injuned up on the three of you. That's him standing in the trees behind you now."

Three cowboys turned as one and saw a man step from the trees behind them. "We've already searched the shacks at the village and came up with a busted flush. The two men left from the ambush at the Lazy J ain't been back here since last night. Did Josh know where we might look for them?" Black Beard stepped closer as he talked.

Barney picked up on his mention of only two men and let his words out in a puzzled voice. "We trailed three men from the knoll in front of the house."

"You trailed three men, all right. They showed up at the village last night, got in a poker game with Hank, then tried to kill him when he bluffed them and won. Shorty's luck ran out when my bullet took him in the head after he tried a second time to get Hank. I figure the three of them stashed Millie somewhere before coming to the hole to get Hank. That's why I asked if Josh had any ideas."

Head spinning, Bob tried to get the hang of what Black Beard talked about. Barney again took over the conversation. "Josh said there were two old prospector's shacks within five miles of here where those scoundrels might of stashed Millie. If we split up, we can search both of them, then meet back here with the results."

Black Beard swung to saddle leather. "You give us the directions to one of those shacks and we'll head for it while you investigate the other one."

Finally Bob found his tongue. "Josh said there was a shack close to the rim north of here about five miles. You check that one out. The three of us will ride to the one about four miles south of here." He didn't wait for an answer but sprinted for his horse tied back in the trees, Barney and Ed close on his heels.

Pounding away from the entrance to the Hole, Bob began to think of the time interval between when Shorty got his pitchfork and the present. He wished they'd waited to ask Black Beard some more questions but he knew there would be no turning back now. If Millie was stashed in a shack, and the two men left for it right after Shorty took a bullet, their time with her would have been ample. Rage boiled through him, followed by despair. Whatever her fate entailed, the seven men riding to find her would surely be too late.

16

The sorrow hanging over the Lazy J this morning permeated Shirley to the bone. No word came from any of the men who rode to find Millie. The distances those men had to travel made it unlikely that any news would reach the Lazy J by this time, but she anxiously scanned the horizon, hoping to see at least one horseman galloping in. A puncher rode to town yesterday to summon Heidi after they heard Hank was recovering from a bullet wound. She wanted desperately to have another woman with her during this waiting period. She knew Heidi wouldn't want to stay around too long once she found out where Ollie took Hank, but at least the two of them could commiserate with each other for a short time.

Her two patients were barely hanging on without much change one way or the other, but at least they were both still breathing. Checking the bandages, she found the wounds looking pretty good, considering what took place. No new spots of blood showed anywhere and she said a silent prayer of thanks for Colt's seeming expert medical care. Mr. Jeffrey woke during the night but his speech didn't make any sense--it was obvious he was out of his head with fever. His wife lay as though her next breath would be her last. Preparing the willow bark, then mixing it with coffee, she gave each patient a dose every four hours as per Colt's instructions. He told her it would help keep the pain down and it did seem to help.

Leaving the sick room, she found her way to the kitchen and began to prepare something to put in her stomach. Visions of Millie in torment came rushing to her and bile rose in her throat. If it weren't for Colt's quick and accurate shooting, Betty Jo would have suffered the same fate as Millie. How could men be so cruel? The Strip always seemed to get along with the outlaws coming to it before men like these arrived. What did they come for? To cold-bloodedly shoot the Jeffreys on their own doorstep didn't jibe with the outlaws riding with Mitch. She knew most of the Hole gang and felt Mitch kept good control over his men when it came to how they interacted with those people living on the Strip.

There must be someone else giving these men their orders, or else they were acting on their own. If they acted on their own and were new to this area, why wait on top of the knoll in front of the Lazy J to kill the Jeffreys? She remembered Colt's parents and their ambush--were the two episodes connected? It was certainly possible, and if so, that someone knew the people living here, and for some reason wanted these two families wiped out. The attempted murder of Hank brought up another question: did this same person want to cause trouble with the outlaws at the Hole, and that's why this new breed of vicious outlaw kept showing up? Could the instigator be living on the Strip, or would he give his orders from a place outside the area?

Her thoughts were interrupted by the sound of riders entering the yard. Glancing out the window, she saw Heidi and Carl, the puncher who went for her, dismounting at the hitching post. She sprang for the door and pulled it open, meeting Heidi as she stepped onto the front porch. The two embraced, and Shirley could see tear streaks through the dust on Heidi's face.

Catching her breath, Heidi anxiously inquired, "Where's Hank? Carl didn't seem to know anything except that Hank took a bullet and Black Beard patched him up. He said he'd been sent to get me and that's all."

Taking Heidi by the arm, Shirley led her into the ranch house, throwing instructions to Carl over her shoulder. "Carl, saddle two fresh horses. You'll be taking Heidi to where Hank's hidden. Then come on in and I'll have some breakfast for the both of you."

Her pronouncement brought Heidi to a standstill. "Why is Hank hiding? Who shot him and the Jeffreys? What's going on and why all the secrecy?"

Exerting pressure on Heidi's arm, Shirley started her toward the door. "I'll tell you all about it while you get around a big breakfast. Then you can hustle off to where Black Beard sent Ollie and Hank."

Fresh tears were cutting new streaks through the dust on Heidi's face as she allowed herself to be led to the kitchen. She reluctantly sat in the chair Shirley indicated, but as soon as Shirley turned to the stove, she bounced up and began to pace the floor. "I can't stand the suspense any longer. If Hank is hurt bad, I'll take a gun to whoever did it."

"Shush now. You won't have to do that. Black Beard already sent the man to the happy hunting ground, or wherever men like that go after they die. He was also one of the men who shot the Jeffrey's. I saw all three of them in town yesterday morning and thought they were up to no good, but they left before I could find anything out about them." Shirley flipped the pancakes over and began cracking eggs in a skillet. Hot sausage waited on the side.

Sobs began to shake Heidi and Shirley left the stove to hold the woman in her arms. "Hank took a bullet in the upper arm, breaking the bone, then it passed on through and traveled along his ribs. Black Beard doctored him, then sent Ollie to lead him to Black Beard's place so Mitch couldn't get at him when he got back."

Suddenly Heidi's sobbing stopped. "Are you crazy? Why would Mitch want to kill Hank? They're good friends. When Mitch leaves, Hank is always in charge till he gets back."

"I'm as puzzled as you are. All I know is Black Beard said the three killers mentioned they were sent by Mitch to kill Hank. I've been trying to think things through all night, but still can't see any rhyme or reason for it. The only thing I can tell you is that if Black Beard thinks Mitch is out to get Hank, then it's true. When he gets back from hunting for Millie, you can ask him more about it. After all, you've only known Hank for a few months and there may be some time in the two men's past when they experienced trouble with each other."

Heidi stepped over and picked up the coffee pot. "It still doesn't make any sense. And another thing: why are all these toughs coming into the Strip? They must be the meanest men on earth to go around kidnaping and killing all the time. I don't believe Mitch would condone the abduction of Millie. There has to be someone else setting these men loose on the people living here. And why cause trouble at the Hole-in-the-Rock?

"I don't have any answers. We've always gotten along with the outlaws that come through. I know it doesn't look right to people living across the line in Kanab for us to go so easy on those men, but what else can we do? At least they respect us and keep trouble to a minimum in town."

"All this started shortly after Black Beard showed up in Fredonia. You think he could have something to do with it?" Heidi really didn't like this sudden thought but someone must be spearheading these things.

Placing a plate full of food on the table, Shirley answered positively, "That's one thing I know for sure: Black Beard is not the one causing trouble. Besides, look how he went into action in town to save Betty Jo. No, if there's a mastermind behind all this, he must have a powerful reason to send such men onto our range."

Heidi sat down to eat, but couldn't get her mind off Hank. "Where's Hank hiding? If he needs more medical attention, will someone be there to help him?"

"That's why I sent for you. You have some experience in nursing in your background, and just having you around will cause Hank to heal faster. Carl will take you there as soon as you both are fed. It's on the other side of the Kaibab mountain at the south end of the Hastings range. Black Beard told me he has a soddy there. No one ever travels that section of the range---Hank will be safe. But no one is to know about it but us. Carl will stay there in case of discovery, or you need to send him for supplies. He can be trusted to keep his mouth shut."

Just then Carl stepped through the kitchen door. "The horses are saddled, Miss Shirley. If you give me directions to this place you're talking about, I'll shovel the grub down fast and we can be on our way."

Thinking back over what Colt told her, she tried to describe things the best she could. "I've never been there, Carl, but Black Beard said to go to the foothills at the eastern side of the Kaibab, then cut south along the flat. He figures its a good thirty miles or more to the edge of the canyon running along the southern border of the Strip. He has a soddy located about a hundred yards back from the rim of the large canyon, so cut east when you reach the rim and you should see the place. Better announce your arrival when you spot it or Ollie might get trigger happy."

The three of them proceeded to polish off all the food without any more conversation interrupting them. Then Shirley bid them good by as they stepped into saddle leather and trotted from the front yard. She returned to the bedroom where the two sick people lay. There seemed to be no change in either person. If they would only wake up enough to take some nourishment, the healing process would speed up somewhat. She'd been able to slowly spoon some broth down both patients along with the mixture of willow bark and coffee, but that wouldn't be enough to hold them for long. Sighing, she sat down in the chair beside the bed to wait for a change, hoping for word from those seeking Millie.

This week had taken its toll on her reserves, what with all the sick she felt responsible for. Why couldn't life just roll along easy-like, without all this hassle coming at her all at once? Her thoughts swung to Colt and a smile began to play around the corners of her mouth. He was one man who stepped into her life and took control. She admitted to herself that his actions constantly reminded her of the place he was filling in her heart. His young age didn't seem to stop him from doing good for others, yet he certainly showed no hesitation to jump into action when it presented itself.

Her head fell forward and her eyes closed as the sleepless nights caught up with her. Startled by a racket in the front yard, she came fully awake in an instant. Her glance swung to the bed and she saw Mr. Jeffrey trying to sit up. His face turned even more pale, if that were possible, and words came from his feverish lips. "Those scoundrels have come back. I gotta get my gun before they kill Millie."

Stepping to the bed, she pushed gently on his shoulders. "Lay back down, Mr. Jeffrey. You're wounded pretty bad and in no condition to even hold a gun, let alone fire one. That's probably Bob returning with the crew." He tried to resist her efforts to push him back to the bed, but he didn't have enough energy to accomplish it.

More words peeled from his lips, "Why isn't Millie in here to help you? Where in tarnation is that girl anyway? Seems she's always off mooning somewhere instead of helping around the ranch. And where's my wife? What're you doing here? You're supposed to be in town taking care of the hotel." She could tell he was out of his head. His breathing became labored as the speech ended, then his eyes closed and she thought he'd died. Abruptly his respiration started again. Very slowly it began to even out and he lay unconscious. Putting a hand to his forehead, she could feel the fever burning, but it seemed to be a little less than before. Hope began to stir in her, then she remembered the disturbance in the front yard. A knock came on the front door.

Her footsteps were quiet as she left the bedroom, going to the door. Who could it be that would knock before entering? Surely if Bob and the crew had returned, he would come in quietly, rather than knocking. Lifting the door latch, she swung the door open enough to peer outside. A relieved sigh escaped when she recognized Captain Gregg standing there.

"Captain, you're a sight for sore eyes. Come on in but be quiet-- the Jeffreys are both pretty bad." She swung the door open wider so he could enter and noticed several troopers still setting saddle in the front yard.

He stepped through the door. "The word reached me as I came in from patrol. I came as fast as possible to see what could be done about this terrible tragedy. My men and I will clean out that gang of killers at the Hole if it takes all the resources I can bring to bear on them."

Her finger touching her lips, Shirley admonished him. "Hold your voice down, Captain. Come on into the kitchen while I fix you something to eat and I'll tell you all I know."

He turned back to the door. "First let me get my men to feed and water the horses, then they can eat at the cook shack. It's been a long ride and both horses and men are pretty much used up."

When he left, she went to the kitchen. Cutting a steak and slicing some potatoes, she dropped them in the fry pan, then stoked up the stove, adding more wood. He came in quietly this time and she felt his arms come around her waist. Thankful for the support he offered, she leaned her head back against his shoulder. "Captain, what's happening on this range is just awful. No one seems to be safe."

"Once I get the order from Washington, I'll take troops into the Hole and clean it up and you wont have to worry anymore. I sent another request for permission to take into custody all outlaws who come into this territory. This time I think those in power will listen because so much has been happening." For the first time Shirley seemed to be putting her trust in him and he felt ten feet tall and that he could cure all her problems. However, his joy came to an abrupt halt as she twisted from his embrace.

The idea that Colt could be branded an outlaw and arrested with the others flashed through her mind and she pulled away from him. "But we haven't had any trouble like this from those outlaws who live at the Hole. It's just this new breed of men causing all the trouble. You know Mitch keeps a tight lid on his men when they're here on the Strip. Oh, I know they rustle a few cattle now and then, but in general they let those living here alone."

Captain Gregg couldn't figure what he'd said that triggered her sudden change of mood. Then the thought went through him that it must be Black Beard she worried about, and jealousy began to gnaw at him. Didn't breeding, looks, intelligence . . . all of which he possessed in abundance . . . count for anything? "You must have a good reason for defending such a terrible group of men. They wiped the Hasting's spread completely clean of cattle, and one outlaw is just as bad as the next. If we don't put a stop to this, all sorts of rough characters will be coming here . . . then things will just get worse. And the people of this town won't have anyone to blame but themselves. If you condone the doings of one outlaw, you condone them all."

Now she felt like a fool for destroying the peaceful feeling she'd had while in his arms. She needed some support and Gregg couldn't see any other way to do things than to bull his way into the Hole and get a lot of men killed. Should she tell him that Colt

had already penetrated the outlaw camp and would be the best
source for finding the answer to the trouble? She started to open
her mouth when noise from the bedroom interrupted her. Hurrying to the room, she saw Mrs. Jeffrey lying on the floor. Remorse
rushed through her. She should have been paying attention to the
sick rather than lollygagging with the Captain out in the kitchen.
The next thing she knew Gregg rushed past her to stoop and lift
Mrs. Jeffrey back onto the bed.

Mr. Jeffrey came awake as the weight of his wife's body sank
into the feather mattress. He spoke coherently. "Captain, thank
goodness you're here. Those men shot up the place and I don't
know what all damage has been done. You'll have to get after
them at once." Then he saw Shirley lean over his wife to check on
her bandages. His glance took in the bandages surrounding her
mid section.

"Oh Christ. Did those fools shoot her too? Why are you here,
Shirley? Why isn't Millie taking care of us?"

Quickly Shirley interrupted before Gregg could say anything,
realizing that Mr. Jeffrey was blocking what had happened out of
his mind. "She's busy doing other things right now, Mr. Jeffrey.
You received a very bad wound and so did your wife. Bob and
the crew are out hunting for the killers. When they return, I'll
send Millie in to look after you, but for now you must take it easy
or your wounds will start to bleed again. Please lie back and let
the Captain and I take care of Mrs. Jeffrey."

He let his eyes roam from one to the other as she finished
checking the bandages on both patients. "That's just like that daughter of mine. She'd sooner be roaming around chasing outlaws
than home taking care of us. I swear I don't know what to think.

All she talked about, all the way home from the dance, was the outlaw Black Beard. He danced with her a couple of times, you know, and it went straight to her head. Now she thinks he's the only man on earth."

The Captain interjected. "That's just young inexperience talking, sir. Give her a few more years and she'll realize one of your cowboys is who she really wants."

"Harumph. Bob would give his eye teeth to have her look twice at him. But no, she leads him on and then dumps him as soon as a new face shows up. I oughtta take a willow stick to her behind . . . then she'd be worth something around here."

Shirley wanted him to rest, so she interposed, "You go back to sleep now, your wife can heal up faster without all this jabbering around her. When you're back on your feet, you can take care of Millie."

He gave her an exasperated look but settled back in bed and let his eyes lock onto his wife lying beside him. Then his glance shuttled back to Shirley. "Smells like something burning, but it don't matter--I'm so hungry I could eat a horse."

"Oh my heart, I left your food on the stove, Captain Gregg." Shirley dashed from the room as the Captain followed, closing the bedroom door quietly.

Entering the kitchen he saw her remove the fry pan from the stove, a dish towel wrapped around the handle. He looked in the pan. A few burned potatoes were beyond saving but the steak might be edible. "Why don't you take the steak into Mr. Jeffrey. I'll eat with the men at the cook shack, then come back in to see how things are going."

Her smile didn't come off the way she wanted. "I'm sorry. I

guess things are piling up so fast my thinking cap isn't on today. I'll get him fed and we can talk more while he sleeps. He docsn't seem to remember Millie was abducted. She's been with those men for almost three days and who knows what might have happened to her in that time. I just wish Black Beard would get back here with her in his possession."

Dusk was settling in when the last knot fell from the rope around her ankles. Horse sounds carried to her, along with the rough laughter of men. Quickly she rolled from the bed, intending to hide under it. As she hit the dirt floor, her glance settled on the hole under the wall left by the porcupine. Would her slim shape fit through it? If not, she'd be stuck in the shack with those repulsive villains, who brought her here. Frantically she scurried toward the hole, going down it head first. If she got her shoulders through the rest of her body would follow. No such luck--her shoulders were a bit too wide.

Her heart sank, then her fighting spirit welled up. Digging with both hands, she attacked the dirt on one side of the hole. It came away in chunks, breaking some of her fingernails in the process. Scooping the dirt up onto the floor, she dug again as the horses stopped out front. More dirt fell from the side of the hole. If she didn't fit through it now, it would be too late to do anything other than hide under the bed. Scooping out the dirt again, she struggled into the hole. It seemed she wouldn't make it this time either. Then she rolled to her back, squirming downward and pulling her shoulders as close to her chest as possible. Wiggling hastily, she felt her upper body move past the bottom of the hole and reaching up, she grasped the lower log of the shack on the outside of the building. Pulling with all her might and twisting to help get her hips through, she felt like a mole crawling from its hiding place. The door opened as her hips, then her legs, came out of the hole. Thank goodness it was a dirt floor: they might not notice the hole right away. Sweat dripped from her hair, rolling through the dirt on her face. Kneeling on the ground, she tried to stand but her legs wouldn't support her. Crawling over this rough ground wouldn't be pleasant, but neither would being discovered by the men after her. The shout coming through the wall made her decision for her.

The twenty feet to the trees dropped behind as the blood began to stream from her hands and knees. Diving to cover the last two feet, she somersaulted into the temporary safety of the trees. She wanted to shout and cry with joy and relief, but now wasn't the time for either. Grasping a limb on the nearest tree, she pulled herself to her feet which finally supported her weight, but were still wobbly from being tied so long. She wanted to run like a deer through the woods but this would make enough noise for her abductors to follow. Carefully, she stepped along the pine needle covered ground, gaining more strength in her legs with each slow step. Her bare feet handled the sticks and stones fairly well. All those years of running around the ranch without shoes on, were paying off.

Head swivelling from side to side, her eyes sought a hiding place that would give her concealment. Instinctively she reasoned that to try to outrun them would be useless. They would expect her to put as much distance as possible between her and the shack, and wouldn't search too thoroughly this close. Stumbling on, she heard them rush through the door and mount their horses, coming around to the back of the shack. They must have found the hole. It would be only moments till they trailed the blood to the trees. She wanted to run. It took all her will power to stay calm and cast about for the hiding place she prayed for.

A log lying on the ground butted into her vision. Old and moss covered, it had been there for years, gradually becoming one with the earth that had given it birth. Hoping it would be hollow, she forced herself to walk softly to it, leaving as little imprint on the ground as possible. By now the scratches on her legs didn't drip blood, so that would help. Rounding the other end of the log, her heart skipped a beat. A fairly large hole glared blackly back at her. Would it be big enough to hide in?

Kneeling down, she gathered the remnants of her dress and backed into it. Her dress tore more and she carefully picked every small scrap from the ground. But at last she could see there would be just enough room for her if she stayed doubled up as tight as possible. Looking out at the ground, she noticed blood on the dirt where her knees left their impression. Quickly she threw dirt over the blood and pulled pine needles over the impressions.

Voices knifed through the air while she held her breath. "She went into the trees. Can't be too far ahead-- that blood's pretty fresh. Let's spread out with about twenty feet between us and ride straight ahead. She grew up in this country and probably knows every foot of the forest around here. Probably find her hiding in a cave somewhere. Keep your eyes peeled for something like that. We'll get her yet."

Horses moved between the trees and one passed within a foot of the fallen log. Its brown legs were plain to see and as it moved farther away, she got a glimpse of spurred boot heels. The man would surely look back and see her, but the horse disappeared in the trees and the hoof falls grew fainter. Why didn't they search for her on foot? If they had, she could've stolen one of their horses and been gone from this terrible place. Then she latched onto the fact that a man on foot would probably have seen her in the log, and she thanked her lucky stars they took the horses.

Waiting for sounds of their travel to completely fade out, she figured now was the time to seek another hiding place, before they came back this way. Crawling from the log, she scooped up some dirt and rubbed it on the scratches covering her arms and legs. This would keep them from bleeding and giving her route of flight away. Only, where to go?

Creeping furtively back through the trees, she studied the shack. Would they look inside again when they didn't find her? It just didn't seem like a good place to hide, even if they knew she wasn't there, and she couldn't bring herself to enter that horrible place again. Nothing about this country rang a bell in her memory, despite what the outlaw thought. Would they expect her to head back toward the Lazy J? Probably. So the best direction would be toward the river; at least water would be there and she couldn't keep from licking her cracked lips in anticipation. It would mean passing by the Hole where the outlaws stayed, but she was willing to chance it.

Glancing at the cool rays of the moon as it climbed toward the top of the sky caused her to wonder if darkness would help or hinder her. It would make it impossible for her pursuers to track her, but could she find her way in the dark and not fall into a ravine or wash? A gunshot sounded behind her. What were the men shooting at? One of them must have seen something move and fired at it. The surprising thing was that the shot sounded a lot closer than she expected. Were they coming back this way? The thought lent added strength to her stride.

She stayed in the trees and tried to hurry, but still not make any noise. If only she were an Indian---she could move without any sound at all. Black Beard mentioned that she came up on him very quietly yesterday morning. It felt like weeks since she talked to him, but only two days and one night separated her from that time. Now the second night enveloped her. The thought of his complement gave her courage and she hurried on.

A good mile lay between her and the shack---hope again rose in her heart. Would Bob or any of the men be able to track the outlaws who abducted her? She figured it was a long shot---they covered their trail pretty well. The darkness deepened and quiet pressed in. Without warning, the air filled with more gunshots from behind her. Had one of the three found her trail and summoned the others? The one thing she must not do was panic and make so much noise they would hear her. Trying to keep her mind calm, she scurried on as silence closed in again.

The pale faced moon crept behind a cloud, hindering her travel, but she kept doggedly at the pace she'd set, being as quiet as possible. If she didn't watch her steps she would fall into one of the many washes covering this upside down land. The man who stated she would be familiar with this country sure missed his mark by a mile. She didn't know anything at all about this end of the Strip, and she wished she'd paid more attention to her studies when the subject of the stars and planets came up. Instead she figured stars were for dreaming and no sensible young girl would be caught out alone in pitch dark anyway. Men knew about the night sky because they always came back to the ranch from town in the wee hours of the morning, but ladies didn't do that. At least not when they were part of the Jeffrey clan. Her father wanted her to be a lady instead of a tomboy. He should be glad that she wasn't--a lady would still be tied in the cabin, weeping and wailing "Oh me, oh my. Where is my hero?" Millie got a much-needed giggle from this thought.

Because she had no idea as to where she headed, she wished one of the crew were with her to show her the way. Would they have tracked her abductors this far? It seemed doubtful. What she wouldn't give for a drink of cold water. Or even warm, or muddy, or brackish water. Anything moist would do. Night helped take the thirst away a little, but it still felt like rabbit fur covered the inside of her mouth. How long would it take to reach the river if her captors didn't catch up to her? Two days and two nights without food or water were beginning to take their toll, and she found she was walking slower. If she came upon a ravine with water below, she'd roll down it till reaching the bottom. What were a few more scrapes and bruises on her already tattered body?

The thought no sooner crossed her mind than gunfire erupted a third time. There were many shots and so close it made her cringe, thinking the bullets were coming her way. Raising her head slightly, she strained to see in the utter darkness. Then a shout from off to her left filled the night. "We sure blundered into a mess. Let's get out of here."

The voice sounded like the outlaw who wanted to stay with her at the shack while his two companions reported to the boss. She saw a horse with a man on its back break from the trees. The man appeared to be looking backward and didn't see her as she dropped flat on the ground. The horse saw her though, and gave a flying leap as it sailed over her prone body, landing with thundering hooves on the other side. Those huge back feet were inches from her and she instinctively rolled to one side as a curse issued from the ground a few feet away: "Damn a horse that jumps at his own shadow. If I catch that crazy animal, I'll shoot it right between the eyes."

The outlaw lifted himself from the ground and started in her direction. Surprise shifted to wrath as his glance fastened on her, and he spit out a vivid oath. Death never seemed so close. Adrenalin raced through her body, and bounding to her feet, she tore off through the trees. The heavy footfalls as he ran after her came distinctly to her ears. Something cut the air above her head as the gun in his hand blasted. It didn't matter--she'd rather be shot than caught by this man again. Her running feet flashed over the ground but she heard the slowly gaining sound of his boots. Another shot sounded and the bullet passed through the cloth of the dress covering her upper arm.

Involuntarily she looked back. Her foot hit a log and she went head over heels, sprawling face down in the dirt. Spinning over, she saw him come to a stop just above her. A spiteful leer severed his lips. "You're the cause of all this mess. Shoulda killed you when we killed your parents. But I can fix that right now." The gun pointed at her and she saw his finger tighten on the trigger and the hammer fall before she closed her eyes, not wanting to see the flame spear from the barrel toward her. Click. The gun either misfired or he'd run out of shells in the chamber. Either way, a slim chance came to her. Grabbing a handful of debris from the forest floor, she leaped up, threw it in his face, and fled.

His footfalls again came close and moments later a bullet hit the ground in front of her. He must have put one or two slugs in the chamber. Another shot blasted so close that it made her ears ring, and she heard a groan from behind. This time she didn't turn to look, but it didn't matter as an arm reached out from the tree beside her, pulling her behind it.

She fought like a cornered mountain lion, beating her fists against the man's chest and sobbing in disappointment. After all her efforts, she must have run right into the arms of one of the other outlaws. His hands came up and grasped her flailing arms, pinning them behind her. Somehow his words got through to her. "Millie, it's me, Bob. You're safe now." Instantly her sobs became ones of joy and she buried her head against his shoulder. His hands let her arms go, then slipped around her waist, pulling her closer. Uncontrollable shakes began to run along her body as the tension drained away. Never in her life had she felt so thankful for the foreman of her father's ranch. His strong arms held her tight until the muscles of her body regained control and the shaking began to subside.

Several more shots sounded from not too far away. "I think they got the other one. Those shots came from the direction he went and that's where Barney and Ed would be. If so, that takes care of the men who kidnaped you. The one who ran you down is laying over yonder."

She didn't want to let go of him. "There must be one more. There were three of them, unless you got two just now."

He stroked her tangled hair with his rough rope-calloused hand. "The leader of the bunch got a one way ticket to the hereafter last night, when he tried to kill Hank. Black Beard sent a bullet through his head. You won't have to worry about that bunch any more." As he finished his statement two horsemen rode up.

"Shoot fire, look who Bob found. If it ain't that ornery daughter of the Jeffreys." A grin spread from ear to ear on Barney's face.

Ed took a more serious approach. "By golly, Millie, you're a sight for sore eyes. Looks like they might of treated you a little rough, but don't you worry none--those men won't ever again eat a beef steak on this earth." He rode over to the shape lying in the dirt. A stream of tobacco juice left his lips, planting itself on the back of the dead outlaw, then he turned his horse back to them.

Bob gave his orders. "Barney, rustle up one of the outlaw's horses for Millie to ride. Ed, you catch the other one and bring it along with us."

Noticing the way Millie was standing, Bob took a closer look at her feet and legs. What he saw made him rage inside and want to kill the outlaws all over again. His eyes moved upward, past the ragged dress, and caught on the rope burns around her neck and wrists, the bloody, scraped and torn skin. Then seeing her small pale face surrounding her beautiful courageous eyes, he felt humbled, and, strangely, almost like crying. His big hand moved to her dirty matted hair, and he carefully removed a few twigs. Then, very gently, he lifted her in his arms and carried her back to where he left his horse.

Setting her softly on the smoothest piece of ground he could find, he pulled off the blanket roll from behind his saddle, and handed it to her. "Here, wrap this around you-- there ain't enough dress left to cover a dogie lamb." Because of his need to control his emotions, his words came out gruff.

For the first time Millie looked down at herself. The dress was shredded and her legs and arms were caked with a mixture of blood and dirt. Definitely not a pretty sight. Gratefully, she took the blanket and put it over her shoulders. "Bob, what am I going to do now, with my parents dead? What I went through seems minor compared to what happened to them."

"Well now, the last time I saw your folks I figured the same as you. But when we met up with Black Beard tonight, he mentioned they were still breathing after he did barnyard surgery on them. Maybe their luck is holding, like yours. At least we'll know the answer sometime tomorrow morning when we pull into the Lazy J. Now lets get you into that saddle and we'll go meet Barney."

He helped her mount, then led the horse toward the spot where Barney disappeared. Soon they heard a whistle from just ahead and Barney came out of the trees, leading a horse. "Got his reins tangled in scrub oak, so didn't run far. I heard Ed still chasing the other one---it might be a while before he catches up to us." His eyes roamed over the blanket-covered figure on the horse and his face darkened in anger. Killing was too good for those outlaws. He wanted one alive. They'd throw a rope around his neck and drag him through the brush. See how he liked it. Then they'd kill him. Just the thought of this brought a satisfied smile.

Bob stepped to the saddle slick of the outlaw's horse. "I'll ride this broomtail, save us changing horses. Let's pick up the pace if you can, Millie."

She held her horse at a stand while she reached down to the canteen on Bob's saddle. The two watched as she tipped it up, greedily gulping the water.

The canteen left her mouth as Bob pulled it down. "How long since you took a drink?"

She tried to pull it away from him as she spoke. "Since those fellers grabbed me. They didn't seem to care whether I choked to death or not, and I sure didn't want to beg from any of them."

A curse left his lips. "Those mangy dogs didn't give you anything to eat or drink in all that time."

He wasn't being mean when he took the canteen away . . . if she drank too much all at once, it would come right back up a few minutes later. "When Shorty grabbed me and threw me over his saddle horn, they were more concerned in covering their tracks and getting to a job their boss wanted them to do at the Hole. They took me to an old prospector's shack and tied me to the bunk, fixed the door and window so I couldn't escape, then left. I ain't seen them again till they came back after sundown tonight. By then I'd managed to get myself untied, and escaped through a porcupine hole under the wall of the shack. They tracked me into the trees. I found a hollow log and they rode right on by while I stayed hid in it. After they went by, I figured if I headed for the river it would be the safest, cause' they'd expect me to line out for the ranch. That's when I heard all the shooting."

A whistle left Barney's lips. "Shoot fire, girl, you sure do beat all. I'd a been scared plumb spitless if those two rode by me while I hid in a hollow log."

Bob handed the canteen back to her. "Just sip it slowly as we ride. When we meet up with Black Beard, we'll stop long enough to fry some johnnycake to fill that empty spot in your gut."

While the horses trotted along, she told them the full story. Bob, with help from Barney, filled her in on events transpiring with them and back at the ranch. Three miles drifted behind when horses were heard coming toward them. A voice sang out, "Looks like you hit the jackpot, Bob. At least I suspect that under that dirty old blanket is a nice young lady."

Millie expected to feel a thrill go up her spine at the sound of Black Beard's voice, but it didn't happen and this puzzled her. Then Barney answered, "We sure did and not any too soon. One of them jaspers tried to let daylight through Millie, but Bob drilled him just in the nick of time."

Colt rode up to them. "We ran into Ed after he finally caught the other horse. He told us about it so I sent him onto the ranch with the news that you were safe. He'll ride the borrowed horse till it tires then turn it loose and switch to his. That way he'll cover more ground . . . should be at the ranch before midmorning."

"Sure makes it easier for us. Millie's been through the mill the last few days and a long rough ride would make it worse. I say we stop for a few hours, get some food down her, then she can rest awhile before we continue. It'd do us all good to off-saddle and rest-- none of us have slept since this shindig started."

Thinking on all that still faced him, Colt said, "That's a good idea for you folks, but I need to get into town to check on Betty Jo, then ride to see how Hank's making out. I'll go to the Hole and trade horses, then light a shuck for town. I'll swing by the ranch to check on your parents, Millie, on my way. You're in good hands now, so relax and let these men take care of you."

His horse wheeled and disappeared in the dark before anyone could answer. Bob's voice broke the stillness. "There goes a man I'd be proud to ride the river with. It sure is hard to figure him being an outlaw."

"I don't think he is an outlaw, not with all the good things he does. I figure him to be a Ranger sent in here undercover to solve the rustling on the Strip." Millie spoke the words, but again she wondered why the feelings she thought she harbored for that man, were gone.

18

The only sound filling the air around him was the hoof falls of his horse cutting through the starlit night. Tension which seemed to be his constant companion for the last several days, peeled from his shoulders and tired body, and his thoughts wandered. At least Millie now rode in safety and with a little tender care from Bob and his men, would pull through okay. Bob's feeling for his boss's daughter were plain on his face this night, and Colt figured the two would find out what each meant to the other after the experience of the last two days and nights wore off. She sure did play her cards right while in the possession of her captors. Growing up tough on a ranch and being around all the cowboys seemed to have taught her some mighty important lessons, and those lessons paid off in spades.

Bone weary, his head nodded forward to rest on his chest while the horse trotted towards the village at the Hole. He apparently went clean to sleep, since the first thing he knew was when the guard shouted, "That you again, Black Beard? Thought you was headed for town a while ago."

He rubbed the sleep from his eyes. "I guess this night-owl work is getting to me. The others went on, but I figured it would be a lot quieter here, so turned back. It's a good thing I did....went plumb to sleep on the back of my horse, and him trotting, too. It's a wonder I didn't fall or get brushed off by a tree limb."

A hearty laugh flew from the rocks above. "I done that once. Figure that's why my thinker ain't as good as it used to be. Woke up sprawled flat on the ground with a knot the size of an egg on my noggin. But when I inspected that limb, I couldn't find a blessed bump anywhere on it." He cackled again at his own joke while Colt rode through the entrance and on to the shack where he'd stayed with Hank. After stabling his horse, he walked over to the corral where the extra horses were kept and roped a fresh grulla. It looked to have plenty of bottom and would hold up for the long ride yet ahead. Swinging his saddle to it's back, he tightened the cinches and stepped into leather.

That guard might be some upset, now that he'd pass him for the third time tonight. He debated whether to try and find another way out of the Hole or bluff his way through. Deciding there were just too many miles to cover, he rode for the entrance. Approaching it, he sang out, "You still up there, Jake?" He wanted to get the man talking again to keep his mind off asking where he headed now.

A different voice came back to him and he heaved a sigh of relief. "Jake's probably poundin' his ear and dreamin' bout wimmin. We changed shifts bout fifteen minutes ago. When his head hits the bunk, he's out so far, the roof could cave in on him and he'd still go on snorin'." The man wanted to talk and went right on. "One of the boys comin' back from town tonight said the Lazy J took some shots day fore yesterday. We cain't figger why anyone'd shoot up that place. They's always been decent to us men when we wander their way. Heard tell young Millie got herself packed off by the ones who done it."

This garrulous man could be just the person to give him some information. Colt hooked his leg around the saddle horn and said, "Must be a right sorry bunch who'd kidnap a girl. Where you figure they took her, and what'll Mitch say when he finds out?"

"Hell, weren't none of our bunch what done it...must of been friends of those three what caused the ruckus at our bar the other night. The boys found one of 'em dead the mornin' after. Some think Hank and Ollie must'a done him in. Them other two left the hole long 'fore Hank and Ollie left. Talk is you might know somethin' about it.. Hank took you to his place and it sounded like shots shortly after." The fellow fished for an answer.

If he wanted any information, he better level with the man. "Yeah, I had a hand in that little caper. One of those punks mentioned Mitch set them onto Hank. How you figure that?"

Silence held for a few minutes, then the outlaw answered, "That don't make no sense a'tall. Why, Mitch and Hank pal round like real friends and Mitch leaves Hank in charge when he goes off on a raid. You figger them boys come here to cause trouble amongst us so's we'd be easier to corral by the law?"

"If those men are part of the law, I'll eat my hat. They're mean as a disturbed rattler and twice as dangerous. No, there must be some other reason. But you may be right about them wanting to cause trouble here at the village. Probably some other outlaw with big ideas wants to horn in on the setup you fellers have and figures if he causes trouble between you, he can walk right in and take over."

Silence again ensued while the man chewed on this notion. "Now that you mention it, there's been a few spats between the men that we ain't had in the past. But who in heck would be roddin' such a deal? Sure ain't seen anyone here who aspires to be a kingpin."

Colt popped the main question. "You don't figure Mitch is rodding the deal and wants to replace all you tame boys with some meaner ones, do you?"

"You gotta be loco. Why, Mitch is the best boss I ever rode with. All the men like him. Ain't no way he'd be givin' such orders. Nope, that tough had to be lyin', or else he wanted to put the blame on someone else. His real boss musta put him up to it."

This was the way Colt figured the situation too, but he wanted verification of his feeling. Someone sure wanted to stir things up here on the Strip and used everything he could think of to do it. "You're probably right. Mitch strikes me as a right nice feller as far as outlaws go. Well, I better be riding on...want to see what bank might welcome me again."

This brought a guffaw from the guard. Colt slipped his boot to stirrup and gigged his horse into motion. One thing for sure: those men doing all the recent trouble were following orders given by either Mitch or someone yet unknown, and if he didn't figure who that someone was, he would not solve the reason for his parent's murder. Ollie admitted to being one of the rustlers of the Hasting's cattle, but after knowing Ollie better, he figured murder to be out of his line of work. It still might be Mitch who wanted things changed, but he didn't think so. Next time he saw Mitch he would brace him with this problem and see what happened.

While the horse traveled toward the Lazy J, his head fell to his chest again and he caught a few winks of sleep before the ranch came into view. He pulled to a stop suddenly when he topped the knoll in front. Below were several cavalry mounts tied to the corral fence. Could they be looking for him or were they on another mission? Maybe something more happened in town or at the fort, and they were chasing whoever caused the trouble. Should he poke his nose into this beehive or wait till the detail left? Too many things remained to be done for him to dodge around this bunch of soldiers. Gigging the grulla, he rode on down.

As he approached the front porch, he saw Captain Gregg and Shirley come from the house. They were talking and didn't notice him at first. Pulling to a stop, he swung down from the saddle, wrapping the reins around the hitching post. The Captain must have seen the movement and now shifted to face the intruder. Surprise spread across his face and his hand dropped to the hogleg at his side.

Colt put one boot on the bottom step, looking only at Shirley. "On my way to town ....wanted to see how the Jeffreys are doing. Is it all right if I come in?"

Shirley quickly stepped in front of the Captain. "By all means, Black Beard, I've been hoping you'd show up soon. Jim brought word that Millie is safe, thank goodness. She'll be coming in later with Bob and his men. Mr. Jeffrey woke momentarily and seems pretty aware of what's going on around him, but his wife just lays there, barely breathing."

Colt hurried up the remaining two steps and proceeded through the front door, Shirley right behind him and the Captain's angry glance pasted on their backs. Going directly to the bedroom door, he opened it softly, then tiptoed to the bed. Mr. Jeffrey's eyes opened and settled on him as he approached. Colt pulled the covers down to examine the bandages, then picked up the man's hand and felt his pulse. It was steady and fairly strong. A hand to the man's forehead revealed some fever but not as much as he feared. "I guess it's hard to knock a tough cowhand down for very long with only bullets, Mr. Jeffrey. You're progressing better than I figured you would. Must be this special care Shirley's been giving you."

A frown creased the old man's face. "She's doing a good enough job, but Millie should be here taking care of us, instead of traipsing all around the country with Bob and the men."

Seeing he still didn't know about the abduction of his daughter, Colt went along with the subterfuge. "I left her and Bob a short time before midnight. They caught up with the scoundrels who did this; after catching some shut eye, they'll be back here at the ranch sometime this afternoon. Not one of your men even took a bullet while finishing off all three of those outlaws, Mr. Jeffrey, so you can rest easy and be thankful you have such good men working for you. Your daughter held up her end of the deal like a real lady. You can be proud of Millie--she's a keeper."

A tear left the old man's eye and fought it's way down the wrinkled cheek. "I guess I shouldn't be so rough on her. You say she's staying with Bob and the men? You figure she'll see what that young man is all about and quit making eyes at you, Black

Beard?"

A chuckle left Colt's throat. "You don't have anything to worry about. When I left them, Bob was doing his darndest to correct that situation. Wouldn't surprise me much if those two have something important to say to you sometime in the near future."

Mr. Jeffrey smiled for the first time since being shot. "Son, you don't know how much it means to me. I been hoping for a long time those two would make the connection and if it took getting shot to have it happen, then it's worth it." His eyes rested on his wife. "She wants the same thing. Sure wish she could hear the news you bring, Black Beard. It ain't fair for her to be so close to death at a time like this."

A weak voice issued from beside him. "I heard all you said, Mr. Black Beard, and if my daughter is safe, then I got a reason to live. And my other reason is right here beside me." Her frail hand crept slowly across the quilt until it was met by her husbands.

Shirley moved into the room with a glad cry, "Mabel, there've been times in the last two days when I decided you were checking out the pearly gates. It's so good to hear you talk."

Jeffrey's hand enclosed his wife's and his voice became choked. "Honey, you had me mighty scared for a spell. Hope you don't let us down and kick the bucket later." He tried to grin but it didn't come off right.

Colt stepped to the other side of the bed, checking Mabel's pulse and feeling her forehead, then lifting the sheet to check the bandages. His fingers probed the area around the wound entrance as he spoke to her. "Looks like your gut's healing okay. No swelling or evidence of infection yet. Think you could get around some beef broth if we fixed it for you?"

Her feeble voice showed some spunk. "A steak would sure taste good, but I don't suppose you'd approve of that."

He grinned. "Not yet. You're going to be on a liquid diet for several days till we know for sure everything inside is working well. When it is, you can have all the beef steak you want."

Mr. Jeffrey patted his wife's arm. "I don't know what all you've done for us, Black Beard, but apparently we have you to thank for our life. If there's ever anything we can do for you, we'd sure like to pay you back in some way."

"Just welcome that youngster of yours when she gets back with Bob and your men. They've given everything possible for you during this unfortunate experience, and your daughter will need a lot of understanding for a while. If there's any thanks to be given, it should be to Shirley, who's been at your side constantly." His words were meant especially for Mabel and he felt sure she got his implication.

Captain Gregg stood in the doorway to the bedroom while this conversation went on. It galled him to think these people would be so appreciative of the help of an outlaw, but he held his tongue, knowing he would be the only one feeling this way. His plans to raid the Hole may have to be put off till this young outlaw left the country; he'd be in deep trouble if Black Beard took a bullet in a raid. Sighing inside, he pivoted on his boot heel and left the house. All eyes were on the outlaw anyway, so he might as well get his men and be on his way.

As soon as he saw the Captain leave the room, Colt trailed behind, pausing to speak to Shirley. "I'll be riding into town shortly to check on Betty Jo. Why don't you ride along since Millie will be here to watch these two? Besides, it'll be good for her to have something to occupy her steadily for a while."

"I'm sure you're right...they all need each other. But you needn't worry about Betty Jo--she seemed to be doing very well when I left and the Captain brought his medical man in to check her over. He'll come in from the fort each day to watch her progress." She saw the fatigue in Colt's eyes. "Why don't you take a break and sleep in the bunkhouse for a while after I fix you a good breakfast?"

He reflected on this for just a moment. "The breakfast I'd really appreciate, but there's still Hank to check out and I need to talk to him and Ollie about what's happening here. So as soon as I change horses and stow away the food you fix, I better get traveling." He strode to the front door and stepped to the porch. Going down the steps, he picked up the reins of the grulla and started toward the corral.

The Captain and his men were just swinging to saddle leather as he crossed the yard. His glance settled on the Captain, who left his men and rode toward him. In a low voice the Captain spat out, "I don't know what your game is, Black Beard, but a lot of trouble has come to this range since you stepped foot on it. If I find out you're responsible for any of it, I won't wait for approval to go after you."

Colt's steady gaze never wavered from the grim eyes of the mounted officer. "You're a straight shooter, all right. Thanks for the warning. If I can ever be of genuine service to you, just holler."

His shoulders straightened even more as he glared down at Colt. "That's the only warning you're going to get. And another thing: Shirley thinks she likes you, but don't count on her feelings keeping me from doing my duty."

"I never let a lady interfere with my outlaw work, Captain. When you get ready to haul me off, just make sure your first shot is your best, 'cause it'll be your last." His voice cracked like a rifle shot at the man on horseback.

The challenge lay naked between them. For the first time in his life, the Captain felt he may be in over his head. This man wouldn't back water no matter what came at him. Even though he hadn't so much as indicated a move toward his gun, the Captain knew it wouldn't take much for it to leap into action. The stories told of his speed and accuracy didn't really make for a safe way to finish a day, so without another word the Captain whirled his horse and led his men out of the yard. Colt put his mind on more immediate problems and continued toward the corral.

Catching up one of the ranch cow ponies, Colt changed his saddle, turned the grulla into the corral and led the fresh horse back to the hitching post. The smell of frying meat filled his nostrils as he stepped onto the porch and his mouth started to taste the steak already. He tried to remember when he ate last, but his exhausted brain wouldn't come up with an answer.

Shirley slid a steak onto a plate already half-filled with fried potatoes when she saw him enter the kitchen. "You set and eat while I feed Mabel this broth, then I'd like to talk to you for a moment before you leave."

She hurried from the kitchen as he sat down at the table. Never had a breakfast tasted so good. He felt like a foundered horse when the last bite slipped down his gullet. Groaning with pleasure, he drank the last of the hot coffee as Shirley came through the door.

She uttered a huge sigh and slid onto a chair. "Well, it looks like the news of Millie being all right has done what nothing else could to put Mabel on the mend. She took the broth without any protest at all and now the two of them are talking about what took place. For the first time Mr. Jeffrey knows what horrors his daughter might have experienced. Did she look all right to you, Colt?"

"Other than her dress being torn to shreds from scrambling through the bushes to get away, rope marks and dried blood on her arms, neck and legs, she looked fine. I don't think they had time to do anything more than stash her in the prospector's cabin before going on to the Hole to kill Hank. By the time the two still breathing reported to their boss and got back, she'd managed to escape. It took a toll on her, but she's young and feisty and should come through this with flying colors."

Sitting at the table with him, Shirley sipped her coffee. "Captain Gregg sent in another request to his superiors to let him raid the Hole-in-the-Rock village. He figures if those men are wiped out, the trouble around here will stop." She glanced at him, wanting his opinion.

Colt knew that if he stayed in this chair much longer, his body would drop off to sleep; he stood up and walked to the kitchen window before answering. "It galls the Captain to have to stand by and see the outlaws live like respected citizens here on the Strip. He's military all the way through, and the direct approach has always been the military way to handle things. The problem comes in when his superiors would sooner see the Rangers handle local outlaws and leave the cavalry to take care of the Indian trouble. The Rangers just don't see any sense in risking men's lives on a piece of land that the Arizona Territory doesn't want anyway."

As she contemplated the straight back of this man standing at the window, Shirley felt the desire to take some of the load off his back. "Why don't you wait to see what his answer will be before you kill yourself trying to find the man behind your parent's murders? After all, he has a whole troop of men behind him."

He slapped his pant leg with his floppy brimmed hat. "His superiors won't authorize him to proceed because it would risk the lives of too many men. No, this is a job for one man and I now have the inside track in getting the information I need. All the signs point to Mitch as being the head honcho of this trouble and that's what the Captain thinks, but I figure there's another man behind all this who wants to own the whole Strip country. He can't do that with the ranchers not wanting to give up ownership. He wants the gang to start fighting among themselves so he can replace them with his own cutthroats. These last two bunches of ruthless men were sent in with specific orders and since they failed, more will be sent in. I have to stop things before that happens. I think Hank may hold the answer I'm looking for. That's why I'm so anxious to see him again."

"Surely you don't suspect Hank of being the head man, do you?" Just thinking this sent chills up her spine. Heidi would be devastated if that were the case.

"No, I figure Hank has other reasons to be here on the Strip, which is why he was targeted to be killed. As to what that reason is, I'll have to wait till I see him to find out." Taking a deep breath and letting it out slowly, he turned from the window, giving her a friendly smile. "Thanks for breakfast and all you've done to help out here. When Bob gets back, tell him another attempt may be made on the lives of the Jeffrey clan. He better keep an eye out and a guard posted from now on. If any strangers come anywhere near this place, tell him to give them their walking papers. Another thing: caution Millie to do all the caring for her parents no matter who comes to help. In their weakened condition, it wouldn't take much to push them over the hill, and if that happened all our work would be for nothing."

"What are you talking about? You don't figure someone would be so bold as to come into this ranch and do something like that again?" She held her breath but he just looked at her. "Do you?"

Turning to the door and clamping his hat on his head, he strode toward it. "Yes, I figure another attempt will be made. This ranch is important to whoever is causing the trouble, just as my folks spread is. I wish I knew who for sure is behind this, but for now you must make Millie and Bob understand that they better error on the part of safety. Maybe when I get back from talking to Hank and Ollie, I can shed more light on the subject."

Colt went through the front room with her close behind him, tramped onto the porch, picked up the reins of the horse and stepped to the saddle. He looked at the beautiful girl watching him, and wanted to tell her many things, none of them appropriate. Finally he settled on "Thanks for breakfast. Stay safe, okay?"

The horse showed an interest in running and he gave it its head, letting it run for a mile before hauling on the reins and slowing to a running walk. It would be after dark before they reached the soddy at the edge of the canyon and he figured Buddy would bark his head off when he saw his partner again. The dog would be a welcome sight when they were back together.

19

The air turned blue with curses as Mitch reread the note slipped to him by the waitress. The bank in Colorado proved to be an easy target and his men were happy at the take, but this note spelling out trouble at the Hole and on the Strip sent all his good feelings up in smoke. The sudden change in his attitude alerted his men that something unusual now occupied his thoughts.

Stopping for the night at the trading post at the Gap seemed like a good bet for some shuteye. They were within twenty miles of the Colorado river and once across that, would be on the no-mans land of the Arizona Strip and completely safe from any lawmen who might be chasing them. Looking up at the scarred face of Butch, who sat directly across from him, Mitch read the note out loud. "Black Beard attempted to kill the owners of the Lazy J. He and his men have abducted their daughter Millie. Later the same day he tried to gun down Hank, who hasn't been seen since. This man is very dangerous and seems to want to take over your job of running the Hole gang. Better be careful when you return. I would suggest you shoot first and ask questions later as he will be gunning for you." The signature at the end said 'A friend'.

Butch cleared his throat. "Sounds like real trouble. You figure that note's on the level? Maybe someone's trying to get you into a gunfight."

Pushing his chair back, Mitch stated. "Won't take long to find out. I'll send a wire to the fort. The Captain will know if these things have taken place. If so, I won't waste any words when Black Beard enters my sights."

While they waited for Mitch to get back, his men continued to eat and discuss what this news meant. The meal finished and Mitch still not back, they stepped to the makeshift bar to have a drink. A short time later Mitch came through the door.

He handed a telegram to Butch. It read: "The attempted killings you ask about did take place but it's not sure who the perpetrators of these deeds were. There may be a connection between Black Beard and these actions, but at this point it has not been established." It was signed Captain Gregg.

"Looks like our friend's tip may be true, so we better hightail it back instead of staying here for the night." One thing Mitch figured on was not giving Black Beard the first shot. But why did the man suddenly turn into a killer? So far he showed remarkable ingenuity in getting his work done without causing anyone any real trouble. Could his quick elimination of the men who tried to abduct Betty Jo be part of a show he wanted folks to see? Then, with his reputation secure in their eyes, he'd start to horn in on the gang and take over all of the Strip country for his own reasons?

A fellow just couldn't trust anyone anymore. He admitted Black Beard's actions and his personality set him off from the rest of the men he ruled, and he liked the man. This latest news made a real problem for Mitch. To simply gun the man down the first time he saw him seemed a little harsh. He knew he wouldn't be able to shade Black Beard's draw; he'd have to surprise the man and get the drop, then do his talking.

The lights of the Gap fell to the rear as their horses pounded over the sagebrush covered landscape. Each man carried his own opinion of the message just received. Mitch set a course that would take them to the Ferry, hoping Josh could shed some light on the things that happened. He picked up a lot of gossip from men traveling on the ferry.

A single oil-filled lamp burned at the loading spot on the east side of the river. On the other side, where Josh and his wife lived, everything was obscured by darkness. Pulling hard on the bell ringer to summon the ferry, the men waited till they saw a lantern move out the door of Josh's house and swing back and forth as he walked to the dock. Moments later the light moved across the water and when it drew closer, they saw Josh working the poles that pushed him forward.

Water splashed as the contraption thudded against the bank. Letting down the bars across the entrance to the ferry, Josh hollered. "That you Mitch? Pile on... it's late and I want to get back to bed." A yawn spread his jaws wide.

Prodding their horses, the men rode onto the planking. Josh lifted the bars back into place as he spat a stream of tobacco juice into the water. "You boys being chased and that's why you're in such a all-fired hurry to cross tonight?"

Mitch hitched up his gun belt. "Nope, we got word things been happening here while we been gone. Coming back to get the straight of it. Seems like that Black Beard feller's been raising a little cain at the Lazy J and at the Hole."

Josh spit again, then squinted in the starlight at Mitch. "Ain't heard anything about him causin' any trouble. Fact of the matter is, word from Fredonia says he's been patchin' up those what took the slugs. It's been three, four days now since I got the story, but seems he saved the lives of both the Jefferys, then helped Bob and the Lazy J crew rescue Millie from some ornery cusses. Nothin' since then's been comin' over the desert telegraph. Word's goin' round that he spirited Hank off to a safe place after those same men tried to kill Hank."

Mitch was truly bewildered by this contradictory story. "You sure he ain't the one done all the shooting or at least hired men to do it?"

"You want your head shot off, just mention that to him or any of the Lazy J outfit. They swear he's the only reason things didn't turn out worse than they did. Who's been fillin' you full of bullcrap anyway, Mitch?"

The ferry bumped the west bank and Butch lifted down the bars so horses and men could disembark. "Some feller passed a note by way of a waitress at the Gap saying Black Beard's been causing mayhem at the ranch and the Hole. We reckoned it best to hurry back and get the straight scoop on things." Butch hacked, then spat after he spoke.

His mind in a whirl, Mitch made his decision. "Mind if we bunk here tonight, Josh? Ain't no use killing ourselves getting back if things been quiet for the last three, four days."

A smile creased Josh's features. "Help yourselves to the hay loft. The missus puts grub on the table shortly after daybreak. Now I'm goin' back to bed and if anyone else wants to cross tonight, one of you boys kin do the work." He ambled off as the men headed for the corral to unsaddle, then feed the horses, turning them into the corral.

"Looks like someone is trying to cause trouble between you and Black Beard. You think he wants to get rid of both of you?" Butch drawled as the men settled in the loft.

"Beats the hell out of me. We ain't seen so much happening around this country for ages, then soon as Black Beard shows up, all hell breaks loose. Must be something to do with him person-ally. Anyway, I ain't going to give him first shot. Figure to corral him first, then find out what he has to say." Mitch tipped his hat down over his eyes and settled into the straw. Soon he was sound asleep.

Sun rays spilling through the cracks of the barn walls splat-tered on Mitch's face, and he came instantly awake, hearing a horse snorting out front. Slapping on his hat, he shimmied down the ladder to the barn floor and poked his head out the double door. Three Navajo's were watering their horses in the watering trough as Josh stood by talking in their native language to them. All four men seemed to talk about as much with their hands as they did with their mouths.

Mitch strolled toward them, trying to make out from the hand movements what the gist of the matter was. He caught the words 'Black Beard' coming from Josh's mouth but the Indians didn't seem to know who he talked about. Shrugging their shoulders, they mounted and rode off in the direction of the Kaibab.

When Mitch got close, Josh said, "Those three come in bout once a week to stock up on supplies, then head back the way they come. Hard to get anything out of them. I speak pretty good Navajo but when I ask, they just shrug their shoulders and talk about somethin' else. Well, don't suppose they're up to anything what would cause trouble. They been round for several months and I ain't heard of any problems from 'em."

Mitch furrowed his brow as he digested this. "What did they know about Black Beard? I heard you mention his name."

"Didn't know a thing bout anyone called that. Said if there was such a man, he must be one of the bad men livin' at the Hole-in-the-Rock." Josh spat a stream of tobacco juice which splattered on the center of a flat rock.

"I heard by the grapevine about some Indians fixing up the Hasting's place...must be what those three are doing. You ain't seen the Hastings come back from the east yet, have you, Josh?"

"Can't figure that out either, those folks been gone a long time. Makes me wonder if somethin' mighta happened to them. You get back in that eastern country and some kook is liable to bash you over the head and take all your money." Josh just couldn't figure why the couple stayed away when Indians were working on their ranch. Someone must be giving those workers orders and supplying them with money to pay for supplies.

"Think me and the men'll swing by their place on our way to Fredonia...might stumble on the answer to where the Hastings are." Changing the subject he inquired, "Your missus still have food available? We slept later than I wanted."

"Yep, still got plenty. We figured you'd eat with us. 'Sides, we never know who for sure might show up here and want to chow down."

Mitch strolled back to the barn to buttonhole his men while Josh headed to the house. He almost made it before the bell rang on the other side of the river. Glancing that way, he saw a wagon with two people sitting on its seat, waiting to be picked up. Grumbling, he stepped to the ferry and shoved it across. When the wagon pulled aboard, he commented, "Ain't seen you people in this neck of the woods before. Just travelin' through or planning on stayin' somewheres on the Strip?"

Words grudgingly pinched through the thin lips of the tallest man. "Got a load of flour, salt, and sugar for the fort at Pipe Springs. Kinda figured there might be a detail of soldiers here to meet us. You seen any around?"

Scratching his head, Josh took a minute before answering. "Hasn't been any soldiers here for several months, and that ain't normal. They're supposed to check on the Injuns sometimes. Guess things been poppin' on the Strip too much for 'em to come this way. But the last few days it's quieted down. They'll git here 'fore long."

When the ferry touched the west bank, Josh took down the poles and the driver slapped the reins, causing the horses to move out at a brisk pace. Josh hollered at them, inviting them to breakfast, but the team didn't even slow. Shrugging his shoulders, he tied the ferry in place then hoofed it to the house. Mitch and his men were just getting up from the table. "Reckoned we better chow down before those other two got here. We'll be on our way. Thanks for the meal and the information, Josh." Mitch clapped his hat on, heading for the door.

Josh's words stopped him. "Those two didn't even stop to say thanks. Said they was takin' a load of supplies to the fort at Pipe Springs, but they sure didn't look like army men. Well, guess it's none of my business. You be careful what you say about Black Beard, Mitch, and you'll live a lot longer." He cackled as he set down at the table.

While they worked on getting the horses saddled, then riding out, Mitch mulled things over in his mind. How should he approach Black Beard? It still seemed the best way would be to corner him and get his side of the story. But if he was the one causing all the problems, what could Mitch do without getting himself in a pack of trouble? Looked like he was caught between a rock and a boulder.

His mind rolling this problem over and over, he missed the significance of the wagon tracks leaving the trail to Fredonia. Butch mentioned it several minutes later. "Thought those men on the wagon were headed to the fort. Looked more like they were going toward the Lazy J."

At first his words didn't sink in, then Mitch hauled back on his horse's reins, causing the animal to rear up and almost unseat his rider. "What you figure they went that way for?"

All three were stopped now, looking off in the direction the wagon had traveled. A small dust cloud lay along the ground a couple of miles out. "Something ain't cut the way it's supposed to be," Mitch stated as he gigged his horse to overtake the wagon.

Normally a wagon would stop if men came up to it, but this one increased its pace as the sound of the horses coming up behind reached the ears of the driver. Mitch motioned his two men to ride on up and talk to the two on the seat, taking their attention off him as he rode to the tailgate and pulled the flap back on the cover. The wagon appeared to be loaded to the top with boxes and sacks of flour. He left his saddle to climb inside but still held on the reins. Inserting his knife into one of the sacks marked flour, black granules of gunpowder ran out. He whistled softly, then jumped back to his saddle and rode to the front of the wagon.

His gun rested on the saddle horn as he pulled up beside the team of horses. "You boys mind telling me where you're going with all that black powder?"

One man reached for his rifle but Butch pulled it from his hands before he could swing it into position. "Mitch figures you boys owe him an explanation. Forget the firearms and pull that team to a stop," Butch growled.

Three guns now covered the two men on the seat. Mitch leaned forward and spoke casually, "You told Josh you were carrying a load of flour to the fort. But those sacks marked flour are full of gun powder. There's probably rifles in the boxes under the sacks, don't you think?"

The tall man shrugged. "If you're the Mitch that rods the Hole gang, then you should know what's in the wagon. Black Beard said you'd be giving these rifles to the Indians when they came to wipe out the Lazy J."

Silence held them, so intense you could hear the prairie grass rustle. The three with guns in their hands sat momentarily stunned. Mitch finally bit out, "You telling a windy, mister?"

"If you ain't the Mitch I mentioned, then it ain't none of your business what we're carrying or where we're taking it."

Sputtering, Mitch tried to get the hang of this suprising information. "Where'd you see Black Beard last?"

Lifting his hat to scratch his head, the tall man whined, "Didn't see him at all. Our instructions came from a letter delivered at the Holbrook post office. The envelope contained the directions and five thousand dollars for us to do the hauling. The guns are old flintlocks....won't do the Indians much good. We figure most of them will blow up in their faces when fired."

Butch butted in. "Something sure as hell is going on around this neck of the woods while we been traveling, Mitch. That man's name comes up a little too often to suit me. He'd only cause a lot of trouble with the Indians and the ranchers if these guns get to where he wants them."

"It ain't a going to get where he wants them till I figure what's his reasons. Now you two climb down and cut those two horses from the wagon. You can ride them back to where you came from. You sure ain't going any farther with this load of trash."

His gun centered on the tall man's chest. The man narrowed up his eyes, then shrugged, climbing down from the seat and cutting out one of the horses. He mounted while the other man did the same. "Don't make no difference to me. We delivered the load to a man named Mitch and that's all we were asked to do."

Dust from the two draft horses kicked up, then settled back to earth. The three outlaws sheathed their guns and sat staring at the wagon. "If that don't beat all. Someone wasted a lot of money on this gig and I mean to get to the bottom of it. Leave the wagon---it ain't going nowhere. We better line out for town. I want to get my hands on that Black Beard skunk as soon as possible." Mitch was so mad he could chew nails and spit them in the man's face one at a time.

Sweat dripped from men and horses when they pulled up in front of the saloon in Fredonia. Shadows lengthened as the last rays of the setting sun dipped below the western hills and darkness slowly settled down. Throwing reins over the hitching post, Mitch darted through the swinging doors. Eyes flashed around the room, hoping to spot the man whose neck he wanted to wring. No such luck. The place contained only five people, all of them clean shaven. Stomping angrily to the bar, he ground out, "Where's that no-good rat that has the name Black Beard hung on him?"

Not even the tinkle of a glass answered him as shock froze everyone to their seats. His two men shouldered through the batwings, breaking the spell. The bartender coughed. "You better have a big drink of whiskey if you plan to tackle that feller, Mitch. What's got you so riled up anyway?"

Mitch took the drink in one gulp when Pike set it before him. "You tell me where he is so I can blast him to the hereafter. That dirty polecat's got bats in his belfry and I intend to let 'em out."

Butch pushed up to the bar, signaling Pike to pour him a drink. "You been pushing awfully hard to get here, Mitch, and I know you been simmering worse and worse the whole time. But Black Beard stands pretty high around this here burg. Don't you think we better tread a little more careful?"

The glass slammed on the bar top. "That friend sure hit the nail on the head when he said to shoot first and ask questions after, and that's just what I aim to do. Then it'll be too late for anyone to do anything about it." The words left Mitch's mouth in a blast of fury.

The swoosh of swinging doors punctuated his statement. " I

hear you want to see me, Mitch. That fits my plans too. I figure any boss who sets his segundo up for a back-shooting is pretty low on the list of savory people." Colt's words dropped sharply into the frigid air. He stood with hand just above the Colt forty-four-forty nestled in its holster. Buddy stood by his feet with his lip curled and the hair on his back standing straight.

Mitch's head spun around and his body followed, hand dropping to the butt of the six-gun hung low on his thigh. Mitch was fast and he knew it, but the surprise he wanted to pull over his opponent didn't come off. His gun barely cleared leather when something struck him heavily in the chest. His body drove viciously back against the bar, then bounced off and his face met the sawdust of the barroom floor. A curl of thin smoke trickled up from the barrel of the six-gun in Colt's hand.

Butch quailed as he remained facing the back bar mirror. He could see the reflection of that deadly gun swivel in his direction and he wanted no part of it. Words as sharp as a knife on whetstone crossed the space of the barroom. "You two figure to let it ride as it stands?"

Looking into those steely eyes shining in the mirror, Butch let his words out easy. "Don't get on the prod, Black Beard. I got no quarrel with you." He motioned to the body on the floor. "Mitch got a note from a friend which claimed you been causing all sorts of trouble here while we was gone. It said to shoot first and ask questions later when he saw you. We stopped that load of gunpowder and rifles you sent for from getting to the Indians so's they could raid the Lazy J. Mitch wouldn't listen to reason after that."

His voice dry as gunpowder, Colt said, "Butch, you boys better stand easy."

The bore of the six-gun muzzle disappeared so fast it made Butch blink and Colt moved rapidly across the floor to kneel by the side of Mitch. His hands moved swiftly to cut the shirt away from the gaping hole in the man's chest. Eyes that were halfway to hell settled on him as he worked. Weak words split Mitch's lips. "What you mean about me having Hank shot?"

Those hands never so much as hesitated in their work. "Shorty said you sent him to the Hole to gun down Hank." He ripped his bandana off, plastering it against the bleeding entrance hole. "Butch, hand me that bottle of whiskey."

A puzzled expression crossed the face of Mitch. "Who's Shorty?" could barely be heard escaping from his mouth. Then his body arched and a last gasp fluttered into the air above him.

The bottle of whiskey still rested in the hand of Butch. He knelt beside Colt. "Black Beard, we've been fed a line a mile long and it looks like you bit on the same bait. I tried to get Mitch to go easy when we found you, but whoever cooked this up played his cards too well. He succeeded in eliminating at least one of you and I bet a pretty penny your number will come up next in his tally book." He glanced into now soft eyes as he spoke.

"It sure seems like the rope is tangled pretty bad, all right. Someone's trying mighty hard to get things in a real uproar with you men at the Hole." Standing up, Colt motioned Butch to follow him as he hurried toward the door, Buddy at his heels.

His stride covered the ground between the saloon and the hotel rapidly, Butch sticking tight with him. It didn't even slow till the door to Colt's room stopped them. Twisting the knob, Colt pushed it open. When they stepped inside, Hank and Ollie stared back at them.

The real shocker to Butch was the Ranger badge plastered to Hank's left shirt pocket. "Howdy, Butch. Heard a gun shot a few moments ago...that your doing?" Hank studied the man closely.

Colt broke in. "Mitch went for his gun as soon as I stepped foot in the barroom. Seems we'd been set up for a shoot-out between us."

Hank's eyes shifted to Colt. "Guess you were right to sneak us into the hotel just at daybreak this morning, and keep us hid all day till you saw Mitch and the boys ride in. You got any bright idea as to who set you up?"

Going over to the window, Colt stood looking out while the three men stared at his back, waiting for his answer. Words drifted quietly to them. "If only Mitch had waited long enough to talk things over, we might have come up with an answer and he'd still be alive."

A somber mood persisted in the room as each man locked onto his own thoughts. Buddy jumped to the bed, lying down to wait for his master to come to a decision. Then Butch broke the silence. "So you been undercover here on the strip, Hank. You played things right tight-- none of us got an inkling as to your real mission. But if someone sent this man Shorty to kill you, the brains behind all this trouble must've picked up a slip of yours somewhere."

Hank swore softly. "That's hard to figure. There ain't been a time when I let anything out of the bag. Colt here guessed it on his ride from the Hole to his place, but it wasn't because of any slip I made. He just figured it out. The man behind all this wanted me dead so I couldn't continue to operate undercover in the gang."

Hanging on the name 'Colt', Butch swung his eyes to Colt and a light went on in his skull. "So, you're the Hastings boy. Mitch's been wondering what happened to you and your folks. We intended to swing by your place today, but when we saw the tracks of that wagon carrying the gun powder and rifles, we kinda forgot all about it. How's the folks doing, anyway? They sure been gone a long time."

Still standing watching the street, Colt's brain slipped into gear as Ollie answered Butch's question. "His parents was gunned down on the road back from Flagstaff. He finished off the killers, then set out to join the gang to see who put the killings into play. It's still a mystery---none of us at the hole knew anything about it. Everything pointed to Mitch cuz we thought he sent Shorty to kill Hank. Guess we all been pretty well bamboozled."

Colt swung around and his words bit the air. "You said those guns were headed to the Lazy J. I knew he'd make another try at the ranch when his first went haywire. Shirley left this morning to go check on the Jeffreys; she'll run right smack into it. Why didn't I tumble to the answer before? That man's been stuck in our faces all the time and we didn't even get a whiff of his stink." Colt ran for the door as he spoke. "Butch, head for the Hole as fast as a horse will carry you. We'll need all the fire power we can muster and those boys are used to gun talk. Bring all you can and meet me at the Lazy J. Hank, I hate to ask you to ride but this time we'll need the authority you carry." He was out the door as his last words rushed back to them.

By the time the three of them reached the porch of the hotel, Colt's horse pounded up the street, kicking dust back at those who stood staring after him. Hank took charge fast. "Butch, make tracks. We'll trail after Colt. He's somehow figured out who the culprit is and apparently he's a mighty big fish, or he wouldn't care about me and my badge. Ollie, let's get a move on or we'll miss the fireworks."

All three of them began running for horses. Butch knew his horse wouldn't take another fast ride, so after pulling the reins from the hitching post, he vaulted to the saddle, angling for the stable. By the time he reached it Ollie and the livery man, who'd done Hank's horse for him, were just finishing tightening cinches. The liveryman kept staring at the badge on Hank's shirt.

"Who you figure it is, Hank?" Butch wanted to know as he vaulted from his saddle.

"How in hell would I know? He ain't told me none of his suspicions. Besides, I figure it hit him while he stood staring out the window."

As his horse sprinted along the dusty road in the semi-dark, Ollie right beside him, Hank's eyes roamed the walks of the town to see what might have tipped Colt off. Only the usual folks appeared on the streets: a few business men, some ladies, hangers out at the bar, prospectors, and a soldier. Nothing else claimed his vision and the outskirts of Fredonia soon sank behind his pounding horse.

20

Nothing rests the soul of a western person quite as much as an early morning ride through the cool desert country. The air still has a little nip to it as the night shadows drift into oblivion and the sun begins to warm the trees and rocks dotted over the surface of this part of the earth. Usually the animals who call this their home are finished with their night's prowl and hunt a place to hide and rest for the day. Woodchucks and prairie dogs set at the edge of their holes, ready to dart back inside if their sniffing of the air warrants it. The deer that have not yet moved to higher ground are seeking the shade of a tree where they will rest till shortly before sunset, unless something disturbs them sooner. Cattle, having chewed their cud all night, get up to graze on the grass growing between the rocks and the sagebrush. Birds begin to sing their songs, fluff their wings, and hunt for food. Chipmunks and mice scurry between tufts of wheatgrass, seeming to be as busy as the bees nosing into the wild flowers opening to the sun. Today a hawk, wings flashing in the sun, circled lazily above the earth, heedful of the woman and horse crossing its land.

The clip-clop of the horse's hooves beating almost in time with the rhythm of her heart, Shirley rode relaxed in the saddle, humming a happy tune. Colt, with Hank sporting a Ranger badge and Ollie trailing behind, had come into the hotel just as she left her room to catch and saddle. He suggested she go on with her plans to visit the Lazy J. He wanted to keep Hank out of sight till he saw the lay of the land in town. When the proper time came, Hank would make it known to the folks living here that the Rangers were working on their problem.

After stowing Hank and Ollie in one of the bedrooms, and checking on Betty Jo, Colt took Shirley aside to tell her about his talk with the two men. His hand laid gently on her arm as they moved down the hall and when he stopped, she'd turned toward him. What happened next took both of them by surprise. Her turn brought her around, his hand still in place, and only inches separated them. The next instant she was in his arms and their lips met. His beard scratched her cheeks slightly, but the happiness filling her soul didn't let a little thing like that keep her from enjoying the moment.

When they pulled apart, he stuttered, "Um...uh...well, now that Hank's going to show his badge openly, it may flush the man we want out of his hole. He'll realize killing Hank will only bring more Rangers into the fray. At least that's what we hope will happen." His eyes remained on hers, saying what his heart felt but his mouth was incapable of.

Leaning back in his arms, she smiled hopefully at him. "Maybe once this is over you can think about something other than finding the man responsible for your parent's death." That statement sure charged the air with a different flavor and she wished she could recall the words, but happiness at his kiss caused her to think of their future together.

"I'm counting on it, but as long as that stares me in the face, I don't have any right to kiss you. I might be his next target for saving Hank's life. I can't mix you up with me till this is over." He turned reluctantly from her to go back to the room where Hank and Ollie waited.

"Colt, with Hank on the Strip in an official capacity, you could leave the trouble to him." She simply didn't want anything to happen to this man now that a lawman would be on the job. Her words brought him around.

"Hank didn't lose his parents to this vicious killer. It's my fight much more than his and I aim to stick with it till my forty-four slug tears out his gut." Those steely eyes bored into her and she winced.

Not giving up, she tried one more time. "Sometimes vengeance can cause a man to rot in his own skin, Colt. Please let Hank handle this from here on out. You don't need another killing on your conscience."

One last glance passed between them, then he turned to the door of Hank's room, slipping inside. She walked back up the hall berating herself for spoiling the moment they spent in each others arms. All that could be done now would be to pray for things to turn out for the best. This thought brought back the feel of his lips on hers and she left the hotel humming the tune she now hummed as the horse carried her toward the Lazy J. Despite his last words, her heart sang for joy. He would be hers once his vengeance rested.

Endless miles drifted behind as a slight breeze ruffled her hair and cooled the horse. Reaching the north end of the Kaibab, she figured there remained only about six or seven miles to the Lazy J. Her glance lifted and what she saw caused her to pull abruptly on the reins, bringing the horse to a hasty stop.

Smoke billowed into the air from the direction of the Bar H. Oh, no. The Hasting's place lay under that cloud of rising smoke. Spurring her horse, she raced toward it. Then reason took over. In this clear morning air the smoke looked close, but she knew a good thirty miles separated her present location from the ranch. By the time she reached there, nothing would be gained. Pulling to a stop, she watched till the smoke died down. Should she change plans and go back to town to alert Colt? What could he do at this late time? Her purpose in riding to see how the Jeffrey clan were making out still needed to be done. By now early afternoon had settled over the earth, so she might as well continue on.

Dropping from the pines, she saw a dust cloud traveling across the flat in the direction of the Lazy J and it seemed to enclose several horsemen. As she watched the somehow ominous shroud move along, she decided it was coming from the Hasting's spread. Would it be the ones who set the fire, or someone who went to check on the cause of the smoke? Aiming her horse so she would remain hidden from the riders but would intercept them after a time, she rode carefully.

It took almost two hours for their paths to cross and by the time the riders were within two miles of her, she began to see flashes of light off metal objects in the group. Surprise lit her face when she finally recognized them as soldiers. Moments later the men drew closer and she saw Captain Gregg leading seven troopers. He must have been traveling in the area and seeing the smoke, went to investigate. Moving from her hiding place in the trees, she waited for them to arrive.

Captain Gregg spurred ahead of his men, coming up beside her. "Shirley, what are you doing riding in this neck of the woods? Some of those riffraff could still be around, and they wouldn't hesitate to carry you off like they did Millie."

Her hand touched the rifle in the boot on her saddle. "Old Betsy here might have something to say about it. Besides, I'm on my way to the Lazy J to check how they're doing. The smoke on the horizon stopped me and brought me in this direction. Looked like it might be the Hasting's ranch house."

His eyes narrowed. "You're right about that. We think the Hole-in-the-Rock gang must have raided the place. There were three dead Indians lying around the burning buildings when we got there. The tracks of the men doing the killing led toward the Lazy J, so we cut straight across country in the hopes of beating them there. Horses are pretty wore out, but it can't be too far to their ranch. We better hurry on."

Ranging her horse along side his, they hurried away before the other soldiers caught up to them. The pace didn't make talking easy as the horses pounded over the land. Riding up the far side of the knoll in front of the Lazy J, they were met by Barney with a rifle in the crook of his arm. The rifle came up to stop the progress of the riders, until he recognized Shirley under her white Stetson, then the gun muzzle lowered as they stopped.

Shirley spoke first. "Barney, I came out to check on the Jeffery's. Black Beard will be out later to see how the healing is progressing."

Staring up at her, Barney hesitated a moment. "Guess it's okay for you folks to go on in. Black Beard gave orders to keep everyone away from the ranch, but I guess the Captain and his men are safe. You go right on, but Millie won't let anyone else see her parents... only you, Shirley."

Captain Gregg spoke up, "The Bar H burned to the ground today and the three Indians staying there were killed. So you keep a sharp eye on our back trail, Barney. The tracks leading away from the Bar H pointed this way."

Surprise crossed Barney's face. "You mean the place was fired a second time? Why that sure beats all. Those Indians almost had the place rebuilt from the last time it got burned out."

"You mean the place burned before this? I didn't know about it. Sure didn't see any sign of the Hastings anywhere around. We haven't been down this way in a long time. You know where the Hastings are, Barney?"

"No sir, they been gone a long time. Most folks figure they went back east to pick up their son from school, but with so much time passing since they left, I reckon something happened to them. After the first time the place burned to the ground, those three Indians showed up and started rebuilding, but I ain't seen anyone else around there. Course I only ride that way occasionally to see if the owners are back yet."

"Well, we better get on down to the house. You stay alert now, Barney. Fire three shots if you see those killers coming this way. You should be able to spot their dust cloud before long."

They rode on into the ranch yard to see Millie sitting on the front porch. Shirley started to swing down from her horse. Millie bounded out of her chair. Slamming through the front door, she pushed it shut with a bang. Momentarily taken back by this sudden disappearance, Shirley dismounted and almost stumbled on the first step. What in the world had set her off?

"You and your men might as well water up and hang around the corral while I see what's up with the Jeffreys, Captain." Shirley hurried into the house. The front room was empty. A deathly silence enveloped her.

Stepping to the bedroom door, Shirley twisted the knob, trying to push the door open. It wouldn't give an inch. Millie's words came harshly through the panel. "Ain't none of you going to get in this room. I got a double-barrel scatter gun and the first one tries to get in here gets it plumb center."

Dumfounded by this sudden turn of events, Shirley spoke through the door, using a soothing tone. "What's got into you, Millie? Black Beard sent me out to check on you folks. He'll be along later."

No answer was forthcoming.. Shirley pushed on the door again.

"Why did you ride in with those killers?" Millie's words were almost a sob.

This young lady must be reliving her abduction and wasn't about to let any man near her. "Millie, you know I took care of your folks after they were shot. I wouldn't do harm to any of you."

"Answer me. Why did you ride in with those killers?" The words from the other side of the door finally got through to Shirley.

"I don't know who you're talking about, Millie. I met the Captain and his men about six miles from the ranch. They were coming from the Bar H, which was burned out again. We rode in together. The Captain thinks the ones who burned the Hastings place are headed this way."

Silence again ensued. "You didn't get a look at the men he has with him, did you, Shirley." Millie didn't wait for an answer. "I don't know what the Captain's slant is on this, but those men are cut from the same mold as the ones shot up this place and took me with them, and they ain't getting anywheres near this room! When Black Beard gets here, he'll take care of those so-called soldiers."

Now it became Shirley's turn to remain quiet as the significance of what she just heard began to settle on her. How could this be? Captain Gregg wouldn't let killers in his cavalry. "Millie, I didn't even look at the soldiers when I met them. You sure you know what you're saying?"

"You ain't been run off with, Shirley. If you had, you'd know those men ain't any part of the cavalry. They're here to finish the job their friends started the other day, and I'll fill the whole bunch of them full of buckshot if they even attempt to get in here."

Standing by the door, Shirley tried to make head or tails of this conflict. Nothing made sense to her at all, but Millie certainly would stand by her convictions. Deciding she better go outside and get a look at those men for herself, she turned from the door. Captain Gregg stood just inside the front door and the look on his face slammed into Shirley like a haymaker thrown by a boxer. Then he drew the curtain over his eyes as he spoke. "Millie must be pretty upset to act that way. You don't think there's any sense to what she's saying, do you?"

It took unbelievable will power to keep a straight face as she turned toward the fireplace where a rifle lay on the mantel. Slowly walking to it, her head down so he wouldn't be able to read her intentions, she answered him. "We've been friends every since I came into the Strip, Captain. A young lady like Millie takes a long time to adjust after what she went through. It isn't any wonder she's showing a little scared right now, with all these men around the place."

As she reached the fireplace, she let her arm rest nonchalantly on the mantel beside the rifle. Thoughts were rushing through her brain like wildfire. The Captain did everything by the book and since he couldn't get any orders from his superiors to wipe out the Hole gang, maybe if he caused enough trouble here on the Strip, they'd finally have to send him what he wanted. But would he go so far as to kill innocent people in order to achieve this? For some reason, even as close as the two of them had been, she'd never felt entirely comfortable with him. Something kept nagging her when she was around him and she ascribed this to his strict adherence to Cavalry rules. Now she tried to look at it all in a new light. Millie stood up to her misfortune without a quibble, so she wasn't spitting in the wind with her actions now. The look on Captain Gregg's face verified that when she had suddenly turned from the door to face him.

His voice cut through her thoughts as his arm also rested on the mantel. "You don't believe all that hogwash she's dishing out, do you?"

Her eyes on the burned logs in the fireplace, Shirley hesitated to answer till she felt the control necessary to speak. They reminded her of the burned logs of the Hasting's ranch house when she first met Colt. If only he were here beside her now, she would feel perfectly safe, but he wouldn't show up till morning at least. He'd be busy with Hank and they didn't know the Captain was really the man they wanted.

When she delayed and didn't look or speak to him, Gregg answered his own question and his voice was cold as death. "So you're against me too. Well, it won't make any difference; the Chaplin at the fort will marry us as soon as we get through here. Then you won't be able to testify against your husband. Once I wipe out the Hole gang with the troops that will be sent to me, I'll be promoted to General and will have total control of all this Strip country."

She couldn't believe it...the man was mad, wanting absolute power over everything and everybody. Anything, even death, would be better than married to a mad man. Her decision moved her to action, and her hand darted up, grasping the rifle and pulling it down from its perch. Her other hand grabbed the lever, jacking a live shell into the chamber. The muzzle came up centering on Gregg's chest as he flinched back, stabbing a hand to his gun. It didn't help any that the holster flap still secured the gun in place.

Her finger tightened on the trigger as a heavy force slammed her right shoulder, spinning her around. The slug from her rifle ricocheted off the stone fireplace and spanged into the ceiling. The gun dropped from her right hand, hanging by the barrel held in her left one. Gregg reached over and snatched it from her. For a moment she thought he would bring it crashing down on her head. His eyes spit fire and brimstone at her. Then he pushed the muzzle into her stomach, causing her to fall on the couch.

"You won't be so all-fired handy with a gun once we tie the knot. You'll do exactly like I say. I keep men in their place all the time and it won't be any trouble at all to do the same with you." Never in all her life had she seen such a wild look on a man's face.

Her left hand went up to her shoulder to assess the damage done by the heavy pistol slug smashing into her. When the slug spun her around, she'd glimpsed one of his soldiers standing in the open front door, a smoking gun in his hand. Tears of frustration almost came to her eyes as she considered how close she came to killing this terrible man in front of her, but she held them back, hoping she would somehow get another chance to finish the job.

Showing her mettle, she hissed at him, "Bob and his men will hear that shot and come running. You won't have a chance to leave this place alive."

His sardonic laugh, edged with a glint of wrath, made her skin crawl, but she managed to gain control, even though his words unsettled her. "My men have already pulled the fangs of the crew, so don't think they'll give you any protection. When this place goes up in smoke, every last man will go with it. You better get used to the idea of obeying your future husband."

"You can try, but when the Chaplin asks if I take this man to be my husband, I'll spit in your face, Gregg." Her whole body vibrated in quiet fury.

Totally ignoring this statement, he unexpectedly changed the subject. "You mentioned that Black Beard will be here later. When do you expect him?"

She wanted desperately to tell him to go to hell. She could

taste the words---slightly bitter, but oh, so sweet, as they lay on her tongue---when, with extreme reluctance, she bit them back. It would only anger him---make him certain Black Beard was on his way, then a trap would be set when he came riding unsuspecting into the ranch.

Calming herself, she replied, "He has a lot of things to do in town with Hank...it may be several days before he arrives." She wanted to shock this man in front of her, so she continued, "Hank is an Arizona Ranger sent here to stop the trouble on the Strip. He and Black Beard are organizing the townspeople to go after you and your men."

This bluff didn't even faze the Captain. "Don't get your hopes up. Hank thinks Mitch is behind all this trouble and Mitch will be gunning for Black Beard with the intent to shoot first and talk later. That smug outlaw will be six feet under soon, if he isn't already. Besides, that's why I sent my men after Hank. It took a while, but it finally came to me what Hank's real purpose was in joining the gang. He'll try to arrest Mitch but it won't do him any good---Mitch is too fast for Hank."

Her mind tried not to grasp his words, but they pounded in her ears. Somehow he must have managed to get Colt and Mitch to shoot it out. How did he work such things and still stay in the background with no one knowing he was so evil? Now he'd wipe the Lazy J off the map, then take on the gang and Mitch would be eliminated. No one would be able to stop him.

He turned from her and spoke to the man in the doorway, taking the rifle with him. "Secure the ranch. Make sure all the men stay alert. I don't think Black Beard will ever get here, but just in case I want a guard kept at all times. Shirley told Millie he wouldn't show till later--that probably means at least not before morning, but don't take any chances. Did you relieve Barney on the knoll of his guard duty?"

The man slouching in the doorway smirked. "Weren't no trouble at all. One of the men took him up a drink of whiskey, knocked him over the head and took his place as guard."

"Get the cook to fixing up something for the men to eat. We'll keep everyone around till we see if Hank, Mitch, or Black Beard show up. Want the place to look as natural as ever when that happens."

Stepping back to Shirley, he growled, "Get in the kitchen and fix some food for us. Don't mind Millie and her parents... we'll leave them there till this is over. Since they don't have long to breathe, they can stay behind that door and starve till the fire cooks them."

Shirley took the handkerchief from her pocket, pushing it against the bullet wound in her shoulder. It hadn't bled much and there was no exit wound; the bullet must have lodged against one of the bones. Because she couldn't move that arm without severe pain, she figured the bone broke when it stopped the slug. "I suppose you and your men set fire to the Hasting's place."She made no effort to get up.

"Just like we're going to do here. When the wagon load of guns and powder arrive, we'll scatter the guns all over and fire the buildings with black powder. It'll look like the crew put up a terrible fight against Indians and gang members. Those power guys back in Washington will fall all over themselves getting more troops in here to clean up the mess, once they hear the Indians and gang have joined forces."

"How can a Captain in the service be such a cold-blooded killer? It seems impossible that you could put on such a goody-goody front when all the time you were plotting and killing. I suppose when I saw you in town the morning the three toughs rode through, you met them to give them orders to raid this ranch."

"You bet I did! I met them outside of town and gave instructions to kill everyone here. They took it on themselves to abduct Millie. I guess when they saw her, the temptation just overpowered them. Now get moving. I told you to get in the kitchen and fix some grub. You want me to poke this rifle barrel in that bullet hole in your shoulder, or are you going to move when I speak?"

She might as well do what he wanted for now, at least Millie still had control of one room in the house. Thank goodness for her quick action when she saw the outlaw soldiers. Anything could happen as long as there was one ace in the hole. Getting up, she stumbled into the kitchen, letting her feet drag as though the wound made her weak. It didn't take much acting since she wanted to fall to the floor anyway. A good heavy frying pan in her hand could put the Captain away for awhile, or hot coffee in his face might work wonders.

21

The cool night air pushed against Colt as he plunged through the darkness, riding as fast as possible toward the Lazy J. His mind worked at the many pieces of the puzzle, trying to fit each piece into its proper place. As the different pieces came to mind, he chewed on them for a while, wondering if he were fitting everything in right. Seeing that lone soldier on the street this morning triggered the answer to his question. The Captain's strict adherence to cavalry rules must have been a burden on him for a long time, to force him to such drastic measures. It seemed easy to understand now why he wanted to apprehend every outlaw coming into the strip. They were men who could come and go as they pleased and he, being tied down by regulations, resented it. Somewhere along the line he'd come up with a plan to solve that little problem, and so far it was working like clockwork. The only fly in the ointment might be his not knowing what happened to the Hastings.

His success in setting Mitch and himself up for a shoot-out succeeded just as well as the rest of his plans. Hank must have tipped his hand somewhere along the line, or else the Captain got some classified information through his army connections. The latter being more likely because Hank played his cards close to his vest. That wagon loaded with guns and gunpowder not showing up as he planned should slow him up for a short time, but at the most would cost him less than a day. He apparently wanted to use it in disposing of everyone living on the Lazy J.

These thoughts began to rub against Colt's patience. Would he arrive in time at the Lazy J? If he did, how could he stall the Captain, being one man against how many troopers? This brought up the question of how many men the Captain would have with him. By process of elimination, Colt tried to figure the answer. Most of the soldiers at the fort were honest-to-God cavalry, not cold blooded killers, so that eliminated a lot of them from consideration. Those with the Captain would be similar to the ones who shot up the Lazy J and abducted Millie, and tried the same with Betty Jo. They were probably former soldiers who were kicked out of the service. A record of all those men would be available to the Captain, but how many of them did he locate and enlist in this task? Already thirteen of that stripe had been eliminated. There may be less than another ten left, surely not more than a couple of dozen. But so far his assumptions were only guesses. His thinking occupied his time to the extent that when he finally became aware of what part of the Strip he traveled over, he figured there were only a couple of miles to the top of the knoll in front of the ranch house. Pale light outlining the hills in the east told him his travels used up all of the night. Would Shirley be all right, or had the Captain already arrived and made his move? This thought brought an ache to his heart. What a crime if the two of them found each other, only to be separated by an evil force like the Captain and his men. The feel of her in his arms still reposed quietly at the back of his consciousness. Momentarily his eyes closed, trying to draw courage from that feel.

The horse unexpectedly came to a halt and as his eyes opened fully, he saw six breach clothed red men surrounding it. The one grasping the bridle of Colt's horse sported two feathers in his headband. "Soldiers kill Running Buffalo and two Indians, burn your teepee."

Thumbing back his hat while Buddy began to romp with one of the Indians, Colt said. "What's my friend Two Feathers mean by that?"

A guttural answer came back to him. "We follow tracks here. Soldiers with Captain burn your ranch again. Killed our brothers and Running Buffalo. We here take scalps."

The import of his speech hit Colt abruptly. Burning the Bar H buildings again and killing the Indians working there would be just one more talking point for the Captain when he requested more authority and troops. Those in Washington would fall all over themselves acceding to his demands with two ranches burned and their entire families wiped out by the Indians, supposedly joining forces with the Hole gang. That man sure knew how to prove his point.

"How many soldiers follow the Captain, and have they taken over the ranch yet?" Colt dreaded the answer.

Two feathers held up seven fingers. "Cowboys stay in sleeping house. Me sneak up, look through window. All tied to blankets. Your woman in house. Face pale white, wrap on shoulder. Me think she try take Captain scalp, he shoot her. Young white girl keep shotgun in room with parents. Bad men no get her."

The growl, low in Buddy's throat, caused the Indians to fade into the trees and Colt followed their lead, glancing up at the top of the knoll which now showed plain in the early dawn. A man with a rifle in his arm stood there, trying to make out the shadows still holding strong in the trees.

Five minutes passed. He felt a hand on his shoulder and Two Feathers voice reached his ears. "We go now. Take scalps of all soldiers."

Colt swiftly faced his friend. "If you do that, white fathers will send many soldiers to wipe out your village. Let your friend Black Beard handle this problem. You stay hidden. If I don't succeed in displacing the Captain, it'll be up to you." He knew sound traveled far on the early morning air, so held his voice low.

Two Feathers stared into his eyes. "You kill Captain. He no good...kill my brothers. I take scalp."

You certainly couldn't blame him for this stand. "Your people say man hanged, his spirit not go happy hunting ground. If I win this fight, the Captain will hang and his spirit will be lost." Colt sure hoped he had the straight of their beliefs.

A smile lit the face of Two Feathers. "You hang Captain. Later I take scalp. You not hang him, he lose hair anyway."

The time to go into the ranch yard would be now while most of the men were sleepy. Colt quickly gave instructions. Grabbing his canteen from his saddle, he sloshed water on his face and hair and the black dye began to run down his neck. "Two Feathers, I know your knife is sharp and cuts clean. Take this beard off my face. The Captain won't recognize me when I ride in without a beard. I'm hoping it'll give me an edge."

"You want me take your scalp?" The Indians were silently laughing at the spectacle that was about to take place. Two Feathers pulled his knife, grasping the bottom of Colt's black whiskers. One whack took most of the bottom of the beard away, leaving exposed pale skin.

"You really white man now, Black Beard," one of the other Indians chuckled.

The knife began to whack away and with each swipe of the blade more white skin showed. Colt kept expecting to feel blood drip from his face, but only beard came away. Now he knew how an Indian could take a scalp so cleanly. It took only minutes until Two Feathers stepped back, holding out his hand. "Two bits."

At first Colt didn't get the gist of this, till he saw grins all the way around the faces staring at him. Reaching into his pocket, he pulled out a silver dollar. Dropping it into the waiting hand, he drawled, "A shave like that is worth more than two bits."

Two Feathers clutched the coin, then slapped Colt on the back. "Me keep. Remember always, no more Black Beard."

Time to get started. Colt vaulted to his saddle. "Can one of you knock out that guard on the top of the knoll? Don't scalp him, just put him to sleep for a while. Keep Buddy here with you or the Captain may connect me with Black beard." He reached up, pulled off his floppy brimmed hat and taking a derby perched on the top of one of the Indian's head, clapped it on his own. He placed his hat on the Indian, who took it off, studied it, then smiled and shoved it back on his head.

Two Feathers had already vanished into the trees. Waiting tensely, Colt gave orders to the Indian who's hat he wore, while watching the guard standing on the knoll. Moments later the man turned as though someone spoke to him. Then his body disappeared in the brush. Colt wasted no more time hoping Butch and his men would arrive before the fireworks started.

Riding over the knoll, he looked for the guard and saw Two Feathers in the bushes grinning at him. The guard was nowhere in sight. Hesitating momentarily at the top to assess the yard, Colt gigged the big buckskin into motion. The next few moments would tell whether he would live or die. To him the sound of the horses hooves on the ground would wake the dead, but he realized his senses were heightened by expecting a bullet any moment.

Clearing the end of the lake, he saw Captain Gregg step out on the front porch of the house, shading his eyes with his hat to see who the visitor could be. The distance between them closed and Shirley stepped to the porch. The buckskin paced steadily onward, reaching the hitching post in front of the house. An undetected sigh went through Colt. So far, so good.

Stepping from the saddle, he drawled in a friendly voice, "Good morning, Shirley. I rode over from the Bar H to let you know someone burned the place down while we were gone." His eyes never touched the Captain.

Captain Gregg butted in. "So you're the Hasting's kid. Kinda grown up since you left. We saw smoke in that direction yesterday; what you figure caused the fire? Are your parents with you?"

"My folks were resting quietly when I left them. You must be Captain Gregg we hear so much about." Colt let his gaze travel up and down the Captain before shifting his eyes to Shirley.

"Hey, you injured your shoulder. Would you like me to take a look at it? I spent a little time helping in the infirmary at the University."

Quickly she answered before the Captain could, "Yes, please do. It hurts a lot and I think the bone may be broken." She didn't know how, but Colt already knew the lay of the land and coming in as the Hasting's boy, caused the Captain and his men to tread carefully for the moment. No surprise appeared on his face when he first saw and spoke to her, but he seemed to be stalling for time. What did he have in mind? It didn't matter-- his presence here meant something would happen soon or he wouldn't have ridden in so boldly. Hope began to rise in her. She'd play along with whatever he suggested.

Going inside, Colt noticed the door to the bedroom stayed shut and he raised his voice slightly so Millie and her parents would know he was on the job. "Sit on the couch there so I can get a better look. How did this happen? "

"It was an accident," Shirley replied shortly as she sat down, sending the Captain a venomous glance. If she said anything more, Colt would be put in an unwarranted position, having to make his move before he was ready.

Colt only grunted at her reply and unwound the handkerchief covering the shirt she wore. His disgust for the Captain grew when he saw the minimal care given to her. His fingers gently probed the edges of the bullet hole, then his left hand took hold of her lower arm and he carefully moved it a short distance. The pain shot through her, causing her to moan despite her best intentions. He moved the arm up, bending it at the elbow. His bandana came off and wrapped around her neck, going down to cradle the arm in a sling. "Your arm needs to hang in this position while I get things ready to fix you. The weight helps loosen the muscles enough to let me align the bone ends. Feels like a pistol ball is lodged against the broken bone. I don't want that to be incorporated in the callous that forms to heal the break-- it'll have to come out. Do you still have some of the willow bark available?"

The pain began to ease off a bit. "I took some in coffee last night and again a short time ago."

"Good girl. I need a pair of tweezers; are there any in the house? I don't have anything with me to get the ball out and not cause more damage to the tissues."

"I noticed a pair in the kitchen drawer when I....um... took care of the Jeffreys before." She almost mentioned 'when she helped him', but caught herself in time.

Colt stepped around the Captain, who'd been watching every move, and went to the kitchen. The Captain stayed right on his heels. After rummaging through two drawers, Colt found what he wanted. Taking a bottle of whiskey from the table, he held it up to the light. Still three-quarters full. Either the Captain drank sparingly or Shirley used it on her wound. Retrieving a cup from the cupboard, he poured some whiskey in it and dropped the tweezers inside. Handing the cup to the startled Captain and saying "Hold this for me", he checked the pantry for bandages before returning to the front room.

Watching her closely, he drew his knife and stuck the point as far as possible into the cup. The Captain had taken a step back when he saw the knife, and his hand shook slightly, sloshing the whiskey. "Hey, keep 'er steady, Captain. We've got to help this girl." The fact that the Captain held the cup in his left hand, keeping his right hand free and near his gun belt, had not gone unnoticed by either Colt or Shirley.

"You better lie down for this next procedure." Colt pulled what appeared to be a root from his pocket and handed it to her.

She recognized it immediately. "Isn't this what the Indians call 'peyote'?" This man was full of surprises--why hadn't she thought of that root?

He grinned at her. "Yep, they use it for their tribal ceremonies, but it really comes in handy when you want to kill pain quickly. I picked it up from Two Feathers when I crossed the reservation. Just bite off a piece of it and chew while I go to work on that bullet."

Gently laying her face down on the couch, he knelt beside her, cutting away the shirt sleeve and pouring whiskey over the bullet wound. Her chewing became more rapid as the sting bit into her. Taking the knife from the cup, he quickly made a crosshatch through the skin over the hole in the back of her shoulder. A groan escaped her lips but it was done so quickly, she wasn't sure what happened.

"This next will hurt more. I need to separate the muscle a little in order to get my finger in the hole and feel the lead ball, then guide the tweezers to grasp it. Are you ready?"

Sinking her teeth into the chew of peyote, she nodded her head. His hands moved rapidly but gently. Still, when the finger went in, forcing the muscle back out of the way, and the tweezers followed down the front of his finger, grasping the ball, she almost lost everything. Then as the ball came out, she fainted.

Taking a clean handkerchief, Colt padded it against the wound to adsorb the blood which seemed minimal, considering what he'd done. "You carry any bandages when you go on patrol, Captain? We need more than what's here."

The man stood staring hard at Colt. You could almost see the wheels churning as the light began to brighten in his mind. "You're pretty adept at that kind of stuff, like maybe you've been doing a lot of it lately."

"Well, now, you got me. Since I arrived back on the Strip, I have been doing a lot. Seems you and your men cause one gunshot wound after another, only this time looks like you planned to burn your victims." It didn't seem worth it to try to keep up the deception after the Captain already figured out the answer. Besides, now that Shirley's bullet wound was taken care of, he needed to get down to the rest of his hastily thought up plan. He only hoped Hank, Ollie, Butch and the gang were in the positions he'd told the Indian to place them. Pouring some whiskey in the bullet hole, he pulled up the hem of Shirley's dress and tore strips off the petticoat, wrapping them over the pad made by the handkerchief. This completed, he glanced at the Captain.

Rocking back on his heels, Captain Gregg began to chuckle, "So Black Beard turns out to be the college educated son of the Hastings. You don't show much smarts for a university graduate, Colt. Riding in here alone when we have the place all signed, sealed and delivered. They teach you any sense at all back in school?" He laughed loudly at his own joke.

Colt ignored him and walked over to the closed door of the bedroom, hollering through the panel: "Millie, you and your folks doing all right in there?"

Her voice came back to him as Shirley lay on the couch listening to all of this, having regained consciousness in time to hear Colt and the Captain's discussion. "Yeah, we're doing fine. A little hungry and thirsty, but it can wait till you skin that polecat out there, Black Beard. Are you really Colt Hastings?"

"That I am, Millie. I remember my first visit here with my father...you sat on the porch the whole time just staring at us."

Her release of breath sounded to all of them. "I guess you're the real Colt, all right. When you get ready to make your move, just holler and this scattergun will do its part."

"I hope the Captain has more sense than to cause you to do that, Millie, but you keep the hammers back, ready to fire instantly."

He turned back to lay a hard stare on the Captain. "I suppose you fed her and her parents like you took care of Shirley's wound."

A slight flush suffused the Captain's face. "Didn't see any reason to bother with them-- they're going to burn before long."

Resting his arm on the mantel, Colt let his voice out softly, "You're the one not showing any sense, Captain. You think I'd deliberately ride in here without all bases covered? Hank, along with the Indians you planned to blame for all these fires, coupled with the men from the Hole gang who you wanted to get rid of, have this place surrounded. You're the one should be shaking in his cavalry boots. The hangman is chomping at the bit to stretch your neck."

The wheels again began to turn behind those black eyes as the Captain digested this. "So, Hank let you know he's a Ranger. I thought Mitch might get the both of you."

"Oh, he gave it his best shot, but his hand became a little slow at the last moment. I have to give you credit: you set us against each other and Mitch took the bait hook, line, and sinker."

"Now I'm supposed to walk out that door, giving myself up to Hank. Is that it?" For some reason he almost laughed and Colt caught on quickly where his thinking took him. The Captain's next words verified his suspicions.

"You're forgetting I still hold the upper hand, young man. The lives of the women here are still mine to do with as I please. You were foolish to ride in when I have them to bargain with. You might as well ride back out and tell Hank if he doesn't move out and leave us, I'll shoot Shirley first, then storm the bedroom with my men and kill Millie and her parents. And this time they'll stay dead!"

The hope rising in Shirley's breast faded quickly. Colt didn't even flinch as the words were flung across the room at him. His boot lifted and he walked across the floor. Despite the pain, Shirley raised slightly to see what was happening. Stopping in front of the Captain, his hand came up, slapping Gregg hard across the face. The force of the blow sent the Captain staggering back two steps and his hand stabbed to holster. Shirley's glance swung in that direction and saw the flap pinned back, making the gun instantly assessable.

The cavalry regulation pistol started to lift from its resting place, then stopped half out, and dropped back. Her glance saw Colt standing with his gun touching the center of the Captain's chest. "You should know better than that, Captain. Mitch could out-draw you any day of the week and he made the same mistake. I figured you for more smarts." Those were the same words Gregg used on Colt only moments before.

Captain Gregg's face looked like something scraped off the

alkali flats out on the Strip, it shone so white against the blue of his uniform. His eyes dilated, expecting to feel the tearing track of a bullet through his chest. "Shirley's right, Captain. Vengeance does rot a man's gut. I been thinking a lot during the night on what to do with you. Two Feathers gave his consent to let us hang you as long as he could take your scalp afterward. Sure don't want to disappoint him, so a court-martial, then a hanging seems to be the best trail to travel." Colt slipped his gun back to holster and deliberately stepped back to the fireplace. The last thing he wanted was a shootout here at the ranch: chances were good that some Indians would be killed and unless the Hole gang had arrived, the women's outlook wasn't so great either. He'd have to play this differently.

Gregg stood there trying to get his courage up. This young man didn't seem to scare at all--- there must be truth in what he said about the number of men surrounding the ranch. He blustered again as he lifted his pistol from it's holster while Colt's back was turned. "You still have the women to consider. A well-placed bullet through Shirley's head might convince you."

Lifting his arm to the mantel and turning to face the Captain, Colt's cool drawl filled the room. "I suppose you rustled all the Bar H cattle to get money to pay your cutthroat men. You figured once the Hastings were killed and the Jeffrey's wiped out, you could take over the ranches and later use them for holding the cattle you'd rustled from the four states. When the blotted brands healed, you could drive those cattle to market. These two ranches are so isolated, a plan like that would work fine. The only problem is you failed to eliminate all the Hastings, or the Jeffrey's either."

Cuss words dribbled from the Captain's mouth. "You son of a bitch. Think you've got it all figured out, don't you? But you're forgetting I have enough soldiers with me to burn this ranch before your men can stop us. The Jeffrey clan and you along with Shirley will go up in smoke before any help gets here. You got to remember, if you try to move the Jeffreys from the burning house, it'll kill them. And if it doesn't, we will. You'll be sitting ducks."

"Yes, you could do that Gregg, but it would cost you twenty thousand dollars. You sure you want to lose that much money?"

The pistol barrel dropped lower as a puzzled expression lit the Captain's face. "What the hell you talking about?"

"When your men took the strong box off the stagecoach that morning, you found it empty. Where do you think the money is? With me dead, you'll never find out. So looks like we got a Mexican stand-off. You have any suggestions?"

"Damn you, Colt! You took that money before we got a chance to, and I needed it to meet the demands of those hired outlaws. Because of that, several quit and went elsewhere."

"I'm still waiting for a suggestion to end this stalemate, Gregg." The cool way this man stood, not seeming concerned at all, convinced the Captain more than anything. Someone facing sure death didn't stand and talk so quietly, confidence oozing from him.

Fixing cautious eyes on Colt, he finally came to a decision. "All right, Colt. What did you have in mind?"

An insolent smile crossed Colt's face. "A trade, Captain. You can walk out of here with me, turn your men over to Hank to take into custody. You and I will go alone to where the money is cached. I give you my word that Hank and the Hole gang will not follow. You go on your way with twenty thousand dollars, which ought to last a long time in Mexico or South America. A lot of lives will be saved, including your own, because if you even start to tighten a finger on the trigger of that gun, I'll put a bullet in your chest before you complete the task." The last words snapped across the room as Colt's body came erect and the forty-four-forty cleared leather and centered again on Gregg's chest.

The color which suffused Gregg's face while they talked now drained away. "You pull that trigger and my men will be in here in a flash, Colt." He stood looking at the huge gun barrel facing him, which a fraction of a second before rested in the leather at Colt's side.

"I know that, Captain, but you'll be just as dead as I will and your men won't last long once the shooting starts. Seems to me a lot of lives would be saved if you and I just walked out of here like I suggested." Then he placed the clincher, "Twenty thousand is a lot better than six feet of fresh turned earth."

A sigh escaped Gregg as he slowly dropped the pistol back to leather. "Things were going my way till you butted in, Black Beard. Why didn't you stay back east and leave us alone out here?"

"Why, Captain, if I'd done that, look at all the fun I'd've missed." The stern look and hard eyes on Colt's face belied the statement.

"Call the guard you have posted up on the knoll. We'll walk up there with your men, leaving the ranch as it is."

A light dawned on Gregg. "If my man is still on guard, it means your men aren't there." Hope began to spread across his face.

"Oh, my men are there all right and so is your guard, but if we walk up there and your men see someone else at first, they'll get suspicious. So your guard will stand there waiting for you, but the look on his face when you get close won't be a pleasant one."

Gregg swore again. "Hell, you thought of everything, didn't you. Hey, why don't you and I split the twenty thousand and go partners on the scheme I cooked up?"

Colt appeared to consider the proposition. "I suppose you'd still want to marry Shirley if I did that. The problem is, she already promised to be my wife, so I guess we'll just have to do it my way."

Rage suddenly took hold of Gregg and he almost went for his gun. Then his shoulders sagged. "You're smart as all get out aren't you, Colt? But you better watch your back, cause one of these days I'll put a bullet through it."

Colt knew the man would be so busy trying to hide his trail so the Rangers couldn't catch him, there'd be no time to stay and dry gulch him. When Hank wired headquarters, every lawman in the country would be on the alert. If Gregg made it to the border, it would be a miracle.

"You win for now, Colt, but I want Shirley to go with us. That way you won't be so apt to go back on your word."

Colt didn't like this suggestion but he could see no way out of it. Turning to Shirley, she beat him to it. "You don't think I'd let you get away from me now, do you, Colt?" She stood up from the couch and walked toward the front door, while the two men followed her outside.

The fake soldiers were lounging indifferently around the ranch yard since no racket had come from the house after Colt's arrival. The three walked to the corral as Colt beat the Captain by talking first. "I saw a wagon loaded with supplies meant for the fort bogged down in the mud this side of the ferry. Told the Captain I'd take you all to get it."

Gregg fell in with this ruse, not really caring what happened to the men he'd enlisted in his scheme. "You boys saddle up--we'll leave two of you up on the knoll to watch the place while the rest of us are gone. Just in case there's trouble, I'd like the two left to have horses available."

The soldiers studied the three, figuring the Captain wanted Shirley along for his own reasons, then turned to catch and saddle. Moments later the party lined out for the top of the ridge. Shirley glanced up but saw no one at first, then the man standing guard appeared at the edge of the scrub oak, his hat shading his eyes. Gregg saw the same thing and they continued up the slope.

Colt sat tense in the saddle. If Hank hadn't arrived yet, there'd be fireworks and he would put his first bullet along the rump of Shirley's horse, causing it to bolt and get her out of the line of fire.

The guard stood quietly till they were almost on him, then he fell backward into the bushes. The soldiers pulled to a stop, confusion spreading across their faces. Instantly a good twenty men with rifles at the ready surrounded the Captain's party and Colt slacked in his saddle, relief running through him. Buddy dashed from the trees, short yips making clear his happiness at seeing Colt. Colt took a moment to lean from the saddle and fondle Buddy's ears.

When the sunlight glinted off the badge on Hank's shirt, one soldier went for his gun. The rifle in Butch's hand crashed and the soldier slumped over, falling to the ground. "The rest of you want the same thing, just go ahead and oblige us." His words cracked sharply in the cool morning air.

Colt rode close to him. "Hank, I know you won't like what I'm going to tell you but it will have to be my way."

Hank's glance plastered itself to Colt, while his mind tried to grasp the significance of this statement. He considered only a moment. "Colt, if you hadn't entered the picture I wouldn't be standing here. The trouble my boss sent me here to solve is almost over, so whatever you say goes for me too."

His eyes shifted to Butch holding the smoking rifle, and Butch answered the unasked question. "Same goes for me. We been talking while waiting for you to come out of the ranch house. The gang woulda been slaughtered by this no good Captain and his men if you weren't bossing this shindig, so fire away and we'll go along with it."

"Thanks, fellows. Gregg, Shirley, and I will ride on out. You'll take his men and do whatever you want with them, Hank. The Captain threatened to shoot the ladies if I didn't go along with him. He wants Shirley along as insurance. That's the bargain we made."

His glance stabbing into the Captain, Hank spit on the Captain's boot. "You're a lucky son of a gun. Anyone else ask that but Colt, I'd turn him down flat and hang you myself." Shifting his gaze to Colt, he spoke again, "You be careful. This sidewinder is mean as a cornered cougar. You sure it has to be this way?"

Not answering, Colt gigged his horse, leading off the knoll as Shirley and Gregg brought up the rear. The sound of men being disarmed and tied to saddles soon faded out behind them. Not a word passed between the three as the horse's hooves plodded along the ground. Shirley could tell Colt didn't like the set up, but she also knew it must be the only way he could solve the standoff without a lot of men dying. A chill went through her as she remembered the cold-blooded way Gregg talked about killing the women. How had he ever gotten as far as Captain in the service? It just seemed beyond belief.

Quick glances back showed Colt she took the ride fairly well, not hesitating to keep up with the pace he set. Crossing the north end of the Kaibab, Gregg hollered up to them. "How much farther we got to go? Won't be long till we raise sight of town."

The horses came to a stop as Colt pulled up. "Why don't we let Shirley stay back here? This ride isn't the easiest thing with a hole in her shoulder."

"Ha, fat chance of that. You'd plug me for sure if she stayed behind. No, she's tough as any soldier I ever saw. Besides, she deserves all the pain she gets because of the way she's treated me."

Disgusted, Colt's heels touched the buckskin's side and they moved out. He began to think once the Captain got his hands on the twenty thousand, he'd sneak back and bushwhack them both. Well, he'd keep his end of the bargain, hoping he was wrong about Gregg, but he didn't think so and with the Captain behind them it made things touchy.

An hour before sunset the party reached a cave wending into the white ledges back of town. Stepping from the saddle, Colt stopped short at the Captain's command. "I have a bead right on Shirley's back. If that cave holds the money, you go in and retrieve it. We'll wait here for you. Throw that gun of yours away first."

Now the man wouldn't have to dry gulch them. As soon as Colt stepped out of the cave with the money, he'd meet a bullet. "No dice, Gregg. You want that money, you're coming in with me and I'll keep my gun. If you shoot Shirley, the next thing you hear will be Saint Peter sending you the other direction."

"You're right, Colt, he wants to gun us both down anyway so don't make anymore deals with him. He either does as you say or we all die right here." Shirley's voice rang with conviction.

Swearing, Gregg stepped from saddle leather but kept his gun in his hand. Stepping to her, he shoved it so hard in her back she almost fell off the horse. Gasping for breath, she slid from the saddle, following Colt into the cave. Their troubles weren't over yet. This man behind them smelled more of skunk all the time.

The money lay in a gunny sack pushed back on a ledge about ten feet into the cave. It's resting place was high enough so that anyone entering the cave would be unable to see it. Taking it down, Colt handed it to the Captain. "You got your money so get on with your travels, Gregg, and if we ever meet again, you better shoot fast 'cause I'll drill you plumb center."

Debating the situation, Gregg finally came to a decision and whirled out of the entrance. Grabbing Shirley by the arm, Colt quickly pulled her around a bend in the cave just as lead slugs slammed into the darkness. The Captain didn't waste any time trying to eliminate them.

When the sound of gun fire died out, Shirley came into his arms, little happy sounds drifting from her to him. Their lips met, holding the joy that infused them both. Suddenly sounds of guttural voices reached their ears. Pulling away from her, Colt rushed to the cave entrance. The sight that met his eyes almost turned his stomach. The Captain dangled from a limb of a pine tree, a rope around his neck and his head cocked at a deathly angle. Blood ran down his face from the hair that was no longer there. Not another soul could be seen and the surrounding air gave back only silence.

Colt sighed, then a slow smile eased over his face at this unexpected but somehow fitting ending. He would bury the body in a hidden spot, and when the horse was found, carrying the bag of money but with an empty saddle, who's to say what happened to the Captain? The Indians wouldn't be blamed, and Colt himself would swear the last time he saw the Captain alive, he was headed towards the border. His parents would rest easy, knowing their deaths had been avenged.

Happy in heart, Colt turned back into the cave to get Shirley, and his future.

The End

L. J. Brooksby

About the Author,
Lyle J. Brooksby

Lyle Brooksby was born and raised on the Arizona Strip where no lawman dared to step on the range and outlaws jumped across the Colorado River or the Utah line in order to be safe from the law. From the age of eight, he worked on his father's ranch, riding with the cowboys with a rifle in his saddle scabbard and a six-gun on his hip, eating his meals at the chuck wagon, sleeping on the ground, and caring for his own horse.

His father had immigrated from Australia, homesteaded six hundred acres of land, which he filled with cattle and sheep. Joseph Brooksby was the first Justice of the Peace on the Strip, which gave young Lyle first-hand knowledge of the outlaws that inhabited the area. Law finally came to the Strip in the 1950s, but the author had already left his father's ranch. At the age of seventeen he attended Colorado State University where he earned a degree in Doctor of Veterinary Medicine. Dr. Brooksby set up practice in Flagstaff, the county seat of the Strip, and flew his own plane to reach the ranches on the Strip to treat the cattle.

After thirty-five years of medicine, Lyle Brooksby gave up his practice to write about the old days on the Strip. To date, he has written seven books, calling upon his knowledge of its history, tales from Indians and "old timers", and his personal love of this desolate, beautiful land. All of his stories are placed in the Arizona Strip country, but with different locations and characters.

"All I know is that the Indians, ranchers, outlaws and women of the old west will keep flowing across the pages of my writing till the big chief in the sky calls me home.

"To my readers — may your trails be twisted enough to give you strength and courage.

"So long and happy reading."

L. J. Brooksby

Member of the Western Writers of America, Inc.